The Jewel in the Christmas Holly

Debbie Kelahan

ISBN: 0692890637
ISBN-13: 978-0692890639

Library of Congress Control Number: 2017908696
Jewel in the Christmas Holly, The, Hellertown, PA

To my family and friends with love.

ACKNOWLEDGMENTS

I want to thank my husband, Joe; my mother-in-law, Kathleen, and Ellen for reading and giving feedback to my story. I appreciate it from the bottom of my heart!

CHAPTER 1

Lamington. A small town in a modest, yet prosperous kingdom of the distant past where knights roamed and castles dotted the landscape. The first day of winter had arrived to this place, which advantageously rested between the shadows of four protective stone walls with a stately castle at its center. This day was like any other in Lamington. Life moved slowly for the people there as they went about their daily affairs, all except for that of one young girl whose name was Nan. She had something very important to do that afternoon as the gray clouds raced across the sky and cold sunlight peaked out over the wintry townscape. Nan was being sent by her mother on a special errand out-of-doors to look for some holly. She did not take long to find a sprig of it when a stranger approached her out of nowhere and handed her one.

"Many good thanks to you!" Nan said, and she went running home with the holly.

Nan lived with her family in a tiny cottage on the corner of a narrow, cobblestone lane near the main street of Lamington where the town gate was visible. Though she was the daughter of peasants, who toiled hard on their small plot of land, she had a happy and secure childhood and never felt the want for anything. With the arrival of winter, Nan's excitement of preparing for Christmas grew, and completing mundane farm tasks became easier with each passing day. Christmas was one holiday of the year where it mattered not whether one was common folk or noble. Everyone celebrated it together and enjoyed each other's company, because of the important significance that Christmas held for Lamington and their entire kingdom.

Reaching for the handle on the cottage door, a northwesterly wind savagely blew at her braided hair and woolen cloak. Nan fought against the wind with all her might, as she pulled hard to open the door, but curiosity got the better of her and she let the door slam shut. She turned and took one last glimpse through the town gate at the forest beyond and the mysterious road it bordered. The tall, leafless trees of the forest were silhouetted against the evening sky, and the road was a black, curving line that went into nothingness that made Nan shudder and look away.

The church bells mournfully rang out their warning. The town's evening curfew would soon be upon them, and the town gate would be secured for the night. Nan felt comforted knowing that Lamington was being closed off from the outside world as the townspeople slept, all except for the few brave souls who chose to live and farm outside the town walls. She was happy her family farmed their plot of land inside the walls behind their thatched cottage. Strange new places terrified Nan and she hoped she never had to travel anywhere far; a common fear of those living in town who rarely went anywhere in their lifetime. Those who had gone even a few miles were very lucky. She was glad she was not one of them, even today.

With one last struggle at the door, Nan freed herself from the violent wind and stepped into the house. Shutting the door behind her, she excitedly held up the holly for her mother to see.

Isabel's soft brown eyes, which matched the color of her hair under her white wimple, lit up at the sight of the evergreen leaves.

"Nan, my daughter! You found it!" her mother exclaimed, taking the holly and hanging it up around the cottage door. "You do not know how happy you have made me today. 'Twould not be Christmas without some holly in the house. I hope you did not have to go too far into the woods to find it."

"Nay, Mama, I did not have to," Nan replied, trying to catch her breath. She went to the hearth in the middle of the room. She rolled up the sleeves of her simple, homespun dress and warmed her cold, red hands. It felt good to be in front of a crackling fire after being out in the cold. "Servants from the castle gave some to me. Lady Catherine had more than she needed. She wanted to share what extra she had with those of us in town."

"God bless her ladyship!" Isabel said, clasping her hands to her breast. "God bless his lordship, too! Lamington would never be the same without them. I am thankful to our Lord above that we have such good people looking after us."

Isabel went over to the pot of soup she was making for her family's supper. The smell of the simmering beans filled the air of the cottage. The soup made Nan very hungry in spite of the fact that they would be eating the same one over and over in winter as certain foodstuffs were scarce. This made Nan long for Christmas when the lord and lady of Lamington opened their hearts and shared their food with the townspeople, including every tasty dessert to make her mouth water!

Nan looked about the whitewashed walls of the cottage with its thatched roof and dried vegetables and herbs hanging from the rafters. Her eyes darted down to the dirt floor where a small wooden storage chest was and where she and her family slept on straw pallets. She then noticed her two younger sisters, Mary and Agatha, playing tug-of-war with a well-worn straw doll with their little brother, Simon, who had just learned to walk. In the end, little Agatha managed to grab it from Mary as she ran and gave it to Nan.

Nan smiled as she took the doll from Agatha and returned it to Mary who came screaming after her. Such was the home life of Isabel and Simon the farmer. They both depended on Nan, their eldest, to help maintain their home and watch over the smaller children. This was particularly true in the spring and summer during planting and harvesting time when she was needed the most. Nan was proud of the fact that she was so depended on for being almost thirteen years old.

Opening the door of the cottage with a jolly laugh, Simon the farmer came whistling into the room. He took off his brown, woolen cloak, which matched his tunic and hose, and hung it up on a peg near the door as his family ran up to greet him. Simon was a thin man of average height whose years of hard work in the fields had given him a weather-beaten face and scarred, callused hands. Despite his appearance, it had never changed the great love and affection that he had for his family. Upon mention of the fine holly Nan found, he praised his daughter until the girl beamed from ear to ear. Simon then sat down on a bench near the fire to warm himself while Nan went back to finish preparing supper with her mother.

"Isabel, I will be leaving after sunup tomorrow to help the other men folk do more butchering of the pigs and fowl," Simon stated. "His lordship has many animals that need to be prepared for the big Christmas feast. He needs as many men as he can find to help him get it done faster, or there will not be enough food to go around for all the town folk on Christmas Day."

"I am so grateful for his lordship's generosity toward everyone during Christmastime," Isabel said, her eyes sparkling with joy. Of all the holidays of the year, Christmastime always brought out the best in her.

"Remember all the other Christmas feasts?" Isabel reminisced. "This one will be better, I am sure of it. I only wish I had gone the other years like I had before the littler ones came along. Now that Nan is older, she can help me out with the younger children."

"Aye, the feasts do get better every year," Simon sighed. "Last year, the tables were filled with all sorts of good-tasting meats, hot pastries, and wonderful pies and such soft, baked bread—but not as good as yours, Isabel. I can still smell the mince pies as the servants ran back and forth, bringing them out from the castle kitchen to put on all the tables in the great hall for the people to take from. What a kitchen the castle has, too! So big that many homes like our own can fit into it. I felt obliged to bring home a large sack of food. I see no reason why we all cannot make the trip to the castle for the Christmas feast this year."

Nan's heart skipped a beat when she overheard her parents' conversation. What a dream it would be for her whole family to walk over together to gather food from Castle Lamington for their own Christmas meal. Nan tried to imagine what her father had seen and smelled the year before when he got the foodstuffs. She only wished she remembered the feasts her parents took her to when she was small. Perhaps if her father took her along for the butchering of the animals, it might refresh her memory of the castle. She might even get to see some of the different foods being made in the castle kitchen before the big day.

"Father, may I come with you to assist with the butchering?" Nan asked shyly.

Nan went over to her father and sat down on his knee. She looked up at him with pleading eyes that matched the same slate blue color of his own.

"Nan, *you* would like to do something like that?" Simon answered, looking back into the eyes of his child. "I do not know what any of the men folk there would say if I brought you with me. A young lady like you should be home helping your mother."

"I know I can do it, Father! I beg of you to take me! I may even learn a thing or two at the castle that will help me here at home."

Simon looked at his wife who was standing nearby, anxiously waiting to see what he would say to Nan.

"Let her go with you," Isabel insisted. "I can manage around the house without her for once. 'Tis time for Mary and Agatha to learn to help me more these days—at least, as best they can for their age, and little Simon cannot go with you as he has many years to grow."

Simon sat in silence for several minutes before deciding what to do.

"'Tis settled then, Nan!" he cried. "Be ready at sunup to go to the castle. Now, let us eat before the good Lord above frowns on us for wasting his good food."

"Oh, Father!" Nan cried out happily, giving Simon a quick hug against his scruffy face. "You are too good to me!"

When the family finished their supper of hot bread and soup, Nan quickly helped put away the trestle table before settling down to sleep for the night. She had an important day tomorrow and wanted to be up early enough to go to Castle Lamington with her father. Nan did not fall asleep immediately after saying her prayers. There was so much running through her head as she lie on the straw pallet next to her little sisters and brother. At length, she finally drifted off to sleep. She dreamt of the grand castle, that she was going to visit for the first time since she was a child when she was brought to her very first Christmas feast, that she had no recollection of.

The blackness of the dawn light was still lingering when Nan and her father left the cottage to go to Castle Lamington the next morning. The sun had not risen yet, and there was barely a hint of it on the horizon. Nan made out the dark figures of the cottages and smelled the smoke rising from the chimneys all around her. Some geese were heard flying somewhere overhead in the predawn light. Nan pulled her cloak closer to herself with her wool-mittened hands as she and Simon walked on the frozen ground that crunched under foot.

They soon came upon the market section of Lamington with its narrow cobblestone street winding down the middle. Nan and her father passed many businesses along the way with their half-timbered fronts, including the mill near Lamington Stream and the blacksmith shop. Nan also made out the most important building of all in Lamington, the Church of the Holy Angels with its large bell tower. She gazed upon the church's stained glass windows and shuddered. They were still enveloped in an eerie darkness as the sun had not yet bathed them in its rays that reflected their myriad colors to the daytime world. She was glad when they went by the church and saw some sign of life around her. Some people were seen going in and out of buildings and carrying on with some early morning chores, including setting up for market day and building the stage for the miracle play that took place every year in the town green. All of the action going on around Simon and Nan was a sure sign that everyone was getting ready earlier in the morning because of Christmas.

"Father, what a joyous feeling there is in the air with Christmas coming!" Nan said, taking in all the sights and smells around them.

"Aye, it is, Nan," her father replied. "I almost forgot to tell you. Your mama will be at market today, so she will be meeting us here after we are finished at the castle."

As Nan and her father passed through the center of Lamington, they saw Castle Lamington rise up in the distance on the hill as a hint of purple and red sunrise came up behind it. They followed a well-worn path that led up the high hill to the castle. Nan shivered when she saw the menacing stone structure with its numerous battlements and watchtowers. Many colorful banners billowed gracefully in the wind above the castle towers. The castle seemed all the more mysterious with the thick morning fog ascending from its moat and making the surrounding area very damp. Castle Lamington was a very important part of their lives as Lord Robert who resided there protected his townspeople from any enemy that might come upon them.

"Ah!" Simon exclaimed. "We are finally here!"

They approached the castle drawbridge and crossed over the moat, with its murky brown water below, before reaching the portcullis. The fog hung so thick in the air that Nan scarcely saw the outline of her father standing next to her. As the portcullis was down, they waited patiently for a guard to let them through the gatehouse so they could get into Castle Lamington. There was complete silence all around them, save for a few birds twittering around the castle walls.

"The castle is very quiet today," Simon observed. He glanced through the portcullis at the empty courtyard in the distance. Nan peeked behind Simon's shoulder to see what he was staring at. "'Tis almost too quiet today with Christmas coming and all. We will wait here for a few more minutes and see if anyone comes out to us."

"Simon!"

A loud voice disturbed the silence as it shouted down to them from the gatehouse above. Looking up, Simon took off his gray woolen cap and waved it upward to the disembodied voice. Nan saw the head of a lad appear from the inside the gatehouse. Another lad came up behind him.

"Good morrow to you, Richard! How goes it?" Simon shouted to one of the castle guards whom he was familiar with.

Simon replaced his hat back on his head as the first lad came down from the gatehouse to greet Simon and his daughter. The guard was unusually tall with fair coloring.

"Good morrow to you, sir!" Richard answered Simon. His enquiring azure eyes kept darting back and forth, first from Simon and then to Nan. "What brings you here this cold winter morn?"

"I come to assist in the butchering of the animals for the Christmas feast," Simon replied. "His lordship needs a lot of meat roasted for Christmas. This is my daughter, Nan, who came with me to help out."

"Good morrow to you, lass!" Richard said, nodding in Nan's direction.

Turning to Nan, Simon explained, "This young lad is Richard. He is one of the castle guards here at Castle Lamington, as you might have guessed. He has seen me come to the castle many a time before to work."

Nan greeted Richard in return. Since Richard seemed to know her father, she hoped he might have some news about the strange silence at the castle that morning.

"I would like to wish you both a good visit to Castle Lamington today, except for an unfortunate message that I have to make," Richard said with a rueful grin. "By your faces, I see that word has not gotten around. I had to make it to the others who have come here earlier to help with the feast, and so I must tell you."

"Oh, something *has* happened at Castle Lamington!" Nan exclaimed. She turned and buried her face into her father's woolen cloak. She did not turn to Richard for fear of hearing what horrible news he had for them.

"I hope that something has not happened to his lord- or ladyship," Simon said with concern. "I had a funny feeling come over me when I looked at the dead-like courtyard from where I am standing."

"Nay, 'tis nothing of the sort, sir," Richard replied. "His lord and ladyship are quite well. 'Tis just that his lordship has called off the Christmas feast."

"How can this be?" Simon asked, thinking that he misheard the lad. "Praise God and the saints that our lord- and ladyship are well, but what is this about the Christmas feast? This makes no sense to me!"

"We have received a message from his lordship today, instructing all his guards to tell anybody coming to Castle Lamington to help with preparations for the Christmas feast, that there will no longer be a feast held at Castle Lamington," Richard said flatly.

"There must be some mistake," Nan stated in disbelief. "His lordship *always* has a Christmas feast. Why, 'tis a tradition that goes back a very long time. Does it not, Father?"

Nan wondered why Lord Robert's generosity toward those on his lands during Christmastime had changed. Surely something had happened and Richard was withholding information, but it did not appear that they would be able to get it out of him that morning. His manner was too practical, and he was only a castle guard imparting information given to him.

Simon shook his head in disgust as he put his arm around his upset daughter. "'Tis a strange thing for his lordship to do—give up the very thing the town folk look forward to all year, the big Christmas feast."

"Sir, I have nothing more to say to you today," Richard said curtly. "I have given you his lordship's message, and so I must ask you to leave Castle Lamington. Good day to you, sir! Good day to you, lass!"

Richard stiffly turned on his heal and went back up to the gatehouse. Simon and Nan had no other choice than to turn themselves around and leave Castle Lamington as they were told.

"Well, Nan," Simon declared, trying to be strong for his daughter, "I suppose that explains why we were the only ones walking to the castle this morning. Everyone else must have gotten Richard's message before we did."

Nan tried to forget what was said at the castle as she and her father walked down the hill toward town. What a sad day it was for Nan, and it was only morning. She wondered when she would ever get the chance to go back to Castle Lamington.

"I do not understand," Nan said, wiping a tear from her eye before it escaped down her cheek. "I got some holly yesterday morning from her ladyship's servants. A Christmas feast had to be planned if she was decorating the castle with it."

"Do not worry too much about the feast," Simon reassured. "'Tis no loss at all. We can still have our own little feast on Christmas Day. Your mama will make sure that 'twill be as tasty as she can make it. Our food might not be as grand as that of the castle, but that does not really matter. Christmas is not all about the food, is it?"

"Aye, Father," Nan nodded, drying the rest of her tears. "You are right. I still find it odd of his lordship, though."

"'Tis odd, indeed," Simon affirmed under his breath. "Mayhap his lordship will change his mind in the future. We may have another Christmas feast, but not this year. When we get to market, we shall see what the others have to say about it."

CHAPTER 2

Nan and her father had entered the marketplace at last. It had become a flurry of activity on that crisp morning with the sun fully overhead and the church bells ringing the hour in the background. No one seemed to notice how cold it was, either. The merchants were selling their wares from the front opening of their shops and some peddlers set up their carts nearby. In the center of the marketplace was a bright, blazing fire for the customers to keep warm. People were already huddled around it, talking to one another after they were done shopping.

"Isabel!" Simon cried out. He saw his wife standing near the fire with little Simon and his sisters.

Isabel waved to her husband and daughter as she continued to speak with some women next to her.

"I have just learned about what has happened at Castle Lamington today," Isabel said with a grim smile, her dimpled cheeks red from the cold.

Nan was unable to hold in her anxiety much longer. "Oh, Mama! The castle guard turned us away at the castle gate. Something awful is going on at the castle. 'Tis so unlike his lordship not to have a Christmas feast."

"There will never be a Christmas feast held at the castle, we were told by the lad who is guard over there," Simon stated bitterly.

"The same has been told to me by my husband when he returned from the castle early this morning," said Cecily, a close neighbor and friend of Isabel's. Lettice, Cecily's daughter and friend of Nan's, was with her as well. "We also do not know what to make of it."

The other wives who stood around Isabel and Cecily repeated the same.

"I will go and see what the men have to say about his lordship's behavior," Simon whispered to his wife. "Mayhap they know more than we do."

Simon left his family's side, but soon came back disappointed. He did not learn anything more than he had when speaking to the women around the fire.

The story of the bizarre event at Castle Lamington began to spread throughout the marketplace. Everyone was astounded and distressed at Lord Robert's decision about the Christmas feast. Even the peddlers and merchants briefly stopped selling their wares and went to join in the conversation with those about them. Rumors began to fly. Some felt that Lord Robert must have fallen ill, but that seemed very unlikely as everyone knew that Lady Catherine was decorating the castle for Christmas just the day before. Others felt that perhaps his lordship had been called away on some unexpected duty for their king and could not have a feast for the foreseeable future, but that did not make sense, either. The feast was cancelled far too abruptly, and the castle guard would have given the reason had it been as simple as the townspeople had assumed.

The crowd in the marketplace became so engrossed in discussion over his lordship, they did not hear the sound of a rider on horseback galloping furiously down the middle of the street. When he reined in his horse, the town folk saw that this was no ordinary rider. The rider wore a fine, plumed hat over his wavy hair while a long green cloak hung from his shoulders. Opening his saddlebag, he revealed a scroll of parchment paper in his beige-gloved hand.

"Good people of Lamington!" cried the rider, vying for the attention of the occupied townspeople. The horse he was mounted on started to neigh and bob its head up and down restlessly.

"I am Bartholomew, messenger from Castle Lamington," the rider continued with a serious expression, his breath white against the winter air. "His lordship, Robert of Lamington, has bid me to come to the marketplace today with a message to all of you here."

Unrolling the scroll that was in his hand, he read, "Robert, Lord of Lamington and its surrounding lands, has had to make the regrettable decision of not only canceling the Christmas feast, but Christmas altogether, now and forever more, which includes feasting of any kind in the home, Christmas plays, and going to church, whether it be on the Eve of Christmas or Christmas Day. Anyone who is caught doing any of these things, either publicly or privately, then woe to him. The consequences will be severe."

Bartholomew glanced from the scroll with an icy stare as everyone else stared back at him in silence. Rolling the scroll back up, he held it tightly in his gloved fist as he said with a nod, "That is all that I have to say to you. Lord Robert's warning must be heeded. I must return to Castle Lamington as his lordship awaits my arrival."

The multitude who had now gathered around Bartholomew were flabbergasted at Lord Robert's message. His proclamation had taken everybody several moments to digest before they spoke out to the messenger who seemed eager to ride off.

"Bartholomew, pray do not leave us!" screamed a woman who stood next to the baker's stall nearby. "What are we to make of this? 'Tis not a thing that anyone ever forced any of us to do, especially his lordship. I do not know if anyone in Lamington can stop celebrating Christmas. 'Tis such a part of all of us here and all of mankind. Does he not celebrate Christmas, too?"

Shouts of agreement rang out.

An old man who stood close to Bartholomew shook his graying head.

"His lordship cannot make this decision for us," he said. "Telling us not to celebrate Christmas, even in our own homes . . . how can this be?"

"Surely you must know more than you are leading on, Bartholomew!" a lad shouted from somewhere in the far back of the horde of town folk.

"Good people, you have heard the message from his lordship!" replied the castle messenger. He had become uneasy listening to the anger and complaints of those around him. Fearing that a violent backlash might soon be coming, Bartholomew quickly stated, "I do not know more than what has been read to you. I must be off. Good day to you all!"

Bartholomew charged his horse into the direction of Castle Lamington and vanished from sight.

Poor Bartholomew! Nan mused. *He is only taking orders from Lord Robert. 'Tis not his fault that we are upset over the message he brought to us. My heart is heavy for Lamington. What has gotten into his lordship?*

Nan pretended that she was not affected by the loss of Christmas like the others. She was too drained over his lordship's message to think. It was too troubling, and the threats that went with it were too much—nay, too extreme—for her mind to handle. She wanted to put them out of her head, but she knew she could not shut out his lordship's demands for long. She would have to live with them and the difficulties they presented for her and the entire town.

"His lordship has surely lost his head!" cried an old woman at Nan's elbow.

"Hush, Alice!" stated another old woman. "Do you want to lose *your* head, too? Who are we to question our lordship? You heard what the messenger said. If we do not abide by his lordship's word, punishment will be severe."

Nan was tired of the people quarrelling over Lord Robert's message. She turned to see her parents discussing Bartholomew's message with Cecily, and now her husband, who had appeared at her side. There was sadness, even fear, in their eyes because Christmas was such a joyful time of the year and now they were powerless to partake in it.

"Isabel, we should gather the children and leave," Simon said, motioning to his family. "If we cannot have Christmas, then what is here for us to buy for it?"

Isabel and the children turned to follow Simon out of the marketplace. Others were doing likewise for the same reason. The festive holiday mood had left the town and the shopping that went with it.

"We will do as his lordship has said," Isabel said unhappily. "We do not want trouble, do we? Of course, we can always close the shutters and celebrate Christmas quietly without anybody knowing."

"I think we should be careful!" Simon warned Isabel. "We do not want a guard from the castle breaking down our door and finding us doing that."

Isabel nodded grudgingly to her husband. His lordship's commands were intolerable, but the penalties would be worse, far worse, and she knew it. She walked slowly, eyes to the ground with a heavy heart, as they started for home.

Moments later, a gust of wind blew out of the northeast. The wind infiltrated the marketplace so strongly, that it nearly knocked everyone off their feet. Nan grabbed onto her brown cloak before it was pulled from her shoulders. She took notice of a very strange blue dirt blowing in the wind. Some of the blue dirt got into her cloak and hair. Nan tried to brush it away, but was unable to. She saw it, but she could neither feel it on her fingers nor grab it in her hand. The oddest part of all was that the blue dirt fell like a fine coating of snow on the townspeople, and only on them!

Blue dirt that fell on anything else—market stalls, horses or other animals, the ground—rapidly disappeared before Nan's very eyes. The blue dirt did not have the ability to stick to anything but people! Nan wondered what it was and where it came from. She had never seen anything like it before.

As Nan's attempt to knock the blue dirt from herself had become more and more unsuccessful, something unexpected occurred. The people in the marketplace became motionless. They froze in whatever pose they were in and did not move, from the merchants in the stalls to the crowd that was still milling about in the market. Nan's parents and her siblings, along with Cecily and her family, had stopped conversing and stood lifeless. She saw her mother standing unresponsive as she held the hand of Agatha, her little sister, who in turn stood immobile next to her other lifeless sister, Mary. Even little Simon was stationary in his mother's arms with his little arms gripped around her neck. What an eerie sight it was to behold! They did not blink or move one finger! The people looked like the very statues that Nan saw in church.

As the strong wind started to die down, it gently billowed through everyone's static body. Not a sound was heard in the marketplace, not even from the birds chirping in the trees above. Save for Nan, there was a deafening silence everywhere. Nan peered down the street of town and as far as the eye could see, there was not one sign of life.

"Mama?" Nan cried out fearfully. "Father?" She caught her breath. "I can only hear one voice—mine! I am the only one still moving! Are they . . . dead?"

Nan feared that a sudden, deadly malady had taken over Lamington and she was the last one not to succumb to it. Relief came over her when she saw the swirling of everyone's white breath, silently inhaling and exhaling the cold winter air. Nan stuck out a trembling finger and touched her father's cheek. He was warm to the touch. Next she touched her mother's face that was also warm. She ran throughout the marketplace, touching each and every person to see if they were alive.

Praise God and his saints! They are not dead! Why is this happening? Why am I not like them?

Nan wanted to sink down on the ground and cry as she had no answers to what had just taken place. She rested her shaking hands over her face and tried to dismiss from her head the unexplainable that was there, but she knew she could not. She was living in reality and this was not a simple, bad dream she could wish away upon awaking from sleep.

Peering from in between her fingers a few seconds later, something astonishing was going on. The market, the townspeople, and everything started to come back to life! Nan was taken aback as she watched everybody move about in their usual fashion. Her parents began speaking to one another, her little sisters began jumping around, and her little brother squirmed in his mother's arms. The merchants in the marketplace continued conducting business at their stalls. Their actions appeared as if time had not stopped in between what they were doing before and after they were frozen for a short time.

"'Tis gone!" Nan murmured with surprise. "All gone!"

Nan looked at her cloak and noticed that the blue dirt had disappeared, too. She scrutinized the townspeople around her to see if any of the blue dirt was still on them. There was no sign of it! The blue dirt was not on her mother. It was not on her little brother. Further still, it was not on her father!

"Mayhap I am seeing things," Nan declared, rubbing her eyes. "'Twas there! 'Twas all over the marketplace . . . I have not imagined it!"

Nan kept twirling around and around to observe those around her, but the blue dirt had vanished.

"I have dreamed it then! I must have!" Nan was indecisive about the existence of the blue dirt and the frozen townspeople and kept changing her mind about it.

"What is that you say, child?"

Nan found her father staring down into her face. She was so fixated on the blue dirt that she did not hear him speak.

"I do not know what I was saying," Nan answered. She did not wish to worry her father about something she was unable to explain herself.

"Nan, be a good girl and let us be on our way home," her mother said. Isabel tried to quiet down little Simon as he started to cry. Her little sisters were becoming fidgety and wanted to go home, too.

15

I do not think I can go home," Nan said to her mother.

"Whatever do you mean, Nan?" Isabel asked.

"You would not believe me if I told it to you," Nan murmured. Her legs became restless. They wanted to carry her far, far away from the marketplace and her home. She did not want to be anywhere near where she saw the blue dirt that morning. She wanted to be somewhere where she could pretend it never existed, but where could she go?

"I must be going, Mama," Nan said.

Nan ran off down the street through the market and up the high hill where Castle Lamington was. She did not know herself why she was making a mad dash for the castle. Some voice deep inside her seemed to be telling her to go there, and Nan had to obey. Her father was shouting to her to come back. Her mother was calling to her, too, but Nan kept going until she reached the summit of the hill where she finally reached the castle gatehouse.

Nan was thankful that the sun had burnt through the fog as she was able to get a good view of Castle Lamington. As she got closer to the enormous structure, it began to make her feel smaller and more insignificant as she stood in its shadows. Nan walked across the open drawbridge and went toward the portcullis that she and her father had peered through earlier that morning. Nothing had changed since then—there was still dead silence in the courtyard. Backing away from the portcullis, Nan decided to wait and see if someone would come and help her.

A familiar voice spoke out.

"Lost something, have you?"

She fixed her gaze upward toward the gatehouse. It was Richard, the castle guard, whom she had met before with her father. She wondered how long he was watching her before he said anything. She trembled at the thought, especially with Castle Lamington being such a lonely place lately. Her father's engaging stories of the castle during Christmastime was beginning to dampen her girlish fancies about it.

"Are my eyes deceiving me, or is Simon's daughter back for the butchering of the animals? The Christmas feast is not to be, as if you have not already heard!" Richard shouted from the gatehouse window before breaking out into laughter.

Nan heard further snickering from someone else in the gatehouse. She recognized it as coming from the companion castle guard. The audacity of them to taunt her for being back at the castle! If they had been aware of the blue dirt in the marketplace and what it did to the townspeople, they would have been sympathetic toward her.

A wave of boldness came over Nan.

"I *must* speak to his lordship!" Nan implored with conviction. "I do not know why he cancelled the Christmas feast, but . . . ."

She did not know how much the two gatehouse guards knew or would believe her about the blue dirt. Nan quickly made up her mind to keep it to herself. But it was not going to deter her from asking his lordship about it! She knew that Lord Robert could still be useful to her when it came to other matters. Her father did tell her many a time that Lord Robert was a wise and just man, even if his decision about Christmas was not the most sensible one.

Mayhap his lordship knows something about what I saw in town today. If only the castle guards will let me into Castle Lamington to ask him!

"Lass, his lordship is not eager for visitors these days!" shouted the second castle guard. "I beg of you to take leave of here. If you do not leave, then punishment awaits. Good day to you!"

The two guards turned their backs on Nan and disappeared back into the gatehouse.

Nan bristled at the guard's scolding and felt dejected.

"Oh, how I would like to climb over the castle wall without them seeing me!" Nan said, thinking aloud. "I must get into the castle, but how?"

She was about to retrace her steps across the drawbridge and give in to defeat, when through the portcullis, she saw a man wearing a dark robe walking across the castle courtyard. He seemed to have been watching the exchange between Nan and the castle guards. He subsequently disappeared from view into a nearby building. Moments later, another man reappeared and ran up to the gatehouse to discuss something with the castle guards. Nan recognized him as Bartholomew the castle messenger whom she had seen in the market. Figuring that whatever was going on in the gatehouse between Bartholomew and the guards did not pertain to her, she raced down the castle hill.

"Lass! Lass! Come back!"

Light snowflakes started to fall into Nan's eyes as she circled back around. Richard was standing at the top of the hill. He had left the gatehouse to find her and was waving frantically for her attention.

"I have a message for you!" he shouted. "I have been told that you are to make the attendance of his lordship. Pray come here! You may enter Castle Lamington!"

Encouraged by his lordship's change of heart, Nan ran with a childish innocence back to the drawbridge. The portcullis was raised and she went inside.

Nan walked into the snow-covered castle courtyard. The wet granite walls of the castle and several silent outbuildings that she could not identify left her with a strange, empty feeling as she wondered where she should go now that she was inside Castle Lamington. She did not know where Lord Robert was, and the lonely stillness of the castle made her eager for somebody to come and retrieve her now that she was inside its walls.

Nan stopped and stared up at the many arched windows in a tall building of many levels that stood in the middle of the courtyard. No one was seen at any of these dark, lifeless windows as all the shutters were tightly closed. She contemplated whether any fire was burning in the building or if anyone was inside it at all. This strong, formidable granite building, which was at the same level as the castle walls, stood all by itself amidst all the other smaller buildings nearby. A flag above the building, with Lord Robert's coat-of-arms, flapped violently against an awful wind that blew in with the snowstorm. Over the top of the building's battlements walked a solitary soldier guarding this building. He seemed to be oblivious of Nan as he walked quietly back and forth in the blinding snow.

The snow was becoming heavier and heavier. The castle courtyard was devoid of any inhabitant. Whether it was because of the bad weather or something else, Nan could not say for sure. Nan's plain, woolen cloak seemed to do nothing to drive out the cold as she shivered miserably. She was beginning to think that her invite to the castle was a joke played by the castle guards. In the meantime, Nan knew she had to act fast and speak to his lordship before her father caught up with her. If only somebody could point her in the proper direction!

"Come here, lass! Come this way!"

Nan saw a figure come out of the tall building that was centered in the middle of the castle grounds. It was the same man she had seen through the portcullis. She saw he was part of the clergy. He motioned to her and Nan went to him, slipping and sliding on the snow in her simple leather shoes.

"At last you are here, Nan, daughter of Simon the farmer!" the priest declared solemnly. A grin came to his wrinkled, pink face as he held out both arms to Nan in a welcoming gesture. "Lady Catherine will be pleased, as I am, when she learns you are here. I am so glad I got to you when I saw you from the upper window of the Great Tower—'tis the building in the center over there where his lord- and ladyship reside. Nan, you are very much like the lass found in his lordship's . . . ."

He let his sentence trail off as if he quickly remembered something he dared not discuss.

"'Tis of no importance. Anyway, my name is Father John. I am a chaplain here at Castle Lamington. I say Mass here every day for his lordship and his lady. I also take care of his official and personal correspondence, too."

The soft hazel eyes and reassuring voice of this man put Nan immediately at ease. He was slightly bent over from age, but he was agile enough and moved about without issue. Nan looked at him quizzically.

"Father, how is it that you know who I am?" she asked. "I have never been to Castle Lamington before. Mayhap you know me from my father who has come to the castle to do work. He is, as you say, Simon the farmer."

"I made a small visit into town not so very long ago and, by the grace of God, I had the great fortune to come upon you there," Father John replied. "I recognized your face at once. I asked a shopkeeper what your name was and whose family you belonged to, and he knew right away. You were going about your business with your mother with whom you were shopping. I cannot go into any particulars about how I was able to recognize your face, but I did."

Nan was unsure how to answer what Father John had shared with her. Nothing seemed to be making any sense to her since being turned away from the castle with her father. Things were becoming more and more puzzling.

"Father, let me explain why I have come to Castle Lamington," Nan said. "Something very peculiar has happened to me in the marketplace today. Something fell from the sky this morning . . . it looked like dirt that was *blue*. I tried to touch it, but 'twould not let me. I could not feel it! Father, it rested on the townspeople there. They . . . they . . . I do not know if you will believe me, but they did not move after that. They were dead like. I moved, but not them. The blue dirt then disappeared—the people started to move again! 'Tis all very confusing why it happened there and to *me*. I *must* speak to his lordship about this! I do not mean to be so bold, but 'tis all very urgent, too. How odd that this should take place, and right after the castle messenger told us that his lordship said we cannot celebrate Christmas in Lamington anymore!"

Father John put a finger to his lips as he looked up at one of the windows of the Great Tower. He scanned it with his eyes and shook his head.

"I understand how you feel, lass," Father John said softly. "'Twould be best if we kept this information to ourselves until a more appropriate time. We have been instructed not to celebrate Christmas at the castle as well. You are not alone in this. 'Tis the book that has caused these troubles. 'Tis not a coincidence that you are here."

"What book?" Nan asked. "I do not know of what you speak, Father."

A worried look came to Father John's eyes. He seemed at a loss for words before promptly changing the subject.

"I tried to get the castle guards to let you in sooner, but one of the guards gave me some trouble about it," Father John said. "He did not heed my request to let you in, so I had to go and ask her ladyship to order him to do as he was told. I was afraid that his lordship would side with the guards if I asked him, so odd in manner has he been as of late, but Lady Catherine knew better. His lordship relented because of her. 'Twas only then that Richard yielded, too. That Richard! I do wonder about him sometimes. He is usually a good lad, but as of late, he has been so unmanageable. Something is troubling him and this is his way of acting it out. Someone had spoken to him about his behavior, but he does not change. He does not take orders well around the castle."

Father John shook his head with dissatisfaction when speaking of Richard. He looked at Nan sadly, which only seemed to deepen the lines in his aged face.

Nan was grateful to Father John for allowing her to make Lord Robert's attendance, though it did take some wrangling to make it happen.

How strange that Richard does not take orders well from those above him, Nan thought. *I suppose I will never really know why, but I will try to avoid him next time if I can. I seem to be in enough trouble with him!*

Father John looked toward the gatehouse and surveyed the castle guards intensely from where he and Nan were standing. The castle guards were walking around in the building and seemed unaware of Father John and Nan in the courtyard.

Nan saw from Father John's reaction that he was satisfied that the guards were busy with their duties and not plotting any further distress.

"We cannot worry about Richard," Father John declared. "There are other, more serious difficulties on our hands to take care of. Come, Nan! Let us go to his lordship. We must hurry before he changes his mind. Lady Catherine is with him. Pray follow me!"

Nan's knees began to knock. She was truly going to see Lord Robert, the most powerful man in Lamington, and it was making her nervous. She played over and over in her head what she was planning to say to him. She only hoped she would not lose her nerve and forget about what she went there for!

CHAPTER 3

Father John started walking up a flight of high, winding steps into the Great Tower with Nan following closely behind. She was ready to take her first step when she saw something that made her stop.

"Father!" Nan cried out as she pointed in the air. "See! There 'tis again!"

Father John turned to see what Nan was indicating to him. The falling snow had immediately changed into the same blue dirt that Nan had seen in town. It fell on both Nan and Father John, but unlike the townspeople in the marketplace, they did not become motionless. Nan wondered whether it was falling and freezing the people in town like it did previously. She tried to brush the blue dirt from her cloak. She could not feel it in any way. The blue dirt clung to her in a perplexing fashion.

"I cannot grab it!" Nan said in frustration. "I tried to once before, but I failed to. It seems to be falling like snow, but 'tis not snow. See, Father! This is what I meant about this . . . I do not really know what to call it. It only stays on *us*, too. I do not know what it is or where it comes from. I pray that what I am seeing is not something of my own mind."

Nan frantically kept seizing for the blue dirt as Father John watched with widened eyes.

The blue dirt quickly stopped falling from the sky and changed back into snow. It also vanished from the hair and clothing of Father John and Nan.

"I believe you, lass," Father John murmured. He stared into the heavens as snow fell into his face. "I have seen it before with Lady Catherine, but we are not sure of its consistency, its origins, or its name, either. I am not surprised it has stopped. 'Twill come down again. We have seen it many a time before. While I have not seen anyone frozen myself as you have, it seems that anyone who is close to his lordship and

22

lives with him in Castle Lamington is not affected by it. At least from what we can gather. Why you are not affected by the blue dust other than ourselves, I am not certain. You must not speak of what I had told you to anyone. Do you promise me this, child?"

"Aye, Father," Nan said. "I promise."

"I must caution you about one thing, lass," Father John said. "In whatever way you decide to present your concern to his lordship, do not demand too much of him. If he does not wish to answer you about something, let him be. His lordship is not himself as of late. I confess that things are not well at Castle Lamington these days."

Nan was becoming increasingly bewildered by his words. She wondered if he were speaking in riddles, but decided not to ask Father John anything more. Nan guessed there was something greater to all this than her simple mind could grasp.

"Not another word, Nan," Father John said. "Come with me— before 'tis too late!"

Nan carefully followed Father John up several flights of stone steps that were built on the exterior of the Great Tower and left to the elements. They had to fight off the brutal winter chill, as it blew their cloaks around, as they climbed before eventually coming to the chamber in the Great Tower that belonged to the noble couple. Nan found herself standing bashfully inside the doorway of a very large chamber with a huge roaring fire in the center of it. This room was at the uppermost point of the Great Tower. The heat rushed out of the room and immediately warmed her cold, shivering body. She imagined herself standing in front of that great fire, drying out her braids, and taking her soggy stockings off as she warmed her feet.

"Nan, this is his lord- and ladyship's chambers," Father John said in a hushed voice, beckoning her to come forward. "'Tis what we call the great hall."

Nan quietly observed the room before her with its high timbered ceiling and shuttered windows in the walls. She could not believe that she was in Lord Robert and Lady Catherine's chambers and was about to meet them face to face! The room had brightly painted frescos and many luxurious and colorful tapestries hanging on the high walls. Brilliantly lit torches hung at various points along the castle walls, yet the room remained dim and shadowy. In the far back of the room, she saw a dais with two sumptuous chairs on it.

"My lord!" Father John announced. "My lady!" His voice echoed loudly throughout the great hall. "Nan, daughter of Simon the farmer, has arrived."

A figure with a neatly trimmed auburn beard and ruddy complexion came around from behind the other side of the fire. Broad-shouldered and tall in stature, he wore a violet blue tunic with gold trimming around the neck and arms. Observing Nan with interest, Lord Robert walked up to the dais to sit down on one of the chairs there. Flickering brilliantly against the firelight, his many jeweled fingers gripped the arms of the chair as he sat.

A petite, slender young woman with an arresting face in a wine red gown of silk followed his lordship to his chair and stood next to it. She had sandy blonde hair that hung down in two long braids that peeked from underneath a long, white veil. Lady Catherine smiled shyly at Nan as she clasped together her many bejeweled fingers.

Nan was awestruck by the prominent couple in front of her. Unsure of what to do next, she looked at Father John despairingly.

"My lord, this lass has come here to speak to you about a problem that has arisen in Lamington recently," Father John said, speaking on Nan's behalf. "It needs your immediate attention."

Lord Robert nodded to Father John and stared ahead at Nan as he waited for her to speak.

"Nan, daughter of Simon the farmer," Lord Robert said in a brusque voice, "pray state your business for what you have come here."

Nan became a little put off by his dolefulness, but remained hopeful of the outcome of her audience with him.

"My lord, a very strange thing has happened to me in town today," Nan said.

She found it odd to hear the sound of her own small voice in such a large room with the intimidating figure sitting in front of her. For a moment she was unable to control her nervousness, but a sudden comforting hand from Father John on her shoulder gave her much encouragement to continue.

"Blue dirt or dust—whatever you call it—fell from the sky in the marketplace this morning while I was there," Nan declared. "Why that is, I cannot say."

On bended knee, Nan tried to explain the blue oddity to the best of her ability. She told his lordship all she remembered in the marketplace and when on to describe the blue dirt coming down in the castle courtyard only seconds before she and Father John entered the Great Tower.

"I thought that mayhap you can tell me what it is and why it had fallen only on me in town," Nan said with beseeching eyes. "Your lordship is very wise and just in all matters, I hear. I know you can help me."

Lord Robert did not respond, but remained completely attentive to the kneeling peasant girl in front of him. Occasionally, he nodded his head respectably as she babbled on. Glancing at Lady Catherine briefly, Nan detected some concern in her face, but it soon disappeared as she gave Nan a sweet smile.

"Your story is very remarkable," Lord Robert said, rubbing his beard after Nan finished. "Nay, very intriguing! You mention that you saw the townspeople become frozen after this . . . this . . . blue thing came from the sky. I do not know if I have ever seen such a thing. 'Tis doubtful that Bartholomew had anything to do with it after he read my decree on Christmas. Such an imaginative girl, you are! I do not think anything like this exists or ever did. With a gesture of his hand, Lord Robert said, "You may arise, Nan!"

"Nan speaks the truth, your lordship," Father John interpolated. "I have also seen this blue dirt—in the courtyard before we came here. Just as she has said."

"Father, you are a bit imaginative, too!" Lord Robert said with a loud laugh. "Do not side with this peasant girl. She does not know of what she speaks of. As far as myself being wise and just in all matter, young lass, 'tis quite a compliment you pay me. However, I am going to have to disappoint you this time. Pray leave Castle Lamington without delay."

Nan's hopes were shattered. His lordship would not help her. His lack of interest in the blue dirt was inexcusable. As lord of Lamington, Nan had envisioned more from him. She was also stunned that he did not believe Father John, his own castle chaplain! Nan wished she had not come back a second time to Castle Lamington. She looked at Lady Catherine who gazed back at her with saddened eyes. She guessed that if her ladyship had her own way, she would be speaking her mind on the matter, but something held her back. Lady Catherine seemed to be in fear of her husband for some reason and said nothing. She looked from Nan to his lordship and immediately turned away.

Mayhap his lordship does not know what the blue dirt is, Nan thought, *and this is his way of telling me. I wish he was not so unkind about it!*

"Pray, Father, take this girl back from whence she came," Lord Robert said firmly. He did not look at Father John when he said it. His lordship ran his hand through his hair as he got up from his chair. Making his way back over to the fire, he rubbed his hands together in agitation.

"As you wish, my lord," Father John said with a bow of his head. "I will escort the lass immediately from the castle."

Father John bowed to Lady Catherine next before calling to Nan.

"Come, child," Father John said. "I will take you back to the gatehouse—you may go home from there."

Nan followed the chaplain out of the great hall and down the stone steps until they reached the courtyard outside. She and Father John hastily walked side by side across the chilly grounds, but did not speak to one another. The snow had stopped, and the cold winter sun had shown itself in bright blue skies overhead.

Nan's feelings were bruised by Lord Robert in the Great Tower. Furthermore, his revolting command at the end to leave the castle was even more hurtful. She did not know what to say to Father John after the incident. He was, after all, the castle chaplain and in close contact with Lord Robert. Father John was perhaps not the best person to complain to about his lordship.

"Nan, lass," Father John murmured to the distraught girl, "do not let what has happened discourage you. 'Tis not like his lordship to act this way. I know he wanted to hear what was troubling you . . . 'tis a long story, but he must be aware of its existence. He must notice it through the windows every time he reads from his book. The blue dirt always falls the moment the words fall from his lips."

Nan stood by patiently listening to Father John. Then, as if he had remembered something, he said, "I should not be so forthright about this, but I have reason to believe there is some relationship between the blue dirt and his lordship's forbidding Christmas here in Lamington."

Nan was taken aback by Father John's speculation and her eyes grew wide with surprise.

"I know you do not know of what I speak, but you soon will. Nan, 'twould mean a lot to us—both her ladyship and I—if you would meet us at the Church of the Holy Angels after the sun rises tomorrow morning. Everything will be explained in greater detail to you there. When you arrive at the church, go inside and you will find a Brother Albert waiting for you. You will know what to do when you meet him. Pray do not speak of your mission to anyone, even to your own family. 'Tis imperative that you do not. Child, I am depending on you to keep your word. Do you think you can do it?"

There was a hint of unrest in Father John's voice. Nan was unsure as to whether or not she should do as the good priest requested. She thought about it and, in the end, decided she would do as he bade her and the rest was up to God and fate if anything should go wrong. Being that it was only the Church of the Holy Angels that she was directed to go to, she could not envision any meeting there being as unpleasant as it had been for her with his lordship at Castle Lamington a little while ago.

"Aye, Father," Nan said excitedly. "I can do it."

Nan even surprised herself when a smile came to her face after all that had transpired that day.

"You are a good lass, Nan," the old chaplain answered with a smile in return. "I will take my leave here."

They were both at the gatehouse by this time. Nan looked up at it, but the two guards there were engaged in an animated discussion with one another and did not seem to care that Nan was there and taking leave of the castle. The portcullis was raised without any trouble, and she walked out with a wave to Father John who was walking hurriedly back to the Great Tower.

Nan pulled her cloak closer about her as she raced down the castle hill as a fierce wind blew against her. She hoped she could get to the Church of the Holy Angels without causing too much suspicion from her parents. After all the distressing events from early morning leading up to the failure of her audience with Lord Robert, Nan wondered what else was in store for her. She contemplated on what was going to happen with Christmas now that the holiday was essentially banned from Lamington and the surrounding lands by his lordship, after he canceled the Christmas feast. Nan did not believe for once that anyone could stop celebrating Christmas, even under the point of a sword. They were indeed living in dangerous times.

Nan saw her father fast approaching from the opposite direction.

Simon looked tired and worn from running up the high hill after her. Nan knew why it had taken him so long to find her. The blue dirt had fallen as she was walking into the Great Tower with Father John, and Simon had probably become frozen until it disappeared.

"Where have you been, Nan?" Simon asked angrily. "Why have you run off? Your mama was sick with worry when you left us in the marketplace."

"I am very sorry, Father," Nan replied, hanging her head. "After Bartholomew left and the blue dirt fell and later disappeared, I became so upset over it that I wanted to return to the castle to see if his lordship could explain what it was. He did not know, Father. What will we do now that his lordship has stopped us from celebrating Christmas? 'Tis so dreadful that we have to live like this!"

Simon was becoming impatient with his daughter's prattling.

"Nan, what are you speaking of?" Simon demanded. "What is this blue dirt? I did not see any dirt fall anywhere, nor any that is blue. Fanciful child! We ought to be getting back home. There is plenty of housework your mama is expecting you to do and here you are, playing silly games instead. I have so many things to do around the cottage today. The fence needs mending before I can do anything else. We are wasting precious time standing here. What is this criticism of his lordship and about Christmas? We do not celebrate such a thing! Do not speak of it anymore!"

Nan was mystified by his reply. She was sure he had seen the blue dirt fall before everyone in town had become frozen.

"Father, it fell in the marketplace today," Nan stated. "Did you not see it, too?"

"Pray, Nan, stop!" Simon exclaimed. He was becoming increasingly angry with his daughter. "This ridiculousness *must* end. Mayhap this is more girlish humor between you and some of your friends, but do not put it over me. I am not becoming senile!"

The fierceness in her father's eyes and his manner of speaking took Nan aback. He had been a happier person earlier today, until that strange happening at the marketplace. She was shocked that he did not see any of the blue dirt falling there, nor was aware of Christmas being halted by Lord Robert. She wondered if Simon had even noticed the messenger that came into the marketplace to announce it.

Thinking back to the marketplace, Nan recalled her father

accepting the fact that they could not celebrate Christmas. Now it looked like he was unable to remember the holiday at all. Would her mother? What of her friends? Her neighbors? Fear filled Nan's heart as she thought of what might be the inevitable. If they could not recall it, then Nan was the only townsperson in Lamington, including a select few within the walls of Castle Lamington, to have any memory of Christmas.

Nan became deeply troubled as she and her father walked steadily down to the bottom of the hill with the shadow of Castle Lamington at their backs. Instead of pressing him further on the matter of the blue dirt and Christmas, Nan let it drop as she knew that she was not going to win any argument with her father. If she wanted to share any of her thoughts on the blue dirt, she would have to wait until she saw Father John.

Back at the cottage, Nan was immediately put to work on several chores throughout the day. Nothing further was said about the escapade to Castle Lamington, which Nan found puzzling, but she did not complain. She worried that some form of punishment would come her way over it, but it never did. Nan rarely caused trouble for her parents as she was generally an obedient daughter, so they let the small mishap drop.

During the mid-afternoon, Isabel filled a basket with food and took the other children to visit an ailing neighbor woman while Simon spent most of the day outside doing repairs around the cottage. As Nan worked on some spinning that her mother instructed her to do on the spindle and distaff, she carefully devised a plan for her visit the next morning to the Church of the Holy Angels with Father John and Lady Catherine.

"I will ask Mama if I can take something to the home of her friend, Cecily, in exchange for something we might need," Nan thought aloud. "What better way to get myself out of the house and to the church! I cannot see why Mama will not allow it."

Nan had not realized how stiff her back had become until she lifted her head up from her meticulous spinning while sitting on her favorite stool near the fire. She decided to get up from the seat. Turning her head in the direction of the doorway, she noticed that the holly her mother had hung up was no longer there.

"Oh, no!" Nan cried out in dismay. She went over to the door and touched the place where the holly once was. Her eyes darted frantically around the cottage for other places the holly might be, but alas! It was gone.

"'Tis a sure sign that Christmas will not be celebrated here or anywhere in Lamington. If we were, Mama would not have thrown it out. I will try and find out if she remembers Christmas at all—I dread to find out what my answer will be. Ooo! I have to get to the Church of the Holy Angels tomorrow! I will not allow myself to be stopped from going! 'Tis painful enough to see the holly missing; to have Christmas missing from our lives is even worse!"

Nan sat down and put her head into her lap. She had lost her enthusiasm for doing any more spinning that day, but her spirits lifted a little when she thought of seeing the others from Castle Lamington. She wanted more than anything to discuss that missing hole in their lives—Christmas. It might not bring Christmas back, but it would help in easing the pain she had deep inside her.

Isabel and the other children returned home later on in the afternoon. Nan was setting up the trestle table for supper and mixing the soup she helped prepare earlier. When Simon returned from out-of-doors, the family spent an uneventful supper together. The rest of the evening was spent sitting around the fire, singing songs and telling of tales and legends of times past until it was time for sleep.

Nan still could not tell if her mother remembered Christmas or not. Her mother was not the sort of woman to hold things inside if anything bothered her, especially after what his lordship had done with Christmas. During other years, a day like this one would have been spent with cheerful holiday chatter, putting up decorations (and not taking anything down like she did with the holly), and endless baking of sweet breads and cooking special foods for the holiday, in spite of his lordship's generosity of handing out foodstuffs from the castle's Christmas feast. She would have been terribly upset and very vocal about not being able to attend to these duties.

I do not think I will bother to ask her about Christmas, Nan said to herself. *I will be wasting my time. She will look at me as if I do not know what I am saying. Father already does not know what I mean, so 'twill be the same with Mama.*

Nan nearly forgot to ask her mother about taking something to Cecily's the next day until Simon went over to the fire to rekindle it for the night and her mother started to put the younger children to bed.

"Mama, why must we always have bean soup?" she asked, staring at the big cooking pot where the leftover soup simmered throughout the night. "Do we not have any vegetables? We can make another kind of soup if we did. Or, add them to the soup we already have."

"We did have some vegetables," Isabel explained, "but we ate them all by the time autumn was over. Do you not remember? Our harvest this past summer was not very good."

"I remember, but I can always go to see if Cecily has any," Nan suggested. "I know they had a good harvest of carrots in the summertime. We can always use some carrots in our soup, and they can have some of our plentiful beans."

"What good thinking, Nan!" Isabel answered with a smile. "You know I hate asking for charity. We can live off the beans for the rest of the cold months if we had to, but if you would like some carrots with our soup, I will not object. Nan, what would I do without you? You do think of things that I do not sometimes. It must be age taking its toll on my mind these days."

"May I take the beans over tomorrow morning?" Nan asked eagerly.

"Aye, you may go," Isabel replied. "I can see the surprise on Cecily's face when you come with a sack full of beans. She will be thanking me for months."

Nan sighed happily. It worked! She could run over to the Church of the Holy Angels and get an important chore done at the same time.

How guilty I am . . . having to get carrots just to see her ladyship and Father John! Nan stated to herself. *From what it seems from Father John, I am going to be told something very important . . . and very secret. I wish I were honest with Mama about where I am going, but I know I cannot without breaking my promise to Father John. She does not mind me stopping by the church a bit to say a prayer or two, but if I am gone for too long, she may send someone after me. How much worse for me if she and father find out what I am really up to! I can expect a punishment for sure! I will try to get to the church and back as quick as I can tomorrow. Things will not be so bad if I hurry.*

CHAPTER 4

Nan did not sleep soundly that night. She tossed and turned on the straw pallet as she dreamed that her undertaking to the Church of the Holy Angels failed, though she still did not know the exact reason she was called there for. When the sun rose at dawn, Nan awoke gratified that what she had experienced was only a dream and she was still at home. After washing her face and hands in a cold bowl of water, she helped her mother with a few tasks before grabbing a sack to fill the beans with from a large barrel at the back of the cottage. She took her brown cloak from the peg near the doorway and went skipping down the lane to the main road with the full sack swinging at her side.

The morning air was crisp and clear as the cool winter sun shone overhead. Nan stopped skipping when the Church of the Holy Angels came into view, the church that her family had worshiped in for generations. Her heart beat wildly when she tried to rehearse what she would say to Brother Albert when she saw him. She did not recall ever hearing of a Brother Albert before. Perhaps he had traveled to Lamington, at the request of the chaplain of Castle Lamington, for the same reason she had been called to the church for.

Nan walked up the front steps of the plain, stone church with its thatched roof and small, deep set windows. She pulled one of the heavy oaken doors and went inside the semi-darkness until her eyes grew accustomed to the surroundings. Nan made out the altar at the front of the church where sunlight streamed in through the high stained glass windows in the walls. There were tall, wax candles around the front of the church where flames flickered and cast long shadows on its heavy walls.

She apprehensively went down the center aisle of the church when she heard footsteps behind her as a hand reached out to touch her shoulder. Nan whirled around as she saw a familiar sight standing before her. He was wearing his simple dark woolen robe with a rope belt. A set of kindly hazel eyes were smiling back at her.

"Father John!" Nan exclaimed, her voice reverberating throughout the empty church. Her eyes darted around in anticipation of another clergyman. "Where is Brother Albert? You said I was to meet him here."

Father John put a finger to his lips to silence Nan.

"Has anyone followed you here, lass?" Father John asked uneasily. "Have you told anyone of your whereabouts?"

"Nay, Father," Nan said. "I kept my promise to you and told no one."

"Good," Father John replied. He anxiously looked over the dark corners of the church before turning to stare for a moment at the front door where Nan entered. With a chuckle, he added, "Pray come with me, daughter of Simon the farmer! We must not waste another minute."

Nan felt a chill in the air as she followed Father John. Whether it was from nerves or from just that, an early morning chill found within the walls of the building they were in, she was not certain. Their footsteps made an echoing sound on the stone floor. They went to the front of the church where the altar was and through a side doorway on the right. Going down several stone steps that led along a stone walkway, they eventually came to a door at the end of it.

What was this room they were going into?

Nan was filled with excitement. A feeling of importance came over her as Father John opened the creaky door and led her inside. She had never been anywhere else in the church except in the main part where Mass was held.

The door shut behind them with a loud slam. Nan saw a woman standing nearby in a gray cloak from head to toe. Hidden underneath the cloak was her long, white veil and familiar sandy braids. Nan recognized Lady Catherine immediately. Accompanying her ladyship was another young woman of the same age, dressed in fashion of similar class from what little was visible under her dark cloak. Nan supposed her to be a servant who tended to her ladyship's every need. She had attentive pale blue eyes and tawny hair that peeked out from underneath her headdress.

"Your ladyship!"

Nan caught her breath as she fell on bended knee before Lady Catherine.

"I . . . I . . . I am so sorry for calling out to you the way I just did.

Father said you would be here, but I did not expect you to be hidden so well under a cloak."

Lady Catherine chuckled softly. Throwing back her cloak, she revealed a beautiful gown of moss green.

"Nay, child," Lady Catherine replied, coming forward. She gently placed a hand on Nan's shoulder. "You have done nothing wrong. You may arise from the floor, Nan, daughter of Simon the farmer."

Lady Catherine paced back and forth across the floor in a dignified manner. Her hands were clasped in the same way as they had been at Castle Lamington.

"If you wonder why I hid myself under a plain gray cloak, 'tis because I did not wish to be recognized and for a reason you will soon find out," her ladyship said. "Yet I could not fool everyone entirely. Nan, you knew who I was because you had recently seen me at the castle."

Nan got off the floor as Lady Catherine had commanded. As her eyes adjusted to the dimness of the room, she scanned it briefly. They were in a small musty room that was surrounded by shelves and shelves of books from ceiling to floor on either side of the four walls. There was a little stained glass window in the wall above where faint sunlight streamed in through the various jewel-like colors of the glass. Candles were placed about for extra light. Nan saw a long oaken table in the middle of the floor with a bench found on either side of it. She had never seen a room like it before. She later learned that they were in the church's library.

Nan at once spied an intriguing book that was lying in the center of the table in the room. She gasped in delight when she saw it. The book was small and thin in size and perfect enough to be transported around in the hand. It had burgundy leather binding, gilt-edged pages, and many faceted jewels set in the leather binding, which seemed to irradiate a strange, unearthly light from the candlelight in the room. The exquisite brilliance from the jewels' colors hurt Nan's eyes and forced her to look way.

"Nan," Father John began, "we are beholden to you for coming to the Church of the Holy Angels this morning. You are a very honest and loyal lass to heed my request to come here. We are also grateful to Father Nicholas, your priest, who graciously allowed us to use the library here today."

Father John fumbled over some words as he stared at the quaint book on the table. A shadow passed over his face as if something seemed to be troubling him.

"Regretfully, I must tell you that there is no Brother Albert here," he said apologetically. "There is a Brother Albert, but there was no plan for him to be at the Church of the Holy Angels today. I did not intend to mislead you in any way yesterday when I asked you to come here. However, for your own good and ours, I had to tell you he would be here. I did seek him out recently for some very important information which, I believe, only he can help us with. If he were well enough to travel, he would certainly have made his best effort to do so."

Nan stood silently and patiently as Father John spoke. She was not upset in the least with Father John about Brother Albert's absence. She told herself to pay close attention to whatever was said about Brother Albert. Whoever he was, he seemed to play some important role over all of them in the library.

Her ladyship stopped walking around the room. She looked directly at Nan in a very poised and noble manner. Her blue eyes became very serious in the very delicate features of her face.

"Father John feared that had you told someone where you were going and with whom you would meet, it might arouse suspicion," Lady Catherine stated. "He thought it best not to take any risks. We would not have wanted your life to be in any danger. So far, everything has worked out well."

"How dearly 'twould cost us if we had been found out," Father John said.

Nan nodded in response to both Lady Catherine and Father John. They both hinted at something serious that was making Nan feel unsettled.

"This is why we are here," Father John said. He pointed to the little book on the table that caught Nan's interest. "The church library seems to be an appropriate place to discuss a book, but 'tis not the real reason why we chose it. 'Tis a very quiet and secluded place to meet. No one would think to search for us here."

"This book shows why you are so important to us," Lady Catherine declared. She smiled warmly at Nan. "There is a task associated with it as well. Father and I have decided that it must be successfully accomplished by you."

Lady Catherine paused before the book on the table. She lightly touched its cover with her fingertips. She fleetingly looked up at Father

John and hesitated as if she did not wish to speak anymore, but did so at the encouragement of the old chaplain's nod to her.

"'Tis a strange, yet beautiful book nonetheless," her ladyship continued. "We have recently acquired it through the death of his lordship's very aged uncle who raised him from a small child. His parents had died from a horrible illness before his uncle adopted him. Lord Anselm, his uncle, was lord over one of our neighboring border regions near the mountains. My husband received the lands of Lamington and its castle from his uncle when he came of age to rule. Lamington was won through a battle between Lord Anselm and the original Lord of Lamington. My husband would not have had a future without the generosity of his uncle. He would have been a penniless ward of his only relative."

Lady Catherine turned away to face the wall as she sniffled with great emotion before composing herself.

"Lord Anselm's eldest son and heir now rules his father's lands and castle near the mountains now that he has passed," her ladyship expounded. "'Twas this eldest son, Lord Eustace, who sent the book and some other things to my husband after his uncle's death. Well, at least, we thought he sent it. I will explain later."

Lady Catherine took the book into her hands and proceeded to open its cover.

"Come, Nan," Lady Catherine said. "See here."

Nan came forward to look at this fascinating book as Lady Catherine lifted the front cover. The jewels from it still did not lose their strange, unearthly brilliance that Nan observed earlier. Nan wondered whether she would feel equally the same way about the book once she found out what lie beneath the cover. So far, what she was seeing had piqued her curiosity.

Her ladyship turned the first few pages. The book revealed beautifully painted pictures of animals, flowers, and birds of all kinds. On the opposite page of each picture was some writing. Nan did not know what the writing was as she was unable to read. There also appeared, on every other page, scenes from everyday life. People, richly clothed, were riding horses in front of a grand castle; lords and ladies having a sumptuous feast at a food-laden table outdoors, or seated happily in a garden where summer flowers abounded. There were scenes of farmers as well working their fields during different seasons of the year. Around each and every picture found in the book was a gilt border adorned with small, intricate flowers and designs.

"'Tis a fine book, my lady," Nan said solemnly. She had never seen such a magnificent book before. She was as awestruck by the inside of the book as she was of the outside of it just moments ago.

"'Tis a fine book, indeed," Lady Catherine said, echoing Nan's words. "We thought it to be a prayer book at first, but after carefully examining each page, we were not able to find one picture of anything pertaining to God, the angels, or saints."

"Furthermore," Father John interposed, "we do not know for what reason the book is for, and I have studied it closely. To complicate things more, 'tis not in a language that any of us are familiar with. My lady, show Nan what we found to be the most incredible of all."

Lady Catherine flipped to a page toward the back of the book.

"Look, Nan," Lady Catherine said. "Tell me what you see there. 'Tis quite astonishing."

Nan stared closely at what Lady Catherine pointed to. It was a picture of a lanky girl, strikingly very similar to herself, with long ginger braids in a brown cloak. The girl was standing in front of a castle that looked identical to Castle Lamington. Something bluish was raining down upon her. A second picture underneath, divided by a gold line, now had the same girl standing in front of the castle without any sign of the blue substance. Around both pictures on the page was a border different from all the other pictures in Lord Robert's book. This time, the border had green holly leaves.

"My lady, I see what you mean!" Nan exclaimed. Her knees started to tremble. "Is this a picture of me? What I see reminds me of what happened yesterday when I came to Castle Lamington. Father John knows of what I speak of."

Her ladyship's eyes were fixed steadily on the girl in front of her.

"Father John has made me aware of the blue dust falling yesterday," Lady Catherine replied. "Do not fear. I am aware of its presence more than you realize."

"Lady Catherine and I have agreed—there is no other likeness but of you, lass, in these pictures," Father John stated. "Coupled with yesterday's occurrence, 'tis further proof in my mind that 'tis you. The holly around the pictures serve as some reminder of Christmas as well.

Mayhap it means you were to come to the castle around Christmas, which you have. I also want to bring something else to your attention, Nan. On the page opposite the two pictures of you is some writing, beautifully and painstakingly done by an unknown scribe. This is the writing that his lordship recites over and over again. Now you see why I was overjoyed to see you on the castle grounds. I could not believe my eyes when you came to us after what we had seen in this book."

There were tears in Lady Catherine's eyes.

"Nan, something dreadful has happened since this book came into our possession. Ever since my husband has been reading the passage next to the strange pictures, he is not the same anymore. I know this, because I know him well as a wife should. I see how he is day and night. He is greatly attached to this book that is almost never out of his hands. That is not all! He barely eats or sleeps. He paces the floor of the great hall, hour after hour. He continually stares out the window for long periods of time for reasons unknown and sweats at the brow when he does. His judgment is not as it should be, as we have all seen with the cancelling of our Christmas feast. The blue dust does not want most of us to celebrate Christmas, except for the very few of us that it has not touched. I do not know what has come over him. His lordship is a heart-wrenching sight to see!"

Lady Catherine bit her lip and was on the verge of tears. She placed the book back on the table.

"I have seen it myself as well," Father John nodded. "His lordship appears as if some great evil has come over him that must be drawn out. From my observance, the blue dust is playing some evil havoc with our minds, and the minds of the people of Lamington. Aye, his lordship most definitely has some connection to it. We do not know what the blue dust is made of or why it comes and goes at will. What we do understand is that his lordship brings it on with his book. Why it has chosen Christmas as a way to do its horrible deed is something else we do not know. Only the devil himself knows the answer to that. One thing is for sure. If evil is as we know it, then 'twill get out of control and lead us into the abyss if we do not stop it."

Nan shivered. She felt her scalp tingle in fear. Nan's mind flashed back to the visit she made to Castle Lamington just the other day. She recalled how his lordship had acted toward her when she spoke to him of cancelling Christmas. Was *this* how evil acted? Nan was startled by the thought.

Lady Catherine paused and made a sigh of despondency. She shook her head as her eyes dropped to the floor. Her voice cracked with emotion, yet she continued to speak of her husband despite the pain.

"His lordship found the book in a chest with many other things that belonged to Lord Anselm," her ladyship said. "He went through all of his uncle's possessions with a long list that came with the chest. Oddly enough, the book was not in the inventory. 'Twas not long after its arrival to Castle Lamington that his lordship began to act peculiarly. I knew I had to act at once after what I was seeing, so I secretly showed the book to Father John when my husband was not reading it. Taking the book from him was not easy to do."

Lady Catherine exchanged a glance with Father John as if they both knew something that no one else did. She discreetly wiped away a tear from her eye. Nan did not blame her ladyship for feeling the way she did. She was a young bride, starting a new life with her husband. The last thing she wanted to go through was something as insufferable as this so early in her married life, even for a noblewoman as herself. Turning her back to the others, her ladyship began to cry openly as her maidservant handed her an embroidered handkerchief. She was unable to hold in her emotions any longer.

Nan sadly watched her ladyship. She wished she could somehow comfort her, but being just a peasant girl, she did nothing for her. Then Emma, Lady Catherine's maidservant with a comely face, came to her aid. Lady Catherine was led to a bench where she sat down as Emma spoke something quietly to her. At length, her ladyship whispered and nodded to Emma in return. Emma, seeing that Lady Catherine had stopped crying, went back and stood behind her silently.

"Nan, I have decided . . . I cannot hold anything back from you!" Lady Catherine said with conviction. "You *must* know the full story of all the goings-on with his lordship."

"Do you think 'tis a wise thing to do, my lady?" Father John asked with concern.

"Aye, Father, I do," Lady Catherine declared. "If I only tell her part of what has been going on, 'twill not make any sense. Nan *must* know. Deep in my heart, I do not think she would tell anyone anything that we tell her here. She spoke to no one before her arrival here or rumors would have been already spread. She is a trustworthy child. She has proven it to us."

Lady Catherine finished wiping her reddened eyes and face with her handkerchief. She took a deep breath and smiled a little.

Father John silently nodded to Lady Catherine.

"When his lordship came across this mystifying book, he instantly took to it," Lady Catherine said in a clear, confident voice. "Immediately he began reading from it, which would not be so strange if 'twas not for the fact that my husband does not know the language 'twas written in! This strange language is the very one that Father referred to earlier. We had written a letter to Lord Eustace about the book, but alas! He did not know from whence it came or even of its existence!"

A somber look came over her ladyship's face. Father John took over speaking for her.

"We often wonder who put the book in the chest that was sent to Lord Robert," Father John declared. "Mayhap 'twas put in there accidentally, but we just do not know. As of this curious language that the book is in, this one has put us at a disadvantage. 'Tis unlike any that we are familiar with anywhere. 'Tis a shame we cannot prevent his lordship from reading this passage that brings on the blue dust, which happens very often!"

Lady Catherine stood up from the bench and walked around the room as she had earlier. She twisted her handkerchief over and over again.

"In the beginning, I did not recognize the blue dust's ties to the book," Lady Catherine stated. "However, after sitting and watching his lordship read the book every day in the great hall, and then seeing the blue dust come down as he read, I noticed a peculiar pattern. The blue dust rained down only for a few moments, but once he stopped reading the passage, it stopped. That is when I called in Father and asked him about it. He saw the same as I! We dared not bring this to the attention of the servants. It would cause quite a stir if they knew. We also wanted to try and catch some of the blue dust to see what it was, but without success. It melts away before it can be touched. The very thing you have experienced, Nan. We believe that, for whatever reason, the blue dust first fell at the castle before it did in town. Otherwise, we would have heard about it long before you saw it, child."

Lady Catherine closed her red swollen eyes. After opening them, she stared off into space and then back at the book lying on the table. There was no doubt to everyone present that mental exhaustion was draining this young noblewoman. The book's significance played heavily on her mind. What Nan's unknown role was in it was especially unsettling to her, as nothing in the book made any sense.

"What is this passage about?" Nan asked. She did not understand how something written in a book could make a dirt of blue color appear.

"We do not know, lass," Father John replied. "As I said before, 'tis written in a nameless language. The language is not found in any kingdom, near or far. Lord Eustace himself does not know what it is, either. If we knew what was written, we can learn much from the passage and what his lordship was telling it to do. I had recently traveled quite a ways to find answers, but came back with nothing. There is no language, past or present, which comes close to what the tongue of the passage is."

Father John sat down heavily on one of the benches at the oaken table. He looked very tired as if he had not slept in a while. He removed the book from the table and placed it under his arm.

"After her ladyship showed me the book, I immediately went to call on Brother Albert about it," Father John explained. "He was the clergyman we had led you to believe would be here, but was not. He resides at the Monastery of the White Friars, which is quite a distance from Lamington. The peaceful monastery is near Meldon, a remote city near our southern shores, and was built on a steep crag. It took me two days to get there. Brother Albert is not able to make great journeys at his great old age, so I had to go to him. Brother Albert knows all languages, ancient and modern, and can decipher many books. He is the most learned man in our country. He studied the book's passage for many days. In the end, he gave up trying. When such a man as he cannot give me an answer, I know I am in trouble. Although Brother Albert was unable to help, he has decided to keep the passage for further study. He said he will write to me immediately if he finds anything. Incidentally, I dared not take the actual book to him. 'Twould not be prudent to do so. Instead, I painstakingly copied the book's passage on a separate parchment. His lordship keeps the book with him at all times. Her ladyship was only able to give me the book at intermittent times to copy or his lordship would know of its disappearance."

"We were not sure how his lordship would respond to it being gone, although we do know one thing for sure," Lady Catherine declared hesitantly. "There was one instance when he thought he had lost the book somewhere in the great hall. He was terribly upset and made such a mess of the room, it took days to clean, so desperate was he to find it. 'Twas very distressing for all of us to see. We never forgot what happened."

Her ladyship closed her eyes and shook her head in humiliation over what her husband had done at Castle Lamington.

"This is why I must get this book back to its rightful owner as soon as our attendance is over," Father John said. "His lordship will not be content if he realizes 'tis missing. This is why we have decided to meet here at the church so early this morning. His lordship is still asleep at this hour and will not know the book is gone. When he awakens, 'twill be back safely by his side."

Nan saw fear in Lady Catherine's eyes when she reopened them. She was terrified that Lord Robert might come after both she and Father John in search of the book. No wonder her ladyship came there in a dark cloak. She did not want to be seen by her husband when she left the castle to go to the church. She noticed that her ladyship looked at the door of the room several times as if she thought that Lord Robert might walk in at any moment in a fit of rage. His lordship must have been who they were worried about following them to the church that morning. After what he had done in the great hall after losing his book, Nan could only imagine what Lord Robert would do the next time. What a precarious life these people had to live at Castle Lamington!

"Brother Albert would have learned much had Father taken the book with him," Lady Catherine said with regret. "He may have been able to study things about it more closely—the covers, the jewels, the magnificent paintings . . . the scribe who created them was truly gifted, as you can see. These things may have given him hints as to whom might have created the book. We were in a terrible hurry to get the passage translated. 'Twould have taken too long to copy anything more. Of course, we do know that two of the pictures appear to be you, Nan. The paintings of the other people and their castle remains a mystery."

Listening closely to those around her, Nan could discern that Lady Catherine was greatly worried about her husband, and it was not so light a matter if such a great lady, along with her private castle chaplain, took time out of their important lives to meet with a poor peasant girl in the quiet of the church library. Whatever was in the book had them gravely concerned, and it shown in their eyes.

"There are not many things left to do in regard to the book, except for one thing," Father John announced. He took the book from under his arm and put it back on the table. He stared at it closely as if he were bothered by his own inabilities in finding an answer to the puzzling object. "We will seek out our own answers about it by having someone travel outside of Lamington until when, or if, we get a reply from Brother Albert. One does not know how much worse things might get around here. We cannot take a chance by doing nothing."

"Nan, you must do it for us," her ladyship said. "His lordship would be upset if Father John took his book and left Lamington with it. Lord Robert has his ways of finding these things out. He would not suspect the book was with you, Nan, as you are not from the castle, but are still familiar with the blue dust as any of us. If you are the girl in the book like we think, 'twould make more sense for you, and not Father John, to take it somewhere and ask questions of its contents. Our only dilemma is to occupy my husband enough with other duties so he can stay away from the book while it goes missing several hours here or there."

Fear flooded Nan's mind. It was difficult enough to leave town to find holly in the forest when her mother asked her to (she was grateful that her ladyship's servants had some before she went), but to leave Lamington altogether was unimaginable. Seeing that it was the will of those who lived at Castle Lamington, Nan felt she had no other choice than to go.

"My lady, I am honored to do the task," she said. She hoped that the smile she presented to Lady Catherine was genuine enough to suppress her own doubts within.

Father John seemed to be intuitive to Nan's uncertainties.

"'Twill not be an easy one, lass," Father John told her, "but you need not worry yourself. You are an intelligent girl. We will prepare you well for the journey ahead."

"You will not be going alone on it, either," Lady Catherine assured Nan. "I have decided to allow my most trusted servant, Emma, to come with you. You will not be leaving until spring at the earliest. The roads are now filled with ice and snow. Winter is not a good time for traveling."

Lady Catherine motioned to the maidservant by her side who

smiled at Nan.

Tears swelled in Nan's eyes. She immediately understood how important this mission was to her ladyship if she was willing to give up her closest servant for a time to travel with a poor farmer's daughter.

"I am most indebted to you, my lady, but . . . but what of my parents?" Nan asked. "They will be so worried about me. What will I tell them?"

"Your parents will not be alarmed by what you are doing," her ladyship said. "In the spring, I will send a messenger to your family asking them to have you at the castle as my servant. 'Tis there, while you are running some errands for us, you and Emma will be going to nearby towns and villages to find answers to his lordship's book. They will be day long journeys. You will always return to Lamington before sundown. Do not let anyone, including your parents, know the true nature of my invitation to Castle Lamington."

"I thank you much, your ladyship," Nan replied, bowing her head to Lady Catherine. "What if I travel with Emma and still do not find anything about the book?"

"I am prayerfully confident that we will," Father John replied. "There are many places near Lamington with people of all trades living in them. Someone may help us learn something about the book. If we need to go further somewhere, I will take it upon myself to go. I am hopeful 'twill not come to that."

"I am well pleased with the arrangement," Lady Catherine remarked. "I believe that nothing but good will come of it. You may go, Nan. In the meantime, do not reveal to anybody that you have been here. Nor must you let anyone know what you have learned here or what has been discussed. 'Tis my command. Godspeed to you!"

"Aye, my lady," Nan answered. "I promise to tell no one about today."

Nan considered the pitiful face of Lady Catherine in front of her. She thought of the pain this dear lady had to endure with his lordship up at the castle. More than anything, Nan wanted to help her ladyship and her family, friends, and neighbors to celebrate Christmas once more. Nan promptly made up her mind. She would be doubly sure not to tell a soul about her adventure with Emma in the spring. If anybody could keep a secret, it was Nan, no matter how unendurable it would be to hold it in for several months.

Lady Catherine signaled to her maidservant. She gathered up the burgundy book that was on the table and hid it under her cloak.

"Do not worry, Father, I will take the book back to the castle," her ladyship said. "'Twould be better if I took it. Come, Emma! Let us go back to the castle before his lordship arises."

Without any fanfare, Lady Catherine went to the library door and strode out. Following behind her was Emma, Father John, and Nan. The three from Castle Lamington disappeared down a different end of the church, perhaps not to be seen leaving through the front like Nan was going to. Nan was not so concerned for herself in leaving the church the same way she came in. No one would think anything of a young girl stopping into church for a quick prayer early in the morning. Nan opened the weighty front door and ran as fast as she could to Cecily's with the little sack of beans swinging by her side.

CHAPTER 5

After making the exchange of beans for a few carrots, which Cecily was all too happy to spare, Nan quickly thanked her before hurrying all the way home. She would have liked to have asked Cecily if Lettice was around, but after her important visit with Lady Catherine and Father John, it dampened her mood too much to speak to her friend that morning. On the way down the lane to her own cottage, Nan glanced over at some snow covered branches and at the brown ground underneath her feet and became thoughtful.

I am so happy 'tis still wintertime. If I begin seeing buds poke out on the branches and the grass turning green, I will know that Lady Catherine will be sending her messenger to the cottage soon. But what if I accidentally tell my parents of Lady Catherine and Father John's secret? What a mess 'twould be if I spoke of it! What long months I have ahead of me before I go to Castle Lamington. I know! I will keep very busy and then I will forget about what happened at the church today. When I start to feel a spring wind blowing, I will allow myself to think of it again. What a good idea I have come up with!

Christmas Day came and went. There was no attending church, no luscious foods from Castle Lamington to eat, or no festivities of any kind to celebrate. Christmas Day had become an ordinary one spent at home doing the usual daily chores. Nan and her family had even gone into town that morning for a few odds and ends, which was unusual, as the shops were always closed on Christmas. While walking from one shop to the next, not one townsperson made any reference to Christmas. The shopkeepers had not even decorated their own shops with holly as Simon the farmer's cottage was before it was taken down. Isabel's friend, Cecily, her husband, and her children paid a visit in the late afternoon, but it was a friendly visit, not one connected with Christmas. Predictably, not one of them uttered a word of Christmas, and Nan did not try to discuss it as none of them would remember it anyway.

Christmas Day left a big hole in Nan's heart. She could not share her feelings about it with her family and friends. She was forced to keep the grief to herself. Nan was grateful that her little brother and sisters did not fully understand the loss of Christmas.

When they are older, Christmas will be restored in Lamington and we can celebrate it like we always did, Nan murmured to herself. *I will just have to be patient.*

Instead, Nan filled the void of Christmas with chores found around the house as she had planned on doing until spring came. She worked extra hard at her duties, as if her life depended on them, and the pain of losing Christmas was lessened, but not gone, during those moments of being occupied.

The winter months moved along quickly and uneventfully for Nan after the encounter at the Church of the Holy Angels with Lady Catherine and Father John. The lives of those in Lamington continued on in the usual fashion as Nan contemplated over that clandestine meeting at the church. Her father and mother went about their business of tending to their daily work that needed to be done in both the cottage and out-of-doors. Her father tended the animals in the yard most of the time and maintained the outside of the cottage and did other repairs that needed to be done. Her mother spent most of her days indoors caring for the children, doing the customary housework, and visiting her friend, Cecily, when the work was slow.

One gray afternoon in early February, Nan stood daydreaming at the cottage window. Since there was no Christmas revelry that winter, it made the season feel odder without any happy memories of it. She found herself obsessing about the blue dirt as she usually did when there was nothing else left to do during the doldrums of winter. No matter how hard she tried blocking the depressing thought of the blue dirt from her mind, it always managed to find its way back. Since that strange day before Christmas when the blue dirt came down twice upon the people and accomplished its mission of erasing Christmas from their lives and minds, Nan had not seen it since.

"Nan, how many times must I tell you to stop opening the shutters to look out?" Nan's mother asked. "'Tis winter, and we must try to keep the house warm."

Isabel went over to the hearth to see if more logs were needed to be put on the fire.

"I am sorry, Mama," Nan replied, closing the shutters. "I was just thinking of Christmas when I opened them and . . . ."

Isabel frowned. "What is that you speak of, Nan? I have not heard of such a word before. What does it mean? I am not familiar with it."

"'Tis nothing, Mama," Nan murmured. "'Tis just something I thought I heard somewhere."

"No matter," Isabel replied, dismissing the subject with a wave of her hand as she poked at the fire with a long stick. "There is no good sense in discussing something that means nothing. Nan, pray get some wood from the back of the cottage. We need more before the fire dies out."

Nan grabbed her cloak and went out to the side of the cottage where the wood was piled up and where she could be alone in her thoughts.

"What a faded memory Christmas is in Mama's mind," Nan said softy to herself as she picked up a few sticks and logs from the wood pile. "How natural 'twas to talk about Christmas in better times. At least there are a few of them at Castle Lamington that know what Christmas is. But they are the only ones that know! How sad that makes me feel. Oh, spring! Come quickly!"

Her father was at the back fence having a lively conversation with a man who lived in the cottage next door. Nan strained her ears to listen to what they were talking about as she busily picked through the wood pile. Dusk was steadily descending upon them as she quickly searched for one last log. Coming from somewhere in the distance, a fast and furious gallop was coming closer. Nan looked up to see where the sound was coming from. She was taken aback when a rider on horseback stopped in front of their cottage door. Against the darkening sky, Nan still made out his wavy hair and plume in his hat. It was the castle messenger, Bartholomew! The bearer of that awful news that came from his lordship around Christmas. Nan felt a bit apprehensive of Bartholomew's presence and went to stand close to her father who had come over to see what the rider wanted.

"Are you Simon the farmer?" Bartholomew asked, glaring down from his horse.

"Aye, I am Simon," Simon replied.

"I am Bartholomew, messenger from Castle Lamington," he said, introducing himself. "I am certain you have seen me before. I have a message for you."

"Mayhap I have," Simon answered again. "What message do you have for us?"

Bartholomew did not bother to dismount from his horse. Nan's heart began to pound in her chest. Why was he here? Would the blue dirt fall after he left? Nan waited impatiently for Bartholomew to proceed with whatever he had come to them for. A thought struck Nan. It was not springtime, so she could not yet be called by Lady Catherine to the castle. Was there another reason for his visit?

Bartholomew did not read from a parchment as he did the time he was in the marketplace.

"Simon the farmer," Bartholomew said, "your daughter, Nan, is hereby requested by Catherine, her ladyship of Lamington and the surrounding lands, to make her immediate presence at Castle Lamington. Lady Catherine is in need of extra help around the castle, including errands that must be accomplished on a daily basis. Nan is to report to the castle at sunrise. When her duties are completed at the end of the day, she will return home. She will know at the end of each day if she needs to return there. Do not worry, Simon. Your daughter will be well taken care of. You may accompany her to the castle in the morning if you wish."

Isabel had come out of the cottage to see what the clamor was about. It had become so dark when Bartholomew finished speaking that she barely made him out in the vanishing light. She was only able to catch the end of what he was telling Simon and their daughter.

"Aye, I will bring Nan to Castle Lamington in the morning," Simon agreed.

"I will let her ladyship know that she will be expecting Nan on the morrow," Bartholomew replied. Nodding curtly as he did in the marketplace, he raced his horse back to the castle.

"Dear me, what was that all about?" Isabel asked her husband and Nan. She started to shiver a little in the cold air without her cloak on. "I wondered why 'twas taking Nan so long to find some wood for the fire."

Nan had forgotten all about the wood as she watched the dark figure of Bartholomew ride away into the darkness. She hastily grabbed a few more twigs and went back into the house as she overheard her father relay Bartholomew's message to her mother.

"Why am I going to Castle Lamington tomorrow?" Nan mumbled to herself as she placed some fresh wood on the dying fire. "'Tis not spring. What does Lady Catherine need me for? Mayhap it does not have anything to do with his lordship's book. But the messenger mentioned errands every day . . . can it be for what I am thinking?"

The door of the cottage opened. Isabel entered the room with her husband straggling behind her. She went over to the hearth and warmed her cold hands near the fire.

"Well, Nan, looks like you will be going to Castle Lamington once the sun is up," she said. "You will do fine over there. You are hard-working. Her ladyship will be pleased with you."

"Aye, Lady Catherine will be pleased," Simon said, reiterating Isabel's words. "I will come and get you from the castle every day, too, Nan. I do not feel comfortable letting you walk home by yourself in the evening."

Nan nodded in response to her parents. She did not know what to make of the next day's visit to Castle Lamington, but she did not dare share her feelings with her parents. If she did, she might have to reveal her future mission concerning the blue dirt that she was instructed not to do. She did not want to worry her father and mother unnecessarily about the bewildering message from the castle.

Tomorrow's visit might be just that—work! Nan thought. *There can be no other reason for it. I am convinced of it.*

After supper was over that evening and the family had gone to bed, Nan did not fall asleep immediately. The whys and wherefores of her unexpected summons to Castle Lamington kept flip-flopping from one minute to the next in her head.

Am I being called there for something else? Her ladyship would not send Bartholomew out so late to tell us that there were dishes for me to wash in the castle kitchen.

The harder Nan thought about Lady Catherine's message, the more exhausted her brain became. One conclusion was no better than the other.

Whatever the reason might be, I shall have to wait until morning to find out more.

Nan's eyes then became heavier and heavier until she fell asleep.

CHAPTER 6

Nan awoke the next morning to the sound of a rooster crowing vociferously in the yard. The cold weather did not seem to deter the bird from having his say so early, which Nan was grateful for as she was anxious to make an early start for Castle Lamington. After breaking her fast on fresh milk and hot bread, Nan grabbed her cloak and was swiftly on her way to the castle with her father as her mother and siblings waved good-bye in the cottage doorway.

"Our walking to the castle is becoming a tradition as of late," Simon said, as he and Nan made their way down the lane to the main road of town.

"Aye, it does seem that way," Nan replied, trying to keep up with her father's fast gait.

The ground underneath them was not as solid as it had been during the last couple of months, but the air was still cool. Not much snow fell since the beginning of the year, and whatever was left were old piles of it lying around. She and Simon then saw the dark profile of Castle Lamington looming in the distance beyond the silent marketplace in the dawn light. They soon ascended the castle's high hill until they reached the castle gate where, unlike Nan's previous visits to Castle Lamington, the castle guards let them through without question. They were about to be escorted by Richard himself into the Great Tower when they saw Father John hastily running down the steps to greet them.

"God be with you, Simon the farmer!" Father John said with a jovial smile as he released Richard back to his post. "We thank you for bringing your daughter to Castle Lamington today."

"God be with you, Father!" Simon cried out. "We came as we were told. Here is Nan, ready to get to work."

"You are a good man, Simon," Father John replied. "Nan will be kept busy at the castle. Her ladyship—and his lordship, too—will be satisfied with the duties she will accomplish here. You have a hard-working family, Simon. Nothing less will be assumed of your daughter. I will take Nan from this point. You may come back for her by sundown."

As soon as Simon left the castle, Nan followed Father John back into the Great Tower. The terrible memory of that fateful day in December, when she had returned to see his lordship about the blue dirt, came back to her. She quickly dismissed it from her thoughts. Nan promised herself that today would be a much different day from the previous one. She walked up the high stairs with a happy step in her foot, eager to start the first job she was sent to Castle Lamington for.

The sun rose higher in the eastern sky as the birds of early dawn began their chirping around the ramparts of the castle. Castle Lamington itself was slowly becoming alive. Nan heard some men in the castle stables tending to the horses there as the busy blacksmith clanged his hammer on an anvil as he worked on a horseshoe in another building nearby. Many servants went back and forth across the courtyard talking and carrying all sorts of things to and from the castle buildings scattered throughout the courtyard. The busyness of Castle Lamington brought home to Nan how much livelier it was compared to Christmastime when she came for the butchering of the animals.

"We must see Lady Catherine first," Father John said, as they walked up the stairway of the Great Tower. "She anxiously awaits your attendance, Nan. She will be delighted to see that you have come to Castle Lamington this morning."

"I am happy to serve her in any way today," Nan replied earnestly.

Father John suddenly stopped on the stairs. He turned and uneasily whispered down to Nan, "There is something else, lass. You will soon find out what that is. Her ladyship will explain more when we see her."

I just knew it! Nan thought nervously. *Nothing is ever good when coming to Castle Lamington.*

She and Father John came to the door of Lord Robert and Lady Catherine's private chambers. The aging clergyman opened the large oaken door for both he and Nan to go inside. The roaring fire that Nan saw the first time was dying out. That, together with closed shutters to keep the cold winter air out, made the room dark and chilly.

Lady Catherine stood contemplatively by herself next to the dying embers in the hearth. She looked up when Father John and Nan entered and smiled sweetly at them. She wore a flattering rose pink gown with gold edging along the sleeves and bottom. Her attire seemed to clash with the unsettling atmosphere found in the room.

Bowing to Lady Catherine, Father John declared, "My lady, I bring you Nan, daughter of Simon the farmer."

The chaplain stepped aside to reveal the young peasant girl behind him who quickly knelt down in respect to her ladyship.

"Once more, I welcome you to Castle Lamington, Nan, daughter of Simon the farmer," Lady Catherine greeted with an air of uncertainty. "Praise be to God that you have answered my request to be here."

Lady Catherine dismissed the guard that stood by the door, leaving only Nan, Father John, and herself in the room. Emma, her maidservant, and his lordship were nowhere to be found.

Is her ladyship afraid of somebody? Nan thought fearfully. *Or, something? I am not fooled by her strange behavior.*

Relieved that the guard was no longer there with them, Lady Catherine returned to the others and forced a grin upon her face.

"Nan, as you may have noticed, you have been asked to come to Castle Lamington before spring," her ladyship began. Locking her arms behind her back, she strode the floor back and forth as she spoke. "Unfortunately, some things do not always work out as we would like them to, do they? I was afraid that you would arrive here at the same time as his lordship, but there is nothing for us to worry about now."

Lady Catherine went to one of the windows in the great hall. She pulled open one of the tall, wooden shutters and looked outside. With her ladyship's back facing away from the others, Nan sensed that she was trying to hide something from everyone—a tear perhaps?

"Last evening, I found out that his lordship had arranged a hunting trip at dawn. I knew I had to act quickly when I heard of his plans. So I immediately sent Bartholomew to your home."

Lady Catherine walked back over to the dying fire and watched the final flicker of light go out from the burning logs.

"Nan, something has happened recently that has forced us to bring you here," Lady Catherine burst out. "We planned for you to come here in absence of his lordship. Things have not been well at the castle since we last saw you at the Church of the Holy Angels. My husband has been in quite a foul mood for the last several weeks. He does not want to meet with people or speak with them, including me! He refuses to play chess or listen to music. As lord of Lamington, his duties are essentially becoming neglected. He wants to take supper by himself, too, which is unlike him. It surprised us greatly when last night, he decided to go on a hunt, which has not happened in many months. 'Tis something he enjoys doing, but his decision was quite unforeseen."

A mournful expression came over her in the dark room. Nan thought that Lady Catherine was going to cry, but she quickly held her emotions in check. She glanced at Father John and gave him a subtle nod to speak for her.

"Lass, his lordship has disappeared," Father John said quietly. "'Tis such a horrific issue. At the moment, only a few of us here know about it. Considering the circumstances, we thought you should know, too. 'Twould be disastrous if those outside the walls of Castle Lamington knew, Nan. You must not divulge it to anyone."

Nan put her hand to her mouth and let out a little cry. A nauseating feeling crept into her stomach as she fixed her eyes on Father John.

Something did happen! Where did Lord Robert go? What did this all mean? Why do they want me to know? Does the blue dirt have anything to do with it?

"His lordship went out very early this morning and came back safely with his knights who went with him," Father John continued. "Afterward, his lordship decided that he wanted to turn back and go on a second hunt, much to the amazement of his entourage that was with him."

There was a long pause as Father John looked toward the window where her ladyship was standing. Pity came to his eyes as he stood staring her way for several minutes.

"After the men had gone out on the second hunt, some of them came back unexpectedly," Father John stated. "They came racing back with their horses. They were very troubled and upset, and there was chaos everywhere in the courtyard. It had many of the servants rushing out to see what the fuss was. I heard the uproar from the window of the chapel, but I did not know what it was at first. One of the men had found Lord Robert's horse empty of its rider, grazing in a field near the town walls far from the woods that the hunt was held."

"One of his lordship's knights came to me this morning to tell me what had happened," Lady Catherine said as she turned from the window. "He said the men had searched and searched everywhere in field and wood, but his lordship was nowhere to be found. They will continue to search throughout the day and for as long as necessary. We pray for Lord Robert's safe and immediate return."

"Woe to anyone if he has been slain!" Father John said. "We will remain strong until he has been found or returns to the castle on his own. We will do our best to keep this unfortunate event as quiet as possible."

"We do not quite know how the people of Lamington will take this news," Lady Catherine said somberly. "'Tis only a matter of time before the townspeople find out. We can only hide things so well before word escapes beyond the castle walls. The stewards of the castle will be under my direction now that his lordship is not here."

Uncontrollable sobbing broke out from her ladyship. The silhouetted form of Emma promptly appeared from a side door and she went immediately to Lady Catherine's side. She led her ladyship to a cushioned window seat to be comforted.

So this is why I was called to the castle! Nan wondered excitedly. *Since I am now servant here, 'twould make sense they would warn me of what happened to his lordship. They wanted to tell me the truth of his disappearance before I heard any of the rumors spread by the servants and town folk outside the castle. I will be careful not to speak of it to anybody, even to my parents, unless Lady Catherine and Father John tell me to.*

"What has happened to his lordship, Nan, was not the main reason you have been asked to come to Castle Lamington this morning," Father John declared. "There is something else that I must tell you. 'Tis equally as unpleasant as learning of his lordship's disappearance. After the furor that his lordship has caused us today, we have almost forgotten to tell you why you have been asked to come here in the first place."

Nan became heartsick upon hearing those words. Her arrival to the castle had been nothing more than a reception to receive news that was becoming more disturbing at each passing moment. Leaving home that morning was a mistake that she had no control over.

"I have just received a message from Brother Albert who resides at the monastery in Meldon," Father John said. "'Twas given to me last night by a brother messenger who came straight from the Monastery of the White Friars. Brother Albert said that he believes he has found the translation to the passage in his lordship's book. Since Lady Catherine and I are uncertain about whether or not the words have anything to do with you, Nan, we have decided that, for your own well-being, you must leave Lamington at once. Brother Albert also fears for your life and does not want you to stay here. My mentioning to him at the time that I believed that I knew who the girl was pictured in the book likely prompted this decision. The only difference is, he thinks you should never come back!"

Nan's eyes grew wide in disbelief. She did not know if she wanted to cry like Lady Catherine or run out of the castle, down the hill, and back into her mother's arms for safety. Leave the home of her birth! Where would she go? Nan knew for sure that she had been asked to come to Castle Lamington for more than simply assisting in domestic duties around the castle. She *was* there for a far greater reason than that.

Can she leave Lamington now that she was faced with it?

Lady Catherine returned from the window seat. She was in better spirits and was more serene than ever. Her ladyship gave them a smile that was genuine, but short-lived. After her husband's mysterious absence, one only imagined how long she could carry on in a proper frame of mind, even for a noblewoman.

"Father, have you told Nan about the message?" Lady Catherine asked.

"Aye, my lady," Father John replied. "But I have not finished telling her what the effects of it will be."

"I will tell her," Lady Catherine offered. "On my orders, Nan, you must leave Lamington for a time. Mayhap 'twould not be as long as Brother Albert had said, but for a little while. I think he is being overly cautious for your sake."

Nan surveyed Lady Catherine with frightened eyes.

Was her ladyship being truthful about Nan going away for a short time? Or, was she hiding something much worse? And here was Nan . . . only getting used to leaving Lamington for just one day at a time!

"Nan, do not fear," Lady Catherine gently assured her. "You will go to the monastery where Brother Albert resides and stay there for as long as necessary, but not forever. 'Tis the safest place there is if 'tis too dangerous for you to be in Lamington. The monastery is secluded near a forest on a high mountainside and is a two day's ride from here. I have been there myself, so I know. Brother Albert did not tell us what the exact translation of the passage was, lass. The risk may have been too great to send by messenger. Mayhap once you settle in at the monastery, he will share that information with you. By the way, I have not forgotten about having Emma accompany you to wherever you go which, in this case, is Meldon, along with one of our trusted castle guards, for safety."

"I will also be going to Meldon so that I may meet with Brother Albert, too," Father John added. "I will arrive after a few days when things have settled down a bit around here."

Father John was painstakingly trying not to refer to Lord Robert's disappearance in front of Lady Catherine. Her ladyship's feelings were running raw after so much chaos at the castle that morning, and she did not need to be reminded of what had happened to her husband.

"I, myself, am determined to find out what the translation of the passage is," Father John said. "It may help put an end to the very odd goings-on in Lamington. We must make hasty preparations. Word will be given to your parents, Nan, as to your whereabouts. We will be honest with them by letting them know that one of your duties was to go to Meldon with Emma, to help us out with something there. There will be no need for them to worry, but they must not tell anyone where you are. You will come back as safely as you have gone. That is our promise to you, lass."

Nan's fatigued mind was many leagues from the castle. She needed time to think over what Father John and Lady Catherine had barraged her with. She wanted to go home first; to sit and think over her options in going to the Monastery of the White Friars. But what were her options? The reality was much different than the world Nan wanted to stay warm and comfortable in.

I will go where they send me, Nan lamented deep down. *I will be strong. I do not want to bring on any trouble where there is too much already—first with the blue dirt and then with his lordship. Was this translation with me in it have anything to do with his lordship's disappearance? How sick I am becoming at such a thought!*

At that moment, a rapid knocking was heard on the door of the great hall. Father John went to open it as a servant rushed into the room and bowed before Lady Catherine.

"Your ladyship," the man's voice trembled, "I must speak to you, but . . . ."

The servant's troubled eyes shifted from left to right on those standing there. His eyes rested on Lady Catherine. "I need to speak to you privately, your ladyship."

Lady Catherine motioned for Father John and Nan to leave the room so she could speak alone to the servant.

Nan welcomed any interruption to take her mind off of going to the monastery. She and Father John had scarcely left the great hall long enough when the servant came back out and ran down the hallway. Lady Catherine called them back in.

Her ladyship whispered to Father John, "Something dreadful has happened!"

Lady Catherine walked to the window and back several times. She did not seem to know where to stand at any given moment.

Appearing to forget that Nan was in their company, her ladyship blurted out, "The stewards of our castle have taken ill. They immediately took to their beds after making some of their usual rounds about the castle this morning. The castle physician is with them in their chambers."

"Lord have mercy on them!" Father John said. He bowed his head and briefly closed his eyes as if in prayer. Before he said more, the servant who had just given them word of the ill stewards ran back into the great hall.

"Your ladyship!" he cried out to Lady Catherine, unable to catch his breath. "Your ladyship!" His eyes frantically darted back and forth from Lady Catherine to Father John as he uttered more terrible news.

"The castle stewards . . . they . . . they . . . are dead!" the servant cried. "They could not be saved."

"How horrible!" Lady Catherine said. The color drained from her face while Father John's had turned ash white.

"Pray take us to the physician who had looked after them," her ladyship stated firmly to the servant. "We must find out what caused their swift deaths."

Nan followed quietly behind as the clergyman and her ladyship followed the servant out of the great hall and down a stone staircase to a different part of the castle. Just as they were making their way down a passageway, a middle-aged man in a dark tunic with a troubled expression upon his face was walking in the opposite direction of where they were going. Nan soon discovered that he was the castle physician. The servant who was walking ahead of them turned to bow and left the physician alone with Father John and Lady Catherine.

"Your ladyship," the physician said, bowing low to Lady Catherine. Seeing that Nan was standing in their midst, the physician became hesitant to speak of the stewards' conditions with Lady Catherine. "I must speak to you . . . alone."

"Come, you may speak to me in my chambers," Lady Catherine said to the physician. "Father, you may be there as well. Nan, you may remain outside the door until we are finished."

Returning to the great hall, Nan waited while the others went inside and shut the door behind them. An eternity seemed to elapse before anyone came out. Nan felt weak from hunger as it was hours since she had left home with her father to come to Castle Lamington. Moreover, she was becoming increasing fearful of her unknown future since her arrival.

Nan had become so preoccupied in her thoughts that she had not noticed the door of the great hall being thrust open. Father John came out with the castle physician behind him. The physician walked off to another part of the castle as Father John followed him at a distance with distress in his eyes. He did not say a word until the physician disappeared from view. The old chaplain tried to force a smile to his tired, uneasy face. Though not in so many words, Nan sensed that the physician communicated something terribly upsetting to her ladyship and Father John that he was not at liberty to say in front of just anybody.

"Nan," Father John murmured gravely, "you must leave Lamington with Emma straightaway! After the passing of our stewards, we must not take any chances. You will both leave under the cover of darkness with the castle guard. Do not speak to anybody on the way to the monastery in Meldon. Stay nowhere where anyone can ask you any questions, either. If you find yourselves somewhere with people around, do not stay long enough for conversation. When it comes to finding shelter for the night, the castle guard will know where to find everyone a safe, yet unassuming, place to stay. Do you understand, child?"

"Aye, Father," Nan answered with uncertainty. "I believe I do."

"I plan on going to see Brother Albert sooner than expected, too," Father John stated, looking up and down the hallway as if concerned about someone lurking in the shadows. "I do not feel comfortable leaving Lady Catherine by herself without a steward or two to help her, but she can be quite adept in caring for Castle Lamington when necessary. Until new stewards can be found, she will have to rely on the other castle staff for the help she needs. In the interim, just promise me that you will take extra care on the road to Meldon. 'Tis a dangerous world out there. With his lordship missing and the stewards now dead, we cannot be sure that more trouble might not be headed our way. Vigilance, Nan. Vigilance. Remember that always."

Nan was becoming all the more inquisitive as to the reason behind the stewards' deaths, but she was too timid to ask. She wished Father John was forward with her about them, but she dared not ask for fear that the reasons might be far from pleasant, and he might not tell her anyway.

"I will be getting to Meldon before you and will leave Castle Lamington without delay," Father John said. "I will not stop until I get there. I may be tired at the end of my journey, but after a good rest at the Monastery of the White Friars, I will be back to my old self."

Father John gave a hearty chuckle that had Nan laughing along with him.

Abruptly changing the subject, he then added, "I must take my leave of you and prepare for my passage to Meldon. Nan, follow me down to the kitchen. Whilst you wait for nightfall to make your journey to Meldon, we must find you something to do in the meantime. There are always a few vegetables to be cut up for the pot down there, so Hugo the cook will make good use of you there."

CHAPTER 7

Nan and the old chaplain made their way across the stone hallway, down a few flights of stone staircases, and to the bottom floor of the Great Tower, where they ultimately came to a large room.

"Here is the castle kitchen!" Father John announced, his voice echoing throughout.

The room was bustling with a dozen or so people standing around and working at a large wooden table in the middle of the floor. Some of the people curiously looked up at Nan and Father John before continuing on with their work. Nan recognized some of the townswomen who were busy with their assigned duties. One woman was plucking a goose, another was cutting up vegetables, and others were kneading dough or preparing meat for the spit.

On one side of the kitchen were enormous ovens and fireplaces with spits and cauldrons hanging in them, while along the wall, on the adjoining side, were dried herbs of various kinds dangling from the ceiling. There were doorways leading to storage areas where barrels and crates of items unknown were stacked. The room was very hot, and the smells of so many good things cooking and baking in the kitchen filled Nan's nostrils, making her hungrier than ever. For a moment she thought she was going to faint from lack of food.

"What a kitchen I see before me!" Nan exclaimed with surprise. She said it so loudly that she received the attention of some of the nearby kitchen staff. "I suppose the castle needs it with so many people to feed."

Father John went up to a tall man with a white beard, who stood at the far side of the work table, and spoke to him while Nan stood and stared at the woman who was plucking the goose's feathers in a hasty, methodical fashion.

"Nan, pray come here!" Father John called.

Nan went up to Father John and the man with the white beard.

"This is Hugo," Father John explained to her. "He is in charge of the castle kitchen and is head cook. He will give you something to do while you are here today."

Hugo looked at Nan with twinkling eyes and a smile so kindly and wide, it filled his entire face from cheek to cheek. Sweat from the heat of the kitchen was dripping down his face.

"I do humbly thank you, Father," Nan said.

"I want to wish you Godspeed on your journey this evening, Nan," Father John murmured to her. "Her ladyship will have someone come and retrieve you from the kitchen before you leave. Do not discuss any of this with anyone in the kitchen. Do not tell them more than is necessary. You are here from the town to assist in the kitchen and that is all. Do I make myself understood, child? 'Tis here that I make my leave of you."

Nan nodded her head in reply.

Father John smiled back at her encouragingly and left the kitchen.

Nan's heart became saddened by the sudden disappearance of the old chaplain. The smile that was on her face, just moments ago, soon left her. Father John was a great source of direction and comfort to her at Castle Lamington during these last, trying hours. Without him there, it left her with a feeling of vulnerability. Nan immediately shrugged off the feeling that was troubling her.

I am here for nothing more than to help in the kitchen, she said to herself. *Otherwise, I might get questions that I cannot answer.*

After cutting Nan a huge slice of hot bread to eat for which she was grateful for, Hugo showed her to the large table she had first seen when she walked into the kitchen. He directed her to some onions that were in need of slicing. Putting a large knife in front of her, Nan promptly got to work. She had hoped she would be given a different duty. The idea of slicing up onions was something she did not enjoy doing, even at home.

A stout, middle-aged woman, with graying wisps of hair coming out from underneath her wimple, was standing next to Nan. She began to chuckle under her breath as she was cutting up turnips.

"Better you than me, lass," she said, referring to the pile of onions that were set in front of Nan. "I would spend my entire day wiping my eyes if I was doing that job, not that I enjoy mine much. I believe your name is Nan. You are Simon the farmer's daughter, are you not?"

"I am," Nan replied as she began to peal the skin off her first onion.

Nan did not know what else to say to this woman beyond those first few words. She knew her to live at the other side of their lane and was something of a gossip. Her mother had always said that if the woman, whose name was Beatrice, could not hold her tongue in, someone else would pull it out for her.

"Come now, Beatrice," another woman, who stood on the other side of Beatrice and helped her cut up more turnips, said. "Leave the lass alone. We all have work to do here. We do whatever is given to us."

The others, who stood around the other three sides of the table, looked up momentarily at Beatrice as they worked steadily at their kitchen duties.

"If you keep up the complaining, Beatrice, I will have some onions waiting for you as soon as you finish those turnips," Hugo the cook sternly said. He had just come from a back room carrying a bowl of strong herbs and placed some of them in a bubbling pot that was hanging in the fireplace.

"Pray, sir," Beatrice pleaded with Hugo, "you know that I do not complain so much."

"I am not so certain of *that*, Beatrice!" Hugo told her distrustfully. "For a woman your age, you should be grateful that his lordship allows for your actions here. You have complained for years here at the castle. Nothing suits you!"

Nan laughed to herself at what had gone on between Beatrice and Hugo the cook. It was apparent that Beatrice's behavior was nothing new to those in the castle kitchen.

Quiet fell over the entire table afterward and no one spoke as they did their work, except if necessary. Nan soon learned that Hugo preferred that no one speak much during their work or the job would slow down. Idle talk had little to no place in a busy castle kitchen.

Nan felt as if she had been cutting up onions for an eternity. Her back ached and her hand was getting red from the knife handle that she held so tightly. Her eyes stung as well from looking at the onions, and the taste of them were now in her mouth. She was bending over the onions for so long that she had not noticed the two men who had entered the kitchen, until whispers about them were being exchanged around the table she

63

worked at.

A young man who was carving meat excitedly said, "The new stewards have arrived! I overheard them talking a little while ago with Hugo when they walked in."

"How do you know that they are our new stewards?" asked another young man who was walking by with a basket full of bright red apples.

"I heard them say so to Hugo," the other young man replied.

"I take it her ladyship wanted them to make the rounds at Castle Lamington before taking on their duties," added a youth who was at the head of the table.

"After all her ladyship has gone through, I feel for her," said someone else.

"I do not see her ladyship anywhere," Beatrice said, looking up from her turnips to see if Lady Catherine was in the room. "I wonder if she is hurting too much to come to the kitchen with them."

"Aye, 'tis very peculiar that she has not come around with the two men," whispered another woman, standing across from Beatrice.

The kitchen staff, try as they may, could not keep silent at the reference of Lord Robert's strange disappearance that spread throughout the castle. Even the deaths of the other stewards could not be kept hidden, and before long, everyone at Castle Lamington knew of their unfortunate fate.

Nan lifted her stiff neck to glance at the two men who were walking about the kitchen.

Both men looked to be in their early twenties and had a very ethereal appearance about them, which had heads turning from every end of the kitchen. They were very slender, yet very strong in face and body. Their height was impressive as they towered above each person in the room, and their skin and hair was very fair and neatly combed at their shoulders. Their clothing was skillfully tailored, too, as they both wore brightly-colored tunics trimmed with fur. The men had stoic expressions upon their faces. They neither spoke nor addressed any questions at anyone.

"I do not feel comfortable around them," Jeanette, a woman who stood on the other side of Nan, retorted. "They stare at us too much."

"They do not even bother to introduce themselves to us," one of the bakers said as he kneaded some bread dough. "Our previous stewards always came into the kitchen to talk to us. For pity's sake, they do not even crack us a smile. Look at them."

The baker shook his head in disgust as he continued on with his work.

Nan had to agree with Jeanette that the two men, who looked like twins to her, kept looking unceasingly in their direction. They were a bit odd.

"Mayhap, now that our lordship is not here," Beatrice began, "they can encourage her ladyship to start up that one holiday we lost not so very long ago. 'Twas a holiday whose name I no longer remember. But I do remember one thing about it. The holiday had gone on in Lamington for generations. I seem to believe that 'twas stopped because our lordship commanded us not to celebrate it."

Nan turned her head sharply at Beatrice as she spoke.

"Do you remember such a thing?" Nan quietly asked. "Christmas, I mean?"

Nan was aware that Hugo did not like it when they all talked, but not seeing Hugo anywhere, she could not resist asking Beatrice about the outlawed holiday.

The two men, standing close to them, deliberately turned toward them as if trying to catch every word between Beatrice and Nan.

Beatrice started to speak out loud without regard to Hugo's kitchen rule.

"Aye, I do remember something, Nan," she said. "'Tis not much, but my mind is not gone completely."

"Why do you speak so loudly?" Jeanette asked Beatrice, now irritated with her. "You will be getting us into trouble when Hugo returns."

Beatrice was too overwrought to pay any attention to the other woman.

"I do not care!" Beatrice cried out. "Mayhap if these new stewards hear our complaints about how things are run around here, they may change them for the better."

"Beatrice!" Jeannette exclaimed animatedly.

Everyone looked up from their station as a young man, with dark hair far down the table, reprimanded Beatrice in a loud whisper. "Pray be silent! Jeanette is right. We will be in trouble soon enough if you keep this up. You also speak treason in the way you speak of our lordship who is gone from us. Wherever he has gone, may the good Lord take care of him and allow him a safe return."

"How dare a lad like you tell your elders how to be proper!" Beatrice declared in exasperation. Ignoring the young man, she continued to speak of Christmas.

"Now, Nan," Beatrice said, putting her head close to the girl next to her, "I think I do remember this holiday to some extent. What was the name that you gave it?"

Nan was able to tell in the way Beatrice asked about Christmas that she was being sincere. The older woman was genuinely unaware of what Christmas was about and was searching painfully for answers about it.

"Christmas the name was," Nan replied, bending over the dreadful onions and speaking low enough so no one would hear her. She only wished Beatrice would do the same.

Hugo was right about the talking. It did slow things down in the kitchen as Nan could tell from Beatrice who had stopped cutting the turnips and was completely focused on conversing with her.

"Aye, it has a strange name," Beatrice said thoughtfully. "I wonder what it means. Do you know, Nan? Was it something our entire kingdom celebrated?"

Nan found it interesting how speaking of Christmas seemed to joggle something in Beatrice's memory, but in the end, Beatrice shook her head.

"I know nothing of this holiday then," the woman concluded.

Nan was not surprised by Beatrice's reaction to Christmas and how she remembered only a smattering of it. She had seen it before with her parents and the other townspeople. The memory of Christmas slowly slipped from their minds until it faded and they remembered no more. Beatrice had spoken the last of Christmas with Nan. Nan had every reason to believe that the blue dirt had everything to do with it. Seeing it was no use in carrying on her conversation about Christmas with Beatrice, Nan abruptly ended their conversation. She fell silent and went on cutting the pile of onions that lie before her on the table. She was also concerned about breaking the kitchen rule of silence between herself and anyone else, especially when it came to Beatrice who seemed to get into constant trouble for one reason or another.

Nan was becoming acutely aware of the two new stewards coming and standing closer to her, with an occasional sideways glance to one another. At one point, she heard one of them speak to the other quietly. Whatever they said was in a language she was not familiar with. The peasant girl found it curious that her ladyship brought stewards in from a different country to run the castle. Surely there were capable men from their kingdom who were able to do it in their place.

Nan felt a hand on her shoulder. She jumped and half expected it to be one of the stewards. She was afraid to look up and face the new steward, but she was happy to see that it was the face of Hugo staring back at her instead. He had returned to the kitchen from wherever he happened to be earlier. The two stewards stepped aside to let Hugo speak with her. Nevertheless, their eyes kept continual close watch on them.

"Pray, Nan, get some onions from the back room over there," Hugo murmured, pointing to the place with the barrels and crates. "You will need more, so you can get them yourself. If you do not see any there, you will find some outside the kitchen door, where the garden lies beyond."

Nan looked down at the large pile of onions next to her. She was perplexed as to why Hugo would want her to get more when she had plenty already.

Without another word, Nan went over to the back room of the castle kitchen. Without looking back, she felt the eyes of the stewards following her. It was all very uncomfortable, and she hoped they would go to another part of the castle soon and leave the kitchen staff alone.

Stepping into the room that Hugo pointed out, Nan did not see any of the onions he mentioned. Unsure of their whereabouts, she decided to try the second place. Opening the kitchen door to the garden, she stepped out into the cold as a strong smell of rotting leaves hung in the air. The door shut quietly behind her as she gazed at everything before her. Nan judged it to be mid-afternoon, but she could hardly determine this as the morning blended in with the drab afternoon that it was. Looking every inch through the doorway, she was not able to find onions there, either.

Glancing up, Nan saw the kitchen garden in the distance—dead from the winter with mounds of old, overturned dirt and brown, wilted vegetable plants and leaves lying about it. A thin fog was beginning to form and hang around the perimeter of the garden, giving it a ghostly appearance. The garden made Nan tremble and want to run back into the kitchen where she felt safe, except when it came to the two stewards who might still be there.

Not sure where to look next, Nan reluctantly decided to go back into the kitchen and ask Hugo to show her where the onions were. Just then, she heard a rustling sound and some horses quietly snorting from a short distance nearby.

Nan anxiously started to head back toward the kitchen door when a damp leather glove came out from behind and covered her mouth.

"Do not scream, lass!" whispered a young masculine voice, firmly yet gently. We are here to help you, not hurt you."

Nan stiffened from fear. She wondered if the lad speaking to her was one of the stewards. She thought she was going to become ill, yet there was something familiar with his expression that she could not place. Perhaps the identity of this lad would come to light at a later time.

A horse appeared out of the fog, with a second one appearing soon after with a dark clothed figure seated on it. Both horses were equipped with items for a long trek somewhere as leather saddlebags were hanging from each animal.

The lad lifted Nan off the ground and seated her behind the rider on the other horse. Nan's knees were shaking as she had never been on a horse before, nor had she ever ridden on one.

The lad, who had lifted her up onto the other horse, mounted his own with great agility. A small, round shield and simple sword was seen hanging from his side.

"Nan, hold tight to the waist of the rider you sit behind," the lad instructed her. "We will be riding fast, so do not let your hands go free at any time or you may fall from the horse. 'Twill be a nasty spill if you do. There is something else, too. Pray keep the hood of your cloak over your head at *all* times. You must not ask any questions or speak to anyone when we leave Lamington. If you do, one may never know what may befall us. Do you understand me?"

He had placed such great emphasis on his words that Nan knew better than to disobey his command.

Nan nodded to the lad. Pulling the hood of her cloak over her head, she could not make out his face as he, too, wore a simple dark cloak similar to her own. The two people on the horses were taking great pains to hide their identity as they kept their heads down or away from Nan whenever she tried to look at them.

Who were these riders? Where were they taking her?

"Now, we go!" the lad called out.

The lad took the lead of the other rider and Nan as he took off at a speedy gallop. They made their way around the kitchen garden and through the castle courtyard as the fog thickened further and swirled about them. As if someone already knew Nan and the others were coming, they crossed over the drawbridge that was automatically dropped for them. The riders sprinted down the hill away and beyond Castle Lamington. Nan closed her eyes as she held tight to the waist of the unknown rider. She was becoming dizzy from the fast motion of the horse underneath her and her stomach felt queasy. Wanting a glimpse of the castle they were leaving behind, her eyes slowly opened as she turned to stare back at the large, intimidating fortress. The castle was eerily surrounded in thick fog on the high hill that quickly dissipated when they got to the bottom of it.

Turning to look in front of her, Nan saw that they were entering town as buildings and houses passed by them in a blur.

I suppose I shall never know which home was that of my family, Nan wretchedly thought. *It went by so fast. Father and Mama might have heard us, but did not look outside to see who was there.*

Nan became even more downhearted when she thought of what Mary and Agatha would say when they learned that Nan had to leave home to stay in a faraway place. They would sadly ask their mother again and again where she was, but as for little Simon, he would be too young to understand.

Leaving? They were leaving Lamington! Where was she going, exactly? Was this the plan that was laid out for her to leave town?

The lad stopped his horse under the gatehouse of Lamington as Nan and her rider came up behind him. He drew out a rolled parchment paper from underneath his cloak as a sentry came to him from the gatehouse. After reading the paper given to him, the sentry gave a nod of approval.

"Godspeed to you all on your journey to Arnon!" the sentry waved.

Nan was bewildered as to why they were going to Arnon when she was supposed to be going to Meldon. Arnon was a small village south of Lamington, which was not so very far away. Nan had never been there, but she had heard of it. Questions crowded Nan's mind faster and faster. The truth was, no one would answer her until they were far enough from town.

"Godspeed to us!" the lad yelled out as the horses picked up momentum after leaving the town gate.

Nan's rider raised a hand in response to the lad's cry.

CHAPTER 8

The horses galloped side by side down the muddy sloped road that led past the town gate. They headed toward the very forest that Nan had peered at from afar whenever the gate was open during the day. The dense forest was filled with many varieties of trees, from broad-leaf to conifers. The deeper they rode into the forest, the denser and darker it became.

The riders soon slowed their horses down from a gallop to a trot. The road was flat and wide as they rode on. After they went a little ways further, the road began to make its way uphill a bit through the forest while an impenetrable fog was beginning to surface from the ground. They heard the cawing of some crows, and the twittering of a few birds in the trees above. There was a soft crack of a twig in the underbrush made by a small animal, but the forest remained largely calm and quiet around them.

"I will never like this forest for as long as I live," Nan said, breaking the silence.

Laughter was heard coming from the lad ahead of them.

"Does it frighten you so?" he asked. "'Tis only an old forest, you know. We are not even half-way through it—we are still in Lamington, you know—and as 'tis so late in the day, we will make camp here. We will be out of the forest by morning sometime."

The lad pulled the hood of his cloak from his head.

Nan gasped with surprise. It was Richard, the guard from the gatehouse at Castle Lamington! No wonder his voice was familiar to her. She should have known all along with those azure eyes of his gazing back at her.

"You look as if you have seen a ghost, Nan, daughter of Simon the farmer," Richard stated. His eyes were still laughing at her as he drew the hood back over his head.

The other rider chuckled at Richard's remark. Nan became aware that it was a girl's laughter. Turning around to Nan and revealing her face, Nan was relieved to see that it was Emma. It was only until they were far enough away from the castle and the town that they openly identified themselves to her.

"I am happy to know 'tis you, Emma!" Nan said with delight. "Lady Catherine did say that I would be riding with you. If only it came to memory back in the kitchen garden at the castle. I would not have been so terrified when Richard put me on your horse after I was snatched up by him."

"I am shocked that you did not realize I was a girl," Emma answered with disdain. "I was riding sidesaddle the entire time. 'Tis something only women and girls do when riding a horse, Nan. But what can be expected of a peasant girl! She does not know of such things as she does not ride horses."

Nan was pained by Emma's words. She was not pleased that Richard was making fun of her, either, as he had done once before when she had come back to Castle Lamington to speak with Lord Robert. She wished that Lady Catherine and Father John had chosen others to take her to the Monastery of the White Friars.

"Emma!" Richard snapped. "Your manners disgust me! I am very surprised at you, being a lady's maidservant that you are! We were given a duty by Lady Catherine to care for the lass until we reached Meldon and that is what we shall do. Now, treat Nan properly or else I shall take you back to Lamington. Even a peasant girl deserves our respect. Lady Catherine will not be pleased with your conduct."

Emma was taken aback by Richard and did not respond. She kept to herself for a while as they made their way around snow piles on the road that were larger than when they had first started out on the road. The air had even become chillier in the higher elevation than it was further below.

Nan's heart leapt at Richard's chastising Emma and was surprised at his change in character. There was hope for him after all, and she was willing to give him a chance to show his better side.

He is still an immature lad, Nan thought. *He has lots to learn, though he looks older than his age. A man-in-training, as my father might have said.*

"Lass, we did not mean to scare you at the castle like we did," Richard said apologetically. "We were told to hide our faces when we came to get you. Father John's orders. He wanted us to be cautious during our journey. He said he had forewarned you just the same."

"Aye, he did," Nan replied. "He told me before he left the castle kitchen."

Nan sat sleepily on the horse and listened to the wind billowing through the bare trees overhead during the first hour or two during the ride. Richard and Emma did not converse much together or with Nan. Since Nan had no one to talk with, she amused herself by daydreaming about what awaited them on their journey to Meldon. She contemplated what Meldon or the monastery on the high mountain was like. She tried not to think too much about her family so far away. Instead, she prayed quietly to herself for a safe return to Lamington.

"Richard, why did you tell that sentry that we were going to Arnon when we are really going to Meldon?" Nan asked, partly out of boredom and partly out of curiosity. "I heard you tell him that back at the gate in Lamington."

"'Twas by Lady Catherine's decree," Richard said. "She told me that she did not want any rabble-rousers following us to Meldon. Just in case they asked the sentry where we were going. Telling them that we were going to Arnon would throw them off. 'Tis just a precaution. Nothing more."

"Do you think we will return to Lamington?" Nan asked with great interest.

"I do not know, lass," Richard answered, much to Nan's dismay. "Since I am so much enjoying our adventure through the forest, I am in no hurry to go back and see it. I have not often been outside of Lamington, so this is quite a change for me."

"If not you, then do you think that *I* will go back to Lamington?" Nan persisted. "If you believe that I will, do you know when that will be?"

"Again, I do not know!" Richard said exasperated. "I do not know how that is any different from my returning there. I assume we will all return together, but only time will tell."

"Well, I hope *I return* to Lamington soon!" Emma chimed in. She was in better spirits, yet Nan guessed that she was still smarting from Richard's tongue-lashing. Emma also seemed to be in the mood to grumble relentlessly. She complained about the forest and she protested about becoming a maidservant to Nan. Though deep down, she knew she was not really maidservant to Nan. She was only accompanying the other girl to the monastery in Meldon by choice of Lady Catherine.

"My highborn lady mother raised my sisters and I to care for someone such as Lady Catherine," Emma declared. "I am not a maidservant to a farmer's daughter. You must understand that, Richard. Nan must be made to understand that, too. You can send me back to her ladyship if you wish, Richard. I do not care. Send someone else in my place."

Emma sat back on her horse as tears welled up in her eyes.

Nan might have been wounded further by Emma's unkindness if it was not for the fact that she had enjoyed listening to Richard putting Emma back in her place. How well he knew how to do it!

"Nay, Emma," Richard answered her with a roguish smile, "I have decided that I will leave you and Nan to the wild beasts of the forest. I will go ahead to Meldon, and you can both find your own way."

He darted so far up the road with his horse that it took both Emma and Nan by surprise. Emma went off after him at equal speed with Nan nearly tumbling from the horse had she not grabbed onto Emma's waist fast enough.

"Richard, do not leave us!" Emma cried out after him.

Richard slowed down ahead of them and waited for Emma to catch up to him. His cloak and horse were heavily soiled with mud that had splashed up from the road after his fast get-away.

"This will teach you a lesson in humility, Emma," Richard said angrily. "And if you had not thought of it before, if her ladyship had not felt you were up to the job, she would have gotten someone else to be with Nan. Consider that a compliment, Emma, and not some laborious task. If we are all going to be together for a while, then we had all better get along with one another. And I would not leave you here in the forest, you silly goose!"

Emma hung her head and said no more on the subject. She even made a weak apology to Nan who accepted it graciously.

"I realize that I am not here to take care of Nan like I do of Lady Catherine," Emma said. "I do not mean to make exaggerations, Nan. I am here as a traveling companion to you, so 'tis an easy enough job for me. I should not be so ill-tempered like I am. Things will be different from now on. I promise."

Emma turned and placed a friendly hand of Nan's shoulder as a small smile came to her lips.

"I see life will become more bearable for all of us, Emma," Richard said with a grin. "Let us continue on our journey to Meldon. I do not want to hear anymore foolishness."

The road became rougher and narrower, with more rocks and heavier piles of snow, as Emma followed single file behind Richard as he went higher and higher up the hill on his horse. The scenery had not changed much since leaving town, except that the trees became more abundant and dripping with water from the fog. Nan did not know whether they were still in Lamington or not at that point. She was becoming tired and hungry and wondered if they would stop soon to eat something.

Richard held up his gloved hand and motioned for them to stop their horses as he looked about to his left and right as if searching for something in the forest. He put his other gloved hand on the sword that was at his side. He sat there silently for quite some time before saying anything.

"Richard, are we lost?" Emma asked.

Richard did not respond, so Emma reiterated her question to him.

"Nay, we are not lost," he replied softly. "I thought I heard something."

Nan immediately became alert as she listened judiciously to whatever the sound was that Richard had heard.

""'Tis a queer sound," Richard murmured. "Listen! Do you not hear it, Emma? Nan, do you not hear it also?"

"I do not hear anything," Nan replied. "I only see trees standing peacefully in a darkening forest."

"Your hearing is excellent, Richard, if you can hear something that we cannot," Emma rambled on. "You have the ears of a fox, if I may say so."

A shrill sound filled the air around them. It was something between a woman's scream and the hooting of an owl.

HOOOO-AHHH!!!

A tingling feeling ran up and down Nan's spine while an apprehensive look came over Emma. Nan had never heard a sound like it before and was unable to place it. Closing her eyes, Nan prayed that Richard would tell them to turn around and go back to Lamington before the unknown creature had any chance to jump out of the trees and attack them.

"What was that?" Nan asked, opening her eyes. She did not see anything, but she sensed something was amiss.

HOOOO-AHHH!!!

The sound came a second time and then a third.

"I do not know," Emma replied. "I cannot tell if I am hearing an animal or a person."

Richard turned his horse around and came toward the others as grave concern shown in his face.

"We have been too long on the road," he cautioned them. "We should have found shelter a while ago. The fog is going to get thicker at any minute, and 'tis starting to get darker out. There is no telling what danger we will find ourselves in afterward. 'Twas foolish of me to wait so long to find us anything. I see a hunter's lodge in the trees over yonder, but I believe we can safely use it. There is no light gleaming from it, and I do not see any smoke rising from the chimney hole. The road we are on does not look like it has been used all that often, either, which leads me to believe that the lodge is empty. These are no-man's lands between Lamington and Arnon, and 'tis not known to have permanent residents. When we come closer to the lodge, I will take a look inside to make sure no one is there."

"I have neither seen a lodge, nor any building anywhere, for the last hour," Emma declared with surprise. "Have you, Nan?"

Emma strained her eyes to and fro in every direction to see if she had missed seeing anything that resembled a lodge or anything close to it.

"Nay, I have not," Nan said. "How do you know 'tis a hunter's lodge, Richard?"

"There are no farms found in this area," Richard said. "Nothing grows here, just the trees that surround us. The lodge also has trees around it and nothing else. What else can you use a building like this for? Only a hunter would use it and only sporadically."

"You not only have the ears of a fox, but the eyes of one as well, Richard," Emma said.

"I have been told as much," Richard said beaming. "My eyes and ears are better than most anybody's. I do not know why, but 'tis true."

"Now we know why *you* are leading us to Meldon and no one else,"

Nan said with delight. "You are a great help to us."

"Now I understand why you are one of the guards standing at the top of Castle Lamington," Emma praised Richard.

"I do not know if that is the only reason why I am castle guard," Richard said, as a sullen look came over him. "I do not wish to speak of this any further. Follow me so we can find the lodge. I am seeing the path for it a little ways into the forest."

Richard let his hand drop from his sword. Taking the reins of his horse, he turned off the road and into the trees with Emma and Nan following close behind on their horse. They had to ride down a sloped hill to get to the path that led to the lodge. The land leveled off a little further below the hill where they found the narrow path, which was equally as muddy as the main road they had just left behind.

"I see that the path has not been used in a while," Richard stated, glancing down at the ground. Save for some old snow, rotting leaves, and pine needles, there was no sign of horse hooves or footsteps. "Mayhap 'tis a good sign as it might mean that no one has been to the lodge in a while. I will also go and hunt for a small animal for our supper once we get settled."

Putting his finger to his lips, Richard looked up at the bare trees and paused. He then put his hands near his ears to listen. The noise they had all heard earlier did not repeat itself. They only heard the wind blowing through the limbs and the horses snorting.

"We should remain silent until we get inside the lodge so we do not attract any unwanted attention," Richard murmured to the girls behind him.

As clear as day, a hunter's lodge came into full view, nestled in the trees just as Richard had said it was, much to the astonishment of Emma and Nan. The building was not very large and was made out of wattle and daub with heavy, brown vines growing around the front door. It was very much like the cottage that Nan lived in with her family. The sealed shutters squeaked in the breeze, and there was no sign of life surrounding the dwelling.

"I will go and have a look here and there," Richard said. "Stay here, both of you."

Richard dismounted his horse and went to take a walk around the building. He was gone for some time, which made Emma and Nan uncomfortable.

"Well, 'tis what I had thought earlier," Richard said when he returned. "'Tis a hunter's lodge after all. I saw a large pile of animal bones left from hunters who had been here previously. I have done some hunting myself!"

He held up a large hare that he had found for them.

"Our supper, lasses!" Richard said with a grin.

"A hare! How wonderful!" Nan replied, clapping her hands.

"We wondered where you had gone to," Emma stated as she started to walk up to the front door of the lodge.

"Wait!" Richard called after her. "Let me do that."

Running out in front of Emma, he knocked on the front door. When no sound was heard coming from the inside, Richard turned the handle as the door creaked open. He gingerly went inside the lodge and looked around.

"All is safe," Richard announced, reappearing in the front door. "I will go and find some wood for a fire. When that is done, I will clean up the hare."

Evening had descended upon the forest. A full moon had come out, but it was soon covered by clouds moving fast across the sky. The cool temperatures were dropping quickly as the girls stood about nervously waiting for Richard who had disappeared again behind the lodge.

"If 'twas not for this blue whatever-it-is that came over Lamington, we would not be here," Emma complained with bitterness as she shivered in the cold. "I am not blaming you, Nan. I suppose I would like to, but you have not asked for what has happened in Lamington. Neither has any one of us. I do not blame his lordship, either. 'Tis that evil book that came to him from his deceased uncle, although I should not speak so ill of the dead."

"I worry about what my parents must have thought when they were told that I was leaving Lamington," Nan said. "I pray that Father John did not tell them that it had anything to do with his lordship's book, or worse, the blue dirt. They would not have remembered seeing it. They do not even remember what it has done to Christmas!"

Tears came to Nan's eyes. She thought of her family in their little cottage eating supper at this hour. She desperately wanted to be with them, rather than standing in a dark forest with fog swirling around her and danger lurking from wolves and highwaymen lying in wait somewhere.

"Do not worry yourself too much," Richard answered, returning with a pile of firewood under his arm. "I do not think Father John has told your parents about the blue dirt or the book. They undoubtedly would not understand Christmas and the blue dirt, even if he did tell them. I do not understand it myself."

"The blue dirt has not affected you, either, I see!" Nan exclaimed with delight. "Had it, you would not be speaking of Christmas. So you know why you are taking me to Meldon?"

"Father John and her ladyship had explained everything to us before going on this mission with you, lass," Richard stated. Emma nodded in agreement alongside him. "You are not alone in this secret."

"We were quite aware of the blue dirt long before this mission," Emma said. "We also do not know why only a few of us at the castle know Christmas and the others, like the townspeople—all except for you, Nan—do not."

Nan sighed. "Someday, I pray, we will come to know why we are the only ones that remember how Christmas was once celebrated in Lamington."

"We will find out," Richard said. "Mayhap once we speak to Brother Albert, he will have answers for us. If not, we will keep searching for them until we do."

After they went inside the lodge, Richard went to the center of the room and started a fire in the hearth while the girls brought in the saddlebags. He then went outside to water and feed the horses, as Nan prepared the hare for the spit, while Emma sat near the fire and waited for supper to get done. The lodge smelled of mustiness and old straw. It was completely bare, with a packed down mud floor and a small, empty loft on the second floor.

"I have almost forgotten something!" Emma cried out excitedly. Reaching into her saddlebag, she pulled out some vegetables.

"From the castle garden," Emma said. She handed Nan a few carrots, a turnip, and two large onions. "Her ladyship insisted that we take some things from the kitchen. To be used during our journey, she said."

Nan made a small sound of disgust at the sight of the onions, but took all the vegetables and began to prepare them for the roasted hare.

"How I did not want to see any more onions!" Nan said with a wrinkle of her nose. "I was surrounded by too many of them in the castle kitchen. They remind me too much of the two stewards. They could not keep their fishy eyes off of us while we worked."

The lodge door opened and Richard came in after caring for the animals.

"Stewards?" Richard asked, overhearing the girls' conversation as he went to the hearth to warm himself. "What stewards do you speak of, Nan? As of this morning, we do not have any at Castle Lamington. You do know what happened to them, do you not? Lady Catherine told us that 'twould take some time to replace those as good as the ones who had died."

Nan's mouth dropped in astonishment.

"How can this be?" she asked. "There were two new stewards taking over the duties at Castle Lamington. The others in the kitchen told me this. I was there when the two men came into the kitchen. I saw them myself."

Richard became completely puzzled by Nan's words.

"Lady Catherine is quite capable, even temporarily, of caring for Castle Lamington without any steward," he insisted. "Before the castle gained more lands around it, and more staff within its walls, there were no stewards up until that time. Her ladyship supervised everything herself."

"I do not believe it, Nan! This is untrue!" Emma cried. She stood up from the floor and shook her head. "Her ladyship would have told me about these stewards. She always confides in me as we are very close."

"'Tis true!" Nan maintained. "When I first came to the kitchen and was told by Hugo to cut up onions, they were not there. Then later on, I heard some of the kitchen help talk about the coming of the new stewards. I looked up, and there they were. I cannot tell you more than I know, except that they were very interested in what we had to say around the table where we worked."

Richard went to lie down on his side near the fire while propping his head up with his arm. He remained silent for a while as a look of restlessness came over him. The lad stared deeply into the flames before him. It was completely dark outside by now, and the fire in the hearth had gotten brighter the longer it burned. The long shadows of the three travelers around the fire played against the walls of the lodge, creating an eerie appearance. Not a sound was heard outdoors, but for the creaking of a tree branch blowing in the wind.

"I do not mean to frighten either of you," Richard said at last, "but

I do not remember letting anyone through the castle gate today that told me, or my companion guard, that they were being sent by Lady Catherine to be our stewards."

CHAPTER 9

The girls' eyes grew round with surprise. They looked at each other quizzically before fixing their gaze back on Richard.

"Are you sure of this?" Nan asked nervously.

"Mayhap the other guard let them through while you were doing something else," Emma proposed. "Or, watching somewhere else."

"As both of you have discovered, my eyes are sharp," Richard said. "I do not miss anything when I stand about in the guardhouse. I can see quite a distance from where I am, and I know who or what comes in, or goes out, of the castle gate. I was not given such a job if his lordship knew I could not handle it properly. Something unsettling is going on at Castle Lamington. I can just feel it."

"Whatever do you mean by that?" Emma asked. "You are worrying me more and more by what you say."

Nan sat back down on the floor after turning the hare on the spit. Turning toward Richard, she carefully observed him in the firelight. Had the subject of the new stewards not been brought up, she might not have seriously considered how frightfully similar he looked in comparison to them. He had the same fair hair combed to the neck and, despite being quite lean, he was very strong in body. Richard was taller than most lads and young men of his age as well. So much so that it made Nan feel dwarfish in his company. However, Richard had something that the two stewards did not have. His skin type was different. Richard's skin was the kind that freckled easily from the sun and roughened from the wind from constantly being outdoors. The stewards had creamy white skin, and that unearthly aura about them that Richard did not have, and were richly dressed compared to the lad's simple tunic and hose.

I would very much like to tell Richard this, but he might tell me that I thought he was one of them and might become upset, Nan thought. *'Tis the last thing I want to bring up here in this hut in the middle of nowhere. I do not need trouble before I ever get to Meldon.*

"Nan, what did these stewards look like?" Richard asked.

He arose from the floor and walked around the hearth as he became immersed in deep thought.

Nan was sickened to have been asked this of Richard after what had just gone through her mind about him. She described the two stewards to the best of her ability, as her mind flashed back to them standing in the castle kitchen. She feared that Richard, and perhaps Emma, might think she was telling them that one of the stewards may have been Richard, but neither seemed to notice anything peculiar about what she had said. Since most men had a similar appearance in those days, her description of them was not all that uncommon. The two stewards were very extraordinary to Nan, too. They were *otherworldly*, but Nan left that part out for fear that Richard and Emma might think of her as a silly goose with quite a fanciful imagination. She was convinced that the others in the kitchen would agree with her, but for now, this was best left unsaid just in case she was wrong.

"I have not seen them then," Richard said, shaking his head. "They must have gotten into Castle Lamington a different way, which seems highly unlikely. Castle Lamington is not easy to get into with so many of us watching at the top of the castle walls. I suspect those stewards were not what they pretended to be. They were spies being sent by another lord from a different castle. Enemies are easy to come by these days as one lord is always jealous of another."

"Spies?" Emma and Nan cried out in unison. They both sat aghast at the thought of such persons running rampant through the castle without anyone's knowledge, even her ladyship's.

Richard was visibly troubled over this as he tensely fingered the scabbard of the sword that he continued to wear at his side. He frantically began walking around the lodge. He snapped his fingers as a thought came to him.

"They must have killed our two stewards!" he exclaimed. "I am sure they did, otherwise why did they show themselves immediately after the others perished? They must have been in the castle long before that in order to make it happen."

"Mayhap they got in during all the tumult when his lordship had gone missing," Emma declared. "So many men were coming and going early this morning. I can see how someone could have easily gotten into the castle."

"Nay, Emma," Richard answered her. "That is not so. I saw *everyone* come and go from Castle Lamington. You do not know me so well. I would have seen them! The other guard, Adam, is not as sharp as I am."

Nan glanced back and forth from Emma to Richard as they spoke. Richard had the utmost confidence in himself, which impressed her a great deal.

"If only I could get back to the castle, I would take my horse and go," Richard said fearlessly. "The safety of her ladyship and everyone else there is at stake. However, as my duty lies in escorting Nan to Meldon, I cannot go. Whatever happens at Castle Lamington is beyond our control."

"Pray do not scare me!" Emma exclaimed. "I am terrified to think that everyone's safety at the castle is at risk. Do not put such thoughts into my head, Richard!"

"Mayhap they were the ones who came and took our lordship from us!" Nan said.

Richard looked toward the door and sharply turned to look at the two shuttered windows as if he had heard something.

"We should not trouble ourselves about such matters," Richard said calmly, sitting back down on the floor. "'Tis this strange place we are in—'tis dark outside, and we are far from home. 'Tis playing with our minds by creating dreadful conclusions to things we are really not sure of. We do not know if these two men killed our stewards or if they hurt our lordship. We also do not know if her ladyship is unsafe, or anyone else for that matter, at the castle. For all we know, mayhap her ladyship did ask for two men to be our new stewards. She does not need to tell *everything* to her servants, Emma. As for myself, I may have overlooked them coming into Castle Lamington. I can make mistakes, too. At first light, we will make for Meldon. When we get to the monastery there, we will speak to Father John about this. I know he will send someone back to the castle to see that all is well. If he allows me, I may like to be the one to go."

What Richard had said seemed to satisfy Emma and Nan that evening in the little lodge. Nan announced that the hare and the vegetables were finished cooking. The food was passed around and everyone ate in silence as they were lost in their own thoughts. After they had finished eating and Nan cleaned up, Emma began to whine that they did not have any entertainment in the lodge, so Richard found a flute in his saddlebag and played it much to Emma's surprise, who was soon carried away by the delightful sounds of the music. No one seemed to object to the flute that covered up any formidable noises that were heard through the walls of the building.

"How well you play, Richard!" Emma praised. "How strange for a castle guard like you to know music like that."

"I have learned from only the best," Richard grinned proudly, but did not elaborate.

After playing two more songs, Richard became tired of the flute and thrust it into his bag.

"I will go and check on the horses," he said, leisurely getting up from the floor and stretching. "'Tis time for all of us to get to sleep. We have a long day ahead of us, lasses."

The girls found some brown woolen covers in the saddlebags to be used for bedding as Richard stepped outside into the darkness.

"I wonder if he should be doing that," Emma said. She looked at Nan with fright. "'Tis hard to see anything out there. I also thought it odd that he knows how to play a flute. Mayhap that is not so strange to you, Nan, since you do not understand these things, but a simple castle guard does not usually know how to play music like that. I am determined to find out more from Richard when I get the chance."

"Mayhap the other guard taught it to him," Nan remarked. "I do not think it so strange for him to go out into the night, either. Most lads and men are never afraid of it. I have seen my father work until dark, or leave for it, before the sun rises. We never worry, and he always comes back to us."

Before Emma could reply, the piercing sound that they had heard earlier on the road echoed throughout the forest. The sound became louder as it came closer and closer to the lodge. Both girls ran and clung to one another as they peered anxiously at the door for Richard to show up at any second.

HOOO—AHHHH!!!

"There is that hideous noise again!" Nan screamed as her eyes darted frantically from door to window. "It sounds like whatever is making it might be moving near the windows! I hope it does not come in."

"Pray, Richard, come back!" Emma called out in fright, but

Richard did not return.

A loud thud was heard outside the lodge door. Richard came racing back inside the room. He slammed and bolted the door shut behind him. He was carrying in some twigs and branches that were falling from his arms. Richard quickly dropped them into the hearth to keep the fire going throughout the night. He ran to each window to check if the shutters were tightly closed before pulling out his sword from his scabbard.

"We thought you had run off on us!" Emma cried. "Did you hear that sound out there?"

The girls, comforted by Richard's presence, let go of one another as they watched Richard's every move. His actions frightened them more than what he said.

"I did not plan on doing anything of the sort," Richard replied. "I came back here as fast as I could, and aye! I did hear the sound. I do not know what it is. Mayhap a wild animal, but one in which I am not familiar with. This deep forest is crawling with dangerous beasts of every kind, especially at night."

"I hope our horses are safe," Nan said, "or we will never arrive in Meldon. I would hate to walk all the way there if a hungry beast gets them. To think of spending another night or two in this forest is dreadful. I cannot do it."

"Lass, do not worry," Richard reassured Nan. "I do not think 'twill come to that. I found an old barn for the horses in the back of the lodge. 'Tis quite sturdy with a good roof and strong doors. I also have my sword here. As a trained guard, I know how to take care of you and Emma. Her ladyship and Father John would not have chosen me to watch over the two of you if I were not fit for the job. From the directions that I have been given as well, we will be in Meldon tomorrow."

Richard sank to the floor and sat cross-legged by the fire as he listened to the strange sound outside. He held his sword across his legs as the reflection from the firelight bounced off the steel blade.

"I must be completely honest with you," Richard began after some silence. "That sound does alarm me. Lasses, get some rest. Do not worry so much about me. I will sleep across the door if it makes you feel safer. I will not leave you. You have my promise."

Emma and Nan went to their beds near the fire, but they could not sleep. The strange sound they heard seemed to stop and start up over and over again only a short distance from the lodge. Not long after, the sound moved further away and then subsided.

"I think it may have stopped," Richard said. "For how long, I cannot tell."

The girls stared wide-eyed from the floor. They did not take their eyes from Richard who made his sleeping arrangement by the door. Nan observed Richard's sword with keen interest. He seemed to know how to wield it with great dexterity. Only someone with great proficiency could maneuver such an object, and she was glad that Richard was there with them.

"You know how to handle a sword quite well, Richard," Nan said. "I know . . . 'tis a silly question. All castle guards can use one, but you seem especially skilled at it. Were you a knight once? Have you ever been to war?"

Richard laughed at Nan's questions. "What strange questions you ask of me, daughter of Simon the farmer. Nay, I am not a knight, nor have I been in a war of any kind. I have been trained to be a knight from a small boy, but I do not know if I shall ever be one."

"So, I was correct about your flute!" Emma exclaimed, sitting up from her bed. "Only a knight-in-training can be taught to play it and so perfectly."

"I am sorry that I deluded you, Emma," Richard answered. "You were correct in assuming that a humble castle guard cannot play music as well as I do."

"You have quite a story to tell us then, Richard," Emma declared. "There seems to be more to you than meets the eye."

Richard chuckled as he stroked his sword. A shadow of sadness passed over his face as he looked down at the object in his hands and stared at its strong, bright blade.

"There is not much to tell, really," Richard murmured.

Nan, who was still lying by the fire and listening intently to Richard and Emma, pulled the woolen cover from over herself and sat up.

"Do tell us!" Nan urged. She did not believe his modest answer, which had stirred her interest.

Richard sat by the door lost in his own thoughts as the fire crackled quietly in the hearth. The girls grew restless as they waited for him to say something.

"Ordinarily, I would not enjoy telling you about my life, but seeing that none of us wants to get to sleep after what we had just heard out there, I will tell you," Richard said. "Only if you vow that once we leave the lodge, what I say to you is not to be told to anyone."

"We give you our word, Richard!" Emma replied. Nan seconded the promise as she got up and sat closer to Emma.

Richard burst out, "I believe that I am the son and heir of Robert, Lord of Lamington."

Emma and Nan were taken aback at what Richard had said.

"Are you absolutely certain of this?" Emma asked, skeptical that Richard was the son of his lordship. "Why have none of us at Castle Lamington been told this? Lady Catherine tells me everything, but this is one thing I have not heard of, not even from her. You fool us, Richard!"

"I fool you not, but you are right about one thing," Richard declared. "'Tis not something that is openly known at the castle. 'Tis why I am sometimes crass with others there. Even Father himself notices and reprimands me when he gets the chance. You do not understand how angry it makes me feel to be a lowly guard. I should be acknowledged by the station I was meant to live in life. I am the child of Lord Robert, not some unassuming lad who walks around the top of a castle in the snow and rain."

Richard got up and irately stormed the lodge as he swung his sword from side to side.

"I admit that I do not have any real proof that his lordship *is* my father. I am not sure if there is even a likeness—I have not bothered to ask anyone, but something is there," Richard said. "I can detect it."

Nan's thoughts flew back to that December morning when Richard treated her so poorly at the castle gate when she came to speak with his lordship. She immediately felt sorry for him.

Now I know why he was so foul with me that day, Nan told herself. *What a troubled life he leads.*

"I understand," Emma said quietly. "You must tell us how you learned that you are the son of his lordship, Richard. I did not mean to accuse you of lying if you are, indeed, telling us the truth."

"I *am* telling you the truth!" Richard asserted. "There are too many strange circumstances surrounding my life, along with rumors I have heard, which tell me this is so. Let me start from the very beginning. I was raised by two good people—farming folk—named Susanna and Peter who lived outside the walls of Lamington. They had a cottage on a small parcel of land there. I did not think much of it up until that time, but as I grew, I started to believe that they were not my parents. Susanna treated me with nothing but love and kindness, but Peter—though he tried to raise me like the rest of their three children—was unable to give me the same love and attention as he did the others. He was often times distant toward me and punished me more than the other children, but he did teach me a lot about farming during my young years. As I grew older, I began noticing that I did not resemble them. They all had dark brown hair compared to my fair hair and skin."

There was a faint mist in his eyes, but Richard stayed strong as he carried on with his story.

"One day, a man in fine clothes on a well-bred horse came by the cottage to take me away. I remember that Susanna was crying and holding me tight. She told me to be a good little lad. She said I was to be taken to Castle Lamington where I would learn many new things. She did not say whether or not I would ever come back to her. Peter did not come out of the cottage to see me off, but I did not care. I did miss Susanna, though, whether or not she was my true mother. Then the man on the horse put me up in front of him and we rode off. I have never forgotten how good Susanna was to me. I did not miss the younger children. As far as Peter went, I did not miss him, either."

"'Tis a very painful story you tell us," Nan said. "Does this Susanna or Peter still live outside the town walls, Richard? I do not recall anybody by those names. As Lamington is not so very big and people do not move very often, 'tis unlikely that they left the area."

"I went back to see them only recently, as I was preoccupied with my new life at the castle for many years, and the strangest thing had happened," Richard declared. "I knocked on their door, but when Susanna came out—she was a little older then—she acted as if she did not know who I was. She made an excuse about supper burning in the pot and hastily shut the door. It became apparent that she was not interested in me anymore. I saw their other children, a little more grown, feeding the animals out in the yard, but when I came up to them, they just stared and refused to talk to me. I heard Susanna call them into the house and that was the end of my visit. I believe she was watching me from the window as

I was leaving. Peter was nowhere to be found, but since we were never close, I did not bother to search for him."

"I would have gone back and knocked again!" Emma said with her eyes flashing. "I agree. 'Tis very odd that this Susanna woman ignored you like that. After all, she raised you as her own, whether she was your mother or not. How insensitive of her!"

"Mayhap I should have pursued things more," Richard added, "but I did not. I returned to the castle and licked my wounds, all the while telling no one of my call to Farmer Peter's home. I will not deny that my feelings were trampled on by Susanna. Let me finish telling you about what happened when I first left Farmer Peter's home. After my arrival at Castle Lamington, I was immediately made a page. I was told that although only a nobleman's son can become one, I was allowed to become a page because I was a *special* farmer's son. Since I was happier at the castle than at the cottage with the farming folk, who I thought were my parents, I asked no questions."

Emma and Nan listened to Richard's mind-boggling tale with their utmost attention. They were both in shock and disbelief. They discerned that he was releasing something that must have been agonizingly hidden from the world for a very long time.

HOOO—AHHHH!!!

Richard and the girls heard that resounding cry start up in the forest. Emma let out a little scream as Nan huddled closer to her.

Richard held up his hand to stop them from reacting. "Do not worry about the creature," he said. "It cannot harm us. We are safe in here. 'Twill go away before long."

The girls had a difficult time listening to Richard's account. No matter how hard they tried ignoring the sound, it grew louder and quieter at different intervals.

"Tell us about his lordship," Emma probed. "What did he say to you when you came to Castle Lamington?"

"He took a keen interest in all I did," Richard replied. "He made certain that I had the best of everything—tutors, books, toys—that the other young pages who came from noble households had. I also learned how to ride my very own horse and to handle a sword like any of the other lads. 'Twas quite an experience for me until I heard something behind my back that not only left me speechless, but very uneasy."

"What might that be?" Nan asked. The girls sat in breathless anticipation on the floor as they waited for Richard to tell them more of his sad life.

"There was a terrible rumor being whispered amongst the lads. It took place when we were old enough to be given to a knight as a squire. They said that I was the son of Lord Robert! I did not know how that could be, but I dared not ask it of anyone, including his lordship. He neither came to me about it, nor showed any sign in my presence that I was his child, so I did not have actual proof that the rumor had any legitimacy to it. At first, I thought that some of the other pages were jealous of my abilities at sword fighting and decided to play a nasty prank on me. So, on a whim, I thought I would seek out the truth of this rumor, just in case there was something to it. I did not believe for a minute that my friends would say such a thing about me. There would have been a terrible price to be paid by his lordship if he found it out. He is not one to tolerate nonsense."

"This is why you went to see Susanna and Peter again!" Nan said excitedly.

"Aye, which is partly why I went to see them after so many years," Richard said. "I still wanted to see them, nevertheless. More Susanna than Peter, actually. I wanted to see if they could tell me if this rumor had any accuracy. If I knew Peter well enough like I did, he would be more than obliged to tell me the truth. Everywhere in Castle Lamington I went since the rumor spread, heads turned and whispers of this shocking revelation followed me. Then the worst happened to me soon after. Instead of being made a squire, I was made the very thing I have become—a guard at the castle gate. I was mortified, but I was told by the castle steward that his lordship felt this was my only fate. I was given no explanation why, except that with my good eyesight, he said, 'twas the best position I could ever get in life. Well, there you have it! I think we should start getting to sleep even with that sound in the background."

"Get to sleep!" Nan cried. "How can I sleep? Pity tears at me after listening to you. I would try to find out more about your parentage, Richard, if I were you."

"What a wonderful idea, Nan!" Emma exclaimed. "Richard, if you know your father is his lordship, then who is your mother? Surely it cannot be her ladyship. She is not much older than me or you."

"I have considered such a thing," Richard commented gloomily.

"Emma, have you ever heard of her ladyship speak of me as his lordship's son? The rumor did make its way around the castle."

"Nay, I have not!" Emma said defensively. "Not a breath of it. I believe Lady Catherine still may not know that you are really his son. That is, if you are, indeed."

"'Tis something that does not surprise me, really," Richard sighed. "You are the only one who is closest to Lady Catherine beside his lordship. If 'tis true, then you and she are carefully being guarded from knowing anything."

"Of course, Lord Robert does not want her to know!" Emma said. "'Tis too painful for him to explain. He does not want her feelings hurt so he keeps it secret from her. I cannot envision why he does keep something like this hidden and for so long. His lordship should have been honest with Lady Catherine before their marriage. There must be something more to this."

Richard paused for a moment to stare at the door behind him. Satisfied that everything was quiet, he leaned his back against it and closed his eyes.

"When we get to Meldon tomorrow, you should approach Father John," Emma said. "Question him about whom your mother is and if Lord Robert is your father. He knows all that goes on at Castle Lamington. I would be shocked if he had never learned of it. Father John is, after all, the next closest person to his lordship."

"I may ask him about my parentage, but not right away," Richard stated. "The subject is difficult enough to discuss with anyone, let alone Father John. I will wait a little while before approaching him—when I feel more comfortable about it. If the monastery is in a secluded enough spot as I am told, there will be plenty of quiet time to mention it."

"Do not be discouraged," Emma consoled Richard. "You will find your answers soon enough. Do not give up hope. Everyone has a need of belonging . . . of knowing their past."

"Your skills as a page have not been wasted, Richard," Nan said sympathetically. "You were picked by Lady Catherine and Father John to go on this journey with us. You were taught well with a sword and can fight with it if you needed to. Your good eyesight found us this lodge, too. Not to mention that you also heard that frightful noise we did not hear at first. Another lad might not have been able to do these things."

Richard's eyes flew open as something outside was pushing violently against the door of the lodge. The door began to shake as the bolt from the inside began to strain against the brute force of the entity.

"We will soon find out if I can handle a sword after all!" Richard cried out. He jumped to his feet and away from the front door of the lodge.

The girls shrieked as they backed away from their makeshift beds and the fire and crawled into the furthest corner of the room. They hid in the shadows as they watched Richard hold up his sword as he looked wild-eyed at the door. The shutters on the windows were also being rattled as if something, or someone, from the outside was moving from door to window to find a way in.

"Richard!" Nan called out. "'Tis coming to get us!"

"Do not worry, lass!" Richard shouted. "I will not let it hurt us."

He ran to the front door and opening it, looked out into the night with his sword held high in the air. Grabbing for his small shield that lie nearby, he turned to the girls as he threw on his cloak.

"I am going to find out what this thing is once and for all!" he thundered. "Lock the door when I leave. Do not open it until I return!"

"Do not go out there!" Emma wailed. "'Tis too dangerous! What if you do not return? What will we do?"

"I will come back!" were Richard's final words. He disappeared into the darkness, slamming the door shut behind him.

CHAPTER 10

Emma ran and bolted the door per Richard's orders and raced back to the corner where Nan was.

"What a foolish lad!" she lamented. "There can be murderous highwaymen lying in wait out there."

"Pray, Emma, do not speak so," Nan replied. Her voice was shaking uncontrollably. "Let us pray that he comes back to us. I fear for him."

Emma and Nan did not speak to each other the rest of the night. They were both petrified as they sat waiting up for Richard. It was not until the next morning, as the fire in the hearth slowly died out, that they finally fell asleep.

Nan's eyelids gently opened to a gust of cool air hitting her in the face. A tap-tapping of a woodpecker was heard coming from a nearby tree. She had forgotten where she was until she saw Emma sleeping soundly next to her in the corner. What had happened the night before came rushing back. The front door of the lodge slowly swung open, and the room soon became chilly. The sun had already risen, as its rays blinded Nan through the doorway. Her heart began to hammer in her chest loudly, as she peered around the room and saw that Richard did not come back from the night before. From the open door, Nan saw through the bare trees and down a small hill.

I should shut the door, Nan said to herself, as she got up from the floor. *'Tis not exactly summer out there. I do not think Emma locked it properly last night. We must get up and find Richard! What an awful night we had!*

Nan walked toward the door and was about to bolt it when, to her amazement, she found herself watching a strange scene play out down the hill. Two girls in long, flowing gowns of blue and green appeared at the bottom of it. Their faces were indistinguishable from afar, but they had waist-length flaxen hair with white flowers woven into it. They were signaling to someone in Nan's direction. Nan thought they were doing so at her until she saw Richard appear from the left side of the lodge. He was carrying his sword limply in his right hand as he slowly walked down toward the two waving girls. As he got closer to them, he dropped his sword. Not knowing if she had blinked and missed something, Nan saw Richard disappear as if by magic. The young maidens who gestured to him were gone, too. All three of them had vanished into thin air!

Were her eyes playing games with her? Where had they gone?

Nan ran to Emma and shook her until she awoke.

"Emma! Wake up!" Nan cried out. "Something terrible has happened to Richard."

Emma's eyes slowly opened to Nan's terrified face as Nan explained, to the best of her ability, what she had just witnessed a moment ago.

"How very disturbing!" Emma exclaimed, trying to make sense of what Nan had told her. She stiffly got up from the floor and stretched. "Mayhap he did return after we fell asleep, only to leave soon after."

"We should go outside to see where he went, though frightened I am to do it," Nan said, nervously biting at a fingernail.

"I think we should, too," Emma said. "I wish I would have seen those two girls you thought you saw. They seem out of place in this forest. Wearing flowers is not likely in winter, either. There are none growing anywhere until the spring."

Emma and Nan cautiously stepped outside the lodge door.

"The morning is so calm and quiet," Emma said. She looked ahead through the trees and down the hill, but saw nothing that Nan had depicted to her. "Nevertheless, we should not dwell out here for too long."

Nan jumped on a giant boulder that lay next to the lodge door.

"Mayhap from here, I can get a better view of the bottom of the hill," Nan declared. Before long, she shook her head. "I do not see anything."

"Let me go and retrieve Richard's sword," Emma proposed. "You said it had fallen from his hand while he was walking. I will feel better knowing that we have his sword for protection, though we are not good at using it. Stay here near the lodge, Nan, while I get it, in case Richard comes back."

"Are you sure you want to do that, Emma?" Nan asked. "You are always more scared than I am."

"I am sure," Emma replied. "I had thought about all that Richard had reproached me about since we had gotten on the road in Lamington, and he is absolutely right. Her ladyship has given me an important duty to watch over you on this mission, Nan. I will honor that all the way to Meldon, though I am a lady's maidservant and you are a farmer's daughter. I am ashamed of how I had acted around you and Richard yesterday."

"I understand, Emma, and I forgive you," Nan said, as gladness swelled within her. "I was worried I was becoming bothersome to you, because of what the blue dirt has forced you to do for my sake. I know how you felt about me, but what you just said has made me so happy. I think we will get along much better from now on."

Emma gave Nan a quick smile and went down the hill to search for Richard's lost sword. Nan felt better since Emma had put her differences toward Nan behind her. However, her good spirits were momentarily squashed as the reality of the missing Richard returned to her. Everyone seemed to be disappearing in one way or another as of late. First, his lordship had vanished mysteriously, then the unexplained deaths of the castle stewards, and now, their guide to Meldon. She did not like the idea of going to Meldon alone with Emma without Richard for safety.

"I found it!" Emma yelled to Nan. She held up the sword for Nan to see.

"It did not take me long to find it," she said. "If 'twas not for winter, the grass would be overgrown and I would not have seen it. 'Tis very heavy, though."

Nan sighed with relief upon seeing Richard's sword.

"We should go back to the lodge and wait for Richard a little longer," Nan said. "If he does not come back for an hour or two, we will leave for Meldon. Richard did say 'twas not far from here, so we should get there by nightfall."

"A fine idea, Nan," Emma answered. "When we get there, we can tell Father John about Richard's disappearance. He can always send someone out to search for him."

Going back into the lodge, they bolted the door tightly as they ate some apples they found in one of the saddlebags.

An hour went by. Then another. And yet another.

"We are here longer than we intended," Emma said. "We should start preparing to leave. If we do not get to the road soon, we will never get to Meldon today."

"I will clean up the lodge while you get the horses ready," Nan stated.

A rustling sound was heard at the lodge door. Then came a loud pounding on the door and a muffled shout coming through it.

Nan went to open to door and stared in disbelief. There was Richard standing in the doorway, tired and soiled with his fair hair disheveled. His voice was hoarse, and he was coughing relentlessly. He tried to catch his breath as if he had run a great distance from somewhere.

"Hurry and gather your things together!" Richard bellowed. "Do not dawdle, you fools!"

"Richard," Emma stammered, "what has happened? We did not think you would come back."

"Never mind that!" Richard exclaimed. "Let us get out of this place!" He grasped his sword from Emma and placed it safely back into his scabbard. "There is no time to explain. I must get to the horses immediately."

Emma and Nan rushed to pack up the two saddlebags while Richard went to the barn to prepare the horses for traveling. When the girls came back around the lodge to the barn, the horses were saddled up and ready to go. Richard was shielding his eyes in the bright morning light and kept looking frenziedly in all directions. He looked terrified as if expecting something to occur at any second.

"Remember to put your hoods up," Richard murmured after helping Emma and Nan mount their horse. "Our faces must not be seen by anyone on the road."

He mounted his own horse and went racing out of the forest and back to the main road with the others galloping nonstop behind him.

"Richard, what is the meaning of this!" Emma demanded, yelling after him. "Is something, or someone, after us? I know we have to get to Meldon, but there is something else going on. I insist that you stop and tell us."

"I saw you from the open door of the lodge," Nan said. "You were following two lasses down the hill. They were dressed in colorful gowns and had white flowers in their hair. I was not imagining it."

Richard slowed his horse down to a trot and waited for Emma and Nan to ride up next to him. The day started out sunny, but it soon became overcast despite the mild winter day.

A grim expression came over Richard as he knew he had to admit the inevitable.

"The cry we heard in the forest and, when we were in the lodge, was not coming from a wild beast of any kind," Richard validated. "There is only one word to describe it. Viwa."

"Viwa!" Emma laughed hysterically in her saddle. "Fairies! How can that be?"

Fairies!

Nan thought it strange that Richard should mention them.

"Richard, there are no fairies around, including the Viwa," Emma said. "No one has believed in such a thing for a long, long time. They are no more than myth . . . legend."

"I know some who still believe in the Viwa where we live," Nan declared. "Mostly older folk, though. They leave food, mainly sweet cakes, outside for them. Fairies were once known to return possessions that they took from people. As long as you gave them something to eat. The Viwa are an unusual sort of fairies; similar in size to either one of us standing here. You might be next to one and not even know it. I am not sure if I believe in them."

"I might not have believed in them had I not seen them with my own eyes," Richard said gravely. "And, aye! They were not so small to elude me. When I stepped outside last night, I did not see anything at first. Seconds later, I saw something in white running through the trees making that repugnant call. I chased after it, but it disappeared. I saw more of the same amongst the trees, but when I tried to catch whatever it was, it ran off again. Thinking it might be a highwayman or two looking to steal something, I feared for the horses so I went to the barn and stayed with them all night. The barn had no bolt from the inside like the lodge, which concerned me, but I heard nothing more the rest of the night. When the sun rose, I went outside and was met with a quiet morning. Then, out of the corner of my eye, I saw precisely the two maidens that you saw, Nan."

"I suppose that was when I saw them waving to you as you followed them down the hill," Nan said with widened eyes.

"Aye, it was," Richard replied. "A strange, overpowering feeling to follow them came over me. I realized that they were what I saw in the forest last night. I went with them into the mouth of a dark cave hidden amongst some trees. 'Twas foolish of me, I know. I heard their strange calling sound again and that is when they went deeper into the cave. They kept motioning for me to follow them. When I went into an inner chamber, I saw more maidens who surrounded me as if they were ready to tear me apart. As they were coming toward me, the overpowering feeling which I had—they likely put it over me—started to lose its abilities, and I was able to get away. They became very angry. They gnashed their teeth and waved their arms as they tried to block me from the entranceway. I escaped without a scratch, thankfully, except that the cave was muddy and wet. I slipped and fell on the way out. They vanished before I got back to the lodge. The Viwa maidens are very beautiful, I must admit, but are nasty when they are unhappy."

"Evil, too!" Emma exclaimed. "Those Viwa *were* after you! They are the fairies who go after lads and young men. Since you are a lad, 'twould make sense. I still have a difficult time believing in fairies, but as this story is coming from you, Richard, I cannot help but believe it."

"You were very brave to get away from them," Nan commended. "When they capture someone, they usually do not let him get away. I do know one thing, though. Leaving the Viwa is not so easy, but you have managed it well, Richard."

"I was not nearly fast enough in my escape, unfortunately," Richard chuckled.

Emma and Nan saw that the jolted Richard was becoming more relaxed now that the lodge they left was further behind them.

"Did they see your face?" Emma asked fearfully. "If so, then they know what you look like. They may pursue you on the road."

"My hood was not on when I walked outside this morning," Richard said with downcast eyes. "I suppose I should have had it on, but I did not."

"Oh, Richard!" Nan cried out. "That is not good."

"Mayhap they disappeared in pursuit of another lad since they did not get to me," Richard said with a grin. "I am going to try and not let it worry me. There was one thing that I found odd when I went into the cave after them. When those wicked Viwa encircled me, they spoke in a tongue that I understood. Do you know what they said? They said something like,

'We will get you! Come with us!' Then to each other they kept repeating, 'Do not let him get away!'"

"I cannot imagine you knowing the language of the Viwa fairies, Richard," Emma noted. "Where would *you* have learned it?"

"Mayhap it only *seemed* familiar to you," Nan said. "Are you sure 'twas not our tongue?"

"I know my mind was not playing tricks on me," Richard remarked. "Who knows—I might have fallen under a fairy spell in that cave and became delirious."

"I should tell you that those stewards that were in the castle kitchen also spoke in a tongue from another land," Nan said. "I heard one of them saying something to the other, but I did not know what it was. I am sorry to only remember this now."

"How very queer," Emma replied thoughtfully. "I do not think Lady Catherine would bring two stewards in from another kingdom to work at Castle Lamington."

"I do not think so, either," Richard agreed. "We can always ask Father John about it."

"You can also tell him that the Viwa language was familiar to you, too," Nan added.

Richard laughed. "Father John *would* think of me as being fanciful, but I can try to tell him about it sometime. Unfortunately, I can expect him to chastise me for it. He will say that 'tis because I am spending too much time at the top of the castle gate. Not that I have any choice being there."

"Well, I think you should still tell him," Nan encouraged Richard. "He is probably at Meldon already."

"He is very likely there and waiting for us," Emma said. "He is a patient man, but he may grow impatient if we take too long to get there. Incidentally, I am not entirely comfortable with those Viwa maidens gone. I feel uncertain about them somehow."

"You do not think they will come back?" Richard teased. "If it pleases you, Emma, we will ride faster. We need to get to Meldon at a decent time anyway."

Richard and Emma rode their horses faster as Nan held onto her companion for dear life. They went a little ways further down the road when they saw a sign at the edge of the forest that read: ARNON.

"Civilization is not so far off now!" Richard exclaimed. "Father

John said that once we got through the hilly road in the forest we would be in Arnon. He described it as a small village and nothing more. After Arnon, we will be in a long stretch of open land. 'Twill take us to Meldon where we will be in late afternoon, just as Father said we would."

Smiles of joy came to Emma and Nan when they saw the sign.

"I am grateful to hear the word, 'civilization'," Emma replied with a sigh. "You cannot imagine how sick from hunger I am. If I had to guess, you must be starving as well, Nan."

"Aye, I am," Nan said. "All we had to eat to break our fast were the apples we found in your saddlebag, Richard."

Richard laughed at the girls.

"Silly geese!" he cried. "We can purchase something to eat in the village. Lady Catherine gave me some coins for our use. Remember what Father John said. We cannot let anything impede us on this journey, so the sooner we find something to eat, the better. There would be too much time wasted if we had to cook it ourselves."

The riders soon came out of the forest to a road that quickly opened up to flat land as far as the eye could see. They crossed an old, narrow stone bridge that went over a small stream where a mill stood nearby. The sun, as if deciding to play hide and seek with the gray clouds, peeked out from behind them and soon disappeared. Some small cottages with thatched roofs and rough-timbered walls were seen dotting the landscape, one here and then one there, with smoke coming from a hole at the top. Behind the cottages, on their small plots of land, some farmers were plowing the soft dirt of the February soil and planting the seeds of their early summer crops. A welcoming farmer or two waved to the group of three as they road their horses into Arnon.

Nan heard that Arnon was very small and so it was, much to her surprise. She was too accustomed to living her entire life in Lamington, a much larger hustling and bustling place than the village of Arnon. Arnon had a small brown wooden church in the center with a stone fence encircling it, a village green next to its place of worship, and a few other buildings that were a combination shop and living quarters on the second level for the shopkeepers. There were a few other buildings of unknown origin that the small group could not identify. One building that caught Nan's eye was one that was as small as the church, but larger than the cottages it surrounded. Richard pointed out that it was likely the lord's manor house as all villages had them.

The riders reined in their horses near the village green as they glanced up and down the main street of Arnon.

"'Tis a very small village all right," Richard said after surveying Arnon. "I do see one shop right over there that may sell us something. It has an open stall, and I can smell fresh bread and meat coming from it."

Richard and Emma dismounted their horses with Nan. They walked the animals down the center of the muddy street to the shop where food wafted in the air. Walking up to it, they saw that it was, indeed, a place for them to get something to eat. The shop had a wooden sign swinging from it with a picture of a loaf of bread painted on it.

An old woman with a pleasant, grandmotherly face attended to Richard and the girls as they purchased some hot pastries that had meat and vegetables baked inside of them. The old woman looked at them questioningly, but did not ask where they were from. Nan was sure that the woman could guess they were not from Arnon. Nan consumed her pastry almost instantly, as she had never tasted anything so good outside the cooking of her own mother. Emma suggested they buy extras for the road to eat later. Richard nodded and went back to the shop to buy several more pastries. They put them in the leather saddlebags that hung from their horses.

"As soon as we are finished, we must get back to the road and off to Meldon," Richard said. "But first, I want to water the horses at the mill stream. We should also get some water ourselves."

Everyone ate their pastries as they made their way over to the stream. As Emma knelt down to fill the leather canteen, she nonchalantly looked over in the direction of the shop they had left. The gray clouds had made way for clear skies and bright sunshine. Shading her eyes from the brightness, Emma saw two girls walking up to the shop stall and were speaking with the old woman who sold them the hot pastries moments earlier.

"Richard!" Emma said excitedly. "Look!" She pointed to the shop they had left behind. "Are those the same maidens who tried to take you prisoner in the cave?"

Richard looked up sharply from his pastry. He turned toward the shop where the girls Emma spoke of were standing. By this time, Nan had glanced in the direction of Emma's finger. Her jaw dropped in disbelief.

The two girls at the shop looked incontestably like the ones Nan had seen beckoning to Richard near the lodge. They were wearing the same blue and green dresses and had the same white flowers in their long blonde hair.

"I wish I knew what they were talking about," Emma said. "They are certainly there a while with that shop woman."

"I do not think they know we are here," Nan whispered.

"They soon will if they turn our way," Richard said. "Our hoods! We are forgetting to keep them up."

"I pray they do not see us," Emma answered uneasily. She pulled her hood up at once. "We must go while we have a chance."

"Aye, I can agree to that!" Richard declared as he began to mount his horse. "It appears they have been following me since leaving the forest where the lodge was. I am in more danger than you are, lasses. We must leave this village—now!"

"I am thankful we have our horses," Emma said, mounting her own animal after helping Nan up first. "We will be gone before they see us."

"That does not matter," Richard replied. "You forget that they are Viwa fairies. We are only human. They have powers that *we* do not possess."

CHAPTER 11

Racing their horses toward the main street of Arnon, the riders went back over the old, narrow stone bridge that covered the mill stream. They passed all the buildings that they rode by when they first came into the village. The small group made their way out of the small village before the fairy maidens turned their heads to see them leave. Richard and the girls reached the main road that would take them to Meldon, but they did not stop riding once they got there. They continued onward through open country where there were low rolling hills and clusters of small unknown villages, no more than patches with a few structures, seen in the distance. The land was devoid of any trees due to excessive farming of the area.

"Whatever you do, lasses," Richard shouted to the girls behind him, "do not look back! Keep riding! We will keep going until we get as close as we can to Meldon."

Emma yelled back. "That may be a long way from here!"

"'Tis better than being captured by those fairly maidens," Richard answered. "We must put a considerable distance between us and those Viwa. I also hope that our speed discourages them from following us further; that is, if fairies care about that sort of thing at all. I do not know what would have happened had we not found something to eat and not given the horses something to drink. 'Twould have been difficult for all of us to keep up our strength."

"I do not understand why they are after you, Richard," Emma said with a toss of her head. "There are so many lads out there to choose from. Why you then?"

"Mayhap they cannot find one as handsome as I am," Richard retorted with a chuckle.

"Listen to you!" Nan said laughing. "I still do not trust them."

"Neither do I," Richard replied in earnest. "They are becoming a nuisance. I fear to think of what they would do to me if I were captured by them."

The small party eventually slowed down the pace of their tired horses. They rode on quietly for quite some time during that afternoon, and stopped only for a brief period when they found a stream to water the horses again and to eat the remaining pastries, now cold, from Arnon.

"How much longer do we have to go, Richard?" Emma asked.

"By the angle of the sun, I would say we have to be close to Meldon," Richard said, staring up at the sky. "'Tis late afternoon already. If we do not get there soon, I am going to think that Father miscalculated our timing in getting there."

"Or, we are not getting there as fast as we should," Emma concluded.

"I do not believe we wasted much time in any one place," Richard stated. "We shall know soon enough if the city does not come upon us. I do not want to spend another night out here with those fairy maidens in pursuit."

"Have either of you noticed that when those Viwa spoke to that woman at the stall in Arnon, they carried on a conversation between each other quite well?" Emma mused. "Did that old woman know the tongue of the fairies?"

"I understand that fairies can speak any language other than their own," Nan replied.

"I suppose I have been sheltered too long with her ladyship to know these things," Emma confessed. "Mayhap 'tis best, seeing how evil those Viwa maidens are. Their kind makes me shudder, to say the least."

"We should go back and ask that woman what they wanted," Nan said.

"Nay!" Richard shook his head severely. "That would not be wise, Nan. We all know what they want. We have come too far to backtrack to Arnon. Father John is expecting us in Meldon."

They continued to ride on the open road that was less muddy than the road further back. The mildness of the day was coming to a close, and the chilliness of the late day air was starting to edge in. Nan, being terribly fatigued on the horse, started to sing some songs from home and from some May Day celebrations.

"How beautiful you sing, Nan!" Emma said delightedly. "Your

voice rids us of the boredom from this road-weary ride. What think you, Richard?"

Richard did not reply. He had become distracted by something he was carefully observing off the road.

"Nan's singing will not be the only thing that keeps us from being bored on this journey," Richard announced, pointing in the distance. "We are about to have company. Look down there."

The small group watched something moving along the wide expanse where the rolling brown hills met the sun low on the horizon. They saw the dark outline of several skilled riders on horses cutting across some of the low hills where there was no road. The four men quickened their speed the closer they came to Richard and the girls.

"Do you really think they are coming our way?" Nan asked. "They can always ride past us."

"They are riding too steadily in this direction for it to be otherwise," Richard noted.

"You seem vexed by them, Richard," Emma said. "They are not Viwa maidens. They may be friendly knights going on an adventure somewhere. The road is always filled with travelers of all kinds, though not always in winter."

"I suppose that is true," Richard answered her. "I am just concerned because Father told us to be vigilant on the road. At this point, we cannot run without looking like we have something to hide. We must see what they want first. They may be friendly knights, as you say. They may nod to us and go back to their business. After those ruses that the Viwa maidens put us through, I am not convinced that I can be too trusting of anyone."

Emma and Richard stopped their horses and waited for the unknown riders to catch up with them. When the riders came into full view, the travelers from Lamington saw that the four men were, indeed, knights. They were wearing chainmail from head to toe and carrying long, shiny swords held in impressive golden scabbards that were intricately decorated with beautiful designs. The knights had large shields hanging from their backs as they sat on strong, snowy white horses. On each of the shields was a coat-of-arms that consisted of a silver background with a white boar on it. In the boar's mouth was one large sword with a small red rose resting on the handle. The four knights encircled both Richard's and

Emma's horse in such a way as to prevent them from passing in any direction.

Since the men were entirely covered in armor, their only physical appearance that was distinguishable were their faces, red from the cold, with bright blue eyes staring back.

Nan, who was sitting and observing the situation around her, fancied their appearance being a bit like the two stewards who were in the castle kitchen.

"Emma, those knights . . . their faces . . . they are similar to the stewards I saw at Castle Lamington!" Nan cried. "'Tis something in their eyes that remind me of them."

Emma nodded, but did not respond back to Nan. Emma had become too petrified to find her voice.

"Good day to you, Sir Knights!" Richard said good-naturedly to the men. "We have seen you yonder down the hill. Where might you be headed this day?"

The men did not speak or smile back at Richard's niceties. They stoically looked on in an eerie fashion at Richard and the girls as if they were studying them. At some point they exchanged some words amongst each other in a foreign tongue.

"I do not know what they say," Emma whispered to Nan. "I am not familiar with their language. They trouble me greatly."

"Nor do I understand them," Nan replied. "I do not like the way they are blocking our way. How will we get by them?"

Richard gave Emma and Nan a nervous smile.

"I will attempt to speak to them, lasses," Richard murmured. "'Tis best if we remain calm. Mayhap they are seeking directions."

"Who are you?" Richard demanded of the four knights. "What do you want? We are peaceful travelers in these parts and want no harm done to us."

One of the knights came forward from the others and rode up to Richard. He started to say something in the same unknown language that he spoke to his companion knights. Richard frowned and did not say anything as he listened to what the knight was telling him.

Turning his horse slightly around, Richard bent his head low and whispered to the girls the message that the knight had imparted to him.

"He has demanded of me that I come with them or else," Richard stated. "If I do not, they will take me by force."

Emma and Nan were horrorstruck upon hearing the knight's threat and begged Richard to find a way for them to escape. They were equally shocked that he had been able to translate the knight's words to them.

"Do you know, then, what he was saying to you?" Emma asked.

An icy chill went up and down Emma's spine as she stared at the knights around her.

"I believe that is what was told to me," Richard replied. "I do not know how I understand them, but I do. 'Tis all very bewildering, I must say. If we get through this, I will tell you more. This is not the best time."

"What will you do, Richard?" Nan said excitedly. "These are not friendly men as we had first thought."

"You will see," Richard said. "Listen carefully and do as I say."

He turned his attention back to the knights who had now removed their swords from their elegant scabbards that hung from their side.

"I will not go with you, Sir Knights!" Richard cried out. "You will have to come and take me by force as you say." Turning around to the girls, he shouted, "Emma, pray take your horse and Nan to safety off the road! There is something that I must do!"

Emma, who was an experienced horsewoman, took her animal immediately into the muddy pastureland a little ways away from where Richard stood with the knights. She turned the horse around just in time to see Richard preparing to charge at the knights with headlong swiftness. He took his simple sword out of his plain scabbard with one hand and grabbed for his little shield with the other. Emma and Nan stood powerlessly watching the perilous scene unfolding in front of them.

"Emma, this terrifies me!" Nan screamed. "I hope Richard knows how to defend himself. If he gets hurt, I do not know what we are going to do."

"Nan, do be quiet!" Emma ordered. "I do not believe he would do this if he was not experienced in what he doing. He had been trained well in the art of war at Castle Lamington."

Nan hung her head dejected. She prayed that Richard would come out of this safely. Nan realized that Emma was also worried about him and was only putting on a good face during a bad situation. First, Viwa maidens. Now, malicious knights. Richard was being hunted down like a wild beast for causes unknown.

If only his lordship had not been given his uncle's book! Nan thought. *How different things might have been.*

The sound of heavy steel clanged back and forth in the air as Richard tried to fight off the scowling knights around him. The four knights all fought together with unlimited fierceness and determination, but Richard had no trouble in matching their abilities. The girls flinched at various moments during the fighting. The battle between the men and Richard went on for some time on the road. As if by some miracle, Richard was gaining the upper hand. He managed to get the knights to turn and run from him with such great panic and speed, he went after them with his horse down the road, all the while waving his sword wildly in the air.

Emma and Nan watched as the four riders faded from sight. Emma hastily rode her horse back up onto the road and waited for Richard's slow return. Perspiring and winded, the exhausted Richard hopped off his horse for a moment. He patted the animal's sweating back.

"Richard!" Emma cried. "We thought you were going to be mortally wounded fighting those knights. Taking on four men at once like that was quite a feat, and a deadly one."

"We will have lots of stories to tell Father John when we see him," Nan said. "You will surely be made a knight after this!"

"I do not know about that, lass," Richard said laughing. "I would probably have to be in a real battle for that to happen. This was nothing."

"Well, we thought 'twas something," Emma insisted. "You saved our lives. There is something to be said for that. We do not know what they would have done with us if you were hurt."

"Those men were more after me than both you and Nan," Richard said. "You did not understand what they were saying. They had come from another country and were looking for me for a very long time. For how long 'twas unclear, but one of the knights who spoke to me kept reiterating that I must urgently go back to their kingdom with them or else. When I resisted, the fighting began. Those were the only words I understood. Anything else said was unknown to me in their tongue. Either way, I am glad to have scared them off."

"Odd how they did not speak to you in our tongue," Emma declared. "I think they did not want us to hear what they were telling you. They are deceitful! Richard, what language did they speak in? You seem to know many. From the Viwa maidens' to this one."

"What country did they say they were from?" Nan asked. "You did not say, Richard."

"'Tis a wonder that I am still standing after all this," Richard said. He mounted his horse and took a long drink from his leather canteen. He was still breathless from the ordeal he had just gone through with the four men.

Emma and Nan were perturbed that Richard seemed to ignore their questions about the knights.

"I must say I was quite impressed by the workmanship of the knights' swords and scabbards," Richard added. "They were no ordinary knights—they were very powerful fighters. I was able to tell by the way they thrust their swords at me. At first, I was not able to fight even one of them. I was trained at Castle Lamington for the battlefield, 'tis true, but I am no match for four other men at the same time, not as they were. 'Twould be impossible to win this fight under normal circumstances. Then something peculiar came over me, which I do not remember ever experiencing before. Further into our little battle, an unknown strength flowed through me to equal all four or more of them. I felt this urge to run fearlessly toward them, which I did. You know the rest."

"'Tis almost like when you broke free of the Viwa maidens!" Nan declared.

"Aye, very much like that except without using my sword that I lost temporarily," Richard stated. "I do not know from whence this power comes from within me, but 'tis there suddenly when the need arises. I hate to say this, but these men were Viwa, too. They spoke the same tongue as the Viwa maidens."

Emma and Nan stared at Richard dumbfounded.

"Do you mean to say that they are fairy men?" Nan asked. "I have had enough of fairies in one day."

"That is what I am saying," Richard answered. "I am not familiar with every coat-of-arms out there but, considering who they are and what they speak, theirs must be a fairy one."

"Then there must be a connection between these knights and those Viwa maidens we saw!" Emma said. "Nan, you told me that the knights' faces looked like the stewards' you saw in the castle kitchen. I hope 'twill be the end of them after this confrontation on the road."

"'Tis not the only thing I remember," Nan said. "Remember how

I told you that the stewards spoke another language? I cannot explain it, but these knights and those stewards sound terribly alike."

"Nan, are you sure about this?" Emma asked.

"I believe so, though I only heard them speak once," Nan said. "These knights act very similar to the stewards as well—they are not pleasant!"

"Our ladyship is in grave danger, indeed!" Richard exclaimed with seething anger. "Had I known this sooner, I might have asked those Viwa knights about those pretend stewards at Castle Lamington. And those fairy maidens that keep following me on the road!"

"Only *if* they were willing to talk," Emma replied. "As Nan said, they are not approachable. Meanwhile, I also have Lady Catherine's life to fear for. There must be a reason—likely not a good one—for the Viwa to be in Lamington, and I would like to know why!"

"I would like to know as well," Nan stated. "If those Viwa fairies are getting through the Lamington town gate, there may be many more there. How frightening!"

"I have thought of that already," Richard answered sullenly. "The life of every townsperson in Lamington may be in jeopardy, not just Lady Catherine's. Though I am tired after this fight, my mind works overtime. There is something very sinister going on that we are piecing together loosely. I do not like it. This unnerves me greatly. We are in desperate need of a proper answer. We must get to Meldon and fast!"

The travelers broke their horses into a dash with Richard in the lead. They stopped only long enough to have a drink and to refill their canteens at a small creek before speedily returning to the road for Meldon. The sun was turning into a ball of fiery red and orange as it dropped lower and lower in the sky at a faster rate.

Nan was becoming alarmed that they might not reach the city before nightfall. She was no longer in the mood to sing as she sat quietly hanging onto Emma's waist as they rode onward. She was too upset thinking about the two stewards at Castle Lamington who might be Viwa fairies and living under the same roof as Lady Catherine. Nan prayed silently for the well-being of her ladyship and for those in Lamington, especially her family, if more fairies were finding their way through the town walls.

Richard and Emma neither spoke to Nan, nor to each other, the rest of the way. They became lost in their thoughts and too plagued from facing the Viwa fairies. Nan understood their feelings and left them alone.

These horses cannot ride fast enough for me! Nan said to herself.

Nan was about to close her eyes to rest them when she caught sight of something a little down the road. What it was, made her heart skip a beat.

"Richard! Emma! I see something!" Nan cried, pointing. "'Tis a sign for Meldon!"

"And so it is!" Richard declared. He briefly reined in his horse. Emma did the same as she happily stroked her horse's head.

"Nan, your eyes are just as good as Richard's!" Emma praised.

The small group of riders sat staring at a sign as the long shadows of red-gold sunlight played upon it. The sign read: MELDON. They had finally arrived at their destination. The road had now split into three directions with the wider road in the middle leading to Meldon. As they rode straight head, the road had become noticeably busier than it had been the entire time Richard, Emma, and Nan had been on it. Pedestrians filled the road, likely headed for the city of Meldon whose walls rose up in front of them, as they traveled onwards.

"Have you ever seen so many people before?" Nan said. She gawked at the city's monstrous gray walls. Nan could only imagine what went on inside Meldon, if only she could get a glimpse. She had never seen such a large city, and it left her speechless.

"Aye, I have," Emma answered Nan. "I grew up near the edge of a city like Meldon. 'Tis in the central part of the kingdom. 'Twas also the home of her ladyship. We are both from the same place."

The city of Meldon noticeably dwarfed Lamington, and Nan felt very small as they cantered along under its shadows. So many strange faces were coming and going out of the gate, both on horseback and on foot. There were so many carts being driven into city by merchants and farmers, that Richard and the girls found it difficult to move through the crowds on their horses. Meanwhile, the sun had already gone down, and the long shadows that the setting sun had cast on the city sign were disappearing fast with the approaching twilight. Suddenly dark clouds began building up in the night sky and a damp chill was coming on fast.

"Bad weather will be arriving soon," Richard said matter-of-factly. "Can you not feel it in the air?"

"I hope we can find our way to the monastery," Nan worried aloud. "I suppose we can stay somewhere in the city if we had to. 'Tis better than staying in a lonely forest."

"We will make it, but we must hurry before it gets too dark and we can no longer see the road," Richard said. "I do not think we want to find ourselves in a position where we cannot see our hands in front of our faces. 'Tis then that anything dangerous can be hiding in the blackness when we least expect it. The weather is worrying me, too."

Emma and Nan knew exactly who Richard was referring to. He was deeply concerned about stumbling across the fairy maidens or the Viwa knights with their heavy swords. The last thing the traveling companions needed was to run into the Viwa in the dark where escape might become more difficult than in the daylight.

"Look!" Emma pointed. "That must be the Monastery of the White Friars up on the cliff!"

"'Twill not be long before we see Father John," Nan stated.

Everyone looked upward to a large stone structure jutting out of a rocky cliff. At the base of the monastery was a large pine forest that they would have to ride up to get there. A rain shower started to fall as they began their trek on the narrow gravel path up the steep forested hill to the monastery.

"We must take it slow with the horses or we will slip," Richard warned, the wind ripping violently through his cloak as he got wet. "Emma, hold on tightly to your horse and guide him carefully. It can be dangerous if we ride too fast. The rain might be turning into ice."

The rain did turn to sleet and began coming down steadily, covering the ground faster and faster. Darkness had most of the way descended over everything. The gravel path looked almost nonexistent in front of everyone as they rode on it.

"Do you think we will make it . . . safely?" Nan asked in a weak voice, holding onto Emma firmly. "I will say a prayer that all goes well."

"As long as we go slow as Richard has said, we should be fine," Emma reassured. "I can still see a little of the path ahead."

Somewhere in the middle of their journey up the mountain, as they wound their way through the pine trees, the icy rain stopped falling.

"The ice has finally stopped coming down!" Richard exclaimed. "I hope you are doing well down there behind me, Emma. Do not fear, Nan.

I see some lights coming through the trees not far off. We must be getting closer to the monastery."

Richard reined in his horse as he whispered to the girls behind him, "Do you hear something? I do."

"I do not hear anything, except if you mean the ice dripping from the trees," Emma called up to the lad. "You forget, Richard, that your hearing is much better than ours."

HOOOO-AHHH!!!

As if on cue, the sound of a piercing woman's scream and that of an owl's hoot pervaded the forest. Both Emma and Nan trembled in fright. The girls felt that they were now doomed to the fate of where the sound was coming from.

"It cannot be . . . ." Emma began, holding forcefully onto the reins of her horse.

"What do we do now, Richard?" Nan asked.

"'Tis coming from those Viwa maidens!" Richard roared. "Even now they try to find me. What do you want from me, foolish maidens? Try and get me if you wish! You will *not* succeed!"

CHAPTER 12

Out of the darkness, from behind some pine trees, came several Viwa maidens with the same colorful gowns and white flowers in their flaxen hair. They seem to have multiplied as there were at least a dozen or so of them coming toward Richard and surrounding his horse. They silently danced around the animal as their gowns floated gracefully about them. Their eyes were half-closed, and they each had a sick-sweet smile on their fair faces.

Emma and Nan sat in frozen terror as they watched the awful predicament that Richard was in. They knew they were helpless to try to get him out of it. Fairies have lots of power and for humans to try and outdo them somehow was a losing proposition, and the girls knew it.

"There are more of them than ever!" Nan screeched. "We only saw two of them in Arnon, and I saw two at the lodge when you were asleep, Emma. Now, they have brought others with them."

"Where do they come from?" Emma asked, watching the fairy maidens whose only interest was the lad in their midst. "'Tis so cold and windy in this forest so high up, and they have only a gown on. I do not understand it. What can we do to help Richard?"

"Mayhap we can scream and somebody from the monastery will come to help us," Nan suggested feebly.

"I do not think that will work," Emma replied. "We are still too far away from the monastery. No one will hear us. We may provoke the fairies if we try to do anything. It may wake them out of their dance if they hear us. Look, Nan! Does it not look like they are sleeping as they move?"

The Viwa maidens were closing in on Richard's horse as the animal whinnied nervously and reared up in fright. Richard pulled out his sword and poked it at the Viwa maidens to push them away. Some of them opened their eyes and moved back a little so they would not be hurt by the blade that was touching them.

"Emma!" Nan cried. "I still think we should do *something* to help Richard! I do not like what I am seeing."

Emma became quiet and contemplative for a second.

"You may be right, Nan," she said. "An idea has come to mind. We should ride up to the monastery and warn the brothers that we are in some trouble. Mayhap they cannot do anything to stop the fairies, but 'tis worth a try."

Emma and Nan slowly continued up the icy path to the monastery door. Emma jumped down from her horse and ran to it. She pulled at the bronze knocker until a brother in a white habit came out.

"I am Emma who has come all the way from Lamington with my companions, Richard and Nan, to see Father John!" Emma cried breathlessly. "On our way up here, something terrible happened to Richard! We are in desperate need of your help!"

The brother nodded and, after disappearing back into the monastery, came back out with two other brothers at his heels.

"Our companion is a little ways down the hill," Emma said to the brothers. "Follow me!"

Mounting her horse, Emma went back down the mountain with Nan as the brothers ran behind them with lit torches. Any remnant of light that was left in the forest was completely gone.

"Richard!" Emma murmured. "Richard, I hope you are still there."

I wonder what we will do if the fairies have taken him? Nan thought. *I pray he can defend himself from them like he did in the cave.*

Chills ran up and down Nan's spine as Emma gently guided her horse back down the slippery path.

"Someone is calling us!" Nan said. "Listen!"

From somewhere in the pine trees below, the girls heard someone shouting their names above the bitter wind of the mountainside.

"Emma! Nan! Where are you?" the voice asked.

"It sounds like Richard!" Emma declared.

"I would be careful, Emma," Nan advised. "It may be a trick by the fairies. They have the ability to do such things."

Emma took her horse and guardedly took him off the path while she and Nan spied out from behind a large truck of a pine tree.

The brothers held out their torches and moved them about in the darkness of the trees. They saw the silhouette of a rider sitting on a neighing horse amongst the pines.

"Richard? Emma called out warily. "Is that you? Unless my eyes cheat me, I think 'tis Richard, Nan."

"Aye, 'tis I," Richard called out. "I am safe now. You can come out from behind the tree there."

Emma brought her horse out of the pine trees as Nan breathed a sigh of relief. The girls were happy to see their riding companion again as Emma acquainted Richard with the brothers who had come to help find him.

"We feared for you when those fairies encircled you," Emma said. "We thought you were going to be captured by them for sure."

"When I saw the brothers coming with their torches, I thought they were Viwa knights coming as reinforcement for the fairy maidens," Richard replied with a chuckle.

"Did you say you saw some fairies, lad?" one of the brothers, whose name was Stephen, asked as he stared curiously at Richard. "I thought they were just stories."

"We did, too, until they showed themselves to us," Richard replied. "There will be many more things to say about them when we see Father John."

"Father has arrived this afternoon," Brother Gilbert, who was standing next to Brother Stephen, stated. "We were made aware of your coming from him. When Emma came to the door, we immediately knew who she was when she gave us her name."

"We are happy to know that he arrived safely to the monastery," Emma said. "After our harrowing experience last night and most of today, we worried about our own arrival. Praise God we have gotten here in one piece ourselves."

"The fairy maidens are gone," Richard announced. "When they saw the brothers coming down with their torches, they disappeared before my very eyes. What drove them away, exactly, is unclear to me. As far as those Viwa knights are concerned, I am glad that they have not come back. They are much more difficult to deal with."

"You will have to fill us in later about these knights whom you speak of," Brother Gilbert said. "I am not familiar with them."

"I am sorry that our introduction has not come under better circumstances," Brother Lawrence said to Richard and the girls. "Anyhow, welcome to the Monastery of the White Friars! We are glad to see that you are unharmed in any way, Richard. The brothers and I did not see anyone else when we laid eyes on you, so we cannot say how we would have dealt with these fairies you speak of—if they exist."

Richard and the girls followed the brothers up the mountain path to the monastery. They were grateful for the brothers' torches that enabled them to find their way in the darkness. Reaching the large stone building, they followed Brother Lawrence inside while the other brothers took the travelers' horses to a stable nearby. Brother Lawrence escorted the travelers from Lamington down a long stone walkway to a locutory, a room where the brothers met with people from the outside world. It was in this room where they found Father John waiting for them. Brother Lawrence then bowed and left the three people alone with him.

Nan blinked back tears as she laid her eyes on the old clergyman. She thought she would never see him after their many misadventures on the way to the monastery.

"God be with all of you!" Father John cried out. "'Tis a happy moment to see you all here. Worry was coming over me the last hour or so when you had not arrived at the monastery after the sun had gone down."

"We have much to tell you about since we left Lamington, Father," Emma declared.

"Much of what had happened was on account of me," Richard said with remorse.

Richard and the girls hovered around Father John, each vying for his attention as they told him their strange escapades on their way to Meldon and ending with what happened on the mountainside near the Monastery of the White Friars. The chaplain listened closely with great interest to their stories. He was especially pained when he heard from Nan that there might be two Viwa men pretending to be stewards at Castle Lamington with Lady Catherine at their mercy.

"Lady Catherine had not asked for anyone's help," Father John said. "She told me quite confidently before I left Lamington that she was able to manage the castle quite nicely on her own. I will ask for a messenger to ride out to see her tomorrow. There is not much we can do about anything tonight."

Father John was grievously concerned about her ladyship as he paced the floor of the room.

"If you will allow me, Father, I will ride to Castle Lamington. I will go and come back without stopping. I can leave at dawn and return by evening. I am a strong rider."

"That is not necessary, Richard," Father John stated. "After what you have told me about the fairies, instinct tells me that 'twould not be a wise thing to do. Your safety is at risk, lad. I do not want to take a chance and have any harm come to you. I do not mean to disappoint you, but 'twould take much energy for you to ride all the way to Lamington and back without a stop."

Disappointment came over Richard, but he soon overcame it and grinned.

"You are right, Father," Richard replied. "Hiding from any fairies is near to impossible. They come to you when you least expect it. When it comes to the world of man, they know where to look. They are clever. They seem immortal, too."

"To learn that your ride to Meldon has had these unforeseen consequences is very disconcerting," Father John said frowning. "I am glad that I warned each of you to be careful on the road. I could not have guessed that fairies would become troublemakers for you on your journey here. I would have expected more disruption from highwaymen and human knights, not fairy knights! Fairies are not immortal like you think, lad. They can become harmed and die like any of us. According to legend, they can run and hide from us easily, but can perish just as easily at the point of a sword."

"I had not known this of the fairies!" Richard said with surprise. "I thought they lived forever. I will remember that if I ever wave my sword at any of their knights. Not that I am eager to end any of their lives. I would like nothing better than for them to leave me alone."

"Whether they will or not remains to be seen," Father John replied dismally. "Praise God that you were able to get away from them, Richard. When Brother Albert sent his letter to Castle Lamington the evening before I left town, he wrote to say that Lord Eustace found a woman who was able to read the passage from his lordship's book—'twas written in the Viwa tongue. I hope this does not come as a shock to you after coming across some Viwa on your way here. I found it all to be quite incredible since I am

119

not someone who believes in fairies. That is, until now. Brother Albert does not know what to make of them, either. Lord Eustace himself went out of his way to say he disregards any fairies as real. But as we needed to find somebody to interpret the passage, he found her despite what he personally thinks."

"Emma did not believe me at first, either," Richard said.

"I soon did after you told us about your adventure in the cave with them!" Emma said defensively. "'Tis just that . . . after being part of story and legend for so long . . . 'tis hard to know if such things like fairies are true or not."

"You are not alone in your feelings about them, Emma," Father John noted. "As I have just told you, some of us held the same stances about the fairies before learning of their actual existence." Turning to Nan, Father John said, "When Brother Albert learned of this woman, he felt it best for you to come to the monastery. 'Twas mainly as a deterrent until we knew more about the passage. Brother Albert is a very restrained man. He said he apologizes if he has frightened you so by hastening you to leave Lamington. After my own arrival yesterday, Brother Albert was doubly relieved that you were on your way here after I told him about his lordship's disappearance from Castle Lamington—not that we know of any connection between it, the book, and you, lass. I am sorry that I did not tell you more of what was in Brother Albert's letter until you arrived here. This information was too sensitive for me to have told you at the castle. With all the turmoil going on over there before I left, I felt it best to hold off until a later time."

"Father, what is this business about Lord Robert's book written in Viwa?" Richard asked. "We cannot seem to distance ourselves from these fairies since we first heard them crying out in the forest near the lodge we stayed."

"Is this woman a fairy, too?" Nan asked.

"Ooo! Indeed, she may be one of those Viwa maidens!" Emma said.

Father John laughed out loud. "Nay, lasses, she is not a fairy woman, which worried me as well. She is a fellow countrywoman. Brother Albert and I made her presence before you arrived. She had only worked for the fairies in their kingdom of Viwa. 'Tis how she learned something of their language and how to read it. I have not learned much more from her than this. She only told us a thing or two about herself and our reception with her was over. This reserved woman was not keen on saying much, but mayhap with some persuasion from the rest of you, she will. She is staying overnight at the monastery and will meet with you tomorrow morning."

"Do you think that Lord Robert will ever be found?" Richard reluctantly asked. "What of his book? Did he take it with him after he disappeared?"

"The knights were still searching for his lordship when I left Lamington," Father John replied. "I will have the messenger ask about his lordship when he goes to see her ladyship. Meanwhile, we did find his book. He did not take it with him. I took the risk of bringing it here with me, with approval from her ladyship. Brother Albert is looking through it curiously as we speak. Even if the book was gone, Brother Albert has copies of the passage that I made for him, which the woman can read, too. However, having the book itself is even better. That is all that I have to say to all three of you this evening. You did well arriving here, despite some of the delays you went through. Richard, you were a brave lad fighting off those fairy knights the way you did."

"And the fairy maidens, too!" Nan added excitedly. "They looked like innocent girls in bright long dresses and wearing white flowers in their hair, but they were evil."

"Aye, they surely seemed that way, child," Father John said, leaving the locutory with Richard and the girls. "We hope to learn more about them soon. The woman you will meet may have the very clue we are looking for." Father John's serious face brightened. "The brothers have made some delicious food for those who are weary and use the Monastery of the White Friars for their night's rest. Come! Put all your worries behind you and have something to eat. After that, I insist you get some rest. Tomorrow will be a busy day."

Father John led them down a passageway into a room where many brothers were running to and fro busily. They were serving food of hot bread and hearty soup to a few travelers seated on benches around oaken tables in a hall brightly lit by a roaring fireplace. Since people did not travel a lot during winter, the monastery did not have many lodgers and the supper hall was almost empty.

When the wonderful meal was over, Richard, Emma, and Nan were led silently by Brother Stephen to some stone outer buildings that he explained were guesthouses for travelers. As they wearily walked across a dim courtyard to the building that would accommodate a room for each of them, an uneasiness came over Richard. The uneasiness became stronger and stronger at each pace. He did not share his thoughts with Emma and Nan for fear of causing unnecessary worry. For all he knew, he might have developed a deep mistrust toward anything, or anyone, after meeting too many fairies in one day!

Upon reaching the guesthouse they would stay at, Brother Stephen showed the girls their room first and then took Richard over to his before returning to the dining hall. As Emma and Nan entered the small room they would share, they became aware of a faint shriek in the air.

HOOOO-AHHH!!!

"Oh, Nan!" Emma exclaimed, wringing her hands in trepidation. "Do you hear it? Tell me that 'tis really an owl out there that I am hearing and not something else!"

Nan was about to reply when there was a soft rapping sound on the door.

Emma opened the door with Nan at her heels. It was Richard with a somber expression upon his face.

"Did you hear that?" Emma asked. "It cannot be *them*, is it, Richard?"

"I have heard," Richard answered. "'Tis them. I came to warn you, just in case, but you know already. They are getting closer and closer, which is very disturbing. Father John told me, before we left Lamington, how secure the Monastery of the White Friars was and how difficult 'twould be for anyone to enter. 'Twas the reason why the first brothers had it built so high on a cliff many long years ago. Nan would be safe here. We all would. It put my mind at ease, up till now. The fairies have not gone away for good this evening."

"No one was thinking of fairies when the first stone was laid at the monastery," Emma retorted. "Of course, they have not gotten into it yet."

Emma went over to one of the windows and opened the shutters to peer out. A vivid moon appeared overhead in a clear night sky, and the grounds of the monastery were dark and quiet.

Nan followed Emma and looked over her shoulder.

"Whatever shall we do?" Nan asked.

HOOOO-AHHH!!!

Richard reached for his sword in his scabbard and pulled it out.

"I will go back to my room, bar the door, and stay there. I think they are reminding us—me, more so—of their existence out there in the forest below. You do not have anything to worry about with them, lasses. If anything should go wrong during the night, tell the brothers and Father John what happened to me. In the meantime, sleep well. I will try to, although the Viwa fairies weigh heavily on my mind."

"I wonder if anybody else in the monastery hears them like us," Emma surmised.

"If they do, they will think 'tis some wild animal out there as we first did," Richard replied. "They will not likely venture far outside the monastery to check on what it might be. Lock your own door, lasses, despite how safe we think we are here. I must be going."

With a nod of his head, Richard left the girls. They had become more frightened than ever as they crawled into their beds and pulled the covers up over their heads as they tried to sleep. Although the Viwa fairies' cry was heard frequently throughout the night, the girls soon became too tired to stay awake. They fell into a deep, peaceful sleep until the sun rose the next day.

Emma and Nan awoke the next morning feeling refreshed from a good night's sleep in spite of the fairies. The sun was shining gloriously in a clear blue sky. The air was cool and damp, but it did not stop a bird from singing happily from the rooftop of the guesthouse the girls were staying in.

"Emma, do you know that I was beginning to dream of those fairies last night," Nan said with a shudder as she rose from her bed. "What was worse, they came into our room and wanted *us* to go off with them."

"I pray that will never happen," Emma answered as she went to the basin found on a nearby table to wash her face. "I was worrying last night that the Viwa maidens might have forced Richard to go with them."

"Let us go and check on him," Nan stated. "'Twill not be a happy morning if he is gone."

When they left their guesthouse room after readying themselves for the day, the girls saw Richard opening the door of his and coming out. He appeared as if he had slept well, although he did yawn twice as he spoke.

"We are happy to see you are still with us!" Nan said excitedly.

"We were worried about those fairies coming to the guesthouse and dragging you off to some nearby cave," Emma declared.

"Nay, they did not catch me this time," Richard replied with broad grin. "I slept on my back all night with my sword across my chest. 'Twas not the most comfortable way to sleep, but I managed."

"When we talked to Father John yesterday, I noticed that you did not tell him about being familiar with the Viwa maidens' tongue," Nan said to Richard.

"And that you understood the Viwa knights when they spoke to you," reminded Emma.

"I did not forget," Richard said. "I am still not ready to ask him about whether or not Lord Robert is my father, either. When I ask Father about these things, I will let you both know. There he is now!"

Father John was coming out of the side of the monastery that served as a dormitory where the brothers slept. He walked straight toward Richard, Emma, and Nan with a bright smile on his face. After an exchange of greetings, the companions immediately told the chaplain of how they heard the incessant calling of the Viwa maidens that night.

"Very troubling, indeed!" Father John said gravely. "I have not heard anything out of the ordinary last night, but then, I do not know what they sound like. I will ask some of the brothers to be on guard for these maidens when the sun goes down. I should have done this last night after your encounter with them on the mountain, but I did not think of it. I have also asked for a messenger to be sent to Castle Lamington. The brother left on his horse at sunrise. Let us pray that his news is good when he returns in the next few days."

"We thank you so much for what you have done for us, Father," Emma said, wiping tears of joy from her eyes.

"Would it be possible for the brothers to be on the lookout for the Viwa knights, too?" Richard begged. "I cannot say that those fairy men will return, but 'tis more for my own peace of mind."

"I will tell the brothers," Father John promised. "For the time being, come and break your fast. The brothers have hot bread and cheese to ease your hunger this morning. After you are finished, come directly to the monastery library where you will be meeting with Brother Albert and I. The woman who I mentioned to you yesterday will be there as well. We hope that much will be gained by our discourse there. We must get to the bottom of the many misfortunes that have happened in Lamington."

"Father, 'tis all my fault!" Nan exclaimed. "If the blue dirt did not fall, none of us would be here at the monastery with fairies chasing us."

"'Tis not your doing, Nan," Father John gently said, patting Nan's shoulder. "I do not know what role you have in all this, but 'twas all connected to his lordship's book."

"The book is straight from the devil himself!" Emma stated angrily. "We should burn it and be done with it. Look what it had done to his lordship! Her ladyship is suffering greatly because of this book, too."

"I do not think that is a prudent idea," Richard said. "And we do not really know why his lordship ran away. Let us be patient until we see what we find out in the library. 'Twill not be long, lasses. Let us eat. I think hunger is getting the better of us. I know 'tis for me."

CHAPTER 13

Richard, Emma, and Nan finished breaking their fast. Brother Lawrence came to take them to the monastery library. Through the many long, dark passageways that twisted and turned as they went, they soon came to a closed oak door. Brother Lawrence went to it and knocked loudly. A few moments passed before Father John opened the door to let them enter. Richard and the girls were startled at the visibly shaken face of the old chaplain. They looked at one another inquisitively, but said nothing. Nodding to Brother Lawrence who turned to leave, Father John said to the others, "Pray come into the library. We are ready to see you."

Nan's mind returned to the first time she saw Lord Robert's book lying on the table in the library of the Church of the Holy Angels. Here she was going to see it for a second time as the mystery of its existence was finally going to be revealed. Or, had it already?

Something terrible must have happened in there!

Nan was afraid to follow the others into the room as Father John shut the door behind them.

The monastery library was even larger than the one Nan had seen before and she was awestruck by it. Beautifully bound books of all shapes and sizes lined the shelves right to the ceiling in a much similar fashion to the other library. This library, with books neatly arranged in their places, was well-kept by the brothers. High up in the walls were four large jewel-like stained glass windows with Biblical scenes found in each of them. Bright sunlight poured into the room from every end of the library. Nan shielded her eyes as she glanced here and there. As expected, his lordship's book was lying on one of the very large tables in the room. Seated on one of the benches at another table was a very old brother with white, thinning hair and withered hands that shook uncontrollably.

"This is Brother Albert who I had spoken to you about," Father John whispered to Richard, Emma, and Nan. "He resides here at the monastery and has done much research on Lord Robert's book."

In a loud voice, Father John introduced the three companions to Brother Albert who got up from the table and slowly came to them. He was bent over and barely walked without stopping a few paces for a breath. As he got closer, he had a very wizened face that shown a pleasant smile.

"God be with you!" Brother Albert said to Richard and the girls. "I want to welcome you to our library here at the monastery. Father John has told me much about you. I hope your stay so far at the Monastery of the White Friars has been well. 'Tis here we will discuss the book over on the table there. Over these past several weeks, I have gone many a time over the extraordinary language of the passage found within it, but to no avail. I could not find any language to my knowledge from which to translate it from. What makes it ironic is that I can read many languages, from very ancient ones down to our mother tongue and those of other lands. I have examined the passage in the quiet of this library to the point of frustration. Praise God that I had to get up several times a day for prayer and food or else I would have lost my mind thinking about it." A humorous smile came to his lips. "I barely sleep since I think too much about the odd words of the book, and I need sleep as I am a very sick old man."

"Pray, Brother Albert, tell everyone about your letter from Lord Eustace that you shared with me yesterday," Father John prompted. "'Tis best they heard from your own lips what was said in it."

Brother Albert nodded. "I did not know that Father John had already sent Lord Eustace a letter from Lamington about the book in which he wrote back saying he knew nothing of it. What is worse, the book was not even in his father's will! In my letter to him, however, I did something that Father here had not done. I had included a small sample of the passage for Lord Eustace to see. I am glad I did because his lordship wrote to me saying that he did find someone who might know something of the tongue 'twas written in. The woman he spoke to said that there was a great possibility that 'twas in Viwa, but even she was not positive until she came here to see the entire book for herself. 'Twas then she confirmed that 'twas indeed in Viwa and from there, she was able to read the whole passage to us. She is sitting here, now, in the library."

Brother Albert limped over to the woman who was seated in the corner of the room, her head covered with the brown hood of her cloak. He whispered something to her that no one else heard. She started to get up and follow Brother Albert back to the others. As if having second thoughts about it, she went to Brother Albert and shook her head as she whispered something back to him. Going to the furthest table she could find in the library, she sat down at it and covered her face with her hands.

Hobbling back to Father John and the others, Brother Albert said, "She does not wish to read the translation of the passage. She would like me to read it for her. Thankfully, I have written down every word that she has deciphered from it."

Father John invited Richard and the girls to sit down at a table while Brother Albert went to a small desk near one of the library windows. He picked up a long piece of parchment paper and brought it back to the table the others sat around.

"I will begin reading the passage for you, but pray do not interrupt me before I am finished with it," Brother Albert said resolutely. Clearing his throat, he slowly began:

> *I hath destroyed through death*
> *My princess, my wife, whom I hath left behind*
> *She seeks revenge, townsman,*
> *With something she places in thy hands*
> *A gift of holly from the Viwa to thee, Lamington*
> *It all begins*
> *My terrible reward for the princess's demise*
> *Keep ridding Christmas bit by bit*
> *Paying the price by hurting those I rule*
> *I will know the annihilation of Christmas*
> *The blue snow falling each time will be my sign*
> *I cannot tear myself from this book*
> *The holly forces me to read these words without end*
> *Day or night*
> *I cannot sleep*
> *I cannot eat*
> *I desire to read the words*
> *Christmas will be of the past*
> *'Tis the final blow*
> *Her revenge will be complete*
> *My princess would be pleased with me*

Those closest to me will suffer as they watch
My people slowly remember Christmas no more
Not even a distant memory the celebrations are
I will know true darkness descending over us
As Christmas is gone forever.

Brother Albert put the paper down after reading those last words and sat in silence.

Father John rose from his seat and went to one of the stained glass windows. He kept looking out as if he had expected the blue dirt, or blue snow, as it was now called, to fall outside the walls of the Monastery of the White Friars, though it did nothing of the sort. Facing back toward everybody in the room, Father John declared, "Well, there you have it! 'Tis a very telling passage that says a lot about why Christmas has been taken from us, but there is a lot written there that is so ambiguous. What does the rest of it *mean?*"

Nan turned a ghostly white as panic seized her. She placed her hands over her face and shook her head vigorously. She cried, "Father, it cannot be! There is something I cannot bear to say, but I must. Both you and her ladyship thought I was the girl in the book that you showed me at the Church of the Holy Angels. I am convinced that I am. There was holly around my pictures, too. I remember it clearly. What I am trying to say is that I am the *townsman* the passage speaks of. I was given some holly around Christmas by two men—I could tell they were by their voices—who told me they were servants from Castle Lamington. They said that Lady Catherine was offering some to the people in town because she had too much for herself."

Brother Albert shook his head sadly at the peasant girl as Richard looked away, not knowing what to say.

"What can I do about the trouble I have made for Lamington?" Nan pleaded. "'Twas not my fault that I took the holly from the servants. I only got it from them because my mother sent me out in search of some to decorate the house for Christmas. We thought Lady Catherine was only being kind in offering it to those in town."

Emma lent Nan a sympathetic gaze as she watched tears fall down her companion's face.

Father John went to Nan and looked pitifully upon her.

"Nobody is blaming you for anything," the old chaplain stated. "I might have taken some for myself had they said they were from the castle and offered it to me. Someone, or something, caused the holly to get his lordship to read the book, not you. Mayhap a spell of sorts had been placed on the holly when you took it, which caused another spell in the book to be read by him. The passage does largely explain his lordship's conduct after reading the book. I wish her ladyship were here to listen to the words of the passage. She would agree with much of what Brother Albert has read to us."

"Except the part about a princess wife being avenged for her death by a husband who has destroyed her," Emma said. "Lady Catherine would be taken aback by this. 'Tis not her ladyship. She is not a princess. Who is this other wife? I have not heard of her!"

"Quite agreed!" Father John said. "Her ladyship did not know about Lord Robert being married before when she married him. I had not known this, either, until today. Hence my distressed expression about it, which all of you probably noticed, when you came through the library door."

"Ridding Christmas is upsetting enough," Nan said bitterly. "They know how much we all love it so. All the town folk do not remember Christmas now, except for me and some of you from up at the castle. I do not understand how that can be."

"We do not understand it, either," Father John said under his breath.

"The holly . . . a gift?" Emma laughed sarcastically. "Ha! Indeed not!"

Richard snapped his fingers. "Mayhap those two Viwa fairies who were in the castle kitchen gave it to you, Nan. They gave you the holly and then went and killed the two castle stewards afterward."

"God help us all if they did!" Nan said, her voice quivering. "'Twas so cold out that day when I took the holly, I did not see the faces of the servants under their cloaks or thought about how many there were until later."

Brother Albert glanced up at Father John. "There is still much to be answered, Father, as you have said. Some other parts I read here make no sense at all. We are at a loss."

"They do not leave me at a loss, Brother Albert."

The words were coming from the woman in the brown cloak. "I

can explain more of the passage's background if you will allow me to."

Getting up from the bench, she walked over to where the others sat. She stopped short and dropping the hood of her cloak, that exposed her white linen wimple that covered her dark hair, she lifted her eyes and looked hesitantly from under long, thick lashes.

"Mother!" Richard said to the mysterious woman as he sprang from his seat. His blue eyes scrutinized her in frozen surprise. "It cannot be! What are you doing here translating his lordship's book?"

Nan and Emma turned sharply to face Richard. A staggering moment for their small group after the discussion Richard had with them in the lodge about his strange parentage. The girls all but forgot the translation read to them by Brother Albert as they watched what was unfolding between the strange woman and Richard.

"Richard, how unexpectedly we meet," the woman declared. Her sad, dark eyes looked at him apologetically. "I knew who you were the moment you walked in. I did not ever think of seeing you here, but as fate decreed, we have. This is why I did not wish to read from Lord Robert's book. I decided that I wanted Brother Albert to read the words from it before you found me out."

"This is Susanna, lad," Father John announced. "You know who she is. I am so sorry it had to be this way. Had it not been because of the translation, you might not be meeting your foster mother like this."

Susanna reached out an arm to place around Richard. She broke down crying as he stood by reacting stiffly to her gesture. She let go of him as she reached for a handkerchief in her cloak to wipe her eyes with.

"I am likewise shocked to see you here!" Richard stated, sitting back down on the bench. He was unsure if he was overjoyed at the sight of Susanna, or angry at her for ignoring him on his return visit to her at the cottage she lived in with Peter and their children. "And what do you mean by *foster* mother, Father? I thought she was my *real* mother. At least, I thought she was when I was a wee one. How much do *you* know that I do not?"

Father John stared at Richard after the realization of what he had just said.

"I know this must come as a shock to you, Richard," Father John murmured. "I did not know more than I have been allowed to at Castle Lamington—until Susanna came. No one meant to hurt you. 'Twas my instructions from . . . er . . . the castle. Pray forgive me."

Father John sat back down at the table. He sighed and then paused as if he were thinking of something proper to say. Richard did not answer. The lad sat in silence, devastated by those around him for keeping the truth of his life concealed from him for so long.

"I know of whom you mean when you say your instructions came from Castle Lamington," Richard barked. "'Twas his lordship that gave them to you!"

"Aye, lad, he did," Father John said ruefully. "He told me that he was bringing the son of a knight he once knew to be raised at the castle and that is who I thought you were after I saw you there. Of course, I had been informed not to tell anyone—not even yourself—from whence you came. I have been silent about it until now. I will let Susanna tell you the whole story. 'Tis best that she do it. She was there with you since your birth, lad. She, better than I, knows your life firsthand."

"I distinctly remember being told, rather harshly, by his lordship never to tell anyone where I had lived, and with whom, before coming to Castle Lamington," Richard said wistfully. "I thought it rather odd at the time, but I realize now why he had said that."

"I should start from the very beginning," Susanna said. She sat down next to Richard as she choked back some tears. The poor woman looked at him with a half-smile as she patted one of his hands that still lie on the table.

"Before you begin, I would like to ask you something," Richard said crossly, retracting his hand from her own. "Do you remember the time when I came to see you after I was taken from you and Peter to be raised at the castle?" He refused to look at Susanna. "In case you do not, I will tell you. You turned and went indoors when you saw me. You knew who I was, but you acted as if you did not. I was considerably hurt and upset by that."

Susanna looked at Richard in startled amazement as her eyes dropped to her hands. "'Twas not done out of maliciousness, you must understand," she said quickly. She pretended not to sound bitter by his painful words. "I had been instructed to stay away from you after you went to Castle Lamington. Lord Robert had insisted upon it. He wanted you to concentrate on your new life, so when you came to see us, I had to do something that would make you want to go back there and put your old life and the people you lived with as a child behind you. His lordship also insisted that we leave Lamington after that, so Peter and I and our children left our farm and went back to the lands of Lord Eustace. Mayhap somebody had seen you come by our home and told Lord Robert of it—I do not know. I am so sorry, lad. I so much wanted to tell you everything—about you . . . your past . . . and everything when you came to see me, but I was sworn to secrecy. His lordship would be most ungrateful toward me and my family if he found out that I went against his wishes."

"You would have expected *me* to forget those who have raised me from birth, just by how you acted toward me when I came to see you?" Richard said incensed. "'Twould be most difficult on that action alone! I may not fully understand what you are trying to now tell me, but go on, say what you must. I am anxious to learn of it. I may yet forgive you. From now on, I will no longer call you my mother as you are not!"

Susanna broke into a new fit of tears. She went off to another part of the library and turned her face to the wall. She cried endlessly into her handkerchief that she held from before.

"Richard, this is not the way to behave toward this poor woman!" Father John said furiously. "Some things in life do not always go the way we planned, lad. You have much growing up to do. May it come fast! Do not judge her until you have heard her out!"

"I am sorry, Father," Richard said, hanging his head. "'Tis just . . . my mind cannot help but think back to the time when I went to see her after all those years of living at the castle. Susanna, I am truly ashamed of myself for saying these hurtful things to you. Can you ever forgive me?"

Susanna dared not look at Richard as she cried, but she slowly responded with a nod.

"I will start where Susanna has left off," Father John said, still annoyed with Richard. "'Tis not an easy task to tell you, lad, but I must after you have soured the air. I will be brief and to the point. Richard, your parents are not Susanna and Peter as you may have already guessed. Their children are not your siblings, either. Your father is none other than Lord Robert of Lamington. I almost cannot say it myself, but 'tis true! Your mother is a whole other matter, which I will elaborate on later. We are taking a great risk telling you these things, but we are prepared to face the consequences from his lordship if he returns to Lamington."

"Is this a blessing, or is this a curse?" Richard asked dazedly under his breath. Getting up from his seat, he went over to one of the library windows. He tried glancing out of the brightly-colored glass as Father John had done earlier. "So . . . 'twas not an ugly tale of malice by another page."

"'Twas as you had told us at the lodge, Richard!" Emma exclaimed. "You *are* his lordship's son and heir to Lamington."

"Only if he makes it publicly known that I am," Richard replied. He rubbed his temples as if feeling a headache coming on.

"You are correct, Richard," Father John said. "Only when he acknowledges you as his son will he make you his heir. Until that happens, you will continue living as guard at Castle Lamington. I cannot force his lordship to openly admit anything. Only he decides that. You must pay attention to what I am going to say to you, lad, as it ties into the passage that was read to us. There is much more to say. Much, much more."

"Do go on, Father," Richard replied solemnly. He then turned to look at Emma and Nan who sat quietly, yet carefully, soaking in every detail that was being discussed.

The girls were embarrassed for Richard. They were forced to listen, out in the open, to Father John speak of Richard's heartrending background. What they did not know is that their companion did not mind as he had already touched upon it that night in the lodge.

"I must know everything, although ignorance is becoming more bliss," Richard stated. "I would like no better than to go back to my post as guard and forget about this place. At least there, my life has not been thorny as this is slowly becoming."

Brother Albert nodded for Father John to continue.

"Susanna was Lord Robert's nurse when he was brought up in the household of Lord Anselm," Father John went on. "She was a very young girl at the time and even when his lordship was too old to have a nurse, she stayed on in the household of Lord Anselm. When Lord Robert married your true mother, lad, he wanted Susanna to come with him to his new household. When you were born, she became nurse to you as she once was to him."

Richard was bemused. "I was not aware that Susanna was my nurse, Father. I find this all very intriguing. How was it that she learned the Viwa language? You told us yesterday that she lived for a time in the kingdom of Viwa, where the Viwa fairies live. How can that be when she took care of me as a mother? I do not follow."

"Richard, there is something that I should be sincere with you about," Susanna said, returning to her old self. She came to the table and sat back down next to Richard. "I have cared for you for so long, I should be the one to tell you. You should know that your father, Lord Robert, married a Viwa princess and that is why I went to Viwa with him. The Viwa kingdom is very small, with only a reigning prince or princess at its head. Somewhere in Viwa history, the title of queen and king was shunned because there was a ruler then who decided that every ruler after him must keep the title of prince or princess, which they received since birth. You see, he found these titles to be more humbling in the eyes of his people, and it has been this way ever since. Strangely enough, the Viwa still call their lands a kingdom and not a princedom, but I suppose an old habit is hard to change." Susanna hesitated a bit before proceeding. "Now, from what I was saying before . . . You are his lordship and the Viwa princess's son, Richard, and I became your nurse as Father John said."

Richard sat quietly at the table and did not reply. When he slowly looked up at Susanna, he met her gaze with laughing eyes.

"What you say, Susanna, is utter nonsense!" Richard said. "Besides, where would a man, like his lordship, meet a *fairy* princess? You cannot expect me to believe something so ridiculous, do you? Along with the unusual strength that I have, which fought off some evildoers lately . . . that must come from my Viwa kinship then. Indeed! I cannot forget about my excellent hearing and vision, also. Are they from the Viwa, too?"

Richard laughed until his shoulders shook violently. Susanna watched in stunned silence at the lad who seemed unable to grapple with the reality of his life's origins since his earliest existence.

"I would not lie to you, lad," Susanna quietly replied. "I know this is hard for you to understand. I am so sorry that you had to hear this. I would not have come to the monastery had I realized that you would be here. I wish you had not heard what was read from Lord Robert's book."

"What a strange coincidence that I come to the monastery not knowing that I myself somehow fit into this abhorrent book," Richard said tersely. "Mayhap you knew this already, Father."

"I had not known that you were a fairy princess's son," Father John said, "let alone his lordship's, until this morning before you and the lasses walked into the library. Lord Robert has outdone himself with hiding secrets from all of us, including dear Lady Catherine. I am just as astounded as everybody else here about your lineage, lad. Where your father met your fairy mother is unknown to any of us. You would have to ask him about it yourself. If you play any part in the book, 'tis implied. Well, you *are* related to the two people in it—the princess and Lord Robert. If there is anything beyond that, we do not know. We are still learning what the passage is about."

"Me? A fairy princess's son!" Richard repeated with a sardonic laugh. "That might explain why I recognized some of the words that the Viwa maidens and knights said to me. At other moments when they spoke to each other, I did not know what rolled off their tongue, which was odd."

"Well, I did speak a few words in the Viwa language when you were a wee one, lad," Susanna said. "You never learned it fluently. You were not in Viwa long enough. Most common folk know that fairies allow you to understand them only when they want you to. I learned that quickly when I lived in Viwa. What was it that these maidens and knights told you?"

Richard related the words of the Viwa maidens and everything he remembered that the knights told him before the altercation between them took place. He also went on to describe their coat-of-arms as Susanna listened carefully.

"They were definitely from Viwa," Susanna verified. "This does not sound good to me. Be careful if you cross paths with them again, lad. I cannot repeat myself enough about that."

"Richard fought them like the bravest of knights, but they fled on their horses and did not return," Emma said proudly. "Nan and I saw it happen."

"Can you tell me more about those Viwa maidens?" Susanna asked.

"They surrounded Richard in a cave near the lodge that we stayed in during the night," Nan declared. "'Twas from the lodge door that I saw him follow them there. They also tried to do the same on the mountain near the Monastery of the White Friars. I am grateful to God that he was able to get away!"

"I wish I can tell you what this all means, but I cannot," Susanna said. "Their behavior is not welcoming toward you. They should be treating you with great respect. You are heir to their kingdom."

"I do not know what to believe!" Richard said. Slamming both his fists down hard on the table, he rose from the bench to leave the library.

Grabbing the handle of the door, Richard turned to say, "Pray do not come after me. This is too much for me to bear. If any of you follow me, woe to you! My anger is not anything to be met with now!"

CHAPTER 14

Silence fell over the room as the door banged shut behind Richard. Everyone in the room listened to his footsteps fade away on the stone floor as he ran off.

Father John said, "Let the lad be. He is in denial right now. He will come around. I will speak to him later. He is confused as well. He needs some time to himself. In the meantime, I still think that Susanna should tell the rest of the story of what had happened in Viwa. Once I get a clearer idea of things, I can always relay them to Richard when he feels better."

"If you think 'tis necessary, Father," Susanna murmured. "I know the lad hates me. I should not have come here."

"Do not agonize yourself, Susanna," Brother Albert said. "Nobody, not even you, could have foreseen this coming."

Susanna wiped her eyes with her hand and started up where she left off before Richard stormed out of the library.

"Shortly after Richard's birth, Lord Robert became homesick. He was eager to see his native land after living in the fairy kingdom for so long. Princess Lavena, his wife, begged him not to go because she loved him too much and would miss him. He quietly devised a plan to leave Viwa for a short period and return there without her knowing it. I knew about the plan, because I overheard him discussing it to himself, while I was in an adjoining room rocking the infant Richard to sleep. He had a strange habit of talking over things out loud to himself in a mirror, but I understood in some ways why he did this. He did not have many friends in Viwa at the time—most fairies liked him, but a few did not. The Viwa are not automatically trustful of men from our world. The night before his lordship left Viwa, he wanted to take a piece of his wife's hair back home

138

with him as a token. When she was asleep, he cut off a few pieces of her long golden hair. Just as he did, she immediately died. A fairy princess's golden hair is her lifeblood. Lord Robert did not know this at the time, however, and was grief-stricken about it."

"My goodness, Susanna!" Emma said, her eyes transfixed in revulsion. "The poor woman! What a terrible way to depart from life!"

"Richard's mother had such a beautiful name," Nan murmured sadly. "If only he were here to learn what it was . . . ."

Susanna paused and then went on, speaking so softly that Emma and Nan had to strain their ears to hear her.

"Except for a few good fairies there, most of the Viwa kingdom wanted revenge for the death of their princess. That meant only one thing. They were going after Lord Robert and he knew it. He decided he was going to escape with his baby and take those of us, who came from the country he was from, with him. Regrettably, some loathsome fairies caught up with us. There was a terrible fight on our way out of Viwa the night we departed. I was so far back with Richard and the train of riders while leaving, I was unaware of what was actually happening in the front with his lordship and his knights. What I do know is that Lord Robert barely managed to push back the angry Viwa, and we were able to get away."

"We hope that his lordship was not taken by the fairies recently," Emma murmured. "He disappeared after a hunting trip two days ago and, as far as we know, he has not been located by his knights who went searching for him. Lady Catherine would be sick at heart if fairies had done that to him."

Susanna gasped as she placed her hands over her mouth. "I am sick at heart that you tell me this! I do not wholly trust the fairies after what we went through with them when we left Viwa."

Susanna sat listlessly staring straight ahead and shaking her head.

"A messenger from the monastery has been sent out to see if her ladyship is well," Father John said. "Two Viwa men have found their way into Castle Lamington and are acting as stewards in place of the ones who have perished by them, or so we think. We pray that Lady Catherine is safe, but as we have not been to the castle in two days, we do not yet know the fate of Lord Robert. May the messenger return to us with good news of them both."

"The more I hear, my heart becomes sicker," Susanna added,

placing her hand over her breast. "Viwa at Castle Lamington! Those fairy maidens and knights can very well be after Richard to find his lordship!"

"Mayhap those two stewards were waiting for me to lead them to Richard when I was there in the kitchen!" Nan cried out.

"Since they were not able to find him there, they must have sent those Viwa maidens and knights after him instead!" Emma speculated. "They think he knows where his lordship is!"

"They can principally be after Richard as well, in which case, I am happy to know he is safe here at the monastery with us," Brother Albert said.

"Pray continue, Susanna," Emma persuaded. "We are becoming too sidetracked by things we are not sure of yet. Our fears are getting the better of us."

Susanna got up and walked around the room as she labored to put a smile on her face.

"I have a lot to tell you," Susanna said, curling her fist. "I *must* tell you! When we left Viwa, Lord Anselm gave Lamington to his lordship to rule and found a new wife for him, Lady Catherine. Meanwhile, Lord Robert did not know what to do with his baby son. He worried about those fairies in Viwa. He did not want them to come and steal the child and take him back to their homeland. The baby was not going to be in their charge, not after what they wanted to do to his father after what he mistakenly did to their princess. His lordship was angry with the fairies! He did not care what his son meant to their kingdom. If Lord Robert was unable to stay in Viwa, then neither would his son. So his lordship changed his baby's name to Richard from a Viwa name, which I cannot remember for the life of me. He also asked me to continue raising him, but not as his nurse, but as the son of farming folk in Lamington. I had married Peter only months after returning from Viwa, so Lord Robert thought it to be a wonderful arrangement for Richard to think of us as his real parents. Peter did not take to this, but he tolerated it as best he could."

"So Richard is a prince, but not just *any* prince?" Father John asked, regarding Susanna seriously. "He was his mother's first born and one to rule Viwa?"

"Aye, that is so," Susanna replied.

"Is this why Richard was brought to Castle Lamington later on to be raised as a page in Lord Robert's household?" Emma wondered. "He told us about this back in the lodge the other night. He said he found it all very odd that he was taken away from you when he was just a child of farm folk. Or, so he thought!"

Susanna nodded. "His lordship wanted to give Richard everything a princess's son could have in all but name. He kept everything quiet about his child because of the fairies. He really did want what was best for Richard, but his lordship was not able to tell him this openly. I do not know if the fairies told Lord Robert anything about coming after Richard, but he was fearful of it."

"Richard said he was awfully upset when he later learned that he might be the son of his lordship," Nan stated. "He thought some of his fellow pages were trying to hurt him."

"There were any number of people around the castle who could have said it," Susanna explained. "There were many from our entourage who went with Lord Robert to Castle Lamington. They were all from Lord Eustace's lands. Someone could have accidentally said something about it where, eventually, it went innocently around the castle. His lordship sworn us all to secrecy about his past, but there are many people who do not keep them. I would never have done such a thing, but I can see it happening. I know his lordship had no intention of telling Richard. Sadly, there is only so much a father can do to shield his child from something, whether good or bad. I said it once and I will say it again. The lad must be *very* wary of those fairies. I do not like the way they are after him, but I am delighted by his Viwa strength. It has helped him overcome them—inherited no less from his mother's side!"

A creak was heard coming from the library door as it slowly opened little by little and then stopped. Nan looked to see that someone was listening behind it. She lightly touched Emma's sleeve under the table to warn her that someone was there. Emma snapped to attention and gazed in the direction that Nan had quietly pointed to with her finger. The door swung open and Richard sauntered into the library. He sat back down at the table next to where his old nurse had sat earlier. Father John and the others stared in amazement at his reappearance.

"I am sorry that I left like I did," Richard sighed. "I did not mean to run off. I was so upset over what was being told to me, I could not stay here another moment."

"I am glad you decided to return, Richard," Susanna said.

"I did not hear *all* you said, but I have been listening for a few minutes out there," Richard replied, pointing to the door. "You can tell me what I missed later on, but I want to say that I am not angry with my father for not letting me stay in Viwa to be their prince. I am much happier in Lamington than I would be in some silly fairy kingdom. It has become clear to me why I am just a castle guard. Lord Robert wants me to stay close to him so no danger comes to me. All except for now . . . after his disappearance . . . I find myself on a journey, which I had not expected to go on, with danger lying in wait at every turn. 'Tis quite a twist of fate for me!"

"Indeed, it is!" Emma said. "Had you not come, you still would have been guessing about your life, Richard."

"Which I am still trying to come to terms with, lass!" Richard said darkly.

Looking down at the table, Nan examined the handsome book belonging to Lord Robert. She timidly reached out and fingered some of the glistening jewels set in the cover. Nan thought of the book's beautiful pictures that Father John and her ladyship allowed her to look at, including the two of herself.

"Susanna, who made this book?" Nan asked. "Back in Lamington, Father John and Lady Catherine allowed me to look inside of it. All but for the pictures of me in it, we are not sure who the other people are. The pictures of the animals and flowers are beautiful, too. Mayhap you can tell us more."

Taking the book into her own hands, Susanna carefully leafed through several of the pages. She smiled to herself as she pointed to some of the pictures, as if recalling something she had overlooked.

"'Tis Viwa you are looking at," Susanna answered dreamily. "I almost forgot what a beautiful kingdom it was—all that grows and lives there is unlike anything from here in our world. Do you know that some of the pictures are of Lord Robert and his new bride? It makes me so sad seeing them so happy in this book when there was such a different turn of events later on. The other people in the book are servants from the princess's castle and farm folk from around it. If you ask me who made the book itself, I do not know. I would guess it to be an artist from Viwa, but that is beyond my knowledge. I only came here to translate the passage, not to tell you who painted the pictures in the book."

Richard hastily grasped the book from Susanna and immediately went to the pages of Lord Robert and his wife. He studied them with great intensity. Princess Lavena was very much like Richard with fair hair, but hers was peeking out from under a long veil. She was slim and tall-looking with a little upturned nose and wore gold-trimmed gowns in some of the pictures. Lord Robert was a younger, more assured, version of himself.

"I am grateful that you are here to tell me what my mother looked like in the book, Susanna," Richard confessed after closing it. "I hope you can tell me more of Princess Lavena, but another time. I have been through too much this morning."

"What do we do about the translation from the book?" Nan interposed. "A spell has been placed on it by me through some holly I got from a Viwa fairy in Lamington. If it can be undone, mayhap everything bad that has happened to us will be gone for good."

Nan desperately wanted to get back to the central reason they were there in the library. It seemed that everyone in the room had something to gain from the passage of the book. For Nan, it was to celebrate Christmas again and to return home to her family. For Richard, this passage was key to knowing his past life that was taken from him at his birth. For Emma, it was to have Lord Robert safely returned to Lady Catherine at Castle Lamington so she could return as maidservant who she once was.

"I hate to say this, lass, but we must wait until the messenger returns from Lamington and tells us the situation with Lord Robert and Lady Catherine," Brother Albert replied, rubbing his aching back. "We do not want to act too hastily."

"We believe in solving one bad state of affairs before facing another," Father John declared. "Depending on what happens in Lamington, it may help us decide what we must do next."

"I understand, Father," Nan murmured.

"I am truly sorry that the Viwa fairies had avenged his lordship by having Christmas taken from the people of Lamington because of what he had accidentally done to his wife, my mother," Richard apologized to Nan. "I am also sorry for what the Viwa had done to you. They are partly my kin, despite how evil some may act, so I feel the need to tell you that. Christmas means so much to all of us and for what had been done to it is intolerable."

"Richard, 'tis not your fault!" Emma cried.

"Aye, lad, do not blame yourself," Father John stated.

"An idea has come to me to help us all," Richard said. "We must find a way to get into Viwa. We will spy on some of the fairies there until we find the one who had put the spell on the book. We will drag him, kicking and screaming, back with us until he undoes it. I will go to Viwa if I have to. If I look something like my mother, I can get into Viwa and pass myself off as one of them."

Susanna laughed at Richard's naïveté. He frowned at her, confused by her response to what he thought was an ironclad plan.

"Lad, you do not just walk into Viwa!" Susanna exclaimed. "You have to be invited there or know beforehand how to get to it. 'Tis not so easy to get there. *I* do not know how to get there. Going to Viwa is not like entering another land by boat, or like crossing a mountain pass into another country. They come and find you and you go back with them, or you manage to find the secret way in, which is not easy to do. You, yourself, would not want to be the unfortunate guest of Viwa, now would you? They would be eagerly rubbing their hands together to see you come back to them, Richard, especially if they are after you. You likely would not be coming back to us if you dared tried to enter their lands. I wonder if you have thought of that."

"I have not thought of that," Richard replied, shaking his head in frustration.

"What about Lord Eustace, Susanna?" Richard urged. "You came from his lands. What does he know about Viwa? Surely he knows something of Lord Robert, who is his own cousin. They lived under the same roof for a time, did they not? He *must* know the way to Viwa!"

"One day while I was working in Lord Eustace's kitchen, there was some chatter about a letter coming to his lordship from a Brother Albert about an outlandish book that was once given to Lord Robert," Susanna said. "There was some question about its origins, and I knew it had to be only one thing when I heard 'twas in a tongue unlike any other. Little did I know how right I was! Though no one came to me about it, I went straight to Lord Eustace and said to him that I might know something of this book and that it might be written in Viwa, a fairy language. He thought 'twas intriguing and only shrugged his shoulders and laughed. He said he did not believe in fairies and thought the book was rubbish, even though he showed me a little of the writing from it that came from Brother Albert, which was not enough to go on for me. I needed to see more of it. Anyway, Lord Eustace was too young to know anything about the life of Lord Robert, his cousin, when he went to Viwa to marry Princess Lavena. By the time Lord Eustace grew up, Lord Robert was out of his life by either living in Viwa or ruling Lamington. What I am trying to tell you is that Lord Eustace does not know anything about Viwa. I was lucky to have convinced him enough to let me come here about the book."

"I will go to Lord Eustace then!" Richard cried out. "I will convince him. I am his cousin's flesh and blood. He will believe me!"

"Nay, Richard," Susanna said sadly, getting up from the bench and walking toward the library door. "Lord Eustace has no interest in Lord Robert's life. He would much rather go about his own business than worry about something that does not pertain to him. Such is the personality of him whose castle I reside and work in with my husband and children. Lord Eustace told me that he always felt that the whole fairy story of his cousin was a figment of his father's imagination—and mine, I suppose, but he did not tell me that. Lord Anselm, his father, had gone to Viwa with Lord Robert and had come back to tell Lord Eustace the story, but he refused to believe anything his father told him. Lord Eustace is a practical man, unfortunately. If you wish me to tell you something more of your mother, Richard, I will be here at the Monastery of the White Friars for a little while longer until I return home."

Susanna smiled and left the room, shutting the door quietly behind her.

Richard placed his fair head down on the table and remained motionless for a few minutes before lifting it back up.

"Nothing Susanna said beyond translating the passage is of any help to us," Richard said tartly. "We are back to where we had started when we came to Meldon."

"Except that you find you are heir to the throne of a fairy kingdom called Viwa," Emma said, hiding a smile behind her hand.

"I do not find that amusing, Emma!" Richard replied. "Other than going there to break the book's spell, which Susanna said would not be wise for me to do anyway, I have no use for the place."

Grave concern came over Father John. Deep down, he had misgivings about having Richard at the monastery. The old chaplain worried that with all his reckless talk, Richard would do something rash without anyone's knowing and create needless trouble for everyone there. It was not the first time he saw lads like him act this way before. Going up to Richard, Father John placed his hand on the lad's shoulder.

"Whatever you do, pray do not leave the monastery for a time," Father John commanded. "We must wait for the messenger to arrive. 'Tis then, and only then, we will decide what happens next."

"If that is your final word, Father, then I shall go and find Susanna," Richard said disappointed. "I am anxious to hear something more of my mother."

"Do not forget what I have told you," Father John said sternly.

"Do not worry, Father," Richard answered. He ran out the door and was gone before Father John said more.

"Father, I do not think Richard will go to Viwa," Emma asserted, getting up from the table with Nan. "We do not know where 'tis located. Susanna does not, either."

"I realize that, lass," Father John said, "but there is always a chance that Richard may attempt it. With the serious nature of the book's passage, I fear for him. Since the fairies know he is here, I also do not want an army of them descending upon the Monastery of the White Friars if the lad does something foolish. I do not think the brothers here will be prepared for it."

The conversation then turned to Lady Catherine. Emma and Father John became absorbed in a discussion about her that was of no interest to Nan. Instead, the girl went to Lord Robert's book and bent over it. The colorful gemstones were so mesmerizing to Nan that she was unable to extract herself from staring at their timeless beauty. Then something caught her eye.

"Father, look!" Nan cried. "Is there a jewel missing from the book?"

"What do you mean, lass?" Father John asked, looking up.

Both he and Emma quickly came over to Nan.

"There is a wee hole in the cover," Nan said. "See! It looks like another jewel might have been there."

Father John held the book up to get a better look. Sure enough, there was a cavity as small as the tiniest pebble on the book's cover that appeared to have once had a jewel. Other jewels surrounded this cavity, but the cavity was not visible unless someone held their nose close to it.

"How curious!" Father John exclaimed. "I have not noticed this before. I wonder where the jewel went. Mayhap it fell out onto the library floor. Brother Albert and I will look around for it carefully, though it may be difficult to find something so small. If not, then we will keep an eye out around the monastery. I will let the other brothers know as well. Otherwise, 'tis gone for good or it may be at Castle Lamington, in which case, we cannot do anything about it. Now off with you, lasses! This day is not so cold for late winter. The brothers have a garden to sit in, although nothing is growing there yet. At least it may take your mind off some pressing matters. We have learned all we can today."

CHAPTER 15

Emma and Nan went to the monastery courtyard where the garden was and sat on a stone bench they found in the middle of it. They discussed, in great length, what was said in the library that morning until they exhausted themselves of it. Sitting in silence, they listened to the birds twittering in the nearby trees and watched as a few of the brothers came out with their hoes to begin planting some seeds for spring. Emerging from one of the monastery buildings moments later, they saw Richard with Susanna. They were talking amongst themselves and seemed unaware of the girls' presence. About a quarter of an hour later, Richard and Susanna turned and went back into the building.

"I presume she is telling him about his mother," Emma said. "He is quite taken by whatever she is saying. He does not take his eyes from her when she speaks."

"I do not think he saw us here!" Nan cried. "Neither did Susanna!"

"That does not surprise me," Emma declared. "Would you not want somebody to tell you all about your real mother if you had been without one for so long? I am confident that everything around him is a blur right now. His mother is what interests him the most, not us."

Emma and Nan did not see Richard that evening when they ate supper or during the next several days, when they went about amusing themselves by either sitting in the garden or walking around the monastery passageways, watching the brothers go about their daily chores. Both girls were anxiously awaiting what news the messenger would bring back to the monastery as well, but none came.

"Where is Richard?" Nan asked Father John when they ran into him the following day.

"We thought it odd that he has not spoken to us since Susanna left, which I assume she has," Emma said.

"Aye, Susanna has gone home," Father John replied. "Richard is around. He seems to be keeping to himself lately. He spends a lot of time in the library—both studying and looking over Lord Robert's book. He is quite captivated by it. He seems interested in the pictures of his mother the most. I caught him doing so when I walked into the library to get something a few hours ago. I would leave him be, lasses. He needs time by himself."

Later that same day, Emma and Nan went to the second floor balcony of the monastery that gave them a breathtaking view of the city of Meldon below, as they listened to the sound of the chapel bells calling the brothers to prayer as it always did several times a day. They even dared to ask Father John if they could, perhaps, go into Meldon for the afternoon to see what was there, but he forbade it.

"That would not be a wise idea, lasses," Father John told the disappointed girls. "Do not go anywhere. If any of the Viwa recognized you from the time you spent on the road with Richard, they may very well follow you here to find him. We have been blessed that none of the fairies have reached us here since the time they followed Richard up the mountain. Mayhap they have given up, but I am not convinced of that. I have one more thing to tell you. Brother Albert and I searched around the library for the missing jewel. Unfortunately, we have come up with nothing. 'Tis so small, likely 'tis gone. We have alerted the other brothers about it, so if any of them find it in another part of the monastery, they are to bring it to us."

Standing about on their favorite place on the balcony one afternoon, Emma and Nan leaned over the stone balustrade. They looked over the tops of the pine trees far below them, where the winding road went down the mountain to the valley where the city was.

"'Tis such a beautiful view up here, but so windy," Emma said absentmindedly. She drank in the beautiful panoramic scenery of endless woods and fields beyond Meldon, while an occasional manor house or castle dotted the landscape on the horizon. "Summer must be lovely up here. I want to stay here forever. 'Tis a lot like standing at the top of Castle Lamington, only higher since the monastery is on a mountain and the castle is not."

"Look, Emma!" Nan called out softly. "There is Richard! He is playing at sword fighting."

"I see he has finally come out of the library," Emma said. "I was becoming worried about him."

They watched with interest as Richard hiked down the mountain path thrusting his sword about in the air. He kept walking further and further down until the girls no longer saw the top of his head amid the thick cluster of pine trees.

"Where is he going?" Nan asked perturbed.

"I thought we were advised not to leave the monastery!" Emma exclaimed. "If Father finds out Richard has left, he will not be happy. He will also be angry with us for not stopping him."

"I think we should go to him right away and tell him to come back!" Nan cried.

"Come then!" Emma declared, grabbing hold of Nan's arm.

The girls ran down the balcony stairs and without getting the attention of any of the brothers, they quietly slipped out the front door of the Monastery of the White Friars.

"Richard!" Emma and Nan called out as they ran down the mountain path to find him.

The path twisted and turned and the girls slipped here and there on frozen patches of ice. Their eyes darted frantically from place to place, but they could not see how far Richard had walked.

"Do not hold onto me so severely, Nan!" Emma said. "If you do, we will both go headlong to the bottom. 'Tis a long way from here to there."

"I am scared to fall!" Nan wailed. "'Tis too difficult to tell what is ice and what is not."

Nan then saw some branches moving, which could not be the wind as there was none. Not a sound was heard but the cracking of the underbrush.

"I see something," she whispered to Emma. "Over there—to the right!"

Before the girls could get away, they looked up and saw a few Viwa maidens twirling toward them from behind some of the pine trees. They were in their recognizable white garments with half-closed eyes and smiling faces.

Emma gave out a little shriek, but it was too late. The Viwa maidens were too powerful in strength for both she and Nan to break free of them. Two of the Viwa maidens clutched the girls' arms with such physical force that they became immobile. To make matters worse, more maidens came from somewhere within the trees making a semicircle around Emma and Nan. The girls were now prisoners of the fairies.

Where was Richard?

"What do they want with us, Emma?" Nan screamed. "I thought they were after young lads, not you and me! I am becoming ill looking at their faces—why do they not open their eyes for once!"

"What do you want, fair maidens?" Emma asked, trying to steady her shaking voice.

One of the Viwa maidens hissed at Emma. "Where is the lad? We *want* the lad!"

"They speak in our tongue for once, Emma!" Nan exclaimed. Turning to the fairies, she said bitingly, "We do not know where he is."

"Even if we did, we would not tell you!" Emma replied furiously.

"So you will not tell us, will you?" asked the Viwa maiden who held onto Emma's arm.

She squeezed Emma's arm a little harder until Emma winced in pain.

"Let me go, you evil thing!" Emma screeched.

"You will not get away from us until we get what we want!" the Viwa maiden said.

"You will not get what you want!" a voice behind the maidens shouted in a high-pitched voice.

Several of the Viwa maidens turned in time to see Richard pull out his sword and swing it at them with all his strength.

"Richard, we were looking for you!" Nan said jubilantly at the sight of the lad.

"You would not dare harm fair maidens as ourselves, would you, Richard?" one of the Viwa maidens asked sweetly. The Viwa maiden who spoke to Richard swiftly transformed herself into the most beautiful maiden whom he had ever seen. "You are too kind and handsome a boy to do it."

Richard's eyes glazed over as he stood frozen still in place. A smile came to his face as he looked at the lovely Viwa maiden. His sword dropped from his side as he became deeply enthralled by her.

"Nan!" Emma said. "What will we do? This is becoming the

worst thing we have been through."

"Richard has been put under a spell," Nan answered under her breath. "'Tis beyond us to bring him out of it, Emma."

The sound of galloping horses was heard somewhere on the mountain path nearby. To the horror of Emma and Nan, a dozen or so Viwa knights came forward and surrounded the girls and Richard.

"We caught him at last!" a Viwa maiden said with glee. "'Twas not difficult at all!"

The Viwa maidens and knights began to speak excitedly with one another in Viwa, leaving the girls upset as they were unable to comprehend them. It did not matter to Richard whether he understood them or not. He was still staring at the beautiful maiden in front of him.

"Richard!" Nan said. "Wake up!"

"We plan on taking you with us, lasses!" one of the Viwa knights stated without emotion, looking down at Emma and Nan from his horse.

Two Viwa knights got down from their horses and attempted to put the girls on each of their horses, but the girls resisted mercilessly. The beautiful fairy maiden was given some rope by one of the knights. She began to bind Richard's hands and legs together tightly.

"Where will they take us?" Nan said to Emma, sweating profusely from fear. "They are telling us very little."

"Do you think we would be so foolish as to tell you our plans, imprudent lass!" the beautiful maiden replied. "You are our prisoners, if you had not guessed already, but you will never return to your lands— ever!"

A light breeze began to blow through the trees as the smell of fire and smoke was detected coming from somewhere above the fairies and the three companions. Some cries were heard and then several white robes of the brothers became visible. They were holding torches as they ran fearlessly down the path to try and save Richard and the girls.

"Go away, you filthy creatures!" Brother Stephen hollered.

The Viwa maidens went running off into the trees while the fairy knights turned their horses around and went riding off the mountain path and were seen no more. The mountain went quiet as the brothers came rushing toward Richard to help untie him and lift him from the ground where he had fallen after he had been bound by the rope.

"Brother Stephen! Praise God you have found us!" Emma said.

"I did not believe in fairies until now," the brother replied.

"How did you know what happened to us?" Nan asked.

"'Twas easy!" another of the brothers answered. "Father John had become suspicious that you three had gone missing. He sent us out in search of you, and we found you here."

Richard rubbed his eyes as he looked up at the others around him.

"What has happened?" Richard asked slowly.

Emma and Nan told Richard of their happenstance of nearly becoming abducted by the fairies of which he scarcely remembered.

"I should have known better than to leave the monastery," Richard declared. "Since we had not seen any Viwa for days, I thought that I could go and take a walk outside somewhere. I suppose I should not have done that."

"Try not to next time," Brother Stephen replied. "We have a garden you can sit in if you wish."

"I will do that," Richard said. "I am truly sorry about the trouble I have caused. I warrant I will be faced with Father John's wrath."

"Susanna was right all along," Emma said. "We must be more cautious when it comes to the fairies. They evidently do not wish to become our allies. We do not need further proof of this after today."

"It still does not explain why they are after me, although Susanna did give us some reasons for it," Richard replied. "For now, I want to get off this path and go inside."

"Did you notice that the Viwa maidens did not scream before they tried to capture us?" Nan said. "They always did it before."

"They wanted to come up behind our backs the way a wolf stalks its prey," Emma stated. "Such is the way these evil fairies think."

"I relish the thought of how just a few brothers can make an army of Viwa knights and maidens run off," Richard chuckled. "I, on the other hand, have to fight them with all the Viwa strength within me, unless it fails, while the brothers use torches and no swords."

"You will fail no matter what when confronted by a *beautiful* fairy maiden," Nan warned. "I have a feeling that is how you ended up with them in the cave near the lodge."

"Aye, 'tis likely so," Richard answered. "At least then I got away. I will try and not stare into those fairy maidens' eyes if I see them again. Mayhap that will help."

"'Tis not the light of our torches that chases them away," a brother named Matthew indicated, "but likely this place, that we, the brothers, live in that scares them off in the end."

"Then we are, indeed, in trouble when we leave here," Emma said. "Who will guide us out of here safely, especially if Richard can only do so much?"

"I would not worry about leaving here yet," Brother Stephen said. "Let us get back to the monastery before it gets dark. Those fairies may decide to come back."

When Richard, the girls, and the brothers returned to the Monastery of the White Friars, Brother Matthew instantly reported to Father John the clash with the fairies on the mountain path. Father John went directly to Richard and the girls and called them to a private meeting in the locutory.

"I do not need to tell you why you are here," Father John said, suppressing his anger. "I am not even going to rebuke you about it, particularly you, Richard. I think the three of you have learned your lesson. From now on, the brothers are going to watch all of you very closely. They will be posted at every doorway."

"Thank you for not admonishing us too much," Emma replied. "I have learned my lesson."

"I know I have!" Nan said emphatically. "I have never been so scared like that."

Richard did not answer Father John, but remained silent as he nodded his head.

"Now I must tell you something that I cannot judge as either being more or less disturbing than what you have gone through already," Father John began in a low voice. "The messenger, who was sent to Lamington to check on Lady Catherine, has not come back. His horse did, but not Brother James. Most of the belongings he took with him on the journey to Lamington were still hanging from the animal, except for a few things that were missing. Even the letter that I wrote to her for him to take was gone. God forbid if he were robbed by a highwayman and left on the ground harmed! Someone will have to go out on the road to see if he can be found. In the meantime, we are going to send another brother as messenger to Lamington. Brother Alexander is a fast rider, and we will instruct him to get to Lamington by a different route to avoid the same misfortune. Do not be anxious by this calamitous turn of events. Our roads are not always the safest, as you have learned yourselves."

"This is truly disconcerting, Father!" Emma exclaimed. "His lordship has gone missing, the two castle stewards have died, and now the messenger from this monastery has been taken from us."

"I pray the new messenger makes it to Lamington," Nan said. "I am becoming worried about what is going on around us."

"So am I!" Father John cried out. "We will say extra prayers this evening that all will go well with Brother Alexander this time. I am hoping that his lordship has come back to Lamington safe and sound by now, but as a messenger is not able to get there safely, we cannot even find that out."

And so it was that Brother Alexander was sent out on his way to Castle Lamington by roads different than the ones taken by Brother James. Boredom overcame Emma and Nan as they waited restlessly for the second brother to come back with news from Lamington. March had arrived. The tiniest of buds on the trees began to form, but most of the trees around them were bare. Emma and Nan longed for flowers to burst into full bloom and for the air to become warmer, but that meant staying at the monastery longer than they had hoped. So they spent most of their time walking along their favorite location on the high balcony of the monastery or sitting in the courtyard garden, but there was little else to do while they waited.

One day, not long afterward, they heard Father John speaking in a low voice to someone below them. Emma and Nan, who were looking out from their usual place on the balcony, ran excitedly across it and down the stone steps. On their way to Father John, they met him making his way up to meet them. He had a grave look on his face that told them that all was not well. The girls exchanged fearful glances at one another as they waited for him to speak.

"Lasses, I have found out terrible news this morning that leaves me with a heavy heart," Father John said. "It has to do with Brother Alexander. His horse has come back to the monastery late last night. I have only learned of it early this morning after Mass from Brother Albert. He is sick with fear as to why the second brother's horse has returned without the rider. Most of Brother Alexander's provisions were still with his horse, except for the letter written to her ladyship. 'Twas exactly like the last time, when Brother James's letter disappeared with him when *his* animal returned to us. We have, reluctantly, told Abbot Osbert about it. He is the head of the Monastery of the White Friars here, and he forbids another messenger to go out to Lamington. He is concerned that a third brother will not return. We must carefully think about what must be done in place of having a brother ride out there. A decision will be made this afternoon. I will be discussing it with some of the brothers and Abbot Osbert who will be there, although we will have to send *someone* out to find the two missing brothers."

"This is bad news, indeed!" Emma replied.

"Mayhap we *can* send Richard back to Lamington," Nan suggested. "He said he would go, Father, when you first spoke of sending a messenger there. He knows how to fight off the fairies well enough, as long as they do not place him under a spell like the Viwa maidens did."

"I had almost given into this notion myself, lass, but I do not yet know if 'tis sensible to do," Father John answered. "On the contrary, I have told Brother Albert that we cannot keep the lad here forever. He is restless, as we can tell by his actions about the Monastery of the White Friars. If he is, indeed, a prince of Viwa or an heir to Lamington, he needs to do more than trudge about here swinging his sword as we have seen. He does spend time reading and studying books in the library and not just his lordship's book, which he did at first. He is very studious as well. Being guard at Castle Lamington is holding him back from more useful endeavors."

Just as Father John had finished his sentence, he observed Richard eavesdropping on the little party in the locutory. His shadow and a little bit of cloth from his clothing was seen in the slightly open doorway. Realizing that the clergyman had seen him, Richard backed away and his footsteps were heard walking off at a fast tempo down the passageway.

CHAPTER 16

"Richard was listening to what we were saying!" Emma murmured excitedly. "'Tis not the first part of our conversation that I am worried about with him."

"I hope he does not decide to go to Lamington like I said he should," Nan said with worry. "What if he does?"

"I will have the brothers watch him even more so than before, so he does not do anything impetuous," Father John said. "I must now get back to what I had originally planned and have an audience with the brothers and Abbot Osbert. I will let you know what our discussion was as soon as we are finished."

Emma and Nan returned to their second favorite spot on the bench in the courtyard. They sat quietly, as they listened to the wind and birds, and watched as the brothers continued their work in the garden. The girls nearly jumped from their seat as a voice behind them said, "Good day, lasses! I am sorry that I have been so aloof lately."

They turned around to see the towering Richard standing nearby with a wide grin.

"You have frightened us so!" Emma said. "Where have you been hiding from us lately?"

"We have not seen you since the incident with the fairies or spoken to you much since Susanna left," Nan declared. "I thought you were angry with us over something. I was afraid to come to you and ask."

"Nay, 'twas no such thing!" Richard replied with a laugh. "I meant what I said when I told you I was sorry about my behavior recently. I was pondering everything that Susanna told me about my mother and wanted to be by myself. Can a lad not have peace without anyone interrupting him? If I were as sentimental as a lass, I would be telling the both of you everything that Susanna had told me. But, if you must know, my mother had been only a good and noble lady. A lot like Lady Catherine. I am only saddened that her people wrongly turned against my father after he cut off some of her golden hair."

"I am pleased to know that about Princess Lavena, Richard!" Emma exclaimed. "Your apology is accepted as well."

"I am slowly, yet unwillingly, acknowledging the heavy burden I am carrying that someday, if 'tis at all possible, I may become Lord of Lamington or Prince of Viwa," Richard sighed. "I would prefer the former than the latter, but until anything of the sort happens, I do not want to be treated as anyone other than Richard, the guard from Castle Lamington. I have told Father John this, and I am telling you."

"I might have felt the same way, had I been in your shoes," Emma stated.

"We will do as you say," Nan answered with a nod.

"There is something else," Richard said. "I overheard what Father said about the missing second messenger. How unfortunate! How much longer do we have to wait until this monotony of being here breaks? Aye, I am bored here, as you both must be, these last several days of waiting and waiting. For what? Father John is taking too long to make a decision about anything, including our fate here. I also feel that if 'tis my father's fault that the two Viwa at Castle Lamington are posing as stewards, then I, as his son, feel all the more obligated to do something about it. I have decided to go back to Lamington and check on Lady Catherine myself!"

"What!" Nan cried out. "You cannot do that without risking your life, Richard!"

"You know very well who will be lurking around the mountain once you leave the monastery door," Emma said. "The Viwa knights have multiplied, in case you have not noticed when they surrounded all three of us down on the path."

"The Viwa maidens were even more frightening than the worst of my nightmares!" Nan said. "We will not allow it. We will tell. I feared you would take up my idea when I said to Father that he should send you to Lamington instead."

"'Twas a very good idea!" Richard replied.

"You are foolish, as Father John says you are sometimes," Emma said. "You will gain nothing when you leave here."

"Except that you will be captured and taken prisoner for sure by the Viwa fairies," Nan added. "I have not heard them cry out since that first night we came here. They want us to think they are not here, but they are."

"I can ride a horse faster than the best knight in Lamington!" Richard boasted. "I remember his lordship telling me this when the pages and I went on a hunt with him and his knights last summer."

"I am happy for you, except that you have to be careful about Viwa maiden spells, even if you do outride them or fight a few of them off," Emma reminded him. "'Tis not like when you fought off those three Viwa knights before we reached Meldon. There were no spells then."

"I know that is my weak spot, but I will take my chances," Richard said.

"The brothers' eyes are on you everywhere, Richard," Nan said. "They are taking special care to make sure you do not leave them unnecessarily."

"They cannot stop me!" Richard insisted. "I will leave at a time when no one is watching. I will sneak into the stable and get my horse when they all go to Mass at midnight. They will never know."

Detecting that the girls were not warming to his proposal in leaving Lamington, Richard became exasperated. Before stomping off, he exclaimed in a tone more fearsome than ever before, "Lady Catherine may be dead before we find out anything about her! If you wish for that, then I give you permission to tell Father or anyone else of my plans. I will go anyway! I do not need your approval!"

When Richard left, the girls looked at each other in fright.

"Mayhap he has a point," Emma said. "I do not want to see any great harm come to her ladyship. If any does come to her, I do not think I shall ever live with myself."

Nan nodded slowly. "I agree. Let Richard go if he wishes to. The last thing we need to know is that the Viwa carried him off to their kingdom, where he is never to be heard from again. Let us pray that his plans work out well for him and nothing of the sort I mentioned ever happens."

A drenching rainstorm came down that evening. The rain was pounding the roof of the guesthouse so forcefully, that Emma and Nan wondered how they would ever fall asleep. Before getting into her bed,

Nan went to the shutters and opened them to look out the window. So black was it outside, that the streaks of falling rain were not visible to the naked eye. She quickly closed the shutters before the room became soaked with water.

What a night for Richard to leave the monastery, Nan thought. *How can he get himself down the mountain path in this weather?*

"I am starting to hear the screams of the Viwa maidens again," Emma said, as she got into bed. "Listen!"

HOOO—AHHHH!!!

"They are telling us that they are still out there," Nan said shivering.

"Just as I was beginning to think you were right when you said that their cries on the mountain stopped just to deceive us into thinking they were gone," Emma said. "They are not gone, and Richard's safety is being compromised. The Viwa will be behind him when he slides down the mountain with his horse."

"Indeed, he is a foolish lad!" Nan said. "I wish we can go after him."

"Nay!" Emma quickly replied, shaking her head feverishly. "'Tis too risky for us!"

"Then we should tell Father right away that he has left!" Nan stated. "Richard may not get too far in the rain before the brothers catch up to him."

"If Richard does not kill himself on the dark mountain first," Emma declared. "'Tis then we will not have to concern ourselves with fairies taking him, though awful that may sound."

There was a soft knock on the door. A muffled voice was heard calling out to the girls.

"Lasses! Are you awake? We need to speak with you!"

Nan went to the door and opened it. Holding out a smoking torch in the pouring rain was Brother Ambrose, caretaker of the monastery stables. Alongside him was Father John and a figure, many heads taller who could only be Richard, walking slowly behind them. They stood in the guesthouse doorway drenched to the skin in their cloaks.

Nan stood stiffly where she stood and was afraid to say anything. She felt Emma glare at her sideways as they waited for someone to speak to them. Nan knew exactly what this meant; Richard's little escapade to run off to Lamington was essentially over. She worried to what extent the trouble was that he found himself in. She could only imagine how livid Father John must have been when he had found out Richard's misdeed. She trembled at the thought, but desperately tried not to show it.

"So, lasses, you dare defy me and my orders to allow Richard to go off to Lamington by himself!" Father John bellowed in the open doorway as the rain came down. "You are just as at fault as he is for leaving. Brother Ambrose found Richard racing off on his horse in the darkness, but Brother Stephen met up with him before he left the courtyard."

Father John stood glaring at the girls with his arms crossed at his chest and feet apart. This gentle old chaplain was clearly pushed to the brink as he shook his head and rolled his eyes upward in disgust. "You should be ashamed of yourselves. You both should have come to me as soon as he made this known to you. I have spoken to the lad already. He knows he should not have been so bold to try and ride off like he did. How shameful, is all I can say! Richard has already been pardoned, but trusting him is another matter."

"Father, we are so sorry for what we have done," Nan said in a small voice. Deep down, she was relieved that the brothers had caught up with Richard before he left the monastery grounds.

"I am truly sorry for my misbehavior, Father," Emma replied. She put her hand to her mouth as she hid a smirk from Richard.

Had they not told Richard this might happen?

"Now that we have cleared the air about this awful incident that was almost in the making, I need to tell the three of you something," Father John said. "I was hoping it could wait until tomorrow, but after this happened, I feel it best not to. After spending a few long hours in attendance with Abbot Osbert and three other brothers, we have decided upon the best solution that we could find in getting someone back to Lamington. We may have been slow in our evaluation of the situation, but we wanted to be thorough about our plans. Unlike your hasty one, Richard."

The girls danced around Father John elatedly as they waited to hear him out. Richard, who had been staring at the wet ground, jerked his head up to listen to the newest development at the monastery.

"After coming up with several unproductive ideas of how we might find out about Lady Catherine's circumstance in Lamington, Abbot Osbert thought of something that should have been obvious to me to do, but was not," Father John began. "I had first thought of going to Lord Eustace and asking him to send some of his knights to Lamington. I then remembered what Susanna had told us in the library. Lord Eustace does not believe in fairies, or in Lord Robert's marriage to a princess from a fairy kingdom. Instead, we decided 'twas best to go to the lands of Siddell that Lady Catherine is from. Those are the lands that you are also from, Emma. I have written up a letter to her ladyship's brother, Lord Roger. I will deliver it to him myself. Siddell is not far from Meldon—I can be there and back in a day. I will explain the situation at Lamington to Lord Roger and pray he will help us. I cannot think of one reason why he would not."

"He is a gentle soul of a man and much like her ladyship," Emma said. "He may listen." She beamed as Father John spoke of her home. "I am pleased that he is not like his father, Lord Fulk, who had an awful temper and would destroy Lamington to every stone to save Lady Catherine from the Viwa."

"Father," Richard spoke up, "if I may . . . I can go to the lands of Lord Eustace. I will plead with him about giving us some knights to go to Lamington. I am living proof of a child born to his cousin, Lord Robert, and the Princess of Viwa. If you do not think 'tis so sensible an idea, then I would like to go along with you to make Lord Roger's presence."

"I would allow you to come with me if the situation had been different," Father John replied, "but if those vile fairies are out there lying in wait for you like they have been, then nay, lad, you cannot come. I am not sure if you can make it down the mountain path without one of them seeing you. I do not want to hear any more arguments! I leave for Siddell as soon as the sun rises in the morning. I promise to be back either late tomorrow, or early the next day after, depending on how long Lord Roger detains me there. I feel confident that all will go well at his lordship's castle."

"I hope the Viwa do not confront you on the way down the path like they did us, Father," Emma said uneasily.

"Do not worry too much about me," Father John answered, turning to leave. "'Twould be worse for me if Richard came along. They know he is here, but I do not think they will stop me from going anywhere. I am not who they are looking for."

Father John and Brother Ambrose bowed their heads and left the guesthouse with Richard, who turned briefly to Emma and Nan and gave them a contrite smile, where he disappeared into the rainy darkness after the others.

Before blowing out the candles and climbing into their beds, the girls said an extra prayer for Father John's journey to Siddell the next day. They stayed up far into the night, chatting about Richard's failure to leave the Monastery of the White Friars, before falling asleep as the early hours of dawn broke.

By evening of the next day, Father John returned to the Monastery of the White Friars with a retinue of knights from Lord Roger. Father John dismounted his horse as Emma and Nan came running to him in the stable yard.

"Father! Father!" they cried happily. "You are back! Safely, too!"

"Praise God, I am here!" Father John replied. "And with a hundred of the finest and bravest of knights from Lord Roger. He listened quietly and patiently while I explained the situation of his sister at Castle Lamington. Without hesitation, his lordship said he would give me the best soldiers in his lands. I could tell by the look in his eyes that he was anxious for Lady Catherine."

"Do you think that the Viwa captured the brother messengers from the monastery?" Emma asked.

"The thought has crossed my mind, especially when the letters I wrote, saying two Viwa fairies might be at Castle Lamington, had disappeared from their saddlebags," Father John murmured.

"Mayhap the fairies do not want Lady Catherine to know they are there," Nan proposed.

"How deviant of them if that is true!" Emma said.

"A search party of brothers went looking for the two messengers, but they went as far as Arnon and came back," Father John said. "They found no one. They were too fearful to go further than that. The brothers did put word out to the towns and villages along the way to Meldon for two missing brothers."

"Did Lord Roger believe you about fairies being at Lamington?" Nan asked.

"At first, he said he did not know of any personally, but to my surprise, he mentioned to me that he already knew that Lord Robert had been married once before to a fairy princess and had a child. He said he did not know the exact details, except that they were tragic and that his future brother-in-law at the time did not want Lord Roger to reveal this to his sister before their marriage. I suppose Lord Robert planned on telling her, but as we all know, he did not. Lord Roger did say that he also believed that Lady Catherine was still not informed of this, and I confirmed it. I was starting to feel knots in my stomach, when I thought I would have to be the one to bring up this unfortunate news of his brother-in-law's former life, in order to ask for Lord Roger's help. I was so relieved to know that he was aware of it."

"We may not have to worry about Lady Catherine not knowing by now, especially if there are Viwa fairies in the castle," Richard said. "They would have to tell her about his lordship's past if they were looking for either him or I."

"If she knows, then 'tis beyond our control," Father John said. "I pray that she can forgive him for something he should have told her himself long ago."

Emma, Nan, and Father John watched as the knights from Siddell took their tired horses to the stables to be given water and rest. Some of the brothers ran out from the stables to assist the heavily-armored men with their muscular animals. Nan studied their large, impressive shields that hung from the sides of their horses. She noted their equally impressive design of the Siddell coat-of-arms that depicted a large bird's wings in indigo blue above a knight's silver helmet with a white plume. Two swords crisscrossed the other over the bird's wings. The background of the entire shield was bright crimson.

"These robust young men have had many years of training both at Siddell Castle and in the battlefield, Lord Roger did not fail to tell me," Father John explained. "We need only the best knights to fend off the ones from Viwa. If both lock swords together, I want to know who will win before one blow takes place from either side."

"When will they be leaving for Lamington, Father?" Richard asked, walking up to the others.

"Tomorrow morning would be a good estimate," Father John stated. "There will be no postponement. You should go with them as well, Richard. Staying at the Monastery of the White Friars does not suit you. I laid out my concerns to Lord Roger about this. He saw no reason why you should be held back here, despite what the fairies had done or plan to do.

You have fresh knights to back you up on your way to Lamington. Neither Brother Albert, I, nor Abbot Osbert can do anything more for you, the lasses, or for Lady Catherine. Those who live here are only brothers who have no army and are a peaceful lot whose main objective in life is not in fighting fairies, though they did scare quite a few away. If you need any more help after leaving here, then Lord Roger is whom you must turn to for protection. Coming here will not help. I do not want you to think that I completely mistrust your fighting abilities. I was secretly worried that as you are Lord Robert's only son, he might not appreciate my sending you back on the road unprepared and open to adversity because of some ruthless fairies."

"I had expressed something similar to the lasses here the morning after you left," Richard replied. "I was beginning to feel hopeless being here, but I am grateful for your permission, Father, in allowing me to leave with Lord Roger's men."

Richard's eyes glowed with enthusiasm as he looked at the knights with whom he would be accompanying the next morning to Lamington.

Looking at Emma and Nan, who were quietly standing about in the stable yard, Richard then asked, "What about the lasses? They do not have any more reason to remain at the Monastery of the White Friars than I do."

"How right you are, lad!" Brother Albert replied. The old brother had sluggishly come out of the monastery and made his way to the stables. "I cannot imagine them being in better company than with you and the knights from Siddell."

Emma and Nan jumped with joy as they ran to Richard's side.

"Before you leave, there is something I must give you," Brother Albert said. He reached underneath his cloak for Lord Robert's book and handed it to Richard. "You must take this back to its lawful owner. We have gotten all we can from it. He would want it back, I am sure, whether he is at Castle Lamington or not."

"I believe that Emma should keep it in her saddlebag for safekeeping," Richard said, taking the book from Brother Albert. "If the fairies decide to rear their ugly heads, I do not wish for them to know that I have it. Whether that matters or not, I do not know, but I feel safer knowing 'tis not on my person."

"I believe this book is something that Lamington does not need back after what his lordship had done after it fell into his hands," Emma pointed out. "It may be safer here at the Monastery of the White Friars."

"Nay," Father John answered firmly, "'tis not safe here! If his lordship is not at Castle Lamington, he cannot read the passage. If he is there, he will be eager to get his beloved item back. After what we had seen of his temperament when he had lost the book once before at the castle, 'tis not something we wish to see again! Susanna has done her deed. She has translated the passage for us. There is no need for the brothers to keep the book any longer. I spoke to Lord Roger about the book and the trouble it has caused. He said that you, Richard, need to confront his lordship about your being his son when you get to Lamington. The translation of the book is all about him. Not you, lad, and not Nan! He needs to be open to you about it. He also must go to Viwa and demand to meet with those who made him feel like he had no choice but to leave their kingdom. He must speak with the fairies and explain the misfortune he had caused his former wife. Their transgressions over it must end toward us. Lamington must not suffer because of their late princess's accident."

"'Tis the only way Christmas will return and how the situation will be remedied," Brother Albert declared. "Lord Robert must not hide you any longer. He must not hide from the fairies, either, and pretend that his past never existed."

"Lord Roger told me personally that he will help Lord Robert if need be," Father John said.

"I am not sure how this can be accomplished without much difficulty," Richard quietly replied. "I also do not know how Lady Catherine will take it."

"Sir Christopher, one of the knights here from Siddell, will speak to his lordship with you about everything," Father John stated. "He has been advised by Lord Roger to do so. You will have all the support you need, lad. Do not fear."

A look of confidence, mixed with relief, spread over Richard's face. Emma and Nan felt happier than they had ever been since their arrival at the Monastery at the White Friars. A well thought out plan was reached by Father John with Lord Roger. Their journey back to Lamington would be more affable and less worrisome. The Viwa fairies would be kept at bay by the Siddell knights and Christmas would be back at Lamington as soon as his lordship resolved his personal matters with the Viwa.

"How soon do we leave in the morning, Father?" Nan asked.

"I would like to get back to her ladyship as soon as possible," Emma said. "She needs me now."

"'Tis not our decision to make!" Brother Albert chuckled. "You may leave at your own discretion."

"At dawn, I should think," Richard replied to Emma. "The faster we get onto the road, the sooner we can return to Lamington."

"I know I will sleep like a baby this night," Emma said. "All the fairies' screams on the mountain will not deter me from it. Not with the aid of many Siddell knights at our side."

CHAPTER 17

Richard was by his horse's side the next morning waiting with Lord Roger's knights for Emma and Nan. It was a cold morning, but not bitterly cold, like it was during wintertime. Father John said a short prayer, with everyone in the monastery stable yard, for a safe ride back to Lamington.

"Will you not be coming back with us, Father?" Nan asked.

The old clergyman did not appear to be in a position to leave.

"Nay, I will be staying here for a little while longer," Father John replied. "I will not be gone from Lamington for too long. I pray that by the time I return, some part of the situation there will be settled."

Emma and Nan were sorry that the chaplain was not coming with them, as they mounted their horses and waved to him and the brothers before they were off.

Nan quietly observed Richard riding in the midst of the Siddell knights. He held himself too upright, almost regally, which made her laugh aloud.

"Why, Emma, I believe Richard thinks he is Prince of Viwa already!" Nan blurted out. "Does he not look it in the way he holds himself on his horse with the knights around him? See how his fair hair has been neatly groomed and his clothes thoroughly cleaned from the dirt and mud. I think the brothers washed his clothes for him, knowing full well that they had a prince in their midst."

"Nan!" Emma reprimanded her companion. "Do not speak so loud! He may not yet be ready to be thought of as such. You forgot that he is also heir to Lamington as well. I am not sure how he will choose between the two someday, but 'tis something he must decide and not us. Well . . . ." Emma hesitated as she surveyed every inch of Richard. "He does seem to act and look the part of a prince or a lord. He has been given a larger shield to carry, too. I see you are very eager to go back to Lamington, Nan, though we do not know what lies in store for us there."

"I *am* very happy!" Nan said with content. "I will be seeing my parents again and my sisters and baby brother. You are right that we do not know what awaits us there. We can only pray that all is well."

"I will sorely miss the Monastery of the White Friars," Emma sighed as her horse walked carefully down the mountain path with the company of knights, some in front and some in back, as they made their way to the main highway near the city walls of Meldon. "I will especially miss the beautiful view on the balcony. I will cherish it forever in my heart."

"I will, too," Nan said. She looked over her shoulder at the monastery for one last time. Only the tiniest piece of the monastery roof was seen amongst the pine trees before it disappeared from view.

"We made it to Meldon without seeing one fairy!" Nan cried out. "Is that not something?"

"Mayhap they became frightened when they saw us with the knights," Emma said.

"Father John did well to go to Siddell to get assistance from Lord Roger," Richard declared. "I could not have done better myself."

The young people and the knights did not stop riding until noontime on the road—which had gotten busier with travelers since spring had begun—to eat some of the food that the brothers packed for them. By Father John's request, the band of riders took a different route back to Lamington to try and avoid meeting the same fate as the unaccounted for messengers. They traveled the rest of the day on roads that went through hills and fields and passed by strange, unfamiliar villages. As nightfall approached, a small tent was set up for the girls in a forest clearing to sleep in while Richard and the knights slept outdoors. Emma expressed her desire to stay in a hunter's lodge, similar to the one they had been in on their way to Meldon, but none was found. As a lady's maidservant, she was happiest sleeping in better arrangements, but she tolerated the tent until the next morning.

"I honestly thought I heard some strange creature sniffing around our tent in the dark," Emma said, after they had all eaten something and mounted their horses. "I hope 'twas not any of the Viwa scouting us out. I did not get much sleep and must pay the price for it by being tired all day."

"The sniffing you heard, lass, might have been the snorting of my horse," one of the knights, whose name was William, said. "I seem to remember him being close to the opening of your tent last night."

The knights, including Richard, roared with laughter until Emma turned scarlet with embarrassment. Nan tried hard to suppress a smile behind her hand, but was unable to.

"Then I am quite happy knowing that last night was the last time I had to deal with your animal!" Emma said in disgust, holding her head up high and ignoring the others as she rode. "A horse, you say. Indeed!"

Richard grew serious. "We have been very fortunate so far that we have not come upon any Viwa, especially last night. I half-expected to see at least one of the Viwa maidens dancing out of the woods with her frightening set of teeth when angry."

"Not with a horse owned by Sir William, would we!" Emma joked. She had gotten past the comment made by Sir William earlier and was keen to show everyone that she was not bothered by it anymore.

The rest of the morning was spent by Richard laughing and conversing with the knights. Since Emma had come from Siddell herself, she joined in on the conversation about how things had fared there after she had left to become maidservant to Lady Catherine. Nan, who was left out of the discussion, looked about her at the strange new sights, but when doing that filled her with boredom, she shut her eyes to rest them for a while, as she did not admit to Emma that she did not sleep well, either, in the forest where they had set up camp for the night.

"We should be arriving in Lamington within the next hour," Richard called out to the others, as they made their way on the road that resembled the same narrow rocky one they had been on when they began their journey from Lamington.

"The road is going downhill now, and I see 'tis becoming wider and smoother," Nan said. "It appears to be the same road we were on when we left town."

"Aye, 'tis the same one," Richard said. "The road we had just left has converged with the one to Lamington. I am glad that Father John suggested we take another route home. At least we have not met up with anything *or* anyone undesirable. Mayhap it helped to avoid Arnon this time. You remember what happened there!"

"I cannot help noticing that as we get closer to Lamington, there are not many travelers on the highway as before," Nan observed.

"Aye, I have noticed this myself," Richard replied. "How odd for springtime. Well, no matter. There will be more room for us on the road then, is that not true, Sir Knights?"

The knights, who rode with the small party, agreed with grins and laughter at Richard's statement as Richard decided to hasten his horse by galloping faster to their final destination.

"One thing that I am not comfortable with is those menacing rain clouds," Emma said, looking up at the sky above her.

Everyone looked in the direction of the fast-moving dark clouds. The day, though starting out beautiful, was soon becoming a different story. The forest, that the road cut through, took on a foreboding appearance. It became difficult to see the road. It was becoming dark as the sun was being covered up by the black clouds. There was a clap of thunder and before Richard, the girls, and the knights could get off the road to run for cover in the forest, the clouds let out a severe downpour that drenched all of them.

"We *were* making good progress for Lamington," Richard said in disappointment as his head got wet. "Too bad the storm came."

The riders sat in the forest waiting for a break in the rain as Richard, Emma, and Nan were soaked to the skin in their clothing. The knights from Siddell, who did not have anything on but their chainmail, sat in stillness on their horses as the rain ran off their gear. They were used to enduring all kinds of weather conditions and did not seem too bothered by the endless amounts of water falling on them.

Sir Leland, one of the knights who sat on his horse closest up front, said, "I have an awful feeling that this rain is not going to let up shortly. We may be in for a long wait. I am very concerned for you, lad, and the lasses. We have our heavy armor to keep us warm, but all you have on are your cloaks. I fear you will become ill if we do not get out of this. 'Tis quite a heavy shower."

Just as swiftly as the rainstorm came, the wind began to pick up. It blew the raindrops at an angle that made them splatter into everyone's faces. The riders bent their heads to avoid the water getting into their eyes. In between the howling of the ongoing wind, a peculiar, yet familiar sound began to penetrate the air. The sound was that of the hooting of an owl and a woman's scream. The knights looked up and stared at each other dumbfounded at what it might be.

"What was that?" Sir Ingram shouted to the soldiers at the front of the line. He was the furthest knight at the back.

"I do not know!" Sir William answered, tilting his head to the sound. "I have never heard of something so queer in all my life. I cannot tell if what I am hearing is man or animal."

"I know what it is, and 'tis not something you care to know unless you knew what it was already," Richard explained. "You are hearing the fairy maidens. Usually accompanying them are the Viwa knights. They are the very creatures you were asked by Father John to defend us against, Sir Knights." Anger and fear edged into his face as he squinted inside the forest as his ears tried to verify from where the sound was coming.

Emma and Nan threw each other a glance as the sound came rapidly their way.

"Viwa fairies!" Nan said. "I was hoping our journey to Lamington would be free of them as we are almost there."

"Ooo!" Emma fretted. "They have ensnared us after all."

"Emma, take Nan and go into the forest somewhere and wait!" Richard cried out.

Richard did not care if any of the fairies had heard him or not. He had had enough of them, and he intended on fighting off the malevolent Viwa until the very last one. "The knights from Siddell and I will drive them away so we can get to Lamington and end the disaster they are imposing upon our people and Lady Catherine. They will not take our Christmas away, and they will not lay one finger on her ladyship!"

In the darkness of the forest, the sound of something rustling amongst the trees was heard. Before Richard and the knights from Siddell could react, out poured many, many Viwa knights on horseback, pulling out their long swords from their scabbards and holding their large shields in the air with the characteristic silver background and white boar in the foreground, that held a large sword in its mouth with a small red rose on the handle.

Their numbers seemed endless as Emma and Nan sat hidden in the brush on their horse, their mouths gaping wide in shock and horror at the battle that was about to ensue. Following behind the Viwa knights were the same Viwa maidens that the girls and Richard had come upon time and again. Instead of there being just a handful, there were dozens of them running behind the Viwa knights' horses, waving their arms around and dancing wildly in a circular motion while making their horrendous call.

Emma took her horse deeper into the forest for fear of the Viwa maidens or the Viwa knights catching sight of them where they were. She found a small, soggy ravine below some thorn bushes and trotted her horse down into it with Nan holding on firmly behind her. Emma soothingly rubbed her horse's head and mane. She hoped this would help him not give away their hiding place by making a sound that the fairies might hear.

"I have never been so frightened in all my life," Emma said. Her heart was beating so loud that she worried the fairies would hear it. "I keep trying to find the most concealed spot there is around here, but even I do not know if this is the safest place. I wonder if that outlandish sound those fairy maidens make has any meaning. It gives me chills just listening to it."

"There are so many Viwa fairies," Nan whispered. "They seem to have come out of nowhere. They also know where we are even when we do not see them." Her voice chattered from the cold wet cloak that was soaking into her skin. "If only we can help Richard, but I know that is impossible."

"Very much like the time when we left Arnon and came across the four Viwa knights," Emma said with a nod. "Richard fought them fearlessly before, so we can only hope and pray that the result will be the same here."

"As long as those Viwa maidens do not put him, or any of the knights, under a spell," Nan added.

From the bottom of the small ravine, the girls sat and watched the fighting that was going on between Richard, the knights from Siddell, and the Viwa knights. The clanging of swords, the sound of shields clashing, and the screams and shouts coming from both the Viwa knights and the others, was unbearable to listen to. Many a time Emma and Nan had to flinch at some of the horrifying things they saw. They were uncertain about whether or not anyone was wounded or killed, so they decided to stay in their place until the fighting was over and they themselves could get away unharmed. The rain became heavier and louder to the point that the girls could not even see or hear what was going on around them.

The rain drowned out the sights and sounds of the battle taking place both on the road and in the forest. Emma and Nan were confused by who was fighting whom as everyone became a blur in front of them. The forest had become so swollen with rain that the horses and the men were being pushed back with Richard to fight further into it. They eventually found themselves sloshing around in a foot or more of unpleasant, soupy mud. The girls were at first able to see a flash of Richard fighting the Viwa knights here and there amongst the trees, but because of the heavier rains, they no longer saw him. They had hoped to be able to spot him during the fighting, to know that he was there and out of harm's way.

"Nan, can you see anything?" Emma called out to her companion behind her. "Where is Richard?"

"I do not know!" Nan answered. "I had seen him but for an instant, but now he is gone."

"Oh, how that sickens me," Emma said, holding her stomach as if in pain.

The girls stared out into the rain, but it was no use. The torrential rains had blocked out everything from view to the point where they could not look up without getting rain into their eyes. At that moment, the rain gradually slowed to a drizzle until it eventually stopped altogether. The clouds had begun to part where they revealed blue skies and rays of sunshine streaming down.

"God be praised!" Emma said, clutching her hands together in delight. "The rain has ended."

"We must be a sight," Nan giggled, relieved at the warmth of the spring sun on her face. "We are dripping like two wet cats." Pulling the hood off her head, she squeezed her soaked hair until every drop of water ran from it.

"Aye, we must," Emma said, also squeezing the water out of her hair. She was soon distracted by something and immediately clutched at the horse's reins. She tried to look above the ravine to see if the coast was clear. "I am glad that the rain has ceased, but our troubles have not ended. We can be down here quite a while if the fighting has not finished."

"I do not hear anything," Nan replied. "All has gone silent."

"I suppose that must mean that the fighting *is* over," Emma surmised.

The girls strained their ears to see if they detected any sign of life coming from above the hole they were in. They then heard heavy breathing coming from the figure of a man, who was prostrated face down on the ground near the front hooves of Emma's horse. They did not know the man was there until the horse neighed at the sight of him. The animal began to back up nervously.

"Who is that lying there?" Nan whispered. "I have not seen him there before."

"I do not know," Emma replied quietly. "He must have rolled down here when we were not looking. I cannot tell who the man might be; he is too covered in mud. He does not seem to be any of the Siddell knights. I will get down off my horse to assess his condition before we can help him. I hope he is not badly wounded. Stay on the horse, Nan. I have his reins. He will not gallop away with you."

"Be careful, Emma!" Nan shrieked. "The man may be one of the Viwa knights. Do not get too close."

Emma nodded and began to dismount her horse. As she hopped to the ground, the figure got up on his elbows and hands and then slowly to his knees. Lastly, he pulled himself up on his long legs. Pushing back the muddy hood from his mud-soaked cloak, Emma and Nan saw it was Richard, dirty from head to toe from all the fighting that had taken place. He coughed uncontrollably and started wiping off the mud that had covered every inch of his face. Only his two azure eyes were seen almost eerily through the caked grime on his skin. He looked as muddy as Nan and Emma were wet.

"Richard!" Emma exclaimed. "'Tis you! We did not know who was lying on the ground below my horse."

"Are you wounded?" Nan asked with growing fear. "We were worried when we did not see you during the fighting after all that ghastly rain came down."

"Nay, I am fine, lasses," Richard answered, continuing to wipe off the dirt from his face. "Just a little shaken up is all."

"After all the battles, both great and small, which you have been in with those Viwa knights, you could very well be dubbed knight by now," Emma said.

"I feel like I should be dubbed more a coward than a knight," Richard stated. "During the fighting, I happened to come too close to this gully. As I was lunging for one of the Viwa knights when his back was turned toward me, my heel bumped the back of a big rock, and I ended up falling backward and landing face down where you both are."

"You did not run away from any of the Viwa knights," Emma said.

"You fought bravely. We have seen all this from my horse."

"I may not have run off, but I wanted to," Richard reluctantly admitted. "We were too overrun by the Viwa knights who outnumbered us. Strangely enough, as I laid on the ground here under your horse, Emma, the fighting gradually started to subside. In the midst of the shouting coming from all the men, I heard one of the Viwa say that he and the others must leave, because they were not able to find me amongst the soldiers of Siddell with whom they were fighting. Then the battle stopped. In a way, I am happy that I did fall down into this gully."

"'Tis a good thing, indeed!" Emma exclaimed. "We must have hidden well from them, too, for which I am now grateful."

Running to the top of the small ravine, Richard looked all around. Calling down to the girls in the bright sunshine, he said, "Everyone is gone! Like into thin air!"

"Whatever do you mean, Richard?" Nan asked. "Are there no wounded or dead men? Fairies can be injured and even die, even Father John said so. Surely somebody must be lying on the ground."

"Nay," Richard said, shaking his head. "Come up here, lasses, and see for yourselves. 'Tis very uncanny. I do not know what to make of this."

CHAPTER 18

Emma mounted her horse and rode up to the top of the ravine. She reined the animal in as she and Nan glanced here and there for several minutes in silence. The Viwa knights and maidens were nowhere to be found. The Siddell men were gone. All that was left was an empty forest next to the road that everyone had traveled on. The soft twittering of a bird was heard in the overhanging branches, and the sound of a breeze blowing through the forest shook some limbs of the trees and made them groan. There was a tap-tapping sound as some rainwater dripped down from the tree limbs onto the peaceful forest floor, but that was it.

"'Twas as if nobody had ever been here!" Emma said. "I know there was a battle here between the Viwa and Siddell knights and you, Richard. Where have they all gone?"

"The Viwa knights have most certainly taken off with Lord Roger's men," Richard said with eyes flashing. "I have doubts 'twould be the other way around. Little do the Viwa know that trouble awaits them for doing this."

"If we can find them," Emma replied. "Remember what Susanna said. They do not have a country that we can easily locate."

"That does complicate things a bit," Richard declared, rubbing his head furiously. "How that frustrates me!"

"Emma," Nan began, "I am starting to think you were not dreaming it when you thought you heard something outside our tent last night. Sir William was mistaken when he said 'twas his horse that made that sound. It may have been one of the Viwa knights or maidens."

"Hmm . . . I had not thought of this!" Richard murmured. "I am sorry we teased you about it, Emma. We were too confident in ourselves after so long in not seeing any Viwa. We all believed that none would materialize, but we were foolishly proven wrong. The men and I should have carefully inspected the area in the forest before we camped last night."

Emma shook her head. "I do not think you could have foreseen this battle with the Viwa knights. They are not from our world. They can see us when we cannot see them and hear us when we cannot hear them. Our familiarity with them has demonstrated that."

"This proves that I am still from the world of men," Richard confessed. "Despite some of the Viwa qualities I have inherited from my Viwa mother, I forget that my father is still human, and I think like one. Now the knights from Siddell are gone and so is my horse, unless I find him around here somewhere. If I cannot, he will find his way back to Lamington without me." Richard felt at his side in desperation. "My sword! Where is my sword?"

Running back into the small ravine, Richard retrieved his sword that was lying in a pile of rotting, wet leaves. He ran back up and proudly waved the object as he held its handle tightly in his grip.

"Some things are not lost after all," Richard stated. "By the way, Emma, where is the book?" Alarm shown in his eyes as he remembered Lord Robert's most precious article.

Emma promptly thrust her hand into the leather saddlebag that hung from the horse and partially pulled out the book to show Richard that she did, indeed, have it.

Richard sighed deeply. "I am glad that I told Brother Albert to give it to you to carry. Those fairies are deceitful creatures. I may be in part their kin, but I do not trust them entirely. I sometimes think that if they had a chance to take the book back, they would."

"As much as I hate to admit it, mainly because I am not fond of the book, I am glad that I have it with me," Emma declared. "The spell would never be broken if the fairies rode off with the book, and Christmas would remain as far from Lamington as from the minds of the townspeople there."

"Do you know that had I not fallen into that hole over there, I might have gone missing with the knights from Sidell, lasses," Richard said.

"The lasses here beside you are thankful that you did," Nan said with a giggle, but she soon became serious. "I want to tell you something, Richard. I did not think of it as important until the fairies took our knights. I believe the fairy maidens made you disappear with them into the cave near the lodge we were in. I mean, *really* disappear. When I saw you walk toward them, I blinked, and you were gone!"

"Nan, you did not tell me that part!" Emma exclaimed.

"I wish you would have told me that earlier, lass," Richard said. "Not that it makes much of a difference. I did get away from them. What makes it strange is that I do not remember anything of the sort happening. Mayhap they do it so fast that no one notices. I wonder if that is what they did to our knights!"

"I am so sorry, Richard," Nan said, and she meant it.

"Nay, do not be sorry, Nan," Richard answered. "There is nothing anybody can do about this, unless you are a fairy."

The lad tried to chuckle off his worry, but it was not fooling the girls. He sunk to the ground and sat on a wet rock as a look of disgust came over him.

"Wait! I have it! An idea has come to me about what has happened here in the forest. Those fairy lasses—and there were many—turned themselves into beautiful fairy maidens to capture their victims, the Siddell knights. They made the knights look into their fairy eyes. That is when their spell took over. The knights became so enthralled by the maidens, that they stopped fighting. Then the maidens, along with the Viwa knights, rounded up our knights and all vanished together—without one scratch! This explains why there are no dead or injured men, both human and fairy, anywhere."

"Oh, Richard!" said a disappointed Nan. "You could have saved our knights from the fairy maidens' spell—they failed twice from putting one over you."

Richard felt remorseful as he shook his head. "I could have warned the Siddell knights, merely by telling them not to look at the fairy maidens' eyes. If only I had remembered in time."

"What do we do now, Richard?" Emma asked, becoming pale with anxiety. "Remember that Father John said not to go back to Meldon, but seek out Lord Roger's help if we needed it."

"We should carry on as before and make our way to Lamington as planned," Richard decided. He wanted to be strong for the girls, while being cheerful and not bothered, over the unexpected assault by the Viwa fairies.

"The three of us . . . alone?" Nan asked. She looked

apprehensively behind and around her.

"Why not?" Richard said. "We started out as three traveling companions from Lamington. We did not have knights with us for protection. We will end up the same going back. Since I do not have a horse, I will walk the rest of the way. My feet will not hurt as we are not far from Lamington now. I have my sword that can help us in time of trouble, as long as an army of Viwa knights does not swoop down on us again, which I am doubtful of. If they failed to find me during this skirmish of theirs, they will be in no rush to come back to the forest. Or, during the rest of our short journey back to town."

"I see justification in what you say," Emma replied. She then said, "How maddening that those strong knights from Siddell could not aid us against those Viwa knights, simply because they did not avert their eyes from a few pretty fairy maidens. I cannot decide if I should be angry or not with you, Richard, for being so forgetful over a fairy maiden spell."

"You can be angry with me if you wish, Emma," Richard said. "You have my permission. Outside of how fairy maidens behave, though we still must be mindful of them, we *can* overtake an army of Viwa knights and win, but 'twill take careful strategy. Fairies are not without flaw. They can become injured and die, right? This means even in battle. We will have to discuss this with Lady Catherine—assuming that his lordship is still missing—when we reach Castle Lamington, including letting her know what has happened to her brother's knights. Word must go to Lord Roger about his men, which, I am sure, he will not be pleased about. He will want to recover his men as soon as possible. Before leaving this forest, I must bathe somewhere. I would not want to make Lady Catherine's presence like this, although there is only so much I can do about my soiled clothing."

Without wasting another minute, Richard went off in search of a nearby stream to wash himself. Nan and Emma quietly waited for him to finish before starting off on the road back to Lamington.

Richard walked alongside Emma's horse as she cantered the animal down the long stretch of road. Nan worried that he would drop from exhaustion, but she knew the three of them could not ride together on the same horse. However, Richard never complained--though the girls did beg him now and then to stop and rest if he felt tired—and he did have a fast stride.

"The sun is rather hot for a spring day," Emma said. "My cloak and gown are almost dry, but my hair does need a good brushing." She quickly took one of her hands off the horse's reins and pointed to something ahead. "Look! I can see the forest coming to an end. The highway will soon take us through farmland outside Lamington. It cannot be long before we see the town walls."

"How I thought I would never see them once we left Lamington!" Nan exclaimed, closing her eyes in relief.

"Nan, I thought you had more faith in Father John and her ladyship," Richard remarked. "Did they not say you would?"

"I have never been so far from home before, so what was I to think?" Nan replied indignantly. "There was always a small chance that they could have been wrong. Look what Brother Albert said! I look forward to Christmas being restored after an army goes into Viwa and breaks that evil spell that took our holiday from us."

"It may not be as easy as that," Richard reminded Nan. "What is Christmas, anyway?"

"What do you mean, 'What is Christmas'?" Nan asked, staring at Richard.

"I am sorry that I ask, lass," Richard answered. "For a minute I almost could not remember what you were talking about."

"I hope you say that in jest, though I find nothing funny about it," Emma declared, stopping her horse. "If not, then the spell is slowly taking hold of all of us. I am afraid to admit this, but when we spoke of Christmas yesterday, I almost did not remember what it was, either, until I thought long and hard about it."

"I am frightened by what you both tell me!" Nan cried. "If this be true, then we must go faster to Lamington and speak to Lady Catherine. It started with the town folk, now 'tis starting with us!"

"You know what this will eventually lead to," Richard said. "The spell will never be broken in Lamington because none of us will care about Christmas anymore."

"What is worse is that this spell may spread beyond Lamington for all we know!" Emma said. "Those fairies are so evil, who can be sure what their plans are. I hope that her ladyship herself still remembers Christmas when we get there or anything we tell her about it will not make sense."

"All this talking is getting us nowhere!" Richard exclaimed. "Emma, ride up ahead and do not worry about me. I will catch up to the both of you."

Emma galloped her horse with Nan to the edge of the forest road, where the highway met the open farmland of Lamington, as Richard followed behind them. They caught a glimpse of a Viwa knight riding quickly across the road in the distance and into the forest. He did not appear to notice the three people coming toward him.

"It cannot be!" Richard stated, rushing up to the girls.

Emma abruptly reined in her horse. She was unsure of what to do next after seeing the knight.

"Keep riding, lass," Richard instructed her, "until we get to the end of the forest. We will turn off into it if we need to."

Nan felt a sudden pang of discouragement. "Not another fairy knight! Do troubles ever cease for us, Emma?"

Emma did not respond. She rode her horse as quietly as she was able to on the road without letting anyone know they were there.

"Do not worry, Nan," Emma murmured. She did not openly admit it, but her fingers were trembling from fright on the horse's reins. "Things may not be as bad as they seem."

"The Viwa may be gifted enough to see and hear things better than most of us, but if we are careful, that knight there might not know we are here," Richard whispered, though he knew in his mind this was wishful thinking. "Let me get ahead of you, Emma, and I will let you know what I see past the forest. Nay, better yet, 'twould be best for you to get off the road and hide in some of the nearby trees. Do not go anywhere until I send you a signal to come out or to stay where you are."

Richard sprinted off down the road with his fair hair flying behind him, as the girls watched him from the trees on Emma's horse. Getting to the edge of the tree line, he looked beyond it momentarily and progressed to go into the nearby forest without turning around. He did not give the girls any indication of what he had seen there, or if he wanted them to stay in the forest or proceed on the road. He did not return for some time, much to the distress of Emma and Nan.

"What shall we do?" Nan asked fearfully. "Richard is gone too long. How dare he leave us like that! I thought we can trust him and he leaves without warning."

"I am very disappointed in him myself," Emma replied in annoyance. "I doubt he went back to Lamington without us, if that is what you are thinking. Mayhap we should tie our horse to a tree here and walk in the forest alongside the road until we get to the end of it. We can then see whatever 'twas that Richard has left us for."

"We should remember to pull up our hoods so nobody will see our faces," Nan stated, pulling up hers.

"That is something we seem to be forgetting to do a lot lately," Emma replied, getting down from her horse with Nan. She threw the hood of her cloak over her head. "Of course, with the Viwa, they seem to find us no matter what."

Emma tied the horse's reins to a strong oak tree far enough from the road. At the last minute, she remembered that his lordship's book was still in the saddlebag, so she took it out and placed it securely in the pocket of her gown. Emma then whispered to Nan to be very quiet as they walked amid the trees until they came to the end of the road. With herself in the lead, Emma dared to look as close to the edge of the trees without finding herself on the open road. What she had seen was a horror beyond anything she had ever encountered before. She put her hand to her mouth as she tried not to gasp too loudly at the startling sight in front of her very eyes.

"Oh, Nan!" Emma softly cried out. "You do not want to see what is there. I do not know if I should allow you to look or not. 'Tis a nightmare which words cannot describe."

Nan came up behind her companion, and before Emma could try and stop her, she peered into the vastness of the farmland where they met the walls of Lamington beyond. What she saw was, indeed, a nightmare. There in the fields were hundreds and hundreds of Viwa knights sitting on their horses, while many white tents were set up around each and every section of the town's walls. It was clear that they were readying themselves to strike upon Lamington without any given notice. On top of the town's high walls and towers, Lamington soldiers were standing silently waiting for the Viwa soldiers to make their first offensive move. There was even a trebuchet standing amongst the sea of Viwa soldiers, as they were lingering about in the warm spring sunshine. Standing gracefully, but not moving, alongside the knights of Viwa were countless Viwa maidens with their long flaxen hair and colorful gowns. They were not smiling this time, but had an evil glint in their eyes as they carefully scrutinized the Lamington soldiers from afar.

"Emma!" Nan squealed. "The Viwa are trying to take over our

town!"

Tears came to Nan's eyes as she watched the terrifying affair. She felt so small and insignificant at that moment. Nan knew that nothing she could say or do could prevent those massive Viwa troops from going away. Stomach pains gnawed at her as she thought of all those inhabitants of Lamington, who were now at the mercy of the fairies at the foot of the town's walls.

"There is not much left for us to do, Nan, except run for our lives," Emma said. "We must get back to my horse and ride nonstop all the way to Lord Roger. He will send troops to Lamington to fight these conniving fairies all the way back to their kingdom. 'Tis our only hope."

Nan pursed her lips and shook her head.

"Nay, I do not wish to go anywhere," she announced, fighting back more tears. "I cannot leave my family and friends. We came this far, and this is where I shall remain."

"Come now, Nan," Emma said gently. "I understand how you feel. 'Tis not any different for me. Lady Catherine is prisoner behind those walls, along with everyone else at Castle Lamington. I do not like it, but we must leave. What choice do we have? If we stay here, we will be captured by those Viwa fairies. I do not believe you, or your parents, would want that. Our only chance to help them and the others would come to naught, too. 'Tis foolish to wander about in this forest and think that we are safe from the enemy."

Before another word came out of Nan, a hand from behind her covered her mouth. Another hand covered Emma's. The girls wriggled free of the person doing it to them. They whirled around and came face to face with Richard.

"When I heard whispering in the trees," Richard said, "I knew I had to investigate it and behold, I found you both here. I did not mean to startle you, but if I came upon you without forewarning, the two of you would have screamed and gotten the attention of the Viwa knights wandering about. Well, lasses, we know where the Viwa went to after our little battle with them in the forest some ways back."

"Richard!" the girls exclaimed. They were surprised to see that he was there standing in front of them unharmed.

"Why did you go off like that when you went to the end of the road?" Emma asked infuriated.

"We thought you left us!" Nan said. "Or, taken prisoner by the Viwa. Instead of waiting for you to come, we decided to see whatever 'twas that you saw, but never came back to tell us."

"'Twas foolish of you to do such a thing," Richard replied with a shake of his head. "You should have listened to me earlier and stayed back in the forest until I sent you a signal of what to do. Something horrible might have happened. Remember the mountain path near the Monastery of the White Friars? We almost became prisoners of the Viwa if the brothers were not there to save us. Anyway, I am truly sorry that I left you for a while. When I got to the end of the road and saw what was going on beyond the forest—and I do not need to tell you what that is—I decided to get a better glimpse of what the Viwa knights were doing around the town walls, so I went to a different part of the forest to have a look."

"Then you should have come back and told us what you planned on doing!" Emma reprimanded.

"After seeing that out there," Richard answered, pointing in the direction of the town where the Viwa knights were, "I doubt you would have come back, either. As far as your plan to go to Lord Roger and have him send more men to fight against those Viwa knights over yonder, I also feel 'tis the best plan of action for us. I, alone, cannot fight them. Nan, do not worry so about your family behind the town walls. If you stay here in the forest because of them, what good will that do? The Viwa are not going to leave Lamington. We must take to the road and get immediate help from Lord Roger in Siddell."

"I know he will help us," Emma declared. "I know he will be very angry about his knights being taken prisoner by the fairies, and he will most certainly want to help her ladyship, his sister."

"The Viwa are certainly going to a lot of trouble to try and find me," Richard said. "On the contrary, there are times when I just do not know whom or what they are looking for."

"I am sure they will not go out of their way to tell us," Emma said. "Even if we tried to find out, *we* would be their prisoners on the spot. Richard, I am amazed how unruffled you are about the Viwa being here. I would be overheated with anger if I were you."

"Anger blinds one from making clear decisions," Richard replied. "That would not be sensible on my part."

"I do not like that those Viwa maidens are always with the Viwa knights," Nan said shuddering. "They sicken me anytime I look at them."

"No doubt they are there to assist the fairy knights by luring the men of Lamington to them," Richard replied. "'Twould be an easy way to bring down the town. Let us not get too caught up in worrying about them. We must turn around and get back to the road. Quickly, too!"

"What about your lack of a horse?" Emma asked.

"This time I will run as fast as I can behind you," Richard replied.

The small party turned and followed the road through the forest. Emma was anxious to get to her horse, except for Nan who had a heavy heart as she trudged behind her two companions. She turned back to glance through the limbs of the trees, but it was no use. She was not able to see the walls of Lamington anymore. Nan had begun to feel as if she had failed her family somehow, but instinct kept telling her that going to Lord Roger was the best way to solve the predicament in Lamington.

"What I find most interesting is that the Viwa knights have not found us spying on them from behind these trees and bare ones at that," Emma contemplated.

"I know why," Nan said, catching up to Richard and Emma. "They are too busy laying siege to Lamington to worry about a few of us watching them from the forest."

"A likely scenario, unless they find out that I am here," Richard added, "then you can be sure that they will be by our side in an instant."

"*Your* side, not ours," Emma said grinning, despite the pain in her heart over Lamington.

"Do not be so assured of that!" Richard countered. "They do not discriminate. Anyone is fair game to them if they want to cause trouble."

"I know I should not be making light of such things," Emma replied gravely. "I will never forget how the Viwa caused Nan and I some trouble on the mountainside near the monastery over finding you."

"Emma, I realize that I had asked you this before, but do you have his lordship's book?" Richard asked in alarm. He became acutely aware that the book might not be in Emma's saddlebag when they got back to her horse.

Without saying a word, Emma put her hand under her cloak and into the pocket of her gown and retrieved the book for Richard to see.

"I had it here all along," Emma answered him. "There is no need to worry."

Relief came to Richard's face. "You do not know how that makes me feel now that I see it with you. I would put the book back before anything *does* happen to it."

Emma replaced the book in its hiding place as the small group stepped up their pace through the forest. Emma ran toward her horse when she saw him standing idly about waiting for his mistress to return.

"I wish there was a better way to get to Siddell, Richard," Emma stated, as she climbed up on her horse. "I will gladly have you ride my horse for a while when you become tired of running. Nan and I can take turns sitting behind you. Siddell is many leagues from here, in case you have forgotten."

"That is not necessary, Emma," Richard said. "I can run faster than most, so do not worry. When I am tired, we will rest. Then we will take up our journey again. I do not think the Viwa are going anywhere, so if it takes us a few days to get to Siddell, then so be it."

"I see that there is no use in arguing with you about it," Nan said, as she was helped onto Emma's horse by Richard.

The three travelers were about to set off toward the road when they heard someone calling to them from somewhere in the trees.

CHAPTER 19

"Lad! Lasses! I am over this way. Do not be afraid. Look behind you."

Turning their heads, Richard and the girls saw a woman standing close by in a patched gray-blue cloak. She appeared to be in her late thirties and had a pleasant smile upon her face. Richard nodded to Emma who then trotted her horse toward the unknown woman.

"I am sorry if I have frightened you," the woman said. Her deep set amber eyes watched Richard and the others curiously. "I am Helene. I live not far from here with my father who is very old. My husband died but two winters ago from a terrible sickness. Since I was alone and without children, I decided to come and live with my widowed father. I happened to see you from the trees here. After what has happened recently at Lamington, I felt I had to come and rescue you before anything unpleasant befell you."

"So you know about the soldiers surrounding Lamington?" Richard asked Helene.

"Aye, I do," Helene replied. "I am glad that my father and I can care well enough for ourselves out here, or we would have long starved because of them. Lord Robert gave my father permission years ago to own a piece of land to farm on in the middle of the forest."

"When have the soldiers arrived?" Nan asked. "I pray that those in Lamington are not starving."

"I pray not, either!" Helene replied. "They have not been here more than a few weeks, mayhap a month at most, from what I remember. We count our blessings every day that those soldiers have not found us hidden deep within these woods. 'Twould be dangerous if they knew of our existence. I stumbled upon them quite accidentally while gathering firewood one afternoon. Until that time, I did not know that Lamington was under siege. Those soldiers do not sicken me half as much as those peculiar maidens who stand around the town walls with them."

"We know of whom you speak," Richard confirmed. "They are strange, indeed."

"They are there during the daytime, but toward evening, they leave and come back the next day," Helene continued. "I wonder where they go. They cannot be going into Lamington, but they do not live or sleep anywhere the woods. I have not heard or seen them anywhere, but then again, neither my father nor I leave our cottage much at night."

"I gather you have watched them a great deal," Emma said. "Do you know who they are?" She was curious to learn how much Helene knew of the men around the town walls.

"Nay, I do not know them," Helene replied. "Do you? Now that you know something of me, what are your names? From whence have you come?"

"I am Richard, and this is Emma and Nan," Richard answered. "We are travelers from Meldon. I am a guard from Castle Lamington, Emma is Lady Catherine's maidservant, and Nan is from the town of Lamington. She is the daughter of Simon the farmer. We had been sent on an errand by her ladyship to Meldon, but have since returned. Had we known about the siege in town, we would have avoided coming back. I suppose one telltale sign of it was when the highway became less crowded with travelers after we got closer to here, but we were given no warning. The other travelers must have been aware of the siege and stayed away from Lamington—all except for us! I sincerely wish we would have met you sooner in the forest so you could tell us this."

"So you are from Castle Lamington then?" Helene asked. "You are blessed to be her ladyship's maidservant, Emma. Lady Catherine is a woman of beauty in many ways. May God keep her safe behind the town walls. I cannot bear to think of her being made prisoner there."

"She has left quite a wonderful impression on those around her," Emma murmured.

"Helene, you asked us if we knew who those soldiers were around Lamington," Richard said. Instead of answering truthfully, he pretended as if he did not know their identity. "We do not recognize any of them. The coat-of-arms on their shields and pendants they carry around on the fields are unknown to us."

Richard did not want to distress Helene by explaining to her that those using Lamington farmland as an impending battlefield were fairies from a strange place called Viwa. Moreover, he was not willing to share certain information with someone whom he was not familiar with.

"'Tis difficult to want to know anything when you see an enemy surrounding your town like that," Helene stated. "What is worse, I saw some travelers being taken prisoner by these soldiers!" She lowered her eyes to the ground sadly and paused for several seconds before speaking. "I saw them overtake what looked like to be a brother who was on the road, too. He was about to leave the forest road and start for the road where the farm fields of Lamington were when two soldiers noticed him. They rode up to him and taking his horse, they rudely escorted him to one of their tents over yonder. I do not know what they did with him after that."

The three young people exchanged knowing glances with one another. The brother who Helene referred to was probably one of the brothers from the monastery who was sent as messenger to Lamington.

"Do you know who the other prisoners were whom were taken by the soldiers, Helene?" Nan asked.

Helene knitted her brow. "I do not remember anymore, except for one thing. I did not stop running until I closed the cottage door behind me. I refused to move from my bench near the hearth the entire day. So full of fright was I! Do you know that those soldiers burned down every farmer's cottage and barn that stood outside the town walls? I saw the flames myself rising up to the sky. 'Twas so cold that day with light snow coming down. I pray that all those who lived outside the walls made it safely inside those of the town. What a terrible tragedy if some did not."

Those who live outside the town walls are brave souls, Nan thought to herself.

She remembered looking through the town gate and marveling at those who lived outside of it. Now they had met with foul play because of the Viwa knights. Nan was relieved that she and her family never lived there, but she was disturbed by the thought of the people running for their lives toward Lamington's walls once the evil fairies came riding along on their horses and burning farms and livelihoods with it.

"I would like to invite you to my home where I live with my

father," Helene said graciously. "We cannot give you much to eat, but 'tis better than standing out here where a soldier or two might sneak upon you. Our cottage has a small space for animals at the back of it, so you may let your horse rest there with our cow."

Emma and Nan kindly accepted Helene's offer of generosity with Richard's encouragement. If anyone was happy to stay close to Lamington, it was Nan. She felt this was the perfect opportunity to be in close proximity to her family and friends, despite the danger of the Viwa knights.

"The lasses and I do not mind a little to eat," Richard eagerly said. "We do not have much food left ourselves, so we appreciate anything you have to offer us since we are unable to return to Lamington. Helene, would you or your father mind it if we stayed the night at your home? The sun will be going down soon and we have nowhere to go."

Deep down, Richard did not mind having a good, long rest before starting off to Siddell the next day. He did not want to have to find shelter for himself and the girls on a dim road during evening where Viwa fairies freely roamed, making it easier for them to capture the traveling group if they wanted to.

"My father would not mind having you as our guests overnight," Helene replied. "He would enjoy your company as much as I would. I can also wash those dirty clothes for you, too, lad. It looks like you took a nasty tumble somewhere. Come, all of you! Follow me!"

Richard, Emma, and Nan merrily followed the woman down a narrow dirt path through the trees. They came to a small, thatched cottage with shuttered windows. Richard took Emma's horse to the attached stable at the back while Helene took the girls around to the main part of the cottage. Going inside, the girls saw a hearth in the center and a wooden trestle table with two wooden benches around it. The cottage reminded Nan very much of her own home and half-expected to see her own mother cooking at the big pot over the hearth.

An old man rose from one of the benches when they all entered. He introduced himself as Helene's father, Walter, and immediately took up conversation with the others. Most of the discussion by the jovial rotund man, whose head consisted of a few strands of white hair left on his balding head, centered on the siege in Lamington. Seeing that they were all still standing, he quickly invited the visitors to sit with him around the table while they talked.

"I assume not many travelers come this way where you live," Richard inquired of his hosts.

"Nay, not many," Walter answered with a heavy sigh. "We do not mind it. We prefer to live this way. I have lived too many years in Lamington and needed a change of scenery. I thank God that his lordship allowed me to go off and live here. He is a good man. We survive nicely here by ourselves, do we not, Daughter?"

"Aye, we do," Helene replied as she busily prepared supper. "We cannot complain about that!"

Appetizing smells came from the pot over the hearth and from the fresh bread that was baking over the embers next to it. The food made Nan homesick and more saddened over her family's circumstance in town.

"I pray that his lordship can fight back against the enemy who has swooped down upon us," Walter said, his eyes becoming serious. "He has a very good army, so I do not understand what is taking him so long in being rid of them. Does he wish this enemy to become tired and give up?"

"You may not be aware of this, but his lordship is not at Castle Lamington, as far as we know," Emma said.

Walter's eyes shot up with surprise.

"What Emma is saying is that before we left on our journey to Meldon a month ago," Richard explained, "Lord Robert went hunting with some of his knights, but failed to return with them. No one seems to know why. Indeed, even now, he may not have returned to Castle Lamington."

"Oh, this is terrible news!" Walter said in shock. "We did not know of this did we, Helene?"

"We did not," Helene declared, echoing her father's words. The large wooden spoon that she held stopped stirring in the great big pot as she looked down at the others seated on the benches. "I suppose being where we are, we are the last to find out such news."

"A search party went out to look for him, but he was nowhere to be found," Emma stated. "Lady Catherine did say that his knights were going to do a more thorough search for him later, but as we have not been to the castle in a while, we are unsure of what has happened."

"I am sure her ladyship has searched long and hard for his lordship," Helene concluded. "Oh, the sorrow the poor woman must be enduring! First, her husband goes away, and now this. Those evil men standing in the shadow of Lamington's walls! What do they want from us?

I cannot fathom what her mind must be like these days. And here we are, poor farm folk, standing and watching those soldiers helplessly from the trees, as they decide the fate of our town. 'Tis a misfortune that words alone cannot describe."

"I share your feelings, Helene," Nan said nodding.

"What are your plans, lad, when you leave here tomorrow?" Walter asked in earnest.

"The lasses and I here would like nothing more than to see the enemy sent running back to his lands, as you and your daughter had said, Walter," Richard responded, angrily slamming his hand down on the table. "I thought if we found our way to the nearest lord in the area, he might come to the aid of Lamington. I am not saying that there are no good men at Castle Lamington ready to bring the enemy down, but our town would be better off with additional soldiers. If his lordship cannot do it because he is not there, then we will do it for him."

"Being that you are guard at the castle, lad, I know they would listen to you," Helene said. "They would come to Lord Robert's service. Now that I am thinking of it, we do have one neighbor living close by with whom you can speak with about those soldiers, but only if you can catch him."

"We nearly thought him to be a ghost had he not been a man of real flesh and blood!" Walter chuckled, much to the confused looks found on the faces of Richard, Emma, and Nan. "You see, 'tis easy to forget about him since he is not often outdoors. If he is, he quickly runs inside when you come upon him. He is a gruff fellow who hides himself well. He does it so well, he does not show his face when he speaks to you. I wish I knew his name. I fear I may never be able to."

"He does sound like an odd man," Nan said, after listening to Walter's strange story. "I reckon that you do not even know the color of his eyes or the color of his hair!"

"Nay, we do not," Helene agreed. "'Tis difficult to find anything out when he looks down or away from you when you get close to him. There is one thing that I must admit about him. He knows a great deal about the soldiers who have surrounded Lamington. At least, he thinks he does. We believe that he must be speaking the truth as he spares no effort in telling us many things."

"I do not follow what you mean, Helene," Richard said.

"Let me explain from the very beginning, lad, then you will understand what Helene has told you," Walter began. "I first learned of his existence when I went out to check my rabbit traps a week ago. There is an abandoned cottage in the forest, a bit down from us, which I thought no one was living in. I do not know when its last owner occupied it, but 'twas empty with overgrown grass and bramble when I first came here. When I went to check my traps that day, I walked by and noticed that the door was opened and with his back turned my way, a man was cooking something over a spit in the middle of the room. He was squatting over the fire and turning the spit slowly as the smell drifted out through the doorway. When I tried to speak to the fellow, he got up with a bent head and slammed the door shut with his leg."

"How rude of him!" Emma said, shaking her head in repugnance. "He does not have proper manners. Not a gentleman at all!"

"You must have seen *something* of his face inside the cottage," Richard stated. "He could not possibly be wearing anything heavy on inside of it."

"He was wearing a very dirty brown cloak with the hood still draped over his head," Walter replied. "Even inside the cottage with the blazing fire in the center! The cloak was so tattered, but I cannot tell you anything more than that. Helene even said that she would make him a new one if he wanted her to. What a poor fellow he is! I never felt so sorry for anyone until I first laid eyes on him. Whenever I see him, he is wearing his cloak, but always with a covered head. I do not know if he is young or old, but he does seem taller than me from what I can figure. The only thing that I am sure of is that he has a low, gruff voice. This is why I consider him a gruff fellow, both in appearance and behavior."

"Mayhap he is a leper who has run away from some nearby town, mayhap even Lamington," Nan conjectured. "I do not know whether or not Lamington has them, but I have heard that there are those with diseases who hide well. Mayhap he is one of them."

"I have not thought of this," Helene said, bending her head thoughtfully to one side. "Then 'tis best we stay as far from him as possible, just in case he has something."

Richard was growing with impatience. He wanted to learn more about this hermit with some personal knowledge of the Viwa knights.

"What is this you say that he knows much about the enemy who has taken over Lamington?" Richard asked.

"I will tell you," Walter said, keen on telling his story. "I was not discouraged by the fellow's reaction to me, so the next day, I went back to his cottage to see if I might make him talk. He had gotten my curiosity, so I was more than determined to start up a discussion with him. He happened to be outdoors that morning and was acting very strange. As always, his back was toward me with the cloak over his head as he stood peering into the forest at something. I went to him and introduced myself. He did not turn around to face me, but told me that I should go away and never come back. He said he was not interested in making friends with his neighbors."

"How intriguing!" Richard said. He slowly took in every word of Walter's account of the eccentric hermit.

"There is more I must tell!" Walter cried. "I did not obey his orders—who was he to tell me what to do, I thought—so I went on talking to him as if he had not said a word. I started speaking about those soldiers around the town walls. Living here in the woods like we do, Helene and I are anxious to find out anything we can about the outside world. I went on to tell this gruff fellow that I wanted to know more about those soldiers. Where did they arrive from, I asked, and what did they have against Lamington? Do you know what he said to me? He says, 'I know of them and where they are from. They will not leave until matters are settled.' When I asked him what these matters were, he says, 'I know how to be rid of them, and I know of this personally. But I have no desire to get myself involved, so they will not go away.'"

"He does seem to think of himself as someone of great importance," Emma said. "Otherwise, why would he act as if he alone can drive those soldiers from Lamington?"

Paying no attention to Emma, Walter continued on.

"As if catching himself by surprise at what he told me, the odd fellow closed his mouth and returned to his cottage. He shut the door so hard that the rotting wood almost split on it. 'Twas the last I have spoken to or seen him since."

"He has told you much," Richard replied, rubbing his chin. "This hermit fascinates me greatly. I am sorry that your meeting with him did not go as well as you would have liked. I hope he has not decided to move and make his home somewhere else."

"Nay, I think he has walled himself up in his cottage for a while,"

Walter declared with his arms folded across his chest. "His shutters may be closed tight, but 'tis just a feeling I get whenever I look at the cottage when I go outdoors. Mayhap the gruff fellow leaves his cottage at night, but as there is nowhere to go in this region, I cannot imagine him doing that, either, especially since Lamington is now taken over by some enemy out there. Do you have any ideas, lad, about this strange new neighbor of ours? You may be younger than I, but you have lived at Castle Lamington, along with having been to more places than I ever will. You have a better understanding of the world than I do."

While the others discussed the hermit, Helene shrieked and grew pale. She pointed to one of the opened windows in the cottage that she had unfastened earlier because the room had become too hot from cooking.

"I think somebody was trying to take a gander inside!" Helene exclaimed. "While checking on my bread, I looked up and saw one of the shutters shake and then creak, like a prowler was trying to move it with his fingers!"

CHAPTER 20

Richard and the girls glanced sideways at one another and then back at their hosts.

Nan began to tremble. Her first thought was that there might be Viwa maidens lying in wait near the window, as they had been near the old lodge on the way to Meldon.

"I will go and investigate, Helene," Richard announced, getting up from the bench. "I have my sword with me. If there is any danger, I can defend myself."

"Be careful, Richard!" Helene cried out. "I do not want to see you get hurt on account of us poor folk."

The others reiterated Helene's concern as Richard opened the door and went outside. Walter got up slowly from his seat and went to look through the window. Not seeing anything, he tightly locked the shutters.

"I hope the lad knows what he is doing," Walter said with a disturbed look on his face. "But he is a sturdy one and knows how to fight with a sword, which is more than I can do with a large stick."

"How terrifying that he is alone out there in the dark!" Emma said, praying that at any moment Richard would come walking safely through the door. "I will go and see where he is at."

"Emma, I would not go out there!" Nan warned. "Richard will come back. He always comes back. We have been through worse before."

Emma refused to argue with Nan. She opened the door of the cottage and stepped out into the stillness of the night. She shivered a bit without her cloak as she squinted here and there to see if Richard was somewhere nearby. All Emma saw was the outline of the trees against a moon-lit sky. Turning around to a cry coming from the cottage, she saw

Nan opening the door and running out after her.

"Emma, do not leave like that!" Nan pleaded as she stood in the shadow of the cottage. "Come back inside. Helene and her father are worried about you."

"Nan, I am glad that you followed me out here," Emma murmured. "Being anxious for Richard is not the only reason I came outdoors. I need to speak to you alone, even if we have to risk the danger of the dark forest to do it. 'Tis not so easy to talk privately inside a small cottage."

Richard came walking up, swinging his sword by his side.

"Lasses, 'tis just me," the lad stated. "I looked carefully amongst the trees and walked down the dirt path that leads away from the cottage. Alas! I did not see a soul, though 'tis too dark for me to see much anyway. A wild animal might have passed the window and brushed up against the shutter, or there was a light breeze moving it and Helene mistook it for a person. I did not want to say this in the cottage, but . . . but . . . I feared that the Viwa found us and prayed in my heart that 'twas not so."

"'This is what I wished to tell you as well, Nan," Emma said, turning to face the other girl. "My first thought was, the Viwa are here! My stomach turned. How dreadful 'twould be to leave Helene and her father because of them. I cannot involve these generous people with our problems. Can you imagine how frightened they would be if they knew the half of what we have gone through because of the fairies? They would tell us to go away. Who could blame them!"

"If we did leave the cottage of Helene and her father, where would we go at a time like this?" Nan moaned. Fear raced through her mind as she thought of them walking aimlessly in the dense forest, not knowing which way to turn, in the dead of night. "We cannot see past our noses out here. The Viwa would, indeed, have an easy time of making us their captives. Oh, Emma! I wish things were not so complicated for us like this. What will we do?"

Richard lowered his voice. "We do not have to worry about the Viwa, lasses. If those fairies were lurking around the cottage window, they would have surrounded me the minute I left the cottage. To be honest, I am starting to believe that what Helene *really* saw and heard was the old hermit. I have more than a passing curiosity about him. Based on what we have heard about this hermit and what he has told Walter, he might be Lord

Robert of Lamington—alive and safe here in the forest near the town walls."

Emma's and Nan's eyes widened with surprise at Richard's presumption.

"Do you really think that the hermit is he?" Nan asked.

"I think so, but without an investigation, I am not entirely sure," Richard said. "But who other than his lordship would know more about these men camped around Lamington? Only he would know as much about them and why they might be here. It makes sense to me, does it not to you? His mannerisms also suggest that he is trying to hide something. The average hermit is not knowledgeable about multitudes of soldiers, and fairy ones at that, who surround town walls."

"I agree with you, Richard," Emma replied. "Of course, the hermit may be lying to Walter about what he says he knows."

"I doubt it," Richard said. "This hermit speaks the truth. Everything he told Walter points to Lord Robert and none other. Walter and Helene must not know what I have told you."

"Walter did say that the fellow seemed to know how to rid Lamington of the Viwa knights," Nan said. "Would that not be wonderful?"

"If only we can find out how," Emma stated. "I do not care to go all the way to Siddell from here, although I savor the idea of going to see my home again."

"Let us not get too far ahead of ourselves, lasses," Richard said, "or get our hopes up too high. We first have to confront the hermit. I will try to locate him tomorrow when 'tis daylight. We have to earn his trust initially, before asking him too many questions, or he may run from us. We may also have to stay with Helene and her father a little while longer before our plan materializes. I need to think of a good excuse to make them want us to stay with them for a few more days. I do not want them to get suspicious or become tired of us being here."

"Oh, they will not mind," Nan answered with a giggle. "I think they enjoy our company already, especially that of yours, Richard. Helene's father is thrilled to have someone from Castle Lamington to talk to. I can tell by how he reacts to anything you say to him. Even Helene was fascinated by you, Emma, being Lady Catherine's maidservant."

"We have been outdoors long enough," Richard reminded the girls.

"We should be getting back to our hosts. I do not plan on telling them about the possibility of the old hermit at the window. I am sure they want to continue living in peace here in the forest, and that is how I intend on leaving things for them. Before I forget, do not ask them anything about Christmas. We would not want our conversation to innocently turn to what we have learned about it at the monastery through his lordship's book, whether they remember it or not."

When Richard and the girls returned to the cottage, Helene and her father were happy to see that the others had returned unscathed. Walter took Richard's word that nothing was found outside the cottage and so the incident was laid to rest. The rest of the evening was spent eating supper and conversing around the table. Walter and Helene were immensely interested in the life that Emma and Richard lived at Castle Lamington. They were equally intrigued by Nan's brief visit at the castle to work in the kitchen, although Nan did not tell them what the main reason was that she was called there for.

Helene, seeing that her newfound friends were beginning to nod and yawn, cleared the table and took the girls upstairs to the cottage loft to sleep, while Richard and Walter slept around the downstairs fire that night. The next morning was bright and cheery with some sun. Richard wasted no time in asking Walter and his daughter if they minded if he and the others stayed on a little longer at their home, upon which they agreed without hesitation.

"I would like to meet this hermit you speak of," Richard declared. "My curiosity has gotten the better of me, you might say. I understand—based on your observation of this hermit—that it might be difficult to confront him because he likes to hibernate so well in his cottage, but I am up to the challenge. If I do not get to speak to him today, I will try again tomorrow, and mayhap the next day after, if I fail. I pray that 'twill not take as long, but we shall see."

Walter raised his eyebrows and chuckled a deep chuckle while his massive body shook with it.

"Aye, Richard, you may stay here with the lasses for as long as you like," Walter replied. "We do not mind having you here. As we said before, we do not get many visitors. We are more than pleased to have you for our company."

"Now off with you!" Helene laughed as she sat near the fire

mending some clothes. "Enjoy your day finding the hermit if you can. Let us know if you have any success since my father has not had any lately."

Putting their cloaks on and shutting the door behind them, Richard and the girls strode quickly down the path that led away from the cottage. After having gone a little ways, Richard turned to Emma and Nan.

"I became worried that Helene and her father would become suspicious about my interest in the hermit," Richard said, his face tight with concern. "I am glad they did not ask us any questions."

"If they do ask us anything, we should be honest with them about the hermit," Emma said. "They will understand and not tell anyone our secret."

"They are good people," Nan affirmed a bit naively. "I can tell."

Richard firmly shook his head, much to the girls' dissatisfaction. "Good people or not, 'twould not be an astute idea. I refused to tell them from the beginning and it shall remain so. I see the old hermit's cottage ahead. Let us go and put our plan into action before we lose our nerve."

Emma and Nan followed Richard toward the hermit's cottage that was well hidden by trees and thorn bushes that had grown up around it over the years. The building's walls were in poor condition with a thatched roof in severe need of repair. The shutters were barely hanging on the window frames as the wood was heavily rotted.

"I wonder how anyone can live here without getting rained on," Nan observed. "My father would get to work immediately on the roof if he had seen this."

"Shh!" Emma told Nan, as the other girl looked glumly back at her. "You do not want anybody to hear you, do you? We do not want to give ourselves away to the hermit so soon."

The traveling party stood by idly for a few minutes and listened to the forest around them. The wind was calm and not a sound was heard coming from the dilapidated cottage. They looked at each other inquisitively as Richard slowly crept up to the front door and started to knock lightly on it. As he waited for the hermit to come out, Richard quickly remembered to throw the hood of his cloak over his head. The girls, taking their cue from Richard, did the same.

"It may be too late, but I do not want the old hermit to see our faces the moment he opens the door," Richard murmured.

After some time had gone by without the hermit appearing at the door, the impatient Richard decided to take a walk to the back of the cottage. He reappeared, after what seemed to be an eternity, much to the distress of the other mates who wondered where Richard had gone.

"Well, I did find something of interest you might like," Richard announced happily. "'Twas not the old hermit, but my lost horse was tethered up to a tree."

"How wonderful, Richard!" Emma exclaimed. "I worried he would find his way into the hands of those evil fairies if he returned to Lamington. Thankfully, he did not. At least your horse proves that someone lives here."

"Are you going to get him?" Nan asked when Richard did not show any interest in getting the animal. "If the hermit is not home, 'twould be a good time to take the horse back with us without his knowing it."

"If we do, then he *will* know that someone has been here," Richard answered. "If the hermit happens to be his lordship, then there is every reason to believe that he knows that my horse has come from Castle Lamington. In case you are not aware of it, our saddles have a special mark burned into them by our castle saddle-maker. The hermit will realize that someone from the castle is in the vicinity. He may try to make a getaway without us knowing."

"We may be in for a long wait no matter what," Nan said. "He hides from Walter and he will hide from us."

"Then we will do what we have to do," Richard stated. He was determined to get to the old hermit if it took them months. Seeing the look of despair in the eyes of Emma and Nan, Richard kept these thoughts to himself.

The small party waited the entire day for any sign of the old hermit until the sun started to set. They ate what little they brought with them while their legs ached from standing.

"I am more than certain that he is in there!" Richard declared, pointing to the cottage. "He is a clever fellow that hermit. He knows we are at his door. He can hear us, but he will not come out."

"If, indeed, he is Lord Robert, then 'tis clear that his intention was to hide away from the world," Emma said. "He has no desire to speak to the castle folk, or anybody else, which might explain why he ran off into these woods to hide after he left his own hunting party several months ago. His one and only reason was to cut himself off from us forever."

"'Tis a foolish reason, but likely the only one," Richard said. "I am sure it has everything to do with the book that was found in Lord Anselm's trunk. He had had enough of the book and wanted to break free of it, so he came here. The book was consuming his lordship's mind."

"I am glad 'twas not the fairies who stole him from us," Nan said.

"Aye, indeed!" Emma agreed. "Which reminds me, Richard, I still have his lordship's book with me, in case you should ask."

"I am pleased to hear it," Richard replied. "Nevertheless, I worry about standing here too close to his cottage with the book on your person, Emma. If he gets hold of the book and reads from it again, there is no telling what further damage it can inflict. 'Tis time to go now. Next time, Emma, leave the book carefully hidden in Walter's cottage. I do not feel comfortable bringing it along."

The three young people turned to go back to the cottage they stayed at. Walter and Helene were disappointed to hear that Richard, Emma, and Nan had neither seen nor spoken to the hermit that day.

"I am so sorry that you have not been able to catch him," Walter said. "He is a funny fellow. You will spot him, but rest assured, he will test your patience before you do. Do not give up trying!"

After a week of going out and lying in wait for the hermit, Richard and the girls had become exasperated at their failure in finding him. They took a nonchalant walk outside the cottage of Helene and her father one early morning to quietly discuss what their new course of action would be.

"We are wasting our time looking for this hermit," Nan whispered peevishly. "If we wait any longer to catch sight of him, things will become worse for those in Lamington. Every day that goes by, the people there suffer more and more at the hands of the Viwa army. Think of Lady Catherine!"

"I agree with Nan," Emma answered. "I do not care what Walter says. I am becoming tired of waiting for this hermit to show himself. I am convinced he has abandoned the old cottage and moved somewhere else. This hermit may not be his lordship after all. I think we should get your horse, Richard, and leave for Siddell as soon as the sun rises tomorrow—as long as the animal is still where he is."

"I understand how you must feel," Richard said, nodding to Emma and Nan. He saw the tension rising in the girls' faces. "If you insist on going to Siddell, then we will go, although I am very reluctant to go just yet.

Let us walk over to the cottage one last time and get my horse. If the animal is there, does it not prove that someone has been caring for him? If not, then 'tis as you imply. The hermit has taken my horse for himself and went off to another place to hide. Mayhap he is tired of strange people bothering him when he would rather be left alone."

Emma and Nan made their way to the hermit's cottage with Richard, relieved this was the last time they would have to visit it. They ran down the small dirt path and when they were about halfway to the cottage, they saw the door of it slightly ajar.

"Look!" Nan cried. "The door! Someone *must* be inside."

Richard silently went up to the door and took a quick look around the inside of the dimly-lit one-room dwelling as Emma and Nan stood closely behind, peering over his shoulder. A large figure of a man was lying in the far corner of the room on a dirty straw pallet, while a dying fire smoldered near it. Seeing the person covered up to his head with his cloak, Richard walked up to the grimy article of clothing that was tattered and filled with many holes. He engaged the idea of having a look underneath it. Pulling back the hood from the sleeping body, Richard and the girls gasped in shock that the hermit who lived there was, indeed, Lord Robert of Lamington. The last several months as a recluse had not been kind to his lordship. His auburn beard had become long and unkempt, and his ruddy skin was becoming rough and affected by the poor standard of living that he was unaccustomed to by living in the forest on his own.

His lordship's eyes flew open as he awoke with a start. Jumping up from the pallet with an angry grunt, he grabbed for something that was lying near him as he backed himself up against the wall with a fearful and dazed look in his eyes. He held up a sword and pointed it at Richard while the girls recoiled behind the lad. Richard backed away, as he held up his hands, to show his lordship that he was in no danger of being hurt by anyone there.

"We come in peace," Richard said calmly. He did not know if he should address his lordship by his proper name, or go along with the charade by pretending that Lord Robert was a hermit and not a lord. "Pray do not hurt any of us. Put down your sword before you hurt somebody with it."

"What do you want?" the hermit growled, his eyes ablaze with anger. "Why do you come here? Leave *me* be in peace! Go away!"

The hermit slunk to the floor with a thud as he dropped his sword from his hand. He had a pitiful look on his face, but he did not look up at the three people who stood before him. He merely stared off to a corner in the room with a faraway look in his eyes.

"My lord, do you not know who we are?" Emma uttered.

Richard turned and shook his head at Emma. He motioned for her not to ask his lordship such questions.

"We did not mean to enter your home unannounced," Richard explained. "We thought this hut was uninhabited and are sorry to have entered it the way we did. Our intent is not to stay long, but we would like some answers from you."

The hermit did not reply at once but after several minutes, looked up at Richard briefly and dropped his eyes to the ground.

"Aye, I will try to answer you," the hermit said with a tired sigh, "but only if you will leave me alone afterward. I am done with my former life and want to live the rest of it out in this wretched place until I die."

"We understand," Emma declared. "You have our word."

"You know what is happening right now in Lamington, do you not?" Richard asked in a low voice as he bent down next to the hermit.

The hermit nodded as a look of fear crept into his face. It was no use in evading the question as the young people had surrounded him, and he felt compelled to tell them all he knew.

"You know who those soldiers are and why they are there around the town walls," Richard continued. "Since you do, then what can be done to be rid of them? You do know that Lady Catherine is being held up in the castle because of them. I am certain that she is living in panic, and in fear, every day for her life and for those in the town."

The hermit slowly rose from the ground and walked over to the window that was facing in the direction of Lamington, though the town was not visible from the cottage. He opened the shutters and silently stared out. His tall, broad self was turned away from the others so they were not able to see his face. At one point, he lifted his left hand and wiped it across his face as if he had shed a tear.

"I was hoping to be left here content with my new life until you arrived," the hermit muttered. "I had not expected this, you know. But as you are here, I will tell you what you want. When you walk out this door, go down the path a little ways. When you come to the end of it, turn to the left where a small gorge awaits you. There you will see a small waterfall. Continue down toward the waterfall, but do not stop. Keep walking past it. Here you will see the forest continue onward, which you will follow until you come to its end. 'Tis there you may have your questions answered for you. I realize this might not make much sense, but you will understand once you get there. I am a coward, but no doubt you will have better luck than I going there. You will see. Be gone with you!"

The hermit trudged over to the front door of the cottage where he held it open for Richard and the girls to walk through. Impatience in his eyes grew as he waited for them to pass. It was clear that he was eager for them to leave.

"You have come in search of answers, so I have given them to you," the hermit said. "You may take your horse as well before you leave, lad. I know he is yours. Godspeed to you!"

Richard, not knowing what else to say to the hermit, walked out the door with the girls into the blinding sunshine as the door was shut behind them with a loud thump. They waited until they were down the path a little and out of earshot of the hermit's cottage before speaking to one another.

"He *was* Lord Robert after all!" Nan excitedly said. "He may not have told us openly, but he was, though his voice did sound a bit off. He could not hide his face, either, no matter how hard he tried under that cloak."

"I do not know what to make of his solution to Lamington's predicament with those Viwa, though," Emma said. Turning around to Richard, she said, "I am so disappointed in you. We had quite the opportunity to ask him many questions, but you refused to. He seemed keen on rushing us out of his cottage!"

"If we had asked him too many things, such as that of my past, which I would have liked to have prodded him about, he might have told us to leave sooner, which he did just a moment ago anyway," Richard said. "Now all we have are those strange directions he gave us. I cannot begin to fathom where they will take us."

"He *is* a coward, as he suggested himself to be," Emma said in annoyance. "What kind of lord do we have residing over Lamington . . . refusing to return to the town he once ruled, especially when a battle is about to occur there at any moment! He should be gathering an army from the outside right now and fighting those Viwa until the very last one. I do not mean to say such things, but after what he had said in his hut, I cannot see him in the same way again."

"Before we invent decisions for his lordship over Lamington, I say we do as he has told us," Richard stated. "We will go and find this gorge and the forest beyond it. First, I plan on getting my horse from the back of his cottage. The old hermit knew who we all were without saying a word or he would not have returned the horse to me."

"I pray that his lordship is not telling us a falsehood and leading us into a trap," Nan said to Emma when Richard left their side.

"We will take a chance on it," Richard replied, overhearing Nan, as he was coming back with his animal. "What do we have to lose? We have come this far, and with the look of such pity upon the hermit's face, I do not believe he would send his only son into grave danger."

"All right, then," Emma said with a frown. "If you wish to pursue going to this mysterious place, we will go."

"As long as we will not be fighting dragons, or giants the size of Castle Lamington, then I feel confident in going," Richard laughed as a sullen Emma and Nan looked on. "We have had many narrow escapes, so how bad can things get? If I am able to fight off evil fairy maidens and knights, then experience tells me that I can fight off most anything."

"Do not be *too* sure of yourself," Emma replied. "Remember what the Viwa maidens had almost done to you, Richard. But if going to this new place means helping the people of Lamington, then I will be happy to come along."

"Promise us one thing, Richard," Nan begged. "If, for some reason, the old hermit's directions lead us nowhere, then we go to Siddell and get help from Lord Roger."

"Agreed," Richard said. "In the meantime, I give him the benefit of a doubt. Before we take a step further, we must go and say our good-byes to Helene and her father. We also do not want to leave without getting his lordship's book and your horse, Emma."

Richard and the girls walked back to the cottage of Helene and Walter. The girls went to find their hosts, while Richard went to retrieve Emma's horse that was grazing on some grass outside. A few minutes later, Emma and Nan came running out to Richard who was standing and waiting for them with the two horses.

"We cannot find Helene anywhere," Nan said.

"We did not see Walter anywhere, either," Emma added, placing Lord Robert's book into her gown pocket.

"Nor have I seen Walter," Richard said, his eyes darting in all directions of the forest in the hope of seeing Helene or her father. "They must be somewhere nearby. They would not risk going too far with the Viwa in Lamington. I wanted to call out to them, but not with the fairies meandering at will."

"Mayhap they went out to have a look at Walter's rabbit traps," Emma said. "Either way, when they come back, they will know we are gone."

"I wish we can tell them we are leaving," Nan answered sadly.

"No matter," Richard said with a wave of his hand. "Someday, if we come through these parts again, we will explain to Walter and his daughter what had taken place with the old hermit. We will also thank those two for sharing their home with us. Meanwhile, we should go while the day is still ahead of us."

Mounting their horses, Richard and the girls looked back one last time at the little cottage as they galloped down the path ahead of them into the unknown.

CHAPTER 21

The three mates rode on for a while in the forest until the horses became tired. Richard and Emma briefly slowed them down to a trot as they went onward in search of the gorge.

"What was that?" Nan whispered nervously, as she bumped along on Emma's horse. She thought she had heard some noise in the undergrowth.

Looking behind her here and there, Emma replied, "I did not hear anything."

"'Twas just a small animal in the bushes, but we should ride quickly nonetheless," Richard replied softly.

"You are beginning to frighten us with your talk!" Emma chastised Richard.

"'Tis better than telling you a falsehood, lass," Richard said grimly.

The riders picked up speed down the path, where it eventually became narrower and more difficult to discern from the brown dry leaves on the ground. In due course, the path faded from sight altogether. Richard and the girls soon entered a deep part of the forest, that had heavy patches of snow lying about on the floor, as thick overhanging trees left them with a sense of foreboding that they had not previously felt. Despite the sunlight coming through the tops of the trees, the air was stiffer and more colder than it had been when the three first started out. Another, yet unfamiliar, snapping in the underbrush had Richard on edge, but he did not want to say anything to the others until he was sure they were not in danger.

"Which way do we go from here?" Emma asked as she shivered and pulled her cloak closer about her. "The path from the cottage is gone, too. I think the hermit fooled us!"

"He said that we should turn left at the end of it," Nan replied, remembering the old hermit's directions. "Do not worry, Emma. As long as we stay together, we shall be fine. This place is not the most friendliest, I admit."

"I believe I am seeing the gorge he spoke of!" Richard exclaimed, shading his eyes from the sunlight. "I can hear water falling as well. 'Tis to the left down yonder, indeed, but that other sound in the forest is starting to trouble me exceedingly. It keeps following us and is getting closer each minute."

"I am hearing the other sound, too!" Emma replied as a frightened Nan held on tighter to her waist.

"I know what I said earlier, Emma, but now I think we should turn around and ride off to Lord Roger!" Nan stated.

Emma nodded, but put a finger to her lips. She knew it was futile to argue with Richard since he had found the gorge. The sound pursuing them did not hinder his enthusiasm for discovering it, either.

"Get off your horse, lasses!" Richard abruptly said. "We do not need our horses anymore. They will become a hindrance to us with their snorting and neighing if things become precarious. All the noise will get the attention of whatever we are hearing out there in the bush."

Emma and Nan looked up with surprise as Richard jumped down from his horse. Taking the saddlebag from the animal's side, he flung it over his shoulder to carry.

"Is that so wise to do, Richard?" Emma asked. It took her several minutes to warm to the idea before giving in.

"I think so," Richard answered. "They will find their way back to Castle Lamington. They are smart creatures. I hate to think that they might be captured by the Viwa fairies, but 'tis better than being here with us."

Emma dismounted her own horse reproachfully and took the saddlebag off.

"What if we have to go to Siddell?" Nan asked, after she got down from Emma's horse. "We do not want to walk all the way there."

"You are right," Richard said. "We might have to do that, but I think the old hermit is not leading us astray. He was not wrong about the gorge and the waterfall, was he?"

Richard slapped the sides of the two horses, sending them off in a gallop. He stood watching as the animals ran off in the opposite direction back to Lamington. Emma and Nan looked on with distraught eyes as their horses disappeared from sight.

"I hope you know what you have just made us do, Richard," Emma said anxiously. "I would sooner have my horse to escape from danger with than to run or walk."

"'Twill take us twice as long to get back to shelter if we suddenly need it," Nan said fearfully. "The cottage we stayed in is a ways back."

"Besides, we do not want to end up sleeping under the stars tonight if things do not work out," Emma added. "Our friends, and you know of whom I speak, will surely find us with ease. If we have a fire going for warmth, they will find us doubly fast. Richard, do not be blind to reason!"

"I cannot get the horses back at this point, lasses," Richard declared. "They are gone."

The girls were annoyed with Richard's unyielding confidence in the old hermit's directions, but the lad was clearly not listening. They had no choice than the follow him, or be left behind in this remote region that they were unacquainted with.

The three travelers found themselves walking down a deep and narrow rocky passage with steep sides that were covered in velvety green moss. The sides of the two rocks were so high, that sunlight could not penetrate in between them, leaving the gorge in deep shadows. At the far end of the passageway, a foamy white waterfall rushed down boundlessly between the two rocks into a shallow pool of water below. The pool, strewn with broken rocks and smooth round pebbles, mirrored back the mossy green passage, giving a false impression that another gorge was found in the water. Weeds and small bushes grew out of the rocks here and there as Richard and the girls stared at the gorge in awe.

"We make for the other side of the waterfall, lasses," Richard said. "'Twill not be pleasant to get our shoes wet in that icy water there, but 'tis shallow enough to get through. I see a little of the forest yonder."

"I wish I knew what we were going to find once we leave it," Nan said.

"Too bad the hermit did not take his time to explain more," Emma said, grimacing about having wet shoes and cold feet.

"We shall soon have that figured out for us," Richard replied, trying to be brave and cheerful for the three of them.

Richard, Emma, and Nan waded through the shallow pool before making toward the forest. They stumbled over the rocks and pebbles in the water as they came closer to the stunning, yet thunderous waterfall that sprayed them as they went past. They were about to step onto dry land when an all-too-familiar cry penetrated the air. Richard and the girls stared at each other in a state of panic.

The Viwa maidens were approaching!

Emma and Nan clung to one another in the water as Richard pulled out his sword from his scabbard. He waited for the evil fairy maidens to present themselves. The fairies' screams stopped and everything went still. A dozen or so Viwa maidens in their customary garb came dancing through the shallow pool and surrounded the others in a circular fashion. Before long, they stopped moving and silently faced their prisoners with their smiling mouths. Following the maidens were a few dozen Viwa knights, with their silver shields depicting the white boar, galloping on horseback through the water, sending it splashing in all directions. Like the fairy maidens, the fairy men surrounded the three companions as they stood in the frigid water unable to flee.

The Viwa knights looked down on their captives with a victorious smirk. Richard, Emma, and Nan were dreading the fairies' next move. Richard reluctantly put his sword back into his scabbard in defeat and held up his hands to the knights, assuring them that he would not attempt to fight back. Fighting a few of them was one thing, but many of them was sure death if he tried.

"So, Aric, we meet again!" boomed one of the Viwa knights at the head of the entourage. He spoke in the common tongue of Richard and the girls. "We knew we would find you here when we came upon your horses grazing nearby. Naturally, we decided to take them both as sort of a reward for finding you."

"Who is this Aric you speak of?" Richard called up with a scowl. He was displeased with himself that their horses had gotten into the hands of the Viwa so soon. "Have we met before, Sir Knight?"

"'Tis the very name you have been given in Viwa that your father had unwisely changed the day he took—nay, stole—you out of our kingdom," the fairy knight explained. "He hid you well all these years, lad, or else we would have claimed you sooner. Let me introduce myself. I am Sir Erling, as I am known in Viwa. Mayhap this will joggle your memory, lad. You fought my companions and I when you were on the road to and from Meldon with these lasses. The best fighting was when you were with those knights, but alas! We lost you, but gained a few extra soldiers to take back to our siege of Lamington, which is where the rest of us must return to shortly if we want to win."

Richard did not answer the audacious Sir Erling. He remained watching him with guarded eyes as he thought back to all the fighting that went on in the forest with the Siddell knights. Richard wished he had a better sense of Sir Erling's face, but the lad could only distinguish two unfamiliar blue eyes surrounded by chainmail on the head of the Viwa knight.

"You were quite a fighter near the monastery, too, I must say," Sir Erling said, as he glared down on Richard. "We were quite impressed with your abilities, even if you are only half Viwa. Even our maidens could not lure you to us as we would have liked. Though we almost had our chance had those brothers not shown up. Well, there are no brothers here now. You cannot outsmart us. You are greatly outnumbered, like a hare cornered by hunting dogs. You seem surprised by your name, Aric. Have we shocked you in some way by it?"

"By learning of it, I come face to face with the beginning story of my past," Richard replied honestly. "I do not care to acknowledge that part of myself, even though Susanna, my old nurse, had told me more than I wanted to hear."

"If that murderer, your father, had not taken you from us, you would not be standing there in that water," the Viwa knight declared with indignation. "You would be in your rightful place, ruling over us in Viwa, as you should be this very instant."

"He was not a murderer!" Richard said in anger. "'Twas an accident that killed my mother. You very well know it! My old nurse told me so, and I would believe her story over yours any day."

"Ah! *Her* version of the story," Sir Erling yelled to Richard. "Of course. The truth is a difficult thing to believe sometimes, especially for a lad like you. You will come to believe us in time, Aric. You will."

"Never!" Richard growled.

"Richard, pray do not provoke them!" Emma exclaimed in a low voice. "Do you want some great harm to come to us? Take care in what you say. We have found ourselves in enough trouble, and my feet are freezing from the water we stand in, though shallow it may be. We can only pray to God to get us out of this mess!"

"Emma! Richard! Look!" Nan cried. "Walter is on a horse behind one of the Viwa knights. How can that be?"

"Walter, they have captured you, too!" Emma fretted. "What a tragedy for us all!"

The large figure of Walter was, indeed, seated in back of one of the soldiers, as he peered down at his recent guests with a haughty grin upon his face.

Walter laughed until his entire plump body shook.

"Aye, I am here, but not as a prisoner. *You* are the prisoners, lad and lasses! Do I dare let you in on my little secret, lass? I told the Viwa knights that you were staying at our cottage. I got a fine reward for having you with us."

Walter pulled out a little cloth bag from underneath his cloak and shook it up and down. Coins jingled inside of it. A payoff to Walter by the evil Viwa. The fairy knight who carried Walter on his horse laughed, too.

Emma put her hands to her mouth in astonishment. Nan turned to Emma and woefully shook her head.

"We were cuckolded by our hosts, lasses," Richard said under his breath. His eyes flashed. "This explains why we did not find them when we returned to their cottage. They were looking for us with the Viwa knights. I can never be too trustful of anyone from now on."

A scream came from one of the horses. It was coming from Helene who was in the saddle behind another Viwa knight.

"Richard!" she cried. "Pray, lad, believe me when I tell you that 'twas my father who put me up to bringing you to our cottage. He wanted me to be on the lookout for you, so he could turn you over to these men. If I did not follow his orders, he was going to throw me out of his house. When I got to know each of you, I pleaded with him to change his mind, but he would not listen. The money was more important to him than anything else. He knew we needed it badly, so he gave in to these soldiers when they came to our cottage one day looking for you and the lasses. They offered a large sum of money to anybody who found you traveling upon the road to Lamington. Pray understand!"

"Be silent, Daughter!" Walter shouted. "I plan on disowning you, *and* turning you out of my house, now that you let the truth be known. Foolish woman!"

"Poor Helene!" Nan whispered. She was unable to retain her feelings anymore. Tears rolled down her cheeks. "If only we can help you."

"Do you know that the movement you saw at our window was really a Viwa knight?" Walter stated with further laughter. "The knight was signaling to us. He wanted to know if we had found you. He stopped by briefly while all three of you left the cottage, but soon left before you came back. He planned on gathering up more soldiers in Lamington before coming back and overtaking you at a more appropriate time. Of course, I told him you were here, much to his delight."

"I do not blame you, Helene, for what you have done!" Richard shouted back to her. The lad had become overwrought with anger at what Walter was telling them. "I have absolved you of any error on your part. Misfortune had driven you to do your father's ugly deed. 'Twas not your fault, so do not dwell on it."

"Foolish lad," Walter said, shaking his head.

"Mayhap I am, but I would not have been so foolish to have given in to some fairy knights who plan great harm to your own people," Richard replied. "Only a fool would care to do such a thing."

Walter did not answer Richard, but sat back on the horse as his face turned a dark shade of purple.

Nan and Emma immediately sensed that Walter did not readily want to admit the grave mistake he had made toward those in Lamington.

"There is only one way to remedy the problem you face, Aric," Sir Erling advised. "Give yourself up and come to our kingdom of Viwa. If you do, we will gladly break the spell that took Christmas from your beloved people and withdraw our troops from Lamington. What say you to this?"

"Indeed, Sir Knight!" Richard replied doggedly. "I would never follow you anywhere—even to the ends of the Earth! There is something so evil in your face that it repels me. I can never take your word for anything. Anyone who tries to capture or fight me in the most brutal of ways is more foe than friend. Your intentions were never good from the start. If they were, you would have come to me in a proper manner and treated me as a royal person should be. You would not keep calling me by that disrespectful title of *lad*, or just *Aric*, if I was someone of such high birth. Why not call me by the title of *my lord*? And those Viwa maidens of yours, baring their nasty teeth at me in the cave some time ago! Do you not think they should have come to me on bended knee? You are forcing me to go back with you to Viwa, not asking or begging me."

"You *will* go back with us!" Sir Erling said authoritatively. "We did not stop searching for you since the first day you left the kingdom. Had we been able to find you then, we would not have needed the help of that little farmer's daughter over there. Not only that, but 'twas brilliant of us to have two of our knights pose as stewards to find you at Castle Lamington—after we poisoned the real ones, which we did not have to do if we found you still in your cradle, Aric."

"You are most evil!" Emma screamed loudly.

"How did you ultimately know who I was?" Richard asked with curiosity. "It took you quite a while to find me. I did grow up, you know."

"That was easy," Sir Erling replied. "The new stewards—courtesy of us—overheard your old chaplain saying that you were leaving to go to Meldon with the two lasses, so they made their move to try and find you within the castle walls. Alas! It did not work because that peasant lass disappeared from the kitchen and went off with you and Lady Catherine's maidservant, missing their opportunity. Our next step was much harsher—taking over Lamington to get you! We already tried to take away Christmas when Lord Robert refused to tell us where you were, Aric, when we met up with him one day in the forest during one of his hunts. What a fool he is! Using him to take away Christmas did not weaken his will to do our bidding, so we decided to go after you ourselves."

"I am glad that his lordship did not tell you where I was," Richard replied. "If he had, I might not have been able to learn the ways of the world fast enough when it comes to understanding those of *your* wretched kind."

"I have sent many fairies inconspicuously throughout the years to find you, but our search was in vain," Sir Erling said, ignoring Richard's remarks. "Until one day when we overheard some young, naïve pages in town revealing that there was a special page at the castle who his lordship doted on quite nicely. It meant only one thing. Aric was there, without a doubt."

"The Viwa fairies seem to be everywhere amongst us," Emma declared in disgust. "We cannot avoid you, no matter how hard we try. It nauseates me to even think of it."

"We have spies everywhere, little maidservant of Lady Catherine," Sir Erling said. "Anywhere you walked, anyone you might have spoken to. They were there, unbeknownst to you."

"I wish my fellow pages had never spoken so freely of me in the public square of Lamington," Richard said, shaking his head. "How much I would have also liked to have entrapped those two knights of yours before they came through the castle gate and killed our two stewards."

"Those innocent friends of yours . . . 'twas not their fault, Aric," Sir Erling stated with laughter. "You would not have been able to find my men coming to your castle . . . they are too conniving for you, lad. On the other hand, you should commend yourself for leaving right under their noses. An unfortunate failure on our part, fairies we may be. We are not always perfect, although we try to be."

"I am glad to hear it!" Richard roared at Sir Erling.

"Do not be so spiteful!" Sir Erling retorted. "We also hoped to find your father after you left Castle Lamington. We had hoped to punish him for his misdeeds against us from the very beginning. He should have done as he was told and handed you over to us when he escaped out of Viwa."

"Punish his lordship?" Emma cried. "How dare you! Her ladyship would be greatly sickened to know what the enemy wanted to do to her husband."

"*Her* husband?" Sir Erling asked, glaring at Emma. "What about our princess? Lord Robert had lost his first wife by his own hand and did not care much that he did. He ran out of Viwa after she died, taking her only son with him."

"*Their* son," Richard corrected Sir Erling. "Again, I say to you, he did not kill anyone. Pray do not spread such lies."

"We spread no lies, lad," Sir Erling answered ingeniously. "We only come here to claim what is ours. Aye, dear Emma, we planned on coming to kill off Lord Robert first, find Aric, and off we would go, back to Viwa with him."

Richard rushed to pull his sword from his side. His face turned scarlet as he angrily thought of Lord Robert being harmed by these malicious fairies.

"How dare you think of killing him for my sake!" Richard cried out. "I would rather die first than to see him perish before me."

"Put your weapon away, Aric!" Sir Erling ordered. "Look around you. What good is your sword when there are so many of my soldiers in your midst? You must begin thinking like a man, not like a page challenging his quintain."

Laughter was heard coming from the other knights around Sir Erling. Richard furiously plunged his sword back into his scabbard. Folding his arms and parting his legs, he stared up at Sir Erling coldly.

"You ridicule me," Richard stated, "but your day is coming!"

"We will see about that!" Sir Erling said with silent laughter in his eyes. "Where is his lordship, lad? Will you tell me? If you do not, we will force it out of you."

"We do not know where he is," Richard answered. He hoped he had sounded convincing enough to Sir Erling. He did not wish to divulge Lord Robert's hiding place at any cost in the deserted cottage. "Not even her ladyship knows where he is."

"'Tis unfortunate that she does not," another Viwa knight, who rode alongside Sir Erling, said. "She was hopeless in gaining information from after our spies, the two stewards, paid her a visit when you disappeared from Castle Lamington. She told them that his lordship's whereabouts were unknown, and she pretended as if she did not know where you were. They threatened her repeatedly for the truth of Lord Robert, which they knew already. 'Twas then that she hesitantly told them of your whereabouts instead, but would say no more. Mayhap when his lordship learns that Lady Catherine is prisoner in his castle, as my men prepare to take it down in battle, he will come out of hiding and face us like he should. But, alas, I think he is too afraid of that. He knows what his ultimate fate will be for him if he does."

"You sicken me more than you imagine, Sir Knight!" Richard yelled loudly until his throat was hoarse. "If any harm comes to her ladyship, you will pay tremendously at the hand of Lord Robert. The men of Lamington will not stand by and let you bring down one stone of our town walls. They are brave. They will fight until the very last Viwa remains at the foot of Lamington. His lordship does not have to be there for that."

"I find you quite amusing, lad," Sir Erling said with a scornful grin. "When we captured those unwary soldiers from Sidell, we thought 'twould weaken your resolve. I was sure you would come out and give yourself up to us, but not so. You are a strong lad, Aric. Very strong. The Viwa is deep in your blood, despite your father. If 'twas not for those soldiers telling us that you were with them, you would have eluded us again. By the by, there was something else we needed from Castle Lamington that we could not find there. Her ladyship was not useful in helping us locate it, though the stewards ravaged the great hall until every last piece of furniture was destroyed before one of them left briefly to impart his findings to us, or lack thereof."

Emma and Nan stared at each other in horror before looking back at Sir Erling. They immediately knew what he was referring to, but said nothing for fear that any reaction they made might evoke suspicion.

"'Tis an object of great value," Sir Erling stated. "Not much bigger than the palm of a grown man's hand. Mayhap you know what I speak of. Walter helped us look around for it in his cottage, but alas! It could not be found."

"He means his lordship's book, Richard," Emma said under her breath.

"What object do you refer to?" Richard asked, pretending not to know what Sir Erling meant and wanting to buy more time to think through his next course of action with the Viwa knights.

"A book, lad!" Sir Erling shouted impatiently. "Do not play games with us! You astound me if you are not aware of its existence."

"I am unaware of any book," Emma replied curtly. "Pray tell us more about it, Sir Knight. If you describe this book to us, we may be able to tell you about it . . . if we have seen it."

Emma slipped her trembling hand into the pocket of her cloak. She hoped that nobody had seen her do it. The book was safely in her pocket as it had been all along.

"What is that you are feeling for, lass?" another Viwa knight asked. "Something very dubious is going on here."

"Oh, Emma, they know we have it!" Nan groaned to her companion. "What shall we do?"

"I do not have anything," Emma replied weakly. She had failed to convince them that she had nothing on her. They would not believe a word coming from those who had lived in close proximity to Lord Robert at Castle Lamington.

"Come here and show me what you have!" Sir Erling demanded. "If you do not, we will make you come to us. You *will* show us what you have!"

Emma gazed at Richard with desperation in her eyes that begged him to help her out of what was becoming a difficult situation.

"If you want Emma to show you what she has, Sir Erling, pray call off your Viwa maidens as you would your guard dogs," Richard pleaded. "How can she come to you if they smother us so in their circle? Do you mind, Sir Knight?"

Sir Erling nodded. He and some of his knights murmured something to the Viwa maidens in their own tongue. The fairy maidens began backing away from Richard and the girls, giving them leeway to move about in their midst. This action forced the Viwa knights to back up as well, loosening the circle even more around their captives.

An idea came to Richard. He saw a grand opportunity presenting itself as Emma nervously started sloshing through the pool of water toward Sir Erling.

CHAPTER 22

Emma came within several feet of Sir Erling's horse before she heard Richard shouting frantically to both herself and Nan.

"Run, lasses! Run as fast as you can!"

Emma looked over her shoulder and saw Richard pointing to a space that the Viwa maidens and soldiers inadvertently made when they moved aside to let her pass. The space was large enough to allow herself and her companions to get through and escape into the forest. Richard ran between two Viwa knights with Emma and Nan at his heels. Racing through the water and toward an embankment, Richard hastily pulled something out of his cloak pocket and tossed it as hard as he was able to in the path of some of the Viwa knights. There was a bright flash and a loud bang. It forced dozens and dozens of the knights' horses to rear up in fright and race back in the opposite direction of the gorge with the fairy maidens scurrying behind them. Richard pulled another of the same thing out of his cloak pocket that created the same outcome. The knights and their horses dispersed so quickly, none remained when Richard glanced to see what had happened to the fairy men. Richard laughed until his sides were ready to burst.

"This will keep them occupied for a while, lasses!" Richard cried out. "Too bad I do not have more of this powder on hand. Sir Erling was unable to manage his horse after the noise. Did you see him go?"

Richard and the girls were exhausted after their narrow escape from the Viwa knights, but they did not stop running once they found themselves back on land.

"What was that you threw at the knights, Richard?" Nan asked, breathing heavily. "'Twas so scary . . . and that sound . . . I never saw anything like it before. Your Viwa strength helped you aim well and throw whatever 'twas you did at them."

"I do not know myself, lass, what I had tossed," Richard replied. "A man sold some strange, reddish powder to me at the fair in Lamington last summer, and I was carrying it around in a pouch on me ever since. He said 'twould scare away a wild animal if I was ever cornered by one. All I had to do was rub this powder together with two rocks and throw it as far as I could. Now I know what it does. 'Tis amazing, 'tis not? Luckily I managed to gather up a few small rocks while we were walking. Had I not, we would have been prisoners of the Viwa."

"Aye, 'tis amazing," Emma agreed. "How terrified the knights were after they saw the flame—or, whatever you call it—light up after you threw that stuff at them. I hate to say this, but scaring them off like that will not stop them from coming after you, Richard. It only slowed them down temporarily, but they will be back. They have horses. We have only our legs to carry us."

"Then run faster, we must!" Richard exclaimed. He sped up more rapidly, as he sprinted through the forest ahead of the girls, down a timeworn path.

After a while, the path became difficult to see as it wound itself around more and more trees and underbrush while snow covered over it in other places. Richard and the girls occasionally slowed down their pace to listen for any fairy cries that past circumstance had accustomed them to.

"Praise God we are only hearing a stray bird or the wind shaking the tree branches," said a relieved Nan. "I would much rather listen to those than to a Viwa maiden."

Emma walked around some snow piles. She said nervously, "I pray we are going in the proper direction."

"As long as the old hermit is correct, we should be," Richard answered. "I have not seen any other path since we entered the forest, so this must be the right one."

"I am beginning to feel like a hunted animal, Richard," Emma said. "I do not like this way of life anymore." She gulped for air as she struggled with the lad's steady stride. "Not only that, but we cannot keep up with you. You are much too fast for us!"

"'Tis your long legs that carry you so well!" Nan said to Richard. "My sides are beginning to ache and my legs have cramps. I can only go so far like this."

222

"We must not stop now, lasses!" Richard exclaimed. "If we go on a little further and there is no sign of the fairies, we will stop for a moment."

"I thought our lives were over when they found us at the gorge," Nan said. "I am still trembling because of it. This forest is dark with many thick trees, but not impossible for them to find us. I believe 'twas the Viwa we heard in the trees when we left the old hermit's cottage."

"Praise God that we have lost them, even fleetingly!" Emma cried out in delight. "I agree with you, Nan. They were following us from a distance before they found us. Nevertheless, we have learned much from them today."

"Aye, they have answered many of the things we suspected or did not know," Richard replied. "Little did they foresee we would narrowly escape them after they proudly admitted a few of their dirty secrets to us. Fools! All of them! Except for Helene. I feel terribly bad for her. Mixed up in this affair all on account of her ruthless father."

"The poor woman," Nan said quietly. "I wish we could have taken her with us."

"We could do nothing for her without getting ourselves hurt first," Emma declared despondently. "Her fate is not in our hands. I pray that she will be kept safe."

"As far as that outlandish name that Sir Erling said I was born with," Richard began, "do not call me by it. I prefer to be called Richard over Aric any day."

"And so we shall!" Emma said with a grin. "Aric does not suit you anyway, Richard."

"I am surprised that the fairies are not aware of his lordship's presence in the forest," Richard mused. "I half expected to see him as their prisoner when they found us at the waterfall, but I am happy that he was not."

"We are fortunate that the Viwa did not already make *us* their prisoners when we returned to our hosts' cottage after we spoke to his lordship," Nan said. "They could very well have been waiting for us with Walter and Helene."

"Oh, do not remind me!" Emma said. "You know, they certainly have a great interest in his lordship's book. I am glad that I have kept it on me at all times."

"I always had this feeling that there was something more special about the book than just what it already did," Richard said. "Mayhap 'tis something in my Viwa blood that has me thinking that. We can stop here, lasses. I do not hear anything except the sound of the forest."

"'Tis a gift that only the Viwa have!" Nan praised Richard, dropping to an old tree stump to rest. "'Twas wise of Father John to have taken the book with him when he left Castle Lamington. Otherwise, the Viwa would have found it."

"I will guard it with my life!" Emma proclaimed happily. She felt around inside the pocket of her gown for the book. Her face instantly went colorless as she looked away from the others.

"What is wrong, Emma?" Richard asked, lying a hand on her shoulder. "You are oddly silent about something."

"Let us try to keep our voices low," Emma murmured. "We never can tell who is hiding in the thicket." She kept looking back nervously in the direction of the gorge.

"Emma, you are not being truthful with us," Richard remarked. "What are you hiding? I can tell by the way you act that something is amiss."

"My heart is weak as I am about to share some very distressing news with you and Nan," Emma replied. She was unable to speak the difficult words to her friends. "The book!" she stammered. "I . . . I . . . do not have it. 'Tis gone!"

Richard and Nan stared back at Emma and blinked several times, hoping that what Emma had shared with them was not true.

"Are you sure, Emma?" Richard asked slowly. "Check any other pockets you have. You *must* have it somewhere. I would hate to lose the book to those evil fairies. 'Twould be a tragedy if 'twas gone. It can make all the difference in our lives if we still had it, especially if it holds some importance that we do not yet know."

"I am so sorry, Richard," Emma said after checking her pockets over and over again. "As I said before, 'tis not here."

Light snow began to fall, quickly covering up the path in front of them.

Emma groaned at the weather. "This is not good. Now we will not be able to find the book at all."

Nan ran back a little ways over the path. She tried to retrace each of their footsteps. The book was burgundy in color and would easily have shown through the snow.

"I do not see it!" Nan cried.

Richard and Emma came running to Nan's side and hastily helped her look around in the snow and in between some of the nearby trees, but the book was not to be found.

"Richard, can you ever forgive me for being so foolish?" Emma begged. She was on the verge of tears. "I do not know where I lost it. We ran so fast when we left the gorge and went into the forest. It might have fallen out of my pocket somewhere along the way. I had too much pride in keeping it safe. I was not careful enough."

Richard swallowed hard as disappointment shown in his face over the loss of the book. He shielded his eyes in the late day sunlight and looked back long and hard at the route from which they had come.

"There is no point in tormenting ourselves over it," he said, trying not to be discouraged. "Not with the Viwa soldiers at our backs. They are mainly after me than the book, anyhow, though I do hate losing the only picture that I may ever know of my mother that was in it." After a brief period of silence, Richard added, "'Tis safe to say that we can walk and not run the rest of the way. I have a feeling we lost them for, at least, a little while. We put quite a distance between us and the gorge."

Emma did not answer Richard, but gazed the other way to hide the sadness she had caused him. Nan gave Emma a heartfelt squeeze on the arm as she conceded to her companion that nothing could be done to bring back the lost article. The snow had stopped falling. Richard quietly started strolling ahead of the girls. The three journeyed through the rest of the forest. It started to ascend to higher elevation as thicker and heavier snow piles were seen lying about on the forest floor. They were becoming very tired from walking continuously. Richard and the girls were becoming keenly aware that there was not a sign of anything that the old hermit might have described to help them out of their predicament.

"This is just a forest and nothing more!" Emma muttered. "I do not know what his lordship has intended for us, but I am not seeing it. We have hiked many leagues already. I do not hear the waterfall anymore, which means that we have left it far behind."

"The hermit did say that we would discover *something* at the end of it," Nan said. "I assume we have not yet walked long enough. The forest does seem to go quite a ways."

Nan's lips were becoming dry and cracked from thirst and the cold air. Her stomach was growling louder and louder from hunger. Whatever was left in their saddlebags was meager and would have to be rationed slowly, if that were at all possible. Had it been summer, she would have been able to find them something good to eat like wild mushrooms or some juicy berries. A small animal or wild fowl would be tasty over a spit, but they would be wasting too much time for that. They had to keep moving.

"I am beginning to notice that the hill is gradually leveling off and the trees are thinning out," Richard announced. "The air is much cooler up here than down below where the gorge is. Do you not notice it, too? Mayhap this hill we have been climbing is turning into some kind of tableland. We will soon find out if my prediction is correct. I believe his lordship is not sending us to our doom. You will see. We need to be patient."

"You must be right about the hill, Richard," Nan said. "I feel less tired walking now. We are not going up anymore."

"I wish we can stop here," Emma stated. "I feel like falling down and resting even with all that snow under us."

"Do not think of giving up!" Richard beseeched her. "I know how both of you feel. I am still sure that we are going in the right direction. Just think. Soldiers live more difficult lives than we do. I have heard plenty of stories at Castle Lamington. We have done well by coming this far."

Richard, Emma, and Nan plodded on as unwearyingly as they could bear with the snow crunching underfoot. They saw the bright red sun beginning to set low in the sky, as long shadows of each of them was being cast over the snow as they walked. When they became too tired to walk, they stopped and looked through their saddlebags for something to eat. All that was left was some cold, brown bread that they took from the cottage of Walter and Helene. After eating the last of it, they drank down the rest of the water that was in their leather canteens.

"Our food and drink is gone," Emma declared feebly. "If the old hermit is wrong, we shall eventually die from want of them."

"Do not speak in such a way!" Richard said sharply. "I still have confidence in the old hermit. We shall find something before long. We can always put snow in our canteens to drink. Soldiers always do it."

"Such a beautiful sunset," Nan said with admiration. "How sorry I am that nightfall is coming with nowhere for us to go."

"Do not say such things!" Emma rebuked Nan as some self-assuredness surged within her. "'Tis not dark yet. We may yet be fortunate to find something as Richard has told us. You said so yourself not long ago."

Richard opened his mouth as if to speak, but quickly closed it. He paused and turned his head to the left and right, as he closely listened to some clattering that no one else heard. In a quiet voice, he said, "I hear somebody. 'Tis not good, lasses."

Nan's heart sunk and Emma's legs began to tremble as they turned around to see whom it was that Richard was warning them about. Within seconds, the thunder of horses and shrill cries of soldiers were not far behind. From a speck of gray to fully formed figures coming toward them, the soldiers were moving at a faster and faster speed, which was more than the little traveling group could do to make a getaway on foot. Richard and the girls knew they were being outrun. How useless to think that they try and hide themselves on a snowy, barren plain!

"Richard!" Emma cried out. "They *must* be Viwa!"

"I am sure that they are," Richard said. "Who else would care to come after us in such haste?"

"What will we do?" Nan asked. "Where can we go?"

"There is one thing we can do—we *must* outpace them!" Richard answered in one breath. "What alternative do we have, lasses? They have found us, but I would rather run from them than be captured by such evil. I am beginning to hear the sound of those Viwa maidens with them as well."

"Oh, I do not like them!" Emma said unnerved. "I do not know who is worse—the Viwa knights or the maidens accompanying them everywhere."

"Well," Richard began, "I do not plan to wait around here much longer to find out. I repeat, we must run as fast as our feet can carry us! Putting the hoods of our cloaks over our heads will not hide us, either. If the fairies catch us this time, we *will* be their prisoners."

Though worn-out and cold as they were, Richard and the girls sprinted across the plain, each of them wondering how long it would take before they were surrounded by the Viwa. Occasionally they fell down on the icy snow, but the aches and the bruises did not thwart the little group from persevering toward that one goal: finding the end of their journey, wherever it was taking them.

Emma slowed down momentarily. Her eyes became glazed as she stared off into the wide expanse ahead of them.

"Come, Emma!" Nan cried, taking the other girl's hand and pulling her. "We cannot stop. You do not want to see those Viwa maidens again, do you?"

"Nan, what are we running from?" Emma asked.

Without waiting for Nan to reply, Richard said, "From the Viwa, of course! Do you not remember, lass? Is the cold affecting your memory?"

"I seem to remember Christmas being a part of all this," Emma declared.

"If Christmas had not disappeared from Lamington," Nan said, "then aye! We would not be here. If that is what you mean, Emma."

A look of confusion came to Emma and then a smile slowly brightened her face.

"Christmas!" Emma said. "I remember it now."

"Do not tell us that you do not know what Christmas is!" Nan exclaimed. "You remind me of my parents after the blue dirt fell."

"Sometimes I do forget what Christmas is," Emma said quietly.

"I fear that his lordship's words are poisoning Emma's mind," Richard whispered to Nan. "Mayhap the book has lent its bad influence over her when she carried it. Or, what has happened in Lamington is slowly affecting the rest of us. Remember, the town folk forgot first. Then I nearly forgot what Christmas was when we returned to Lamington not long ago. Emma said as much about herself at that time and 'tis happening once again. You may be next, Nan, if this continues."

"Oh, Richard!" Nan cried, chills running up and down her spine. "How horrible that would be!"

"If that be the case, we must find the end of this plain to the place where the old hermit spoke of," Richard remarked. "I, myself, thought we would already be there. We are already long past the forest. Keep going, lasses! The end *must* be here somewhere! It must be!"

"Aric! Aric!"

It was the voice of Sir Erling.

Richard, Emma, and Nan also heard the Viwa maidens calling out to them.

HOOOO-AHHH!!!

The three travelers dared not stop to look back. Fighting against the vicious wind that whipped at their cloaks, they continued to swiftly race out ahead of the evil fairies.

"Aric! We *must* talk to you!" Sir Erling implored loudly. "We came back to personally thank you for this most desired gift that you left us in the forest!"

Riding ahead of his knights, Sir Erling was holding up an animal horn in one hand, which he used to summon Richard with, and in the other, he held up Lord Robert's book.

"All we need now is for you to return to Viwa with us. You are the last piece of what we are missing, lad. Come back!"

"With all my life, I will not answer him!" Richard cried as he ran with Emma and Nan. "Keep the book, Sir Erling! 'Tis me that you will never find going back with you and your criminal knights. And those maidens at your side . . . they will never again get the better of me!"

"If you want him, you will have to come and get him yourself!" Emma cried out in a shrill voice.

"Come back here, Aric!" Sir Erling shouted in anger as he rode on. "You *will* come with us! We are gaining on you, you insolent lad."

"Do not waste your time with him, Richard," Nan advised. "He will slow us down more if we continue to argue with him."

The shadow of Sir Erling and his soldiers grew larger and larger in the snow behind Richard and the girls. The Viwa fairies were within reach. Richard, the prize who the cunning fairies were seeking after many years, was there for the taking.

"We are not going to make it!" Emma screamed as she held tightly to Nan's hand. "'Twill mean only one thing for you, Richard, but what will become of Nan and I?"

The three companions staggered in the snow as they kept hurrying along, unsure of the fate that would soon await them at the hands of Sir Erling and his fairy knights.

CHAPTER 23

Nan and her traveling mates took another step forward. Something unexpected happened. The snow-covered plain they had been going across disappeared before their very eyes. The sounds of the galloping horses and the soldiers' screams were no longer heard. There was dead silence. They had crossed a strange, invisible line. Richard, Emma, and Nan found themselves standing at the edge of a white shoreline with soft sand, while brilliant sunshine shown directly above. Nan turned to see if the plain was behind them. In its place were endless, rolling sand dunes.

The bone-chilling air that the youth had breathed in earlier had changed. The air around them was now balmy and pleasant, quite unlike what the small group was used to even during Lamington's warmest summers. Great strong waves lapped the shore rhythmically while barely hitting the tops of Richard's and the girls' shoes. The waves were sapphire blue with glints of sparkling light bouncing off of them as the sunlight hit the water. The blue was an almost unearthly blue not found anywhere. The color impressed Nan greatly as she and the others stared at one another, spellbound by the incredible sight. Nan had never seen the sea, nor had she ever smelled the strong salty air. She had heard of the sea from travelers and peddlers coming and going through Lamington, but she had never imagined it to be this magnificent. Were they witnessing a dream and nothing else? Richard, Emma, and Nan did not know what to make of it.

The waves began to part slowly and a very grand, high bridge came out of the water. The bridge was made of fine stone, all glistening white with beautiful cascading flowers of innumerable pastel colors growing out of its sides. The bridge seemed to call out to Richard and the girls with a sound that they heard only inside of their heads.

The presence of the strange bridge made Emma apprehensive. She whispered, "What do we do now?"

Uneasy about the weird, yet wonderful, place they had arrived at, Nan gripped Emma's arm for safety as she waited for her companions to come to some decision about it.

"We go over the bridge and see where it leads," Richard replied. "It seems to want us to."

The girls nodded to Richard and followed him across the bridge. They were surprised to see a small castle rising out of the sea as they were walking to the other side. When the castle had fully emerged from the water, diamonds were seen covering every inch of its four walls. The castle was set on its own island with unusual bushes and trees exquisitely landscaped around it. Many sea birds were seen flying and encircling about in the sky above the diamond covered turrets and battlements of this peculiar castle. Coming to the end of the bridge, Richard, Emma, and Nan stepped onto the island where the castle stood. The land was dry, though it had come from under the water a few moments ago. Hearing a quiet splash, the trio turned and watched as the bridge submerged back into the sea.

"What do you make of all this?" Nan uttered, as they got closer to the castle. "'Tis all very odd to me."

"We are trapped here!" Emma cried fearfully. "How do we get back to the shore with the bridge gone?"

Richard carefully scrutinized their new surroundings. He stared up at the diamond castle and then studied its grounds from where he and the girls stood.

"One thing I can say is this castle had not been created to withstand a war," he said. "'Tis too slight and not enclosed very well by the thin walls around it. There are no guards anywhere, either. In fact, there is only a simple, unattended gate without a gatehouse above it! From here, you can see the castle gardens right there in the back. Castle Lamington's gardens are within its walls. This castle is here for some other purpose."

"So where are we, Richard?" Emma asked, wiping her forehead from the heat. She took off her cloak and draped it over her arm. "Is this the place where the old hermit told us to go to? 'Tis so warm here, and yet, *so beautiful.*"

Richard shrugged his shoulders.

"It can be if those Viwa knights are no longer pursuing us. It seems to me that they were prevented from coming after us once we crossed over here from the plain."

"Let us go and see what awaits us inside the castle!" Nan said excitedly.

"Indeed, we should," Emma said. She was unable to resist the splendor that the castle's diamonds illuminated. She reached out and touched a large one set in the castle wall.

"Wait!" Richard exclaimed. "Be careful! This may be where his lordship sent us, or it may not be. I would like for somebody to come out and speak to us first. Where is its owner, if it has one? The castle looks deserted to me, though 'tis well cared for."

The girls, charmed by their new surroundings, ignored Richard's warning and impulsively ran off to the diamond-covered gate much to his dismay. They merrily jumped up and down in front of it as they waited for Richard to join them in their adventure.

"I am afraid her ladyship would not be pleased with my behavior right now," Emma confessed. "Nan, you and I are acting like wee ones. 'Tis this land we come to, making us feel happier than we have been in many days. Come now, Richard! You must feel this way as well."

Richard wanted to try and temper Emma's naïve enthusiasm, but he knew he was losing his argument about being cautious as he himself was quickly being taken in by everything around him.

"I admit I do feel at peace here," the lad said reluctantly.

"Richard, look!" Nan cried out.

The door of the diamond gate, which was covered in smaller diamonds, opened completely on its own without anyone standing there to do it.

Richard and the girls glanced at each other in total surprise.

Not knowing what else to do, they went inside as the door closed behind them. They wandered down a long corridor, brightly lit by torches in the walls. At the end of it, they entered a great hall where a long table with a white tablecloth was set up with food for a feast. In the background, music was heard strumming from somewhere, though musicians were not visibly playing instruments. Torches were burning intensely as sunlight streamed weakly through a few windows high up in the walls. The walls themselves were painted with various scenes of unknown battles and mythical creatures while long, heavy tapestries hung intermittently between the high windows.

The food smelled wonderful to the hungry visitors of this exotic castle. They nervously stood around, unsure of their next move.

"Do we dare sit down?" Nan quietly asked the others. "Is the food for us?"

Richard looked around the room to see if he saw someone, but no one was there.

"I wish I can answer that."

The castle seemed to read their minds as a young servant in a green tunic with black hose and pointy-tipped shoes came out from somewhere. He bowed deeply to Richard first and then to the girls and signaled at them to sit down and eat. He did not speak, but immediately started to serve some of the food from the table to each of them. Additional servants came out from a side door and brought several more courses of food, including roasted pheasant and piping hot pigeons on silver platters.

Nan's eyes grew wide. "Have you ever seen such food in your life? And so much of it, too! I do not think they will serve me. I am just a lowly peasant girl." She was about to protest the reception of the food from the servants, but they motioned firmly for Nan to sit down and eat with the rest of her friends.

"I have not had such great food since Castle Lamington!" Emma said laughing.

"Indeed, I do not think I will be able to eat for many weeks once we are finished here," Richard stated as a smile brightened his face.

After the food was finished, down to the very delectable cakes and pastries at the end of the meal, the servant who had first invited them to dine came out and gestured at them to follow him down a different corridor of the castle. The young man took Richard to a bedchamber nearby and then led the girls to another one, where beautiful new gowns were laid out for each of them. A table was there as well for washing and grooming. Emma immediately reached for her gown and fingered it enthusiastically.

"We are surely being spoiled here," Emma declared. "I suppose that the gowns are meant to be worn for our presence with the lord of the castle, whoever he is. I think he saw us on the shoreline and immediately put his servants to work preparing for our arrival."

Nan was in shock that she, a farmer's daughter, should be forced to wear a gown of blue silk and refused to put it on. After some persuasion from Emma, she reluctantly slipped it over her head. Gazing at herself in a hand mirror that she found lying on the table, she changed her mind and took the gown off.

"Nan, why did you do that?" Emma asked in disappointment when Nan put her old dress back on. "When our visit is over, we can put our old clothes back on. Our old things need the attention of a laundress, anyway."

"I do not want to put that thing on!" Nan said defiantly. "Pray do not make me. I will not do it." Changing the subject, she said, "This *must* be the very place that his lordship was sending us to."

"No doubt this is," Emma agreed, as she admired herself in the mirror at the becoming Robin egg blue gown with silver trim she had on. "I cannot believe Richard's sudden doubt about where we were! Look at how he reacted toward this castle, too! Did he think the evil Viwa were here? How very opposite of that lecture he gave us. Now, what was it . . . I know! He said that his father would not send his only son into danger somewhere and not us to our doom. Pshaw! What a strange lad he can be sometimes. Where *did* he finally think we ended up?"

"Those fairies put him through a lot," Nan reminded her. "No wonder he was worried. Can he be blamed? Mayhap he thought an empty castle was luring us to some evil knights who were hiding in back, ready to attack."

"Nan, if we are being deceived by somebody in this place, he is slow to act upon his deception," Emma stated. "I am not concerned about where we are and neither should Richard, although I could tell he seemed better when we entered the castle. I certainly enjoyed the food here. The lord of this castle has cooks just as wonderful as those at Castle Lamington."

"If the lord of the castle did see us on the shore, then where was he?" Nan said. "I saw not a soul anywhere. There was just water, as far as the eye could see, before the bridge came out of it. Whoever he is hides himself well, almost like the old hermit. I confess that I enjoyed the food as much as you did, Emma. It reminded me of what the Christmas feast at Castle Lamington must be like."

"Ah!" Emma exclaimed with a forlorn smile. "The Christmas feast! You would have liked it, Nan."

Nan unhappily dropped her eyes to the ground. "If 'tis ever held again."

The girls went silent. They were mulling over what had happened to their beloved holiday in Lamington when Richard came and knocked on their door.

"We are to be escorted somewhere," Richard said in a muffled voice. "The servant said we must hurry. Those were his only words."

Emma and Nan grinned. They knew where they were going. The girls finished brushing their hair and came out to join Richard to make the attendance of the enigmatic lord of the diamond castle.

CHAPTER 24

Walking out of their bedchamber, the girls saw by Richard's expression that he was taken aback by Emma's gown. His eyes took in every detail of her appearance as he complemented the blushing girl.

Emma and Nan were equally impressed by Richard's lavender tunic with a gold border all around it. His hose was ivory white and he had soft charcoal gray leather shoes on. He was unmistakably looking more and more like the prince he was born to be, but the girls did not share their thoughts with him on this. They did not want to upset the lad who might be repelled by the idea.

"You are dressed very fine this evening, lass!" Richard remarked to Emma with a bow. Noticing that Nan was wearing the same dress she wore to the diamond castle, he asked, "Where is your gown, lass? Were you not given one?"

"I *was* given a gown, but I did not want it," Nan replied curtly, as she and the others started to follow the young servant from before down a torch-lit corridor away from their bedchambers. "A farmer's daughter does not wear such things. The lord of this castle does not know me very well."

"I am sure the lord here will respect your wishes," Richard said as they walked. "I hope his feelings are not hurt by them."

"If need be, I will explain who I am to him," Nan said. "He will understand."

"Do you wonder why he gave us such finery?" Richard mused. "When I found these garments in my room, the servant insisted they were for me. I had not expected to be given something like *this* to wear. I am dressed as good as, or better than, his lordship in Lamington. He would be shocked by how I look."

"I felt similarly when I dressed in this gown," Emma replied. "The only difference is that I thought of her ladyship. I am sure there is some plan behind the things we were given to wear. This finery is far too splendid for me. Of course, the lord here might just have a charitable heart."

"If that be the case," Richard chuckled, "I will have to be careful not to tell anyone back at Castle Lamington. My fellow guardsmen will want to know where I was and decide to come here themselves, if just for the clothing. Not to mention the food as well!"

The servant took Richard, Emma, and Nan to a doorway near the great hall where they had previously eaten in. By this time, the food and table had been cleared away and a small fire was crackling in the fireplace against the wall. They were then led out-of-doors to the castle gardens. The air was still warm, and it playfully blew through the leaves of the small ornamental trees found in the gardens. Paths of stone were laid out in different directions across the soft green grass where many colorful flowers bordered alongside them.

There were arbors of white, pink, and red roses growing in various parts of the gardens with a few round pools found in the outermost reaches of it. There was one predominantly large pool in the center of the gardens with a fountain. The fountain comprised of two stone lions seated back to back, adorned with stone birds and vines in their fur, as water spewed from each of their mouths. Enjoying this paradise were twittering birds and brightly-colored butterflies that happily flew from flower to flower, drinking the sweet nectar from them.

Emma and Nan were awestruck by the beauty and serenity of the environment around them. Richard himself marveled at what they had stumbled upon as he exhibited a smile at the butterflies he had stopped to watch. As the three companions walked about the gardens, they saw a tall commanding figure of a man standing nearby with his back toward them. His arms were folded loosely across his torso. He was dressed in a silver and red tunic that fell to the ground, covering the very tips of his red shoes that were concealed underneath it. He had long curly white hair that hid some golden strands leftover from his youth. Turning to the young people, he bowed and smiled to each of them as his eyes sparkled brightly in a face worn with age.

"Welcome, Emma! Welcome, Nan! Welcome to you, Richard!" he called out in a pleasant voice that reverberated throughout the gardens.

"My lord, 'tis our utmost pleasure that you have taken us into your castle for food and rest," Richard said, bowing to the aging man in return.

Emma and Nan knelt briefly to this mysterious gentleman.

"Your castle is most unusual," Richard continued. "'Tis not typical to come to one where there are no guards at the gatehouse, or a courtyard to walk through! Your gardens are also curious. They are not within castle walls, which are quite unlike ours at Castle Lamington."

"There is no need for such things here, lad," the gentleman murmured. "We are a peaceful lot. Evil will neither penetrate our lands nor our castle. There is never a necessity to defend our realm like you do in your own world."

"Where are we, exactly, your lordship?" Emma asked shyly. "Do you know that when we came through your castle, Christmas has returned quite clearly to my mind? So unlike before we came here."

"I quite agree with you, Emma," Richard said. "It has for me as well."

"And me!" Nan declared happily. "I never have to worry about forgetting it now."

"Very good," the elder gentleman answered. "My home has done wonders for all of you. 'Tis just as I have said. Evil does not find its way here, especially if forgetting Christmas is one product of it."

Richard and the girls stood watching this most interesting man who had a face as peaceful as his gardens. The warmth that irradiated from him was most comforting and unearthly. He seemed to be a sort of grandfatherly person with an alluring character all his own.

"Are we in Viwa, your lordship?" Nan asked. "You . . . you are lord of this castle, are you not?"

The man laughed out loud and held his stomach as he did. "Do not be frightened, lass. Neither should any of you. Let me explain. This is not the Kingdom of Viwa, but 'tis not far off. You are in the Land of the Diamond Sea, and I am lord of this castle, if you think of me as such. In case you wonder who I am, well, I am he who is above all that is evil. There is one even a greater step above evil than I am, but I am not he. I am his helper, you might say. He needs many helpers, and I am one of them. I only look out for your goodness and well-being. I cannot prevent you from making mistakes in your lives, but can only assist you in times of trouble. You may call me Eolande."

A look of fright came over the girls as Richard eyed this eccentric gentleman closely. Richard wanted to trust this man with his life, but he also wanted to be certain that they had nothing to fear. Deep down he could not imagine Eolande wanting to lead them astray. This Land of the Diamond Sea seemed too perfect and wonderful to anyone visiting it. Richard had no desire to let his guard down, just in case they were walking into a snare.

"How did you know who we were?" Richard asked. "You must have foreseen us coming, though how, I know not."

"Dear lad," Eolande said in a consoling manner, "I see you do not have faith in me. I completely understand how you must feel. You had fought and escaped many Viwa lately, though not good ones. After all you and the lasses had gone through, it has taken a great toll on you. 'Tis difficult to know who is friend or adversary. Your father, Lord Robert of Lamington, wanted you to come here. His only desire was to do what was best for you. You saw that all along. You must not doubt me, Richard."

Richard let his tense shoulders drop. He closed his eyes briefly before opening them and staring down at the stone walk under his feet. He was ashamed to have doubted this man from the beginning and was too embarrassed to admit it. He hoped Eolande would forgive his lack of common sense.

"We did not expect to come to a place such as this," Emma said. "We were not told we were going to the Land of the Diamond Sea. His lordship was very vague in telling us where he was sending us until we got there. Your land is like walking into a dream, my Lord Eolande."

"Why, the sun was setting when we walked across the cold, snowy plain," Nan noted. "Then, we came to a land where the sun was still up, the sky was blue, and 'twas summer-like. It *was* a dream. Are we still in it, your lordship?"

"You are not in a dream, Nan," Eolande said with a smile brighter than the golden sunrise of the morning. "'Tis a very real place. Very much like Lamington that you have come from, just different."

"What is the Land of the Diamond Sea?" Richard curiously asked. "Will we ever go back to Lamington?"

"You will soon learn what this land is," Eolande replied. "*If* all goes well, you may go back to Lamington. I will not lend you false hope, lad."

Eolande walked over to a flower and lightly lifted up a butterfly that landed on it. He surveyed the yellow creature briefly as it fluttered awkwardly off his hand and onto another flower nearby. Richard and the girls studied Eolande's actions and pondered the elusive words he used to describe himself. They then wondered what would become of them in the Land of the Diamond Sea, but were too afraid to ask this formidable, yet very considerate and surreal, man.

"I am dreadfully sorry, my young friends," Eolande remarked absentmindedly, "but for a moment, I was deep in thought and forgot you were here. Sometimes a beautiful living thing can make me forget about the problems of your world . . . so full of pain and unexpected tragedies."

"How did my father know to send us here?" Richard asked. He walked around the stone fountain impatiently before stopping to stare into it. "He said that where we were going, we would find a solution to our problems. We are now here. Pray, Eolande, what can you do for us? There is so much that the Viwa did to Lamington that is not good. Now they want to attack it."

"I am saddened that you have met with more evil Viwa than with those who are honorable," Eolande said, going over to the water fountain and sitting down on its edge. "Remember how I said that I am above all that is evil? I am not of *their* ilk. I am one of the highest order of Viwa that there is. Only good can come from me and never anything wicked. Do you understand that, lad? I will help you in every way that I can."

Richard occasionally nodded when Eolande spoke.

"Your father already knew about the Land of the Diamond Sea before your birth, Richard," Eolande explained. "He learned of it when he married your mother. He knew where to send you. This is how I knew a son of his would arrive here. I prepared for that day with a little foresight of things going on in the world outside of mine. Lord Robert will always be grateful that you have made it here safely and are out of the hands of those who would have prohibited you from coming."

Eolande got up and went back over to the flowers and watched as a butterfly landed on his shoulder. The elderly man laughed with gusto as the insect flew off a moment later. Richard and the girls joined in the laughter.

"I see relief in three pairs of eyes staring back at me!" Eolande exclaimed. "In this world, beauty and goodness work hand in hand. Nan, I see you have decided not to wear the gown that was set out for you."

"I cannot, your lordship," Nan said quietly. "I am only a farmer's daughter from Lamington."

"I suppose I do not completely grasp what you do in your lands, lass, anymore than you do mine," Eolande said contemplatively. "You do not have to wear it if you do not wish to. If you change your mind, 'tis there for you. Does that make you feel better?"

"Aye, it does, your lordship," Nan replied. She was thrilled that Eolande gave her the option of not wearing the gown.

"You must call me Eolande," Eolande insisted. "Not *your lordship* or *Sir Eolande*, although some still do it anyway. I am neither. Eolande will do."

"Eolande, when will Christmas return to Lamington?" Nan inquired.

Christmas was always on Nan's mind, and its nonexistence at home was troubling her relentlessly. Finally, here was somebody who might have answers. The girl's eyes sparkled at the prospect of the holiday being restored.

"You should know that Christmas can never go away," Eolande declared. "Nothing can ever really take it from you."

"But what about what happened to us in Lamington?" Nan asked in desperation. "Christmas is not there. 'Tis not that the people there can celebrate it in hiding. They cannot even *remember* to celebrate it. We were on the verge of forgetting it, too, until we came to you. You must know what his lordship, Lord Robert of Lamington, had done to it."

"And we were never frozen!" Emma added. "Neither was anybody from Castle Lamington."

"I am aware of the spell that brought this about when Lord Robert read it from his book," Eolande said. "'Twould have taken hold of all of you soon enough. You need not have been frozen to have it happen. Some folk are frozen, some are not. Such was its design, regrettably."

"So you do know?" Richard said. "You know how deeply we are embroiled in this disastrous mess?"

Eolande raised his white eyebrows in surprise. "Aye, lad, I know many things! This is why I had mentioned your world as having so much pain and tragedy. I know as many things as I am permitted to see. There is yet a higher order of Viwa who can see even more, but that is not I.

Occasionally, I come together with others like myself in these gardens to address the events going on in your world, especially when it relates to the Viwa who go there. The higher order sometimes arrive here as well and there is a great discussion."

"I am so happy you can help us!" Nan exclaimed.

"Have I not already said that?" Eolande asked. "'Tis what I am here for."

"We were able to take our book before that awful Walter could find it and hand it over to the evil Viwa," Emma said. "I feel awfully sorry for his daughter, Helene, who was a part of his evil plot to have us captured. 'Twas not her fault, Eolande. We have forgiven her."

"'Tis kind and noble of you to forgive Helene," Eolande agreed. "I would have done the same. I sense that you are trying to hide something from me that you do not wish to tell. You do not know how happy 'twould make me feel to hear that you have this book. I can help you all the more if 'tis in your possession. Do you have it, Emma?"

"Nay, I do not," Emma confessed. A painful look of guilt was in her eyes as she hung her head. She waited patiently for Eolande's wrath to come crashing down around her. "I accidentally lost it on the way to the Land of the Diamond Sea."

"We were in such a hurry to get away from those evil Viwa knights, that it somehow fell out of her pocket," Richard said, coming to Emma's defense. "Pray forgive her mistake, Eolande. We would have brought it to you had we not been so careless."

Eolande stayed silent. He gazed at Richard, Emma, and Nan as if reflecting over about their misfortune. He did not become angry, but gave a heartfelt nod to each of them as he walked back over to the garden fountain.

"I do not doubt you about this terrible incident," Eolande finally said. "Accidents do happen. Do not worry that the book has been lost. There is always hope for its recovery. For now, I must introduce you to those of whom the three of you might find of interest, especially you, Richard."

Glancing over the heads of Richard and the girls, Eolande beckoned to someone.

"Come, come!" Eolande called out. "He is here. 'Twill be a most jubilant reunion for all of you!"

Richard and his two companions turned to see who Eolande was speaking to. The lad froze in horror at the sight of the men walking toward them. He reached for his sword as the girls ran behind him, cowering and shaking in fright.

"Stand back or I shall slay you right where you are!" Richard shouted. "Do not come any closer . . . I am warning you!"

There in front of them stood several Viwa men, very much like the evil Viwa whom Richard and the girls had crossed paths with time and again. These Viwa men had the trademark appearance of the Viwa fairies with their pale skin and shoulder-length fair hair. They had light eyes and lean, strapping bodies, which were quite tall. She wondered if tallness was part of being Viwa, too. In Nan's eyes, they were the spitting image of the two stewards who were standing in the castle kitchen. For Richard and Emma, their faces were akin to the Viwa in armor, except these men were not dressed for any battle. They wore brightly-colored tunics and hose and had leather shoes on their feet.

"Do my eyes deceive me?" one of the Viwa men said ecstatically, as he laid eyes on Richard.

"My lord!" cried out another. "You do not know what it means to have you come back to us, grown to almost manhood. You are, in many ways, much like your mother. There can be no doubt of who you are."

A third Viwa who was at the head of the entourage of fairies commanded, "Pray put away your sword, Aric! You are with friends, not enemies. I am Lord Hallam from the Province of Hallam in Viwa. I once held a position in the royal household during the reign of Princess Lavena. These other men are from other regions and provinces of Viwa. Like myself, they have been living in the Land of the Diamond Sea. There are also some younger men who have recently become disenchanted with their lives in Viwa and have left. We are gratified with their decision. There are not many their age, but they are here ready to champion our cause."

Lord Hallam and the other Viwa dropped on bended knee at the foot of Richard. They did not move from their place until Richard, becoming uncomfortable with this gesture, told them to arise as he returned his sword back into his scabbard. There were at least one hundred or more Viwa men surrounding Richard to near suffocation. Emma and Nan warily came out from behind Richard and stood next to him. The girls became remorseful about the mistaken identity of the good fairy men.

"You should know that I am not fond of being called this 'Aric'," Richard said in disgust. "This name has only brought me one misfortune after another. You may ask the lasses yourselves. Had I not been born as Aric, then I might have had a much better life as Richard. Richard is the name I prefer."

"Indeed we understand, my lord!" Lord Hallam replied. "If you do not wish to be called by your birth name, we will abide by it. We would not want to displease you. But it does not have to be this way—this living in fear of who you really are. Your rightful throne in Viwa will be yours one day—you will see!"

"*If* I want it!" Richard said brusquely.

The lad's head was throbbing. Things were happening too fast for him to understand. The unexpected meeting with these Viwa men, though good they might be, was more than he could handle in one day. He wished to be alone in his thoughts, so he meandered away from the fairies to a different section of the gardens. He wanted to peacefully mull over his life without any distractions.

CHAPTER 25

Emma waited until Richard was out of earshot. She went directly to Lord Hallam and begged, "Your lordship, Richard has been through so much as of late. Pray do not be offended by his actions. We thought you were Sir Erling and the other Viwa soldiers who were following us all the way to Meldon and back. We did not realize you were somebody else. You and your men look very much like them."

"Apology accepted, lass," Lord Hallam stated with a bow. "I fear that Richard is not eager to speak with us. You may tell him that he does not have to return to Viwa if he has no desire to. Being Viwa ourselves, there is no guesswork as to whom we would choose to rule over us. We would like nothing better than to have the direct bloodline and son of our dead princess on our throne. Since we have not been in Viwa for some time, we cannot easily do this. My men and I have been unfairly banished from our lands by Sir Erling and his scheming followers. He is an upstart and a usurper and cannot be trusted. He must be disposed of immediately!"

Richard was passively listening to the discussion between Lord Hallam and Emma until he heard the name of Sir Erling. He quickly rejoined the others from the corner of the gardens.

"Pray tell me your story, your lordship," Richard said to Lord Hallam. "I must warn you that I can be terribly stubborn at times. The lasses can attest to it. I sincerely believe I would not make a very good prince because my stubbornness. You would not be fond of my weakness."

Lord Hallam and the other Viwa men laughed and exchanged smiles with each other.

"No one said you had to be perfect!" Lord Hallam answered. He was clearly amused by Richard's comment. "From what I see and hear of you already, you are far better than Sir Erling can ever be. Let me tell you everything from the start."

"Good!" Richard replied. "I am very interested in this Sir Erling. What little we learned of this nemesis of mine was when we were waylaid in the gorge by him. Luckily, we were able to get away with a little help from a secret powder that I kept in my pocket."

Putting an arm around Richard's shoulder and taking him aside, Lord Hallam chronicled Richard's life from his birth in Viwa as Aric to how his mother accidentally perished at the hand of his father when he took some of her golden hair from her head. The story ended with the escape of Lord Robert with his infant son out of Viwa when the fairies wanted retaliation for his unintentional misdeed.

"Nothing you say, my Lord Hallam, is dissimilar to what Susanna, my old nurse, had conveyed to me at the Monastery of the White Friars," Richard declared. "We had gone there in hope of finding answers to the mysterious book that belonged to my father. We needed to have it translated, which Susanna had most graciously done for us. This book has only brought sorry upon Lamington. Christmas has been barred from it, and now, Sir Erling and his soldiers have decided, for one purpose or another, to bring down Lamington at any moment."

"Aye, that is so," Lord Hallam replied sadly, "and I will tell you why. When your father was in Viwa, there were very few fairies there who did not like him. He was quite popular with everyone, and they were delighted that he was happy with our Princess Lavena. Their lives were so perfect together. I shudder when I think of what had happened after your father took you out of Viwa after her death. Sometimes I feel that 'twas best that Lord Robert did. Had he not, the two of you would assuredly not be here today. If you have not guessed already, there was one fairy who was not thrilled with your father's existence there. His name was Sir Erling. Sir Erling wanted nothing better than to be rid of anyone who got in the way of the Viwa throne. Not that Lord Robert was ever in the way of it, but Sir Erling was angry at his cousin, the princess, for marrying someone by whom there would be children, pushing him further down the line as heir. He eyed the throne for himself!"

"My lord, how much you know of Sir Erling!" Emma said, her curiosity deepening about the evil fairy.

"I know more than I care to admit, lass," Lord Hallam said, shaking his head. "When the princess died, Sir Erling did everything in his power to turn the good Viwa against Lord Robert. This worked in Sir Erling's favor when Lord Robert innocently took a few hairs from Princess Lavena's head. The rest of us, though few in number, were able to see through his thin veil of deception. It pains me deeply to think that there are many young Viwa there that have no memory of the Princess Lavena and Lord Robert and the baby born to them—you, Richard! They only know of being ruled by Sir Erling, who is trouble, indeed. When he found out that there was but a few of us who did not believe that Lord Robert deliberately killed your mother, he had his loyal soldiers exile us from Viwa. He brutishly rounded us up and told us to leave, which he succeeded in doing. He set himself up as Prince of Viwa and will not share the throne with anyone there. He was always a vain creature. I cannot imagine that he will ever declare an heir on his deathbed. He likely believes himself to live forever! Thankfully, with your coming to the Land of the Diamond Sea, Richard, it changes everyone's fate in staying here because of Sir Erling."

"He knows I am alive and well," Richard remarked. "His greatest wish is to dispose of me as quickly as possible, though the reasons were vague until now. He has been pretending all along that he wants me to come back to Viwa as prince. I was almost starting to believe him!"

"You are learning fast about Sir Erling!" Lord Hallam stated. "I understand that he does not rule Viwa well. He is cruel to the fairy folk living there."

"I would not be shocked by someone of his caliber," Richard replied thoughtfully. "He is not treating those in Lamington so well, either, by lying in wait around the town walls until the people there starve. I realized back at the monastery why my father wanted me to remain as an ordinary guard at Castle Lamington rather than a knight. He wanted me near him, only working at a job that no one would think of me as having. He did not want to call attention to me. Had he, I might have been taken away sooner by Sir Erling and those who follow him blindly."

Nan, who was next to Emma, strained her ears to hear what Lord Hallam was saying to Richard. She liked nothing more than for Sir Erling to be punished to the highest degree for his wrongdoing.

"So 'tis Sir Erling's fault that we are not celebrating Christmas in Lamington, is it not?" Nan asked Lord Hallam.

"Aye, Sir Erling *is* the instigator for prohibiting Christmas there," Lord Hallam replied. "He believed that once Lord Robert read the book and realized how much the spell was affecting his people, he would send his son back to Viwa. Unwittingly, he would be handing his child over to Sir Erling, the one and only ruler there."

Richard shook his head in disgust. He circled around the stone fountain as he listened to Lord Hallam.

"He and his knights desperately tried to capture Richard several times, but praise God, he has failed!" Emma declared. "Even at the Monastery of the White Friars, too."

"I am not too surprised they have failed there," Lord Hallam said. "A holy place such as that would scare those evil Viwa away. They can only try so hard in such a place, so they have to go elsewhere to do their evil work. This is why they are encamped around Lamington. They cannot get you, Richard, so they want their final revenge on the town and all who live there. We can thank Eolande for telling us this. Without his foreknowledge, we would not know what Sir Erling was up to these days."

"Brother Matthew was on to something when he said that the Viwa left because of the monastery," Emma added.

"Pray do not remind me about what happened there on the hillside!" Nan cried. "If the brothers had not found us . . . Ugh! I do not want to think of it."

"Would my father had known that the book's spell was meant for him to turn me over to the evil fairies?" Richard said, also trying to dismiss those awful events of the Viwa from his mind. He pondered all that Lord Hallam had told them so far. While some things made sense, others did not.

"The spell would have driven him to do it," Lord Hallam answered in earnest, "but as we all know, Sir Erling did not get his wish. In the meantime, there is only one way to end these tribulations once and for all. Do you have the book?"

Richard and the girls glanced at each other in embarrassment. They refused to answer Lord Hallam. Emma flushed a rosy red, as she stared at the good Viwa lord, before finally looking away.

Seeing the three young people's difficulty in admitting anything about the book's disappearance, Eolande came to their aid.

"Richard and the two lasses here had it until they escaped from Sir

Erling and his soldiers, Lord Hallam. 'Twas not their fault. After what they had gone through to get here, some things did not work out as planned."

Lord Hallam looked dejected at this delivery of negative news.

"We will go and search for it then!" Lord Hallam stated. "If it fell somewhere in the forest, or is lying somewhere in the snow, it can easily be retrieved. My men and I will take that chance if we have to. What say you, Eolande? 'Tis important that it be found."

"You would be wasting your time if you did, my lord," Emma interrupted. "'Tis now in the hands of that brute, Sir Erling. He held it up for us to see when we were being chased by him. I am sorry that my carelessness had caused this. I was the one who was carrying the book all along. It fell out of my pocket without my knowing."

Lord Hallam did not know what to say as he broodingly rubbed his chin. The other Viwa men said nothing as they watched him closely, waiting for him to find the right words in regard to the lost object.

"Here and gone in an instant," Lord Hallam replied with a long sigh, dropping his hand from his chin.

Some of the fairy men who were near Lord Hallam shook their heads and groaned in disappointment at the loss of the book.

"If the book were here," Lord Hallam declared, "the lost jewel that rested inside its front cover could be reclaimed. The spell would be broken. The return of Christmas is the return of all good everywhere. Sir Erling is well aware of it."

" "I remember something of the like missing from the book when we were at the monastery!" Nan said excitedly. "Father John and Brother Albert said they would look for the jewel when I mentioned the small empty hole for it. Unfortunately, they did not find it anywhere."

"'Twould not be at the monastery, lass, and you will soon see why," Lord Hallam responded. "Before we were banished out of Viwa, we sent some of our spies to listen in on some of Sir Erling's evildoings. We found out that he had arranged a meeting with the One from the Onyx Gate. The One from the Onyx Gate is a dark spirit who wields great power. For those Viwa who want to go the way of the wicked road in life, he is eager to assist them. Sir Erling and his men now had the ability, with the power of this dark spirit, to create this book with a removable jewel. The book was then given its evil spell, woven into the words that Lord Robert would eventually say at the opportune time."

"I just knew there was something about the book when Sir Erling's interest in it seemed more than a passing thing!" Richard exclaimed.

"We can assist you in locating the jewel, Lord Hallam!" Emma said with great anticipation.

Lord Hallam shook his head and without answering, he strolled over to some red climbing roses and engaged himself for some time by smelling their sweet fragrance.

Sir Ivo, one of the many fairy men who was in Lord Hallam's company, came forward to speak.

"How kind of you to offer help in finding the jewel, lass, but you are not the one to find it," Sir Ivo said. "His lordship here is too troubled to tell you what must be done. 'Tis easy enough for us to find the book, but not if 'tis in the possession of Sir Erling. Getting it back from him will take careful preparation. We cannot go and ask him for it. Nay, that will not work! However, to replace the jewel in the book is not a job for any of us here. There is only one who can do it and that is you, Nan. The little jewel is an emerald, shaped in the form of a holly leaf. We understand that this jewel was placed in some real holly, which was given to you, lass, in Lamington. While the real holly was in your hands, the emerald leaf in it triggered a power within the book. Lord Robert, sitting in his castle, immediately started reading the passage found there. And so he would— again and again! Once some blue snow fell out of the sky, 'twas a sign that his lordship was reading from the book. Thus, every tragedy that had happened afterward was its consequence. This holly *must* still be in your home, if you took it there. Therefore, you must be the one to go and bring back the emerald so it can be placed into the cover of the book, ending its wretched power it has over everyone."

"Similar conclusions about the book were made by some at Castle Lamington," Emma said. "How painful to hear how correct those conclusions were! How much more painful to hear what Nan must now do!"

"And how I thought coming here to the Land of the Diamond Sea would only bring an end to my troubles," Nan replied half-heartedly. "I see it has not! What you have just said proves what Brother Albert translated from Lord Robert's book at the Monastery of the White Friars. Why was I, and not somebody else, chosen to do this?"

"Because you are young and unsuspecting, lass, which is why you had the great misfortunate of being picked out single-handedly to do their evil deed in Lamington," Eolande murmured. "Nothing is ever done by accident with these evil individuals. It could have happened to any innocent lad or lass in Lamington, if that is some comfort to you, child."

Nan looked up at Eolande and nodded her head in understanding. She knew deep down that it would take years to fully understand this horrific and unintentional action that she had performed and many more to expel it from her mind completely.

"They must have been spying on Nan for a while," Richard said "The picture of the girl in the book is a remarkable resemblance to her. They did their planning with the book and the holly exceptionally well, indeed, even going so far as to impersonate servants from Castle Lamington when they gave the holly to her. Those two false stewards placed the book in the chest that came from his lordship's deceased uncle, Lord Anselm, so everyone would think it came from him. 'Tis starting to make sense to me."

"Very likely they had been scouting Nan out and did the very things you say," Sir Ivo admitted. "The evil fairies knew how to scheme well their parts in this."

Nan broke down in a fit of sobs. "I do not care what anybody tells me. 'Tis all my fault for what has befallen Lamington! Why me? Why? Why? I live in peace with my family. We do not bother anybody. I did not deserve this to happen to me!"

Lord Hallam finally wandered back to the others and looked at Nan with pity.

"Do not feel that way, lass," Lord Hallam said softly. "As Eolande had said, they could have sought after any lass, or lad, to do their bidding." Looking at Richard, he stated, "Those two false stewards most definitely would want you to think that the book came from Lord Anselm. After all, he is dead and cannot answer for it. Those criminal Viwa would not want fingers to be pointed in their direction, if it were ever found out the book came from them. In their own eyes, why should they be blamed for such evil? Do they want a multitude coming after them over it? What cowards they are! Sir Erling is not perfect, though he touts himself to be."

Richard kept shaking his head vigorously with downcast eyes.

"Nan, you must not fault yourself for the predicament we are in," Richard said. "Had I not been born, none of this would have happened.

We would not be standing here in these gardens squabbling over a book with a spell, which must be broken to bring back Christmas, that was unknowingly cast over Lamington by my father because of— "

"Lad!" Eoland said sharply. "Calm yourself! I command it! You were born with a purpose and that purpose you must live out. You cannot blame yourself, either, for what happened to your father. Sir Erling was taking advantage of a tragic situation. He wanted the throne of Viwa. He found the perfect opportunity to get it through the death of his cousin, but he will not be on the Viwa throne for long as 'tis not for him to have. Your father did well to guide you here to the Land of the Diamond Sea. 'Tis here that this squabbling, as you call it, will end. A solution will be found to right all wrongs. Everyone should stop blaming themselves for the loss of Christmas, or for being born, and so forth. Let us go into the hall. 'Tis there that we will think of something with a sane head, and we will not leave until we do so."

CHAPTER 26

Eolande wandered out of the gardens and back into the great hall. Following him were the three young people, Lord Hallam, and the other fairy men. Eolande went up to the dais at the front of the room, while the others sat down on benches closest to him, or stood lining the walls of the hall. The hall had become so crowded, it soon became oppressively warm from the many bodies breathing together, as the fire continued to burn in the wall nearby.

Nan secretly wanted these fairy men to go to Lamington and, while overtaking Sir Erling and his army, bring back the emerald they so needed to break the spell. There were so many of Lord Hallam's men! Why could *they* just not do it? She silently prayed that she could somehow avoid going back to Lamington, if they still insisted upon her to get the emerald. Searching for it seemed like such a dangerous feat. Getting past Sir Erling and his men without being noticed was near to impossible. A feeling of dread crept over Nan.

After what seemed like many hours of discussion and debate in the hall, it was decided that Nan *would* return home to Lamington to find the holly leaf-shaped emerald. It was further decided that Lord Hallam and his fairy men would go into Sir Erling's camp and, while trying to bring him and his army down, find the book that was taken by the evil fairy leader.

"With Lord Hallam being there, 'twould also serve as a distraction for Nan to find her way into the town unnoticed," Eolande stated. "There! 'Tis settled. I knew we could come to some agreement if we remained composed and thought this out carefully."

"Eolande, is there no other who can go in my place to recover the jewel and bring it back here?" Nan asked, getting up from her bench and coming closer to Eolande on his dais. "I do not have the courage to take on such a task. See my hands tremble with fear. What if I fail?"

"If you have courage, you will not fail, Nan," Eolande replied with a smile. "I will find one of the best men in Viwa to escort you as far as the town gate. From that point on, you will be on your own. It must be made clear. I, myself, will not be there, but I will watch out for you and protect you from afar as much as I can. Never fear something you think you cannot accomplish, lass."

Nan went to sit back down on the bench and nodded with optimism. She was happy to know that Eolande would be there watching over her in his own peculiar way. She could not ask for anything less as she sighed in relief and prayed that the mission would go well.

Richard, who was leaning against the wall near the dais, asked, "What about my father, Eolande? We talk about him here, but I am not sure if anyone knows of his situation. Well, I will tell you. He is hiding as an old hermit in the forest right outside the walls of Lamington. He had disappeared from Castle Lamington before Christmas during a hunt that he was on with some of his knights. He never returned. Lady Catherine was terribly upset by this. We must find his lordship before Sir Erling does!"

"Rest assured, your father will be brought to safety," Eolande declared to Richard. "I know where he is. One of Lord Hallam's soldiers will bring him back to the Land of the Diamond Sea while the rest of them are on their way to Lamington."

"I am all for our decision in going back to Lamington, Eolande, except for one problem," Lord Hallam said with reservation. "'Tis somewhat suicidal for us to do. I can only make several hundred soldiers out of the men whom I have, but Sir Erling has many thousands of them! We are outnumbered greatly. Even the blades of the swords we brought with us to the Land of the Diamond Sea are now old and dull. Our horses are too old and tired to move. Sir Erling and his soldiers are fresh out of Viwa with new equipment and weapons, and animals that are sprite and young. We will be outrun before Nan can ever make it back here. Sir Erling will have the last laugh. How can this be done?"

"You forget that you are dealing with Eolande here," Eolande replied with a chuckle. "I will provide you with the best armor and swords that Sir Erling has ever seen. I will also get you the best horses you have ever encountered in your lifetime, Lord Hallam. Even if there are less of you, there is a way to do things as long as I am there with you. You may also take some time to practice for this battle out back behind the castle. There are plenty of open meadows to learn the art of war. With me, 'twill not take long for you to sharpen your fighting skills. Does that suffice your needs, my lord?"

"Aye, it does," Lord Hallam replied with a grin. He stood up from his bench and bowed respectfully to Eolande, much to the cheers and smiles of the other fairy men in the room who shared his feelings on the matter. "You are very generous to us, Eolande. 'Twill not be forgotten!"

Standing up from his seat, Eolande walked down from the dais toward Nan.

"There is one thing that I have not told you yet, lass, but I must, no matter how trying 'tis for me to do it," Eolande said, stopping in front of Nan. He fixed his gray eyes on her for some time before his smile slowly faded from his mouth.

Everyone's curiosity heightened.

What was Eolande secretively referring to?

Though the fairy men in the great hall had that excellent Viwa hearing they were well-known for, they strained their ears so they would not miss one word from Eolande.

"You may think 'tis difficult to get the jewel from your home, but that will be the easy part of your task," Eolande stated. "The most demanding part is bringing it here so you can place it back into the hole of the book cover. Nan, the One from the Onyx Gate will be closely watching you at all times while you are carrying the jewel. No amount of help from us will prevent that from happening, even if all of Lord Hallam's soldiers escorted you from Lamington back to the Land of the Diamond Sea. No harm will come to you, except that which comes from playing with the mind. The One from the Onyx Gate will aggressively try and convince you, despite my best protection, that there is no need to bring the emerald leaf here. He does this best through temptation. I know him well and his deeds, too, which are less than desirable to any man or beast."

Nan's eyes flew open wide. She quivered over what Eolande was warning her about. She did not like the sound of this at all!

Who is this One from the Onyx Gate? Was he the one Lord Hallam spoke of as creating the book that Lord Robert read from so Christmas could be destroyed in Lamington? From where would the One from the Onyx Gate be watching?

She rethought the matter. She decided that she definitely would not revisit her family's cottage to get this jewel. She would insist that somebody else go. But would Eolande be so duped by a farmer's daughter such as herself? Likely not, and she knew it. He was too clever and too powerful for the antics of a mere peasant girl from Lamington, but she was willing to try and persuade him anyway.

"Eolande, if this jewel is in the sprig of holly somewhere at my home, then I cannot be sure that 'tis still there," Nan said with a flustered smile. "When Christmas was banned from Lamington, I did not see the holly strung up over our door like it was before it. I do not know if my mother threw it away or not. She may even have burnt it in the fire. If she did, then the jewel is gone forever."

What a perfect excuse for Nan not to go back to Lamington! She only hoped that Eolande would accept it. He would have to. Yet, if she wanted Christmas and the old way of life to come back to her town—along with seeing those evil Viwa gone from there for good— she must face the fact that she would be journeying to Lamington, no matter how much the idea did not appeal to her. If the jewel *was* gone, she would be the one who would have to check the ashes in the hearth.

Eolande knitted his brow as he wagged his finger playfully at her. He shook his head while the curls on his head flew this way and that.

"'Twould be difficult to burn up any jewel in a fire, especially one that fairies use," he said. "They would not find one so inferior, if there ever was such a one, especially when 'twould be used to evoke a spell to suit their own ends. If the emerald was thrown in the fire, then I can guarantee that 'tis still lying there in the cinders. The jewel will be sparkling bright and new, just like on the first day 'twas taken from the book that Lord Robert read from and placed in the holly that was given to you."

"I did not realize that," Nan replied, as she dropped her eyes from Eolande. She became thoughtful and sullen. Eolande had gotten the best of her. She unenthusiastically had to go through with the original plan.

"You cannot do nothing Nan!" Emma exclaimed. "Look at the pain and suffering this emerald has brought us! If you wish, I will go back to Lamington with you to get it."

"Nay, Emma!" Eolande answered sternly. "You will not go with her to get the emerald leaf. You will stay here in the Land of the Diamond Sea until Nan returns. My assignment from the one who is above me is to only watch over one of you. Nan's daunting task is more than what I can handle. The One from the Onyx Gate would like nothing more than to have more people working Nan's mind to return the emerald to him who placed a fiendish spell over it. You would be of more help to him than you know! He enjoys evil for the sake of it. There is no other purpose to his existence. If he gets his hands on the jewel, then the problems in Lamington will remain in place forever."

"I cannot leave her, Eolande!" Emma objected. "We have journeyed together from Lamington to the Monastery of the White Friars and finally here. So much had happened to us in between. We have become close companions. I cannot see why I cannot try to help her until the very end. What harm can come of it? Mayhap that One from the Onyx Gate will have a change of heart."

Richard got up from his seat and walked over to Emma. He looked down at her with pity as she sat there pleading with Eolande.

"Emma, the One from the Onyx Gate is *very* powerful," Richard whispered to her. "Lord Hallam had filled me in further about this darkness just a moment ago. The One from the Onyx Gate is more evil than you or I can ever imagine. If the One from the Onyx Gate tempts you, 'twill be easier for him to convince Nan through you to bring the emerald back to him, especially if Eolande is not able to protect the two of you together. I would not want to see either of you lasses harmed by this evil influence. Do you not understand that?"

"I do not care!" Emma said. "I will take that chance and go with her. Neither you, Richard, nor Eolande can stop me!"

Emma tossed her head in disgust and turned away from Richard.

Richard turned from Emma and looked at Eolande helplessly.

"Things will work out well for Nan, as long as I am there," Eolande said, placing a tender hand on Nan's shoulder. "Remember to stay focused on your quest when you leave Lamington with the jewel, lass. There will be much fighting going on around Lamington then, but those in combat will not notice your taking leave of town, except for the one we spoke of. Just find your way to the Land of the Diamond Sea by way of which you came the first time. When the One from the Onyx Gate sees you, keep up your courage and strength."

"How will I know when he is around?" Nan asked. "What will he look like? When will he show himself?"

"His plans change all the time, so how they materialize is up to

257

him," Eolande replied. "You will know once you leave Lamington. I will do all in my power to keep you from his temptations, but as you are from your world, even I can only do so much to help you, if you do not want that help."

"You are more certain of me than I am of myself," Nan said sighing. "I hope you are right, Eolande, but as you are greater than I, a poor farmer's daughter, then there is something to that. You know more than I will ever know, though much of what you say about the One from the Onyx Gate is like riddles to me."

Eolande let out a booming laugh that echoed throughout the great hall.

"Nan, you amuse me! I will only doubt your ability to get back to the Land of the Diamond Sea if you start paying attention to the One from the Onyx Gate. If you do not, then a painless journey 'twill be. Is that agreed? It may not be as simple as this, but think of it as similar to the time when you tried hard not to taste a little of your mother's best sweet pies cooling on the window sill before supper. You wanted to, but you were able to overcome the enticement of doing it."

"Eolande, how did you ever know I tried to taste one of my mother's pies?" Nan asked, her spirits lifting a little. "That has not happened since I was a wee one."

"I know lots of things, lass," Eolande affirmed. "Now, remember what I said and no harm will come to you."

CHAPTER 27

A loud crash came from somewhere within the castle. Nan looked over at the door of the great hall. Lord Hallam's men were stepping aside to make way for a bent figure, stumbling around and wheezing loudly as he entered. The figure was wearing a very familiar cloak, unclean and threadbare. As the hood fell off, a disheveled head of auburn hair and an overgrown beard in a grubby face was visible. Nan and Emma jumped from their bench as the old hermit fell down before them on his knees, his sword falling out from underneath the cloak he was wearing.

"His lordship!" Nan shrieked.

"He has found his way to the Land of the Diamond Sea!" Emma said.

The old hermit tried to raise himself on his elbows as his eyes darted around the room searching for something. Richard left the girls and ran to the hermit's side.

"Richard! Richard!" cried the old hermit.

He tried to stand up, but crumpled to the ground. Lord Robert the old hermit coughed for a long time before he continued to speak.

"My son! I am so sorry about what I have done to you all these years. If there is even a shred of pity in your heart for me, pray forgive me. I had to get here! I just had to be . . . ."

"My lord!" Richard said, reaching his hand out to Lord Robert.

Eolande immediately rushed forward to help Richard pull his lordship up from the floor. He then began to shout out orders to his servants.

"Take Lord Robert to a bedchamber so he can rest!" Eolande bellowed. "He has come a long way and is not well." Speaking to Richard, he said, "There will be plenty of time later to converse with him, lad, once his health improves. It may take several days or weeks, but he is safe here. Life has not been kind to him lately, and he can use a hot meal and a good bed."

Richard and the girls watched as some servants led his lordship out of the hall. Eolande waited patiently as Lord Robert disappeared from sight before turning to the others. He encouraged them to go back to their bedchambers to get some rest of their own.

"We will speak more of things tomorrow," Eolande announced with a bow. Pulling Richard aside as everyone was clearing the room, he added, "Richard, you and the lasses have been through much recently. Get some sleep. Your minds will be sharper after that. Since our plans have been laid out, there is nothing further that can be done today. Lord Hallam and his men will begin preparing for battle. Your time has come, lad, where you will join the others on the battlefield as you should have been all along. You will become a squire alongside your father there. I doubt he will want to stay here in the Land of the Diamond Sea once he gets back to his old self. He will want reprisal for the evil deeds of Sir Erling and his spiteful men!"

"I can only pray that I am ready for what I will be encountering," Richard replied, unsure of himself. "I feel like I already had a taste of the Viwa and their fighting to and from the Monastery of the White Friars."

"You will learn, and learn well, with Lord Hallam and his men as they refine their skills in our large meadows here," Eolande said with encouragement. "They will involve you in every aspect of fighting. You will become experienced in everything there is to know on the battlefield. Your father will help you as well. He has fought a few wars himself. Once you gain enough skill as a squire, other options await you. I cannot imagine that you will stay a squire forever. You are too brave and clever a lad for that. I do not believe that becoming an ordinary knight is something you will want for yourself, either. Your future has many prospects. Do not forget that."

"I suppose you mean that I will want to go back to Viwa and become prince to the fairies there," Richard quietly said.

"Do not worry about whether you should be a prince there or not, Richard," Eolande advised. "At least, not now. Take one step at a time and see where things lead. You may change your mind yet."

"I know," Richard answered. "Lord Hallam has said just as much."

Just moments before, Nan and Emma left ahead of Eolande and Richard. Before going back to their bedchamber, they decided to wait for Richard in the shadows of the dimly lit corridor. While they waited, Nan eavesdropped on the muffled conversation he was having with Eolande.

"Do you hear what Eolande is telling Richard?" Nan whispered with a grin.

"What do you mean, Nan?" Emma asked quizzically. "I cannot hear a word. I am too exhausted. I want nothing more than to drift off to sleep in a proper bed."

"I have a feeling that the clothing he was given today was deliberate," Nan replied. "He is being prepared for his future as prince of the Viwa. You wait, Emma! He will be Prince of Viwa. I heard Eolande suggesting it to him."

"That is not a surprise, is it?" Emma said, stifling a yawn behind her hand. "Of course, 'tis only if he wants to be prince. He is not eager for it. Has he not said so?"

"Aye, he has said so," Nan stated. "But I am starting to think we were given beautiful gowns because Eolande *does* know something. 'Tis sort of like how he will protect me from afar when I go back to Lamington, whatever that means. The gowns were meant to prepare us to be in the presence of someone great, although I do not know why I should be given one to wear."

Emma brooded over Nan's words. "There may be some truth in what you say, Nan. Outside of that, we are not really sure of the future, are we? I am not sure Eolande is, either. Or, if he does, he is not telling us. One thing I do know is that you will soon have quite an ordeal going back home to get the emerald. I meant it when I said I would accompany you there. That Eolande! He is wrong not to let me."

Emma stood staring ahead of her, angry at Eolande's response. "If I can find a way to do it, I will!"

"I believe you, Emma," Nan replied. "Eolande has given a very good reason for you not to go. You would not want to find yourself in trouble with me, would you?"

"I . . . I do not care to wait for Richard anymore," Emma mumbled unintelligibly and disappeared down the castle corridor.

Nan was left miffed at the other girl's words. Richard came walking out of the hall just in time to catch the end of their conversation.

"Do not fret," Richard reassured Nan. "I heard what Emma said. I will have Eolande speak to her. You are a capable and strong girl, lass. I also believe you will return to the Land of the Diamond Sea without anyone's help and unscathed by the One from the Onyx Gate. Eolande will be watching both the men and I from afar, too. He will be anxious for our welfare, both on our way out to Lamington with you and when we find ourselves on the battlefield."

"I pray you are right about me, Richard," Nan murmured. "If not, then everything you are fighting for will come to naught. What a tragedy that would be."

CHAPTER 28

The first few days spent in the Land of the Diamond Sea went by peacefully for Emma and Nan. They explored Eolande's beautiful castle gardens and wandered the castle corridors aimlessly, until Emma found the castle library, which she lost herself in, while Nan went off in search of her own fun. Nan also took note that Emma did not bring up the idea of leaving with her to Lamington. She assumed that Richard made good on his word and had asked Eolande to speak with Emma about her foolhardy plan, making the matter moot. After a week had gone by, the girls began to notice Richard's absence. He had not gone out of his way to search for his companions, which left them baffled as to his whereabouts. They soon learned from Eolande that he was spending much of his time with Lord Robert in his sick room. Richard had no desire to leave his lordship's side until he became well.

"There is much for them to catch up on after all these years," Eolande told the girls. "Do not feel slighted by this. Richard will come around when he feels the need to be with you again. His father is his first and foremost priority right now."

"Eolande, do you think 'twill not be long before Lord Hallam and his men fight Sir Erling?" Nan asked. "I worry that if they do not go soon, Sir Erling will enter Lamington and destroy it before anyone else has a chance to get there."

"I also worry about Lady Catherine," Emma said. "She is a captive of the castle now that the Viwa had taken over Lamington. I grieve for her day and night. I wonder what she is doing and thinking—praying that she has gotten over the distress the Viwa stewards have placed upon her. She must also be wondering what has happened to us as we have not been home in months."

"Do not worry, lasses," Eolande reassured the girls. "If I foresee anything that Sir Erling and his men may attempt to do, which will further threaten the safety of the people of Lamington, I will warn Lord Hallam that he will have to ready himself and his men immediately. But I do not see that happening there yet. Before Sir Erling ever strikes Lamington, he will likely surround the town walls for many months before doing so. What he does not know is what we have in store for him. You also forget that Richard himself needs to get to work on perfecting his battle skills once he is able to tear himself away from his father. Lord Hallam and his men are already in the meadows this morning perfecting theirs. Now, I must be off as I have much work to attend to."

With a hasty bow of his head, Eolande strolled off to another part of his vast castle before Emma or Nan had anything else to ask of him.

"He is a strange man," Nan stated as she watched Eolande disappear from view. "What work does he need to do? He never seems to be very busy to me. He is rarely away from us for very long. I do not know what to make of Eolande, do you?"

"Nay, I do not," Emma said wistfully. "He is very good to us, though. A most trustworthy and sympathetic man without a doubt."

"He is a good man, but I do not have the nerve to ask him *what* he is exactly," Nan said.

"Nor have I, but we know *who* he is," Emma noted. "He did say he is the head of the highest order of Viwa. Though we hear him speak in our language, he also converses with Lord Hallam and his fairy men in the Viwa tongue when they are alone. In fact, I heard them doing so early this morning in the hall. I know what language it is, because I asked."

"He is not the head, Emma," Nan replied, shaking her head. "When we first met him in the gardens, he mentioned that there is one who is above him and that he is *one* of the highest order of Viwa, so he is not the leader of the good fairies."

"He is too grand a figure of power and interest to have a plain maidservant asking such questions of him, anyway," Emma declared with a wave of her hand. "'Tis best not to worry too much about who or what he is. I like him just as he is, and so should you."

"You, Emma! A *plain* maidservant?" Nan was taken aback by Emma's humble observation of herself. "You said yourself your own mother was a highborn lady. Why, no doubt, you can become something greater than a maidservant to her ladyship."

"So true," Emma answered. "One thing I would like better to do is to get the best horse that Eolande has here in the Land of the Diamond Sea, grab a fine sword, and go into battle against those evil Viwa outside of Lamington. They disgust me the more we stay here doing nothing."

Fear crept into Nan's mind.

Here she goes! She is bringing up becoming a battle maiden again. I hope Eolande has had a long talk with her. Mayhap she is fuming over the Viwa and this is her way of doing it.

"Emma, do not speak of fighting the Viwa!" Nan scolded. "The men are in the meadows practicing their fighting skills as we speak. A moment ago, Eolande told us they were."

Emma nodded her head. "I will try and put my worries behind me, Nan. If I do not, then I might do something rash that I will regret. Eolande does not need to burden himself with the foolishness of a maidservant when there are more pressing issues that need attention."

Nan patted Emma's arm as she said, "'Twill not be long before Richard joins the other men in the meadows. When he does, we can rest our minds. Sir Erling's last days in Lamington will be getting near their end."

Not for another week longer would Richard emerge from Lord Robert's sick room in search of Emma and Nan. Finding the girls in their usual place in the gardens, Richard sat down next to them in the cool grass as he apologized for his recent aloofness.

"I am sure Eolande has already told you where I was all this time," Richard said.

"He has," Emma answered. "I hope Lord Robert is feeling well and more himself these days."

"He is doing much better and has finally made peace with me as I with him," Richard explained. "Most of what he has said to me was either private or not too much different than what was told by Susanna and Lord Hallam, but . . . there were a few things I had not known."

"What wonderful news, Richard!" Nan said smiling. She was genuinely happy for Richard knowing that the heart-rendering story of his young life was turning out for the better since Lord Robert's arrival in the Land of the Diamond Sea.

Emma and Nan sat impatiently waiting for further details from

Richard.

"Well, what have you learned?" Nan pressed. "You will tell us, will you not?"

"Indeed, I will!" Richard exclaimed. "His lordship said that he deliberately hid from Walter and his daughter—though 'twas not the only reason why—because he saw Sir Erling speaking to Walter in the forest one day. He suspected that their conversation was about him whom it undeniably was. He heard enough from a distance to learn that the Viwa knights planned on scouring every end of Lamington Forest and the kingdom, if necessary, to find Lord Robert after his disappearance from Castle Lamington. Once they did, they would take him back to Viwa and have him placed in a dark dungeon, never to be released, as punishment for things he did not, or would not, do!"

"They are very evil!" Emma remarked, shaking her head relentlessly. "All the more reason I do not care for those Viwa. I am grateful they had not found him."

"There is something else!" Richard continued. "His lordship also said that while he was living in the forest, he had many a chance to see those Viwa come and go regularly from Lamington. He had seen them on the road taking the knights from Siddell, who had come with us, and making them prisoner in the camp they have made around Lamington. He had also seen a Viwa knight take as hostage one of the brothers from the Monastery of the White Friars. He only saw one being taken by them, but 'tis likely the second one was taken prisoner as well. At least we know for certain of their fate. I would rather know the truth by his lordship than by Sir Erling. Helene was also not wrong in seeing a brother taken by the Viwa."

"I pray that they are safe and well," Nan said softly, as she folded her hands and briefly closed her eyes. Her mind flashed back momentarily to the kindly brothers who had taken such good care of them at the monastery. Opening her eyes, she said, "I have often thought of Father John since our leaving Meldon. I wonder what has been his fate. Has his lordship said anything of him?"

"He has said nothing to me of Father John," Richard answered. "I can only assume that he has not seen him or surely he would have told me."

"Dear Father John!" Emma said. "I have almost forgotten about the gentle chaplain. I remember he said he would be coming back to

Lamington once the trouble there ended."

"We can only hope that word has gotten back to Meldon by this time from travelers about the capture of Lamington," Richard said. "At least he would be wise enough to stay away."

The girls nodded in agreement as they sat quietly thinking about Father John and what had become of him. Seeing the forlorn atmosphere of his companions, Richard quickly changed the subject. Though the next topic did not have a ring of cheer anymore than the first, it would get their minds off the chaplain they came to know and love so well.

"There is one other thing that made me sick at heart," Richard stated. "His lordship told me that had he not escaped out of Lamington after barring Christmas from it, there was a strong possibility that, in time, the spell would have permeated into other areas of the kingdom where Christmas would have disappeared from there, too. He said he kept hearing voices over and over in his head, while reading the book's passage, telling him so, in addition to insisting that he send me back to Viwa, which he was against. He felt he had no other choice than to leave before the evil spread far and wide, even if it meant leaving behind Lady Catherine. He thought she would be safe in Lamington if he removed himself from there for a time, but when I told him about those Viwa stewards and what they had done inside the castle, he became terribly upset and worried about her ladyship. However, he is glad that I had left the castle not long after he did."

"We must forgive his lordship for leaving Lamington," Emma said. "'Twas not his fault for doing it."

"Indeed! 'Twas not my fault! How that accursed book tried to ruin me. The spell in it kept spinning the absurd lie that Princess Lavena wanted to punish me for her unintended death, though this spell did force me to take Christmas from my people. The spell had other motives, too. Through it, Sir Erling wanted to impose pain and disaster upon me for his own ends. Had I not read from the book, I would not have lived like an animal in that filthy hovel all those months. I do not want to see the book again!"

Standing over everyone was the tall, imposing form of Lord Robert. No longer did he look like the untidy hermit they had found in the old cottage. His auburn beard and hair was neatly trimmed and combed. He wore a fresh tunic with bright hose to match.

Richard and the girls arose from the ground to face his lordship. Richard bowed as the girls came and knelt briefly in his presence. Nan wondered if Lord Robert remembered her when she came to see him at Castle Lamington. If he did, he made no indication of it.

"I hope you are feeling well, my lord," Emma said.

"I am feeling much better, Emma," Lord Robert replied. "I see Richard has told you something of what was said between he and I during these last several days together. I feel grateful to have survived the escape I made from the forest to the Land of the Diamond Sea. I was uneasy the whole way, thinking that I would find myself in Sir Erling's hands. I will have Sir Erling's and those two peasants' heads when I capture them, both for what they had planned for me *and* for you, Richard!"

"I would not blame Helene for what could have happened to me or to you, my lord," Richard pleaded. "She was acting against her will and according to her father's threats. She told us so when Sir Erling and his group of knights came upon us in the gorge. Walter took offense to Helene telling on him and threatened her yet again while they were with the fairy knights."

Lord Robert did not answer. He nodded slowly as he listened to what the lad was telling him. Nan prayed that his lordship would spare Helene any punishment if she and her father were taken prisoner by him.

"I must admit my folly for not doing anything after I ran away from Castle Lamington," Lord Robert stated with regret as he walked about the gardens, examining the beautiful flowers with great interest. "I should have come here to the Land of the Diamond Sea after I left, but I did not. Instead, I went away licking my wounds in the woods and wishing that all the bad things I had gone through would disappear on their own. But, nay! They did not, did they? I should have been wiser in helping you, Richard, after all these years. None of what we are presently going through would be taking place. There is something else that I have not yet told you, my son. What prompted me to finally make my move to come here was something that I overheard Sir Erling tell one of his soldiers on the road. He said that Lady Catherine is going to have a child."

Emma's eyebrows shot up with surprise as Nan's heart leapt at the good news of Lady Catherine's impending child. Nan stole a look at Richard to see his reaction, but she was unable to read anything from his face.

Will this baby become his lordship's heir to Lamington? Nan asked herself. *Or, has Lord Robert made Richard the future lord of Lamington during their conversation in the sick room? If so, what would Lady Catherine think once she learned that Richard was his son? Would she let Richard stand in the way of her child?*

"What news!" Emma said, her eyes sparkling with joy. "I hope she is well. I have only her best interest and happiness in mind, my lord. I am also worried about her condition, and the stress she must be enduring with the enemy nearby."

"Aye, Emma," Lord Robert responded. "I am gravely concerned for her well-being, too, but she is not the only one I fear for. My people need defending, and where is the lord of Lamington? Here, where he should not be! They need a strong leader, but they are leaderless. My soldiers can only hold out for so long—though some would do well enough without me—but I need to be with them."

Turning back to Richard, Lord Robert declared, "I need to improve my battle skills, and you need to learn yours, so we can return to Lamington without delay and reach out to those in need. Come! Where is Lord Hallam? We need to get together with him and his men to prepare for our war against Sir Erling. This despicable tyrant must be driven back to Viwa, unless the point of my sword gets to him first!"

Lord Robert turned to exit the castle gardens with Richard hastily behind him. As if remembering something, his lordship stopped sharply and looked at Nan.

"You are the lass that came to Castle Lamington," Lord Robert said. "I remember you well. Eolande has told me what your mission will be once we return to Lamington. Pray do not disappoint us when you return there. You know what you must do. 'Tis crucial that you perform your job exactly as you have been told. We will be awaiting your safe return to the Land of the Diamond Sea with the emerald safe in your hand."

"I will, my lord," Nan answered, lowering her eyes diffidently as Lord Robert bowed and left. Emma and Nan stayed behind to discuss Lady Catherine in private.

"Something troubles me, Nan," Emma said, sitting back down the grass.

"I wonder if 'tis the same of which troubles me," Nan replied.

"It came to mind when his lordship announced the upcoming birth of their child," Emma stated, looking over her shoulder nervously. "Lady

Catherine may not know the true identity of Richard . . . that he is the son of Lord Robert. We talked about this with Richard in the hunter's lodge that night when we heard those fairy maidens' screams."

"I remember," Nan said, sitting down next to Emma. "The same has come to my mind, too. Mayhap the Viwa stewards already told her after they entered the castle. She would already know if they did."

Emma shook her head as she watched a hummingbird fly from flower to flower.

"Poor Lady Catherine," Emma said softly. "His lordship was not honest with her about his life. She *would* have learned this horrible and painful truth from those stewards. I can see her now . . . sitting all alone in the castle with no one to share her innermost thoughts with. I wish Father John were there to comfort her. I wish I had never left Castle Lamington. Nan, if 'twas not for you, I could have been there with her! I could have protected her from them!"

Emma crossly jumped up from the grass and ran off, leaving Nan by herself. Nan felt stung by Emma's words as her eyes filled with tears. She got up to sit on a stone bench near a flowering bush.

"That blue snow was not my fault!" Nan found herself saying out loud. "Had I not been told that it could have happened to anyone? Those evil Viwa are so troublesome! Emma is right about one thing. She would be with Lady Catherine if her ladyship did not tell both she and Richard to take me to the Monastery of the White Friars. But Lady Catherine *commanded* her to go with me. She should be upset with her ladyship, not me!"

"You are right, Nan! Emma should be, but her ladyship had not done anything wrong by sending her with you to Meldon. Lady Catherine was only doing what was best for you."

Nan turned with a start to see Eolande standing next to the bush where she sat.

"Eolande, I did not see you there!" Nan said.

"I did not mean to pry on you," Eolande stated. "I was walking nearby and wanted to say something about what I heard you express. My gardens are where I come often to connect with the beauty of nature, as you can see. You are taking delight in it as well, which pleases me. As far as what you and Emma were saying—she nearly struck into me, when I came around the other side of the hedgerow, by the way—you have no need to worry about Lady Catherine. Aye, she is aware of Richard and his relationship to Lord Robert. You and Emma are correct. Her ladyship had learned of it through the two Viwa that got inside Castle Lamington. She is strong and has already forgiven her husband. I have been allowed to read her heart from afar. Unfortunately, it should have come from his lordship's own lips, not someone else's. I will mention it to him when I get the chance."

"I am relieved to hear of it!" Nan exclaimed. A smile shown through her tears as she wiped the last of them from her cheeks.

Turning his head to the sound of clanging swords and men shouting, Eolande remarked, "I believe I am hearing the very work of men fighting in a mock battle. Do you not hear it, Nan? We should go and see how much has been accomplished. In the meantime, lass, do not worry about Emma. She will come around, when she has been given some time to think."

Nan grinned. "There is never a reason to doubt you, Eolande, ever!"

CHAPTER 29

Nan rose from her seat and went with Eolande to some meadows far behind the castle gardens, with its lush green grass and beautiful wildflowers of dramatic colors blowing playfully in the warm wind. They saw Lord Hallam and his men, along with Lord Robert and Richard, executing mock battle tactics against one another, both on horseback and on foot. Sweat endlessly poured down each of their bright, overheated faces during the intense, imaginary scuffle. They also used life-sized quintains that hung from poles to fight with. Richard and the men used swords, daggers, axes, and long lances against the quintains, fiercely tearing the objects apart as they rode toward them.

During the mid-afternoon, servants came walking up from the castle. They set up several tables with white tablecloths and laid out vessels and pitchers of refreshments for Richard and the men to drink. Everyone stopped what they were doing and came to the tables, where it became very crowded and noisy from loud conversation and laughter. Eolande himself walked over to the men to take up in the merriment and drinking. Nan observed the activity from a distance until she felt a light tap on her shoulder. She circled around to see Emma standing behind her with a half-smile.

"Nan, I am terribly sorry for my behavior toward you before," Emma said. "I acted like a child in the gardens. Will you forgive my foolishness? Being foolish is the only way I know how to act these days, it seems."

"Of course, Emma," Nan said, returning a smile. "I forgive you. Since nothing is happening as quickly as we would like, we are being driven mad by it."

"Nan, do not patronize me so!" Emma said. "'Tis best to ask

Richard himself about that very thing. I see him coming toward us this very minute."

Walking up to the girls with a drinking vessel in hand, Richard dropped on the grass in exhaustion. His fair hair was matted with perspiration as endless sweat dripped down his face.

Richard contritely said, "I must apologize for my sorry appearance, lasses." Looking back toward the men, he continued, "I was becoming tired of the constant chatter with the others and wanted to come over here for some of your company instead. Sometimes the mind needs a break from the subject of war, war, and more war. Why, Emma! You have yourself another beautiful gown on. It must be . . . how many different ones have you worn so far? Two . . . three? I had been in the sick room for too long, so I am unsure. I am sorry not to have noticed before you came out here. I must have been too distracted at the time."

Emma reddened. "I have lost count of the gowns myself. Eolande keeps providing me with a new one for each day that we are here. I never find the same one twice. He is spoiling me too much."

"I do not think he can spoil you enough," Richard said with an exuberant grin before turning his attention to Nan.

"I see you have decided not to change your mind about wearing a gown, lass. You are still wearing the same dress you had on since we left Lamington."

"I have not changed my mind, Richard," Nan stated. "I never shall, so do not waste your time bringing it up after this."

"Richard, did his lordship ever mention to you that he plans on telling Lady Catherine that you are his son?" Emma asked inaudibly, looking to see that Lord Robert was not in earshot of them. "Nan and I were discussing this a little while ago in the gardens."

Richard shrugged his shoulders as he played with a blade of grass between his fingers. He thought back to the long discussions he had with his lordship in his bedchamber.

"I pray that he tells her soon or she will be in for quite a surprise. Although I am not sure how that can be done with what is going on in Lamington. A letter would not get there safely."

"Richard," Nan began, "Eolande told me that she already knows about you. Those Viwa stewards who entered Castle Lamington revealed it to her. There is good news, however. She has forgiven his lordship for everything he hid from her."

"Ah, Eolande!" Richard sighed. "What would we ever do without him? He has that gift to see things that others cannot. Always on the lookout for all that is good and never fails to inform us about it."

"Do you think his lordship will make you heir of Lamington?" Nan asked hesitantly. "I know there is this new child, but mayhap Eolande can ask his lordship for you about his plans."

"I am afraid that Eolande may not want to interfere in something that is out of his authority, lass," Richard said. Lowering his voice, he added, "Lord Robert has not said a wit about who his heir will be. 'Tis not something that has entered my own mind until you brought it up. I do not *really* know what my fate will be, though at times I thought I did. This is not a proper time to be asking my father about it. I am sure he will make a decision when that time comes. Until then, I plan on dismissing it from my thoughts. First, we have a battle to fight with Sir Erling, or *Prince* Erling, as he is known in Viwa. And you, Nan, have a job to accomplish by locating the emerald."

Jumping up from the grass, he bowed to Emma and then to Nan. Finishing the last drop of his drink from his vessel, he laid it on a nearby table before going off. Grabbing a lance, he mounted a fresh horse that was given to him by a servant and galloped off to the meadows where a few of the men had already returned.

"How can he not worry about his future, Nan?" Emma said. "His answer mystifies me, does it not you? He has a strong opportunity to be declared heir of Lamington, and he acts indifferent about it. How odd of him!"

"A little mayhap," Nan answered. "He may be more certain of his life than we know, but is not willing to share his secrets with us. He does not have to. If he is not worried, then we should not be. And there is the baby to consider, too."

"Well, no matter," Emma replied. "If anything pleases me most, 'tis to hear that Lady Catherine has forgiven his lordship about Richard, even if she has not heard it from his own lips. A saintly lady, she is."

"Indeed, she is," Nan said.

"Truly I would not mind it if the baby was made heir of Lamington, Nan. But I would still feel awful for Richard if he were not at least given the chance first. He deserves more than remaining a castle guard."

Emma slowly turned her attention to two of Lord Hallam's men who jumped from their horses and landed on their feet to face one another. They decided to have a hand to hand combat with their swords. As they raised their swords high in the air, Emma cried out excitedly, "What think you, Nan, if I were able to fight with a sword as well as those fairy men?"

"What!" Nan exclaimed, turning to Emma with a blank expression on her face. She did not understand what Emma was trying to tell her.

"If I were strong and brave enough, I would do just as they were doing out in the meadows there," Emma replied somberly. "Nay, I *am* strong and brave enough. You will see!"

Nan laughed out loud until tears streamed down her face. "'Tis the silliest thing I have ever heard, Emma. How can *you* fight like those men out there?"

Richard and a few of the Viwa men turned their heads in the direction of the girls to see what the laughter was about.

"I meant what I said!" Emma said angrily. "I know this does not make much sense to you now, but it soon will. Either way, there is no need for me to say more than I already had. You do not take me seriously, Nan."

Jumping up from the grass, Emma stormed off toward the castle.

"Where are you going?" Nan called out to the other girl. She had become dumbfounded by Emma's baffling discussion with her.

"I will be back before supper," Emma answered without turning around. She swiftly picked up her pace and disappeared into the castle.

Where did she go? Nan wondered to herself. *Eolande gives her beautiful gowns to wear every day, and she is still not happy. Richard has even noticed what she is wearing. She is becoming a strange one as of late . . . speaking as if she should have a sword hanging at her side! Her silly notion of being a battle maiden is wearying me.*

Shaking her head with exasperation, Nan nimbly got up from the ground and returned to the castle to find Emma. After unsuccessfully searching the corridors for most of the afternoon, Nan gave up and went to her bedchamber to rest before supper.

Emma did not appear when Nan joined the others in the great hall as food was busily being laid out by the servants. Richard, Lord Robert, and Lord Hallam sat down next to Eolande on the dais as the rest of the men filed into the room behind them and took their places at the tables below it. Although the fairy men had cleaned and dressed themselves properly before their arrival in the hall, their faces looked worn-out from the active day spent in the meadows. Nan sat at the farthest end of the lower tables as she watched the last man take his place at his bench and ravenously drink the wine that was poured out for him. She did not see her companion anywhere amongst them and, as Emma always sat next to Nan, her place setting was left untouched. Eolande, seeing Nan's worried expression on her face and the empty space that was Emma's, he got up from the dais to speak to her.

"Where is Emma?" Eolande asked with concern. He gazed over the entire hall in search of the missing girl, but he, too, did not see her.

"I do not know, Eolande," Nan replied. "She said she would be here before supper, but there is nothing more I can tell you."

Out of nowhere, Emma came hastily into the room and sat down winded and laughing with glowing red cheeks. Although she was dressed attractively and groomed flawlessly for the meal they were about to eat, Emma had a look about her as if she had been hiking many leagues from somewhere and was just returning at the end of a tiring day. Eolande gave her a curious look, but said nothing. Nan was surprised at Emma's appearance as she nonchalantly sat there without any explanation of her whereabouts.

"We were beginning to worry about you, lass," Eolande declared. "Well, wherever you were, we are happy to see you have returned."

Eolande smiled and nodded at both girls before returning to the dais.

"Emma, where have you been?" Nan asked. She looked around to see if Richard or any of the others had noticed Emma's late arrival. Seeing this was not the case, Nan said, "You do realize that not one morsel of the meal can be eaten without everyone being here."

"I am deeply sorry about my disappearance," Emma replied, although Nan did not detect any sign of remorse coming from her. "I do not believe I was gone *that* long. I was busy doing something, but no matter. 'Tis nothing to be concerned about, Nan. I lost track of time, but I promise that I will be more punctual next time."

Seeing that Emma was not willing to share any of her secrets, Nan began to eat the tasty fare that was in front of them. She felt snubbed by Emma's lack of interest in sharing whatever it was she was doing.

Recognizing that Emma led a much different life from that of a peasant girl, Nan decided that, perhaps, it was none of her business and did not question Emma any further. As they finished their meal, the girls spoke of trivial matters until the end of the evening.

Richard did not pay much attention to Emma and Nan during the feast. When the long meal was over, he bowed his head at them before leaving the hall with Eolande and the other men who walked out of the room in haste, leaving the girls to themselves. During evenings past, some men would break up into groups to take part in games of chess after the tables were cleared and put away. Others retired to far corners of the room to relax and listen to musicians who were brought in to sing and to play instruments. But this time was different, which Emma and Nan found odd.

At long last, the girls rose from their bench and walked out into the hallway. The loud, echoing sounds of the men's footsteps and talking had trailed off as they heard the shutting of a door not far away. Nan mused what these discussions were that did not include herself and Emma.

"So this is why they left so quickly out of the hall!" Emma said.

"I wonder if they will eventually tell us what they are talking about," Nan stated curiously.

"If not, word will leak out somehow," Emma replied. "I overheard Eolande say that everyone should retire early to their bedchambers tomorrow evening. Something is afoot or he would not suggest this."

The two traveling companions soon found themselves tired after a long day, particularly Emma who was being coy about her busy afternoon, so they returned to their bedchamber where Emma was the first to fall asleep.

The next day and the next, which ultimately resulted into an entire week, Emma once again mysteriously disappeared. She was gone before early afternoon and returned with the others when supper was served in the great hall. Emma would first spend the morning walking with Nan in the castle gardens. She would then insist that they go and watch Richard and the men in the meadows during their fighting practice, which she watched with great intensity. After a mid-morning meal, she would be off without telling Nan any of her plans. Like clockwork, she was back at suppertime and tired as usual. Her appetite was quite enormous as she finished off her entire meal peacefully and looked as if she were ready to fall asleep at the table long before the girls returned to their sleeping quarters. Emma was covertly happy that Richard had not noticed her strange behavior, which was her worst fear. But it did not prevent Nan from being concerned about it.

"Emma, I wish you can tell me what you have been up to lately," Nan pleaded. "At least you are arriving early enough to eat."

"Someday, Nan, you will find out," Emma promised. "For now, do not worry so much about me. And whatever you do, pray do not speak of this to Eolande or anyone else, particularly Richard. I do not want him to become suspicious of me. He may try to stop . . . ."

Emma's voice trailed off. She pursed her lips and refused to tell Nan anything else.

"What are you trying to tell me, Emma?" Nan asked with uneasiness. "Pray tell me! Are you in some kind of trouble? If you will not say, I still promise not to speak to anyone of whatever odd thing you are doing during most of the day. I will also assume 'tis something trustworthy unless I hear otherwise. If you ever need to be honest with me about anything, I am here for you."

"You are a good friend to me, Nan," Emma smiled, trying to suppress a yawn behind her right hand. "Now, I must go back to our room. If I wait for you, Nan, I will be shutting my eyes and falling down in the corridor before we get there."

Emma hurriedly left Nan's side to return to their bedchamber. She was soon fast asleep before changing out of the orchid satin gown, with its long flowing sleeves and ermine trim, which she was wearing.

One early afternoon while Emma was up to her usual vanishing acts and Nan was left wandering the castle alone, she saw Eolande come toward her from the opposite direction. He always seemed to be in a great hurry, but this time he took a moment out to have a few words with her.

"Nan, you look as if you have lost something!" Eolande noted.

"In some ways I have, Eolande," Nan answered. "I never know what else to do after enjoying your gardens and watching Richard and the men in the meadows afterward. I spend most of my time walking around your castle. The view is so picturesque from the towers—the ocean is so peaceful and the flowers in the gardens are so breath-taking. Your flowers are as colorful as the lovely gowns Emma wears. I greatly envy her, but I wish I knew where she was . . . ."

Nan let the words slip. She did not mean to suggest anything about Emma, but she was not thinking when she said it. Nan hoped that Eolande did not figure out what she was trying to tell him, but Eolande knew everything. Nothing could be hidden from him.

"I know where she is, but I do not approve of what she is doing," Eolande replied, shaking his head slowly. "She has her own free will, so I cannot interfere completely. I have tried to dissuade her in some ways, but she refuses to listen. She knows what she must do, but she will not do it. It must be the very drops of the Viwa blood within her that causes such behavior."

"What do you mean, Eolande?" Nan asked excitedly. "Why will you not tell me what she is doing?"

"'Tis up to her, and her alone, to tell you, not me," Eolande reluctantly said. "You will find out in time. This Viwa blood . . . I doubt her parents even know of this ancestor whose name is lost to time . . . it makes her so strong-willed that she cannot be stopped from what she is doing. Pray do not tell anyone this secret, not even to Emma. I tell you this, Nan, because 'twill make more sense to you in the future. Emma cannot be helped any further, and we must accept that. Meanwhile, I must get back to Richard and the others. The time is getting near for their departure and yours. They have done well in practicing for their surprise attack upon Sir Erling. Sir Erling's impatience grows. He may attack Lamington at any time and we must be ready."

"I suspected that preparations were being made for it when you, Richard, and the men were leaving the great hall earlier and earlier the last few evenings," Nan said.

Eolande nodded and quickly meandered down the corridor, leaving Nan with much on her mind.

CHAPTER 30

Sitting down at her usual place in the great hall, Nan quietly waited for Emma as she watched the fanfare of servants bringing in plates of roasted fowl and boar. Out of the corner of her eye, she saw Emma running in behind them. She was wearing a gown even finer than she had on the day before. Emma's cheeks were burning red as if she was having quite an active day.

"Emma! You are back!" Nan cried out, as her traveling mate sat herself down on the bench next to her. "I was beginning to worry about you. You look so beautiful today, too."

"Nan, do not say such things!" Emma said firmly. "I wish we can leave this place already and go back to Lamington. You cannot imagine how much I want to find the gown I came here in. I am starting to feel like you, Nan. If you happen to see it anywhere in the castle, pray let me know. I cannot wait to put it back on. These gowns are starting to get everyone's attention, even Richard's. I do not like it!"

Nan chuckled inwardly.

Well, they should find her beautiful. She is partly one of them, so why should they not think so?

Nan did not disclose her thoughts to Emma. The other girl would have been mortified to learn of her background. Likewise, Nan also promised Eolande that she would remain silent on the secret he let her in on about it.

"I assume you will not tell me where you have been all afternoon?" Nan asked.

Emma did not reply. She started to eat a piece of roasted fowl as if she did not hear Nan. Whether it was because she refused to answer or due to being hungry because of her clandestine adventures, Nan did not know.

Nan studied her companion closely. Emma did, in some ways, resemble someone from Viwa. She was a slender, fair girl with light eyes, which seemed to be a common trait of those fairies. Even Lord Hallam and his men, including Richard to some degree, had Emma's looks, all except for their taller stature. Some of the men had hair that was more a light-brown or a pale reddish color, but generally, their hair was fair. Nan pondered on whether or not Emma had any special Viwa abilities that Richard had, like good eyesight or hearing or strength, but nothing Emma had seemed to be out of the ordinary that Nan noticed so far.

Mayhap since her Viwa blood was from so long ago, she might not be like Richard, Nan said to herself. *Richard might be more like the Viwa since his mother was a fairy.*

"Nan, are you well?" Emma asked. "I have been trying to speak to you, but you just sit and daydream."

"Aye, Emma, I feel like I have been in a dream of some kind," Nan stated as she snapped to attention. "I have been thinking too much as of late."

"Then you must put aside whatever 'tis going on in your head," Emma whispered. "Eolande is about to tell us something important. See there? He has just stood up from the dais."

Facing the others who sat below him in the great hall, Eolande announced the very thing that everyone was waiting anxiously for the last several weeks.

"Men, I want to extol you for your tireless work on our crude battlefield in the meadows," Eolande said, as a smile formed on his lips. "What an achievement! There was not one day when I had not stood there watching you myself as you trained for war. My wisdom tells me that you are more than prepared to go back to Lamington tomorrow. Be up and ready before the dawn light descends upon the Land of the Diamond Sea!"

Tears came to Eolande's eyes as he took the goblet he was holding and held it up to everyone.

"Godspeed to you all!" Eolande cried. He took a drink from his goblet and returned to the dais.

Cheers and shouts of joy resonated from Richard and the men as they raised their goblets in turn. Lord Robert and Lord Hallam stood up and made some speeches of their own in regard to their endeavors in the meadows. Lord Robert also spoke of Richard's great accomplishments at learning the art of war. He glowed with contentment at Richard as he went about making a longwinded discourse of the son he came to know and train as a soldier. Emma and Nan silently watched the excitement around them grow louder and louder.

"This must mean that I will be exchanging my comfortable life here for the unforeseen undertaking in Lamington," Nan said. "Emma, you will be left behind here in the Land of the Diamond Sea. How sad that makes me feel."

Emma did not answer, but sat quietly watching the men in the room.

She ignores me, Nan thought. *I do not understand why. I thought she was my friend, but she has become cold and distant. How anxious I am to find this jewel and bring it back to the Diamond Sea! When I do, I can return to Lamington for good—if everything works out that way. What fun 'twill be to share my adventures with those at home!*

Nan sat listlessly and refused to eat another morsel of food from her plate. She was too upset with Emma. She stared at Eolande sitting on his dais. He nodded at her and smiled. Getting up from his chair, he made his way down to the table where the girls were. Looking at Nan reminded him of something important he should have done earlier.

Bowing before Emma and Nan, Eolande said for all to hear, "There is one person whom we must pay homage to before she takes leave of us. 'Tis you, Nan! May you go to Lamington safely and come back with that which will save us all—the emerald that will destroy what the wicked Viwa have set out to do. May Christmas return to Lamington soon, and your way of life there be all the more peaceful afterward. Godspeed to you, lass!"

The sound of jubilation filled the hall. Eolande lightly patted Nan on the head before going back to his seat. Richard grinned broadly from the dais as he held his own goblet up to her.

"Farewell to you, Nan!" Emma said, reaching over to embrace the girl next to her. "I am sure the men here will take good care of you on your journey back to Lamington. May you find the emerald as Eolande has said."

Surprised by Emma's sudden, kindly reaction, Nan replied, "I pray that I will find it. I do not want to fail anyone in this room, especially Eolande. How awful 'twould be if I did."

"Do not think that you will not find it!" Emma chastised her companion. "Have the rest of them not told you that already! You *will* find the emerald, which will find its way back here. I am sure Lord Hallam's men will find the lost book as well. I was foolish enough to lose it, but they will find it. Eolande has helped prepare them well for what is to come tomorrow. I feel so certain of this, Nan."

"I will come to realize my success, but at a later time—when I am back in Lamington with Christmas all around," Nan said, smiling weakly at Emma. She was amazed by Emma's absolute certainty of uncovering the holly leaf. If only she could share the same optimism.

After the feasting had ended, there was one last evening of merriment for everybody. Some troubadours were brought in to play various instruments for the guests. They also sang and told exciting, and sometimes funny, tales of days gone by in Viwa and even in Lamington. Nan laughed along with the others, but at the same time she was saddened that this was their last evening in the Land of the Diamond Sea before going back out into the harshness of the real world before the sun rose. She would be forever grateful for what Eolande had done for them and she would never forget it. After the entertainers had finished and left, most of the men circulated throughout the hall in search of his own entertainment, either by conversing or playing games. Emma and Nan were seated in one of the window seats when Richard left the crowd of men he was speaking with and came over to them. He stood straight and tall, as he usually did in anyone's presence these days, and a grin lit his face.

The lad was handsomely dressed in a dark green tunic and black hose with his fair hair neatly in place. He was so unlike the Richard they were used to seeing in the fields with the men, sweltering from all the activity there.

"How goes it, lasses?" Richard asked. "You will do well tomorrow, Nan. While you are off pursuing the emerald, Sir Erling will be hunted down in battle. He will be no more. If his army begins losing to us and he dares to escape back to Viwa, he will not get very far. Lord Hallam will send some of his fastest men to intercept him before he reaches the fairy kingdom."

"I pray that will be so," Nan replied. "Sir Erling has not done much good for any of us, has he?"

"I would prefer that he does not escape the edge of my sword," Richard stated with determination. "I seem to remember his lordship saying something of the like. We all want a part of Sir Erling for one reason or another." Anxiety passed over his face. "I also hope to be knighted on the battlefield . . . as long as I do well enough during the fighting."

"May it be so," Nan said softly. "Is that not something we all want of Richard, Emma?"

The seat next to Nan was empty. Emma had carefully and quietly gotten up during the time when Richard had come by to talk with the girls.

"Where has she gone?" Nan asked in surprise. She stood up from the bench and called out loudly, "Emma? Emma?"

"I do not see her anywhere," Richard said, his eyes darting about the great hall. "We were so engaged in conversation, she managed to steal away right under our noses."

"She has been acting so strange—"

Nan abruptly stopped. She did not want to explain Emma's late entrances to the evening meals. She had promised Emma that she would tell no one, especially Richard, of whatever it was she was doing. Nan almost ruined it around Eolande, but Eolande was another story. He knew Emma's secret.

"Mayhap she is tired and has decided to go to sleep," Nan hastily said, trying to cover up her previous words.

"Or, she may still be a bit upset over not going with us to Lamington," Richard declared, not noticing what Nan had tried to express to him. "I must be getting back to my father and the other men, Nan. There are a few more plans to finalize before leaving for home tomorrow. We will see you before dawn in the courtyard. I hope Emma will be there to see us off. Godspeed to all of us!"

"Godspeed to us all!" Nan said, repeating Richard's words.

She quietly slipped out of the hall and returned to her bedchamber where she found Emma fast asleep. Had Emma been awake, Nan would have liked to ask her why she had left the great hall without her. Since the other girl was deep in slumber, Nan let the matter drop.

Nan did not sleep that night. The next day's mission to Lamington was racing through her mind at nonstop speed. She tossed and turned the entire night and slept only intermittently. Lying in bed, she could not tell whether it was still night or right before dawn as it was still dark in the room. She lie fully awake until the sound of a servant came knocking on the bedchamber door to rouse her, which did little good as she was already conscious. Arising from her bed, she saw that Emma's bed was vacant.

"I wonder where she went this morning," Nan said. "She must be turning into a mouse, so quiet she is. I should have heard or saw her leave the bedchamber—I was up most of the night. Mayhap she decided to go off to the courtyard before me."

Nan dressed and went to the courtyard where she stepped out into the predawn light. Richard, Lord Robert, and the fairy men were already in the stables making preparations for the journey. They were clad in chainmail from head to foot, while heavy swords hung from scabbards at their sides. The Viwa men held weighty shields with the coat-of-arms of Viwa, while Lord Robert and Richard held shields with the coat-of-arms of Lamington.

Nan saw that Lord Hallam and his men's coat-of-arms looked quite similar to Sir Erling and his men's, apart from some slight color variations. Instead of a silver background, it was gold. The white boar had become brown. The sword in its mouth became smaller with a large pink rose, rather than a small red one, resting on the handle. Nan later learned that this was done deliberately so Lord Hallam and his fairy men would not be mistaken for Sir Erling's army. She also watched as many servants ran tirelessly back and forth helping others. The courtyard had become so busy that Nan feared she would be left behind like Emma.

A pleasant voice called out to her. It was Eolande.

"Nan, lass! Pray come here!"

Looking at his kindly face above the others' heads, Nan went to join Eolande and the others who stood around in the dewy grass where a low ground fog hung. In the distant sky toward the east, there was a tinge of bright ruby red and purple beginning to show through the darkness.

"I had become worried that you would not rise quick enough this morning, so I had a servant come to awaken you," Eolande said. "I hope you have slept well. You have an eventful day ahead of you. A servant will bring you some bread and some drink shortly. You must not leave here hungry."

"I did not sleep well at all," Nan admitted. "I had too much on my mind last night."

Eolande laughed at Nan's honesty. "Lass, you are delightful as usual! I will be sorry to see you leave here this morning, but you will find yourself back in the Diamond Sea once you reclaim the emerald."

A familiar voice came up behind Nan.

"Where is Emma? I thought she was with you."

Nan turned to see Richard standing in front of her in chainmail. She would not have recognized him if it was not for the sound of his voice.

Nan was afraid to give Richard the abysmal news.

"I did not see her when I awoke," Nan murmured. "I do not know where she is, Richard."

"I have not seen her anywhere myself," Richard said disappointed. "Mayhap she will yet show up."

Richard asked a servant to help locate Emma for him. The servant ran off as Richard stood watching after him. After a short period of time, the servant came back to tell him that she was nowhere to be found.

"If she is not here, so be it," Richard declared. "We must make for Lamington in good time. Nan, you will be riding along with Pell. He is Lord Hallam's most experienced rider who will take you through the town gate to your family's cottage. You will also be hidden underneath a blanket when we get in sight of Lamington and Sir Erling's men. We do not want them seeing you as they will suspect something. We will ride alongside Pell so Sir Erling's men do not cut him down in the process. This difficult feat must go as planned. Do you understand, lass?"

Richard had become so fervent while speaking to Nan, that every bit of confidence that she had earlier about the success of the quest melted away. She could only think of the horror that might come upon Pell and herself if Sir Erling's men broke through to them, killing them with their sharp swords before they reached Lamington's walls.

Eolande grinned and laid a hand on Nan's shoulder.

"I have much faith in you," Eolande stated. "You must have it within yourself as well, Nan. Failure only comes when you lose that faith."

The self-assurance Nan had lost in that moment was restored. A certain calm that words alone could not describe came over her.

"I can always depend on you, Eolande, for support," Nan said beaming.

A distant sound of men on thundering horses was heard coming from the bridge beyond the castle. Nan stood on her toes to see who they were, but the courtyard full of men and horses blocked her view. Eolande turned sharply as he waited for the unknown visitors to come within reach of his castle. Richard looked at Nan in astonishment when they recognized the figure of Father John seated dignified upon one of the horses at the head of the train of soldiers. Every soldier with him carried a bright crimson shield that had a picture on it of a large bird's wings in indigo blue above a silver knight's helmet with a white plume. Two swords crisscrossed the other over the wings.

"The shields of Siddell!" Richard exclaimed with glee.

"And so they are!" Lord Robert said, letting out a loud chuckle. "They are from Lady Catherine's lands. If my prediction is correct, nothing but good comes from this visit. I am certain of it."

"Welcome, men of Siddell!" Lord Hallam cried out.

Nan, who did not take her eyes off the entourage for one second since they arrived, was jumping with excitement. If only she could find Emma so she could see what was happening, too, but Emma was nowhere to be found. Where she went was anyone's guess.

Father John rode up toward them, his cloak billowing in the morning breeze behind him. He looked both relieved and happy to see them all standing there in the courtyard. He dismounted nimbly from his bay horse and came toward Eolande and the others.

"God be with you!" Father John exclaimed to Lord Robert with a nod of his head. "My lord, you do not know how much it pleases me to see you alive and well. Richard! Nan! I am also pleased to see you. I had worried and prayed a great deal for your safety when you left the Monastery of the White Friars. Where is Emma? I do not see her here."

"She is somewhere inside the castle," Richard answered Father John. "She refuses for some reason to see us off to Lamington, but she is doing well."

"I see," Father John said. "'Tis a shame she is not around, but no matter. Let her be."

"Father, what brings you here?" Lord Robert asked. "How did you ever find us here in the Land of the Diamond Sea? I see you have brought many soldiers with you from Siddell."

"Not so very long after Richard and the lasses left the monastery with the other knights from Siddell, we had the fortunate return of Brother James," Father John explained.

"Brother James!" Richard said in shock. "Not the first of the two messengers who was sent to Lamington while we stayed at the monastery?"

Nan watched Father John fervently as she waited for his reply.

"He was the first of the two," Father John confirmed. "He came back to us tired and very weak with hunger, but the Lord above brought him back to us in one piece. Brother James said he had barely eaten the entire way he walked back to Meldon, except for what little he found in the forest."

"Poor Brother James!" Nan cried out.

"Brother Alexander, the second messenger, has been taken by the Viwa fairies in Lamington," Richard stated.

"I had heard some of the Viwa say so themselves," Lord Robert said.

"Aye, he has been taken by them," Father John answered sadly. "'Twas after spending an entire day in bed resting and getting nourishment that we learned the worst from Brother James. He said the Viwa positioned themselves in the fields and around the walls of Lamington. Brother James also told us that he barely escaped with his life from his captors. He was unsure how he did it, but he managed to run away in the dead of night, especially from the all-powerful Sir Erling who was fast asleep. Brother James was deeply sorry that he was not able to bring Brother Alexander back with him. He had a glimpse of Brother Alexander once in the Viwa camp around Lamington, but when the opportunity came to escape, he either had to get away or be caught finding Brother Alexander. He said that Brother Alexander looked well from what he could tell, so praise God for that."

"What did he learn while being prisoner in Lamington?" Lord Robert asked with impatience. "Surely Brother James has had much to tell if he was in the presence of Sir Erling. We are en route to Lamington to seize it from him."

"Aye, Brother James did learn something of great importance," Father John replied. "He had told us that by late spring, Sir Erling planned to bring down the walls of Lamington and obliterate all in its path, including the people and every living thing there. You do not know how ill the rest of the monastery and I felt when we were told this. 'Twas then that I took it upon myself to go to Siddell and beg Lord Roger, if I must, for an army of knights to take back with me to Lamington. As you can see, I was able to do it and deliver them to you myself. They come to join yours."

Richard and the men groaned with anger and disgust while Nan trembled at the thought of what Sir Erling's diabolical plans were against

Lamington.

"You did well, Father, by going to Siddell!" Richard praised the clergyman.

"Aye, you have!" Lord Robert said to Father John. "In what way have you found us? You still do not speak of it."

"Brother James told me," Father John replied. "He warned me that going directly back to Lamington with Lord Roger's knights would not be possible. He had seen the other knights from Siddell as prisoners in Sir Erling's camp, so I knew we had to travel by a different route. Brother James then mentioned how he overheard Sir Erling speak of a place called the Land of the Diamond Sea and that you and the lasses may have run off there after you got away from him. I have never heard of a land by that name before, but with some vague directions that Brother James figured out from Sir Erling, these soldiers and myself were able to find it. This also gave me much leverage with Lord Roger when asking him for more soldiers. I told Lord Roger everything that Brother James had seen and heard when he was in Lamington. Lord Roger had become quite upset when he learned that his soldiers were taken prisoner by those malevolent Viwa. He did not hesitate in giving me five hundred more of the best ones he was able to find within his lands."

Lord Hallam whistled as he surveyed the fresh soldiers.

"Five hundred, you say? Added to my men, we shall have at least as many soldiers as Sir Erling has."

"In fact," began Father John, "Lord Roger has plans on arriving himself with even *more* soldiers. He will be waiting for us near Lamington before the sun rises. He will be hiding with his men in the forest surrounding the farmland where the Viwa are. He did not say this to me openly, but I suspect that 'tis because his sister, Lady Catherine, is prisoner at Castle Lamington that he has become quite motivated to help us, even being so courageous as to linger so close to town."

"Lord Roger is a worthy man," Lord Robert said. "I applaud his generosity and the love he has for his sister by providing us with so many men."

"Bless Lord Roger's heart!" Nan murmured loud enough for Eolande to hear. "We may win this battle with Sir Erling after all."

"Not entirely," Eolande warned with a firm conviction. "Not without the emerald and finding the missing book. You know of what I speak of, Nan."

"Aye, I do," Nan answered, lowering her head.

"If 'twas not for the fact that this book must be found, I would feel joyous that the thing I read from has been lost," Lord Robert said.

"Which book is lost, my lord?" Father John asked hesitantly. "You do not mean . . . ."

"The one that you took to the Monastery of the White Friars," Lord Robert clarified. "Nay, Father. I do not condemn you for taking the evil book there. I understand why you did and it made perfect sense to do it. 'Twas lost afterward when it left the monastery with Richard and the two lasses."

"That is not good," Father John said as his face clouded. "How did the book get lost?"

"It fell out of Emma's pocket on our way to the Land of the Diamond Sea," Richard replied. "'Tis now in the possession of Sir Erling, much to our dissatisfaction. We hope to find it hidden somewhere in enemy camp."

"From what I am hearing, the little empty hole in the book is where an emerald fits into," Father John declared after Eolande explained to him the meaning of Lord Robert's book and the jewel absent from it. "Here I was all along looking around the monastery library for a stone we thought had fallen out somewhere. How little we knew 'twas purposely taken out for a reason not good. I see it has greater significance than any of us might have predicted, too."

"Father, we need to stop here," Lord Robert interrupted. "Once we leave the Land of the Diamond Sea, we will fill you in on many things," Lord Robert stated. "I am afraid that the sun is going to rise shortly. We need to get going to make our surprise attack upon Sir Erling. 'Twill not do us much good standing around here and talking together like a bunch of old women in a marketplace."

Lord Hallam mounted his horse.

"Let us be on our way!" he cried. "We make for Lamington immediately! I can smell victory already in the air against Sir Erling!"

CHAPTER 31

Richard and the remaining men mounted their horses. They began to disperse from the courtyard of Eolande's castle as they resounded Lord Hallam's sentiment for the retaking of Lamington. Nan, who was now seated behind Pell, turned to look for Emma, but there was no one. She only saw Eolande standing and watching them leave. She smiled at him as she watched him raise his hand to wave good-bye. Nan kept staring back at Eolande until her neck ached and she was no longer able to see him. She overheard Richard recounting to an attentive Father John what had occurred when he, Emma, and Nan had left the Monastery of the White Friars. Since Nan already knew the story, her mind drifted to what lie ahead of her.

The riders soon came to the edge of land where it met the beautiful, unearthly blue water of the Diamond Sea. They waited until the white bridge came up out of the water for them to cross over to the world of man. As they rode their horses single file over the bridge, Nan wanted to reach out and pluck one of the colorful flowers that grew out of the sides of it. She felt it might be her one last chance to have something from the Land of the Diamond Sea before they returned home. As they were going too quickly over the bridge, Nan was unable to reach out fast enough to take one. Doubts about the mission suddenly descended upon her, as it did now and then, but Nan caught herself.

I am glad I did not take one! Nan said to herself, withdrawing her fingers from the bridge. *'Twill force me to work harder at bringing back the holly leaf, and I will see those flowers again! How pleased Eolande would be with me for thinking this.*

When they got to the other side of the bridge, the bridge dropped back down into the water with a big splash and disappeared. The army cut across the sand dunes where that peculiar, invisible line was crossed as it had for Richard and the girls. Nan and the soldiers found themselves surrounded by a vast snowy plain with a gray, sunless sky above. The air around them was cool and clammy, forcing Nan to pull her cloak more tightly around her. Nan wondered if it was all a dream—her finding and living contentedly in the Land of the Diamond Sea. She was leaving it much too quickly and having to come back to a world in which she would rather not face made her sad.

The horses galloped furiously at nonstop rapidity across the whole plain. The soldiers rode on in silence as if speaking at all would slow down their progress. It was clear that the soldiers were making good time on horseback, certainly much better than Nan, Emma, and Richard themselves had made across the plain on foot. The knights soon trotted their horses down the large hill that Nan recollected as walking up to get to the plain. The land became dotted with trees again—a little here, a little there, with less snow and more ground showing underneath it.

They were back in the forest where the waterfall in the mossy gorge was heard trickling down the rock from whence it came. Memories of that awful event came flooding back to Nan when she and her companions were caught standing in the middle of the chilly water as Sir Erling and his henchmen surrounded them. She laughed to herself when she thought of how, at the end, Richard threw that nameless substance at those awful men so he, Nan, and Emma were able to make a desperate escape from them. Nan did not want to think of what the circumstances would have been if Richard had not done that. She wondered if he was thinking the same thing this very moment as they went splashing through the pool where the gorge was.

Nan recognized the path they were now taking as they passed the old cottage that his lordship had hid in, and she shuddered when passing the empty cottage of Walter and his daughter, Helene, with its shutters sealed tight. She contemplated what consequences lie in store for them once they were made prisoners by Lord Robert.

"I pray that Helene will not suffer the same punishment as her father," Nan said loud enough for the others to hear.

Richard, overhearing what Nan had said, came up alongside her with his horse.

"I will make sure Helene gets a lesser punishment should she and her father get captured," Richard assured her.

An unexpected snap of a twig coming from somewhere deep in the forest got the attention of Richard and Nan. The soldiers around them immediately pulled out their swords in anticipation of whatever danger might be lurking nearby. Out from behind some tall trees, several knights came riding with one at the forefront dressed in armor more splendid than the rest of them. Nan became filled with fright. She feared that these soldiers might be those of Sir Erling's until she recognized their shields with the familiar coat-of-arms of Siddell.

"Good morrow to you, men!" cried out the soldier at the head. "I recognized you immediately, even from a distance. I am Lord Roger. My men and I come from Siddell to help you recapture Lamington from your enemy. We have quietly camped here since yesterday evening so we would be up and ready to meet you at dawn."

Lord Robert was the first to speak to his lordship of Siddell. He was moved to see his brother-in-law after so many years.

"Good morrow to you, my Lord Roger! You come as Father John had told us. We are pleased to have your service."

"Good morrow to you as well, my Lord Roger!" Lord Hallam declared. "Come, my Lord Robert, there is much to be discussed with Lord Roger before we come in sight of Lamington. Let us go to him."

"Aye, let us do so!" Lord Robert replied. "Come, Richard! You must speak with him, too."

Lord Hallam's and Lord Roger's armies stood face to face with one another as the head of each came forward to address each other. Richard bolted his horse from Nan's side and went to the three lords. He and the lords got off their horses and took a short walk in the forest to converse together, while the other soldiers waited patiently for them to finish. Already the sky had become crimson and purple, as the sun began to rise a little more in the east.

Nan watched and waited as Richard and the men continued to talk and talk and talk amongst themselves. She started to fidget anxiously in the saddle behind Pell.

"Oh, how I wish they would stop speaking and start riding!" Nan fretted to herself. "I so want to get to town and do what I was set out to do. If I do not, I will lose my nerve before we get there."

Nan stopped herself when she noticed that Pell seemed aware of her irritability and turned sideways to look at her, but he said nothing much to Nan's relief.

In the end, Richard and the three noblemen came out of the forest and mounted their horses. Father John then came forward to say some prayers for a successful battle. Nan bowed her head with the men and before she was able to glance up and react after the prayers were completed, Pell was throwing a heavy woolen cover over her head.

"I am sorry to do this to you, lass," Pell apologized. "'Tis an order from Lord Hallam. He does not want the enemy to know you are with us. Whether or not Sir Erling may try to harm you, we cannot say. 'Tis my duty to get you to your journey's end safely."

"I understand," Nan replied in a muffled voice. She was enveloped in darkness, and it was too stuffy to properly breathe beneath the cover. Nan felt the horse under her start to gallop furiously. She heard other horses running alongside the one she was on. She found it disconcerting not to be able to see as she held tightly onto the back of Pell. Nan went bumping along uncomfortably when within seconds, she heard bloodcurdling screams and hundreds of swords clanging as if in one fell swoop. She knew it meant one thing. Both armies of soldiers had met one another at last. The battle had begun!

There was a periodic, loud thud as a soldier fell here and there to the ground. Death was now upon them. Nan shuddered to think of it underneath the encircling blackness. Who was the first victim of this senseless brutality that must be accomplished because of Sir Erling? Was it Richard or Lord Robert, or someone else? They did not have the same shields of Lord Hallam and his army and would stand out from all the men when Sir Erling saw them approach in the distance. Nan was sure that Sir Erling would race toward Lord Robert and Richard first, with the point of his sword waving high in the air. Nan wanted to tear the woolen cover from her head and see what was happening, but Pell warned her to keep it on at all costs. His mission with her must be accomplished. It must not fail or all was for nothing. A battlefield was no place for a peasant girl like herself, and Nan knew it. But what could she do when her life took a different direction as the blue snow fell in the marketplace that uneventful morning and brought about those strange chain of events? Nan could only imagine the anguish her father and mother would go through if they knew where their daughter was. Her mother would cry in fear for her daughter's life and her father, well, he would take that perilous chance in finding her, even if it meant losing his own life.

Nan sensed Pell fighting off some soldiers around him as the sound of a sword close to her ear was ringing endlessly with another, and then another, nearby. She was gravely concerned for Pell's life. Then she remembered that Richard had told her that several of Lord Hallam's soldiers would be right there with Pell, protecting him with Nan as he rode. Nan found solace in this, but she knew she was not safe until they got to the other side of the fighting. But what if Pell was injured or killed? What would happen to Nan? She did not want to think of these things, so she tried to block them from her mind, though it did little good. The sounds of the battlefield did not allow her to mentally shut out these fears.

"Nan, you are safe!" Pell called out exultantly. He pulled the cover from her head. Dropping to the ground from his horse, he lifted Nan from her seat and put her onto her feet. "We made it here at last."

Looking around, Nan saw that she was on the main street of Lamington near the town gatehouse. Up ahead, she saw the lane and the cottage where she lived with her family.

"How did you ever do it, Pell?" she asked with surprise. "May God be with you for risking your life for someone such as I."

Pell smiled down at Nan. He seemed not much older than Richard and here was this lad, barely a man, bringing her back to her home, which she was beginning to believe she would never again see in her lifetime.

"The Viwa—the good Viwa—have the adeptness of helping those from your world in ways that you cannot even begin to envision," Pell replied proudly. "I cannot believe that I actually made it through the town gate. The soldiers of Lamington saw the shields of Lamington on Lord Robert and Richard, who were with me and some of Lord Hallam's men, so they immediately knew that we were not coming to aid Sir Erling. They risked opening the gate for me after Richard signaled at them to let me through it. Once I did, they managed to quickly close it so Sir Erling's men would not follow behind. Sir Erling and his men were caught off guard when they saw us charging toward them as the sun was rising behind us. The sun must have blinded them good. They fight bravely, I must say, but they will soon lose. We have overwhelmed them and their Viwa maidens. Those vile lasses have no chance to distract us from our fighting now! We have made excellent headway, Nan."

"I pray that the emerald will be found as easily as getting through the town gate," Nan said.

Pell nodded and mounted his horse. Turning to Nan, he said, "Godspeed to you, lass! I also pray that you find the emerald. I told the sentries that you must be allowed to leave Lamington at once when you return to the gatehouse. I know they were puzzled by this odd request, but those are the orders of Lord Hallam, so it must be done."

Pell lifted his gloved hand and waving to Nan, he dashed off with his horse. Nan watched as he shouted to the sentries in the gatehouse to permit him to return to the battlefield, which had become louder and louder at each transitory minute. Nan held her ears to prevent the frightful sounds coming from it, but she was unable to. She let her hands drop to her side.

Well, I must do what I was left here for, Nan told herself. *Dilly-dallying will not find the jewel. I wish Pell had not left me here by myself.*

Nan nervously looked up and down the main street before walking down the cobblestone lane where she lived.

"This is all very strange," she said aloud. "I do not see one living soul around. 'Tis so quiet here, too—almost dead-like. I do not hear anything, except for the fighting that is going on beyond the walls. The streets, the lane, and even the cottages are quiet. Where can the town folk be?"

Peering in the direction of the castle, it suddenly occurred to Nan that everyone abandoned their homes in town and took refuge at Castle Lamington.

"How sad that I will not see my parents," Nan said tearfully. "On the contrary, 'tis truly a blessing. They would be quite suspicious of me coming to them like this just to look around for a missing piece of holly. To be sure, they would demand an answer to where I was going after finding it, especially since I have been away from them for so long. They might not have let me leave, either!"

Running up to the cottage, she apprehensively crept to the door. Her heart was banging violently in her chest as she slowly pushed the door open and went inside. What little light there was in the room filtered through cracks in the cottage walls or came from Nan opening the door. The fire inside the hearth had long since died out and a table, set as if for supper, was left untouched by those forced to leave it. A big pot of soup was still hanging over the hearth.

Nan sat down on one of the benches and wanted to cry. Not just any cry, but a long, hard one as she stared at the stale bread and cold bowls of soup on the table. She had half a notion to start the fire again and eat the food herself—the very soup and bread that her mother had made that was now wasting away, left to the mice and rats that were wandering about the cottage floor.

The emerald!

She had almost forgotten what she was there for until her eyes settled above the doorway, where her mother had first placed the holly that cold winter day in December—the day that had started everything.

Jumping up from the bench, Nan decided to look for the jewel behind the cottage where the garbage pit was. The very place where her mother threw all the waste at the end of the day.

"I am certain she must have thrown it in there!" Nan declared. "I will have to look hard in the pile as it likely got deeper since the holly was put in it."

Nan found the rotting heap out back. Finding a long stick, she began to move it around in the pile in the hope of finding the jewel. Some time had passed before she decided that her effort in looking for the emerald in the garbage pit was becoming futile.

Thoughts raced quickly through Nan's mind as she desperately looked around in the garbage.

"If I do not find the jewel soon, I do not know what I shall do," she said out loud. "But Eolande was so sure I would find it!"

Returning to the cottage, Nan's eyes darted here and there around the room.

"What did Mama do with that holly?" Nan agonized. "I have only so much time to look for it."

Nan put her hand to her head as she stood there thinking feverishly. She felt a terrible headache coming on. Her eyes fell on the cold pot of soup in the middle of the room and then to the burnt ashes of the hearth underneath it.

What if she threw it into the fire? Nan mulled over in her mind.

She jerked with a start as she heard a creaking sound coming from the partly-closed door. Dismissing the sound as just the wind blowing against the cottage, Nan rolled up her sleeves. Getting onto her hands and knees near the hearth, she moved the ashes here and there with her fingers. Not finding anything still, she grabbed the stick that she used to search around in the garbage heap outside. Pushing around the ashes with the stick and digging deep into older ash, a glint of something caught her eye in the faint light of the room.

What was this that she found?

Nan's heart began to thump excitedly. Feeling for the glimmering object lying there in the old ash of the firewood, she pulled it up from the hearth. Wiping the gray powder from it, there it was lying in the palm of her hand. A tiny object, brilliantly green in color, was sparkling profusely against the streaming light that forcefully made its way through a crack in the cottage wall behind her. Nan wanted to get a better look at the object. She arose from the floor and opened the door of the cottage. She held up the little leaf-shaped jewel to the bright sunshine and gave a cry of joy.

"The emerald!" she exclaimed. A rush of happiness swept over her. "I found it! Eolande will be so proud of me and so will all the others. Christmas will be back yet again in Lamington!"

She clenched her hand around the jewel so it would not get lost.

Thinking aloud, Nan said, "I must find something to hide it in for my journey back to the Land of the Diamond Sea. 'Tis so small a jewel, indeed. Finding it *was* the easy part. Here is where my real troubles start. I must get out of Lamington somehow. Then I must get around the Evil One—the One from the Onyx Gate, whomever he may be. No matter what happens—good or bad, I must go on. I shall not be stopped!"

"You speak too loudly for your own good, lass!"

Looking up from the emerald, Nan glanced about the cottage as she tried to discover where the voice was coming from. Somebody had stepped into the room from the outdoors. She was so startled by the figure's presence, she did not recognize his face at first.

"'Tis one of the Viwa stewards I saw in the castle kitchen!" Nan cried out.

The surprised Nan covered her mouth with her hand. She then saw the second Viwa steward appear next to the first. They both stood looming over her with their distinctive fair hair and piercing blue eyes. They were not speaking Viwa anymore, but in Nan's mother tongue—as clear as day.

"I suppose you think we will let you get away with what you are hiding there in your hand?" the first Viwa fairy asked her, his eyes narrowing. "We were continuously on the lookout for someone such as you to return to this hovel searching for the emerald. We have been correct in our thinking. You may be here, but you will not leave!"

The two Viwa filled Nan with apprehension. She reprimanded herself for not locking the cottage door as her stomach became tied up in knots. She had not expected to come face to face with those two evil fairies that day. Her heart sunk as she knew that there was nowhere to run. If she did not give them the emerald, they would undeniably force it from her. She wished that Pell had escorted her to the cottage first before leaving her not far beyond the gatehouse in town. Nan wanted to break out into tears. She knew that she had to remain strong in those fairies' eyes. She did not want to appear vulnerable to them, even if she did lose the jewel.

"Give us the emerald, lass, and your life will be spared!" one of the fairy men ordered. He came closer and closer to Nan and thrust out the palm of his hand.

"You *will* give it to us!" the second counterfeit steward declared. "You will not win in this situation, so do not try and act brave. Marden here is stronger than you. He will know how to get it from you if you do not behave like a nice girl and give it to me."

Nan looked from one steward to the other and shivered. Her knees started to knock. She had only moments to spare before they came after her. Nan tried to make a daring escape through the cottage door, but the two Viwa fairies swiftly blocked the entranceway. The one whose name was Marden grabbed her arm to prevent her from taking another step. He tried to force the emerald from her by squeezing her hand until she winced in pain, but Nan was reluctant to give it to him.

"You are making a terrible mistake, lass!" Marden hissed. "You will not get away with this!"

CHAPTER 32

A shadow rose from behind the two stewards and there was a loud neighing of a horse. Nan looked up in time to see one of Lord Hallam's men through the doorway. He was seated on his horse with a sword drawn in one hand and a shield held high in the other. The soldier was ready to pounce upon the two fairy stewards who were ready to harm Nan for the sake of the precious stone.

"Let her go or you will pay for *your* mistake!" the soldier shouted to the cruel Viwa.

Nan did not recognize the voice of this strange soldier. It did not sound like Pell's, though she could have forgotten it after all the mayhem that went on. She wondered who this soldier was who had come to her aid.

Did Pell suddenly decide to turn back when she made for her family's cottage?

The Viwa fairies were taken utterly by surprise. Marden promptly let go of Nan's hand. He and his companion ran out the door and angrily drew their own swords as they faced their challenger. The two fairy men then looked around frantically for their horses, which they had left outside the cottage.

"If you are looking for your steeds, I have sent them running back to the stables," Lord Hallam's soldier announced to the Viwa. With these words, the two fairies bounded toward the soldier with full force of their weapons.

The two fairy men struggled on foot as they fought the other soldier high up on horseback. Lord Hallam's soldier struck back with his sword, but it soon became clear that he was having a grueling time trying to fight off the Viwa who were now gaining the upper hand in the scuffle. The soldier began backing up with his horse to circumvent their swords being plunged at him. The sight was becoming amusing in Nan's eyes.

The soldier appeared to regain some of his strength. He lifted his sword high in the air and let it come crashing down upon Marden's sword, knocking it from the steward's hand. Lifting his sword a second time, he hit the other steward's shoulder with the tip of his blade. The other Viwa howled out in pain as the sword cut through his tunic. In spite of the wound he had received, he courageously continued to fight back as fiercely as he was able to on foot.

"Nan!" screamed the soldier. "Get onto my horse! We must leave here this instant. I do not know how much longer I can keep fighting like this. I am no match for these Viwa!"

Nan gasped in surprise.

The voice had a familiar ring to it. Did she dare to think that this soldier, who sounded and dressed like one of Lord Hallam's men, was Emma?

It cannot be! Nan thought with skepticism, but she was unable to place the voice as anyone else's.

Nan ran up to the horse and pulled herself up with the help of the soldier's hand. Plopping herself down in the saddle, the two Viwa fairies hurried toward her and the soldier. They attempted to swing their sharp swords at the horse's legs to prevent him from carrying off Nan and her mysterious rider.

"Emma?" Nan asked cautiously. "Are you . . . Emma?"

A closer look revealed the face to be very like that of her companion, the maidservant of Lady Catherine, despite the chainmail covering her head.

"'Tis I, Nan!" the soldier shouted in a raspy voice. "Pray no more questions. My strength is failing me. These men are much, *much* stronger than I!"

Emma sped her horse hastily with Nan toward the direction of the town gatehouse. Getting in sight of it, she signaled to one of the guards to open the gate. When the gate was pulled open, she rode nonstop through it as the Viwa fairies who were chasing them on foot gave up.

"We made it!" Emma laughed. "Nan, do you have the emerald?"

"Aye, 'tis here in my hand," Nan replied. She crimped her hand tightly around the little object.

"Mayhap you had better place it in your pocket if you have one," Emma stated. "'Twould be safer there than in your hand. I am grateful to

God that you found it today."

Nan placed the jewel safely into one of the deep pockets of her dress.

"I want you to hide your face and well, too, with your cloak," Emma advised. "Remember, I am not Pell. I do not have the cover that he had. And whatever you do, say no more. You have many questions for me, I am sure. I cannot answer you until we leave Lamington and are safe outside the boundaries of the fighting going on. We must reach the forest. 'Tis then that we will be out of danger."

As Nan pulled the hood of her cloak over her head, the girls entered the farmland-now-turned-battlefield with consternation. Emma tried to keep her horse close to the town wall for the moment and away from the center of the terrifying conflict that was encompassing them. The shrill screams, the unending sound of weapons, and the smell of death was enough to nauseate Emma and Nan, but Emma diligently kept herself focused on the direction of Lamington Forest ahead.

"I will soon have no choice but to take my horse through the thick of battle," Emma shouted to Nan above the noise. "I cannot ride within the shadows of the town wall much longer. The enemy will soon see us no matter what. I admit that I do not know how I managed to get beyond all this to find you." Flinching at the sight of an injured soldier being thrust from his horse, Emma declared, "Things may become unpleasant shortly, Nan. Pray that I get us through the horror without any bodily harm. One thing I have learned is that the life of a soldier is not an easy one."

Emma maneuvered her horse in between the fighting with all the spirit and bravery she was able to gather. It was becoming increasingly difficult to avoid getting hit or bumped by someone or getting attacked from behind. There were several instances when Sir Erling's men galloped toward her in time for one of Lord Hallam's men to come between the rival and Emma and take him down. On one occasion, Emma saw the enemy charging from behind. She raised her sword and shield in preparation for what was to come. A struggle ensued! Excruciating pain developed in her arm from the sword fight. Emma was incapable of holding up the object. She wanted to drop her sword and admit defeat, but admitting defeat meant certain death. Death was not an option that she was willing to take. With one last stroke of her sword, she came down on the opposing soldier's arm with all her might.

Emma heard the soldier's pitiful cry, but without giving a second thought to the injury given, she forced her horse to ride faster and faster out of the maelstrom they were in. She fleetingly turned her head and saw the figure of Sir Erling approaching at the rear of Lord Robert. What happened next made her come to a frightful stop. Lord Robert swung his horse around and met the oncoming Sir Erling. He locked swords with his greatest enemy as they commenced to fight to what seemed to be a mortal end. With one swift blow of his sword, Sir Erling came down on Lord Robert. Blood flowed from Lord Robert's fatal wound as his body fell limply off his horse and to the ground. His lifeless form lie face down amidst all the horses and men battling around him.

Through the corner of her eye, Emma caught a glimpse of Lord Roger rush to Lord Robert's side. Sir Erling turned his sword on Lord Roger who had come behind him with his horse. To her utmost shock, Lord Roger fell to the ground on his knees. Sir Erling jumped from his horse and drove his sword into his lordship, ending his life. Emma let out a little cry and hoped that what she had seen was neither Lord Robert's nor Lord Roger's demise, however she knew in her heart that it was, though removing their deaths from her mind was no easy task. She was amazed, yet disgusted, at Sir Erling's agility at using the sword and prayed he would soon get his due. Emma attempted to see if she could find Richard in the melee, but he was nowhere to be seen. She prayed that he was well and had not lost his life by one of Sir Erling's men. Or, Sir Erling himself! Emma looked up just in time as a soldier was coming toward her with a lance. Realizing she had spent too much time idling on her horse with danger all around her, she bolted off in the direction of the forest.

"Nan!" Emma cried out as her horse careened through the trees. "The battle is behind us! We are safe for now, but we should not stay here for too long. One never knows if an enemy spy is lurking in the trees nearby."

Emma slowed her horse down and trotted him deep into the forest. She reined the animal in and patted his side. Jumping down from her mount, she stretched her tired legs and rubbed at her sore fighting arm.

"Here, Nan," Emma said. "Let me help you down, too. We need a little rest before moving on to the Land of the Diamond Sea."

Pulling off the hood of her cloak, Nan looked at Emma in complete shock as she allowed her companion to help her from the horse.

"Nan, you look as if you had seen a ghost," Emma said with a devious smile.

Nan shook her head several times before uttering a word.

"I cannot believe who I am seeing," Nan muttered. "Emma, 'tis you! You were told not to come and help me. And yet, you are here!"

"Aye, I am here," Emma replied.

Emma pulled a canteen from her saddlebag and took a drink from it. She could tell by the look in Nan's eyes that Nan did not approve of her being outfitted like a knight.

"I am not well from this, either," Emma declared. "As I told you before, this has not been easy for me to do. Eolande knew what I was doing and was angry. Richard would be terribly upset with me as well. I can well imagine what he would say if he knew of my charade. I do not believe his words would be pleasant to my ears."

"I would not blame him," Nan agreed, trying to hold back anger. "You could have been killed, Emma! We both could have been in that battle. You are a lady's maidservant, not a soldier. If those men out there knew you were a girl underneath your armor, they gladly would have carried you off as their most prized prisoner. 'Twould not have been any better for me."

"I know that," Emma said. "But what was I to do, Nan? Let you get the jewel and find your way back to the Land of the Diamond Sea on your own? I cannot see how you could have left Lamington without soon finding yourself under the tip of a sword. I wonder how any of the men, whether it be Lord Hallam or Eolande himself, thought you could have escaped safely back to his castle without being seen by Sir Erling's soldiers. 'Twould have been sheer imprudence to try to get away from all that. I had my doubts, Nan, no matter what any of them said."

"It had crossed my mind, too," Nan admitted, "but they had enough faith in me to allow it to be done that way. You know, Emma, I thought you were Pell coming back to help me. Little did I know 'twas not him. You have fooled me well."

"I observed what he did with you when he entered the town gate," Emma explained. "When he left Lamington, I came out of the shadows and pretended that I was he. The town guards let me through without any difficulty. I was holding one of Lord Hallam's shields and was dressed like one of his men, so who else could they think of me as? Are you not pleased that I have come to your rescue, Nan? Pray say that you are or all that I have gone through for you has been in vain. Do not be angry with me."

"I am grateful," Nan said, trying to force a smile. Her anger toward Emma started to dissipate. "I am even more grateful that we have survived this ordeal. I prayed all the while when you rode us across the battlefield. I was almost certain that death was soon upon us. Emma, I wondered what happened to you this morning in the courtyard. Were you hiding somewhere in that crowd of soldiers waiting to leave Eolande's castle?"

"I was riding at the far back of Lord Hallam's army," Emma answered. "I was greatly concerned when we left that I would be caught and sent back to the Land of the Diamond Sea, but thankfully, I was not. I blended in quite nicely with the men, do you not think so?"

Emma stood there in her chainmail and grinned, revealing a set of perfect white teeth. She seemed quite proud of herself for becoming one of Lord Hallam's soldiers.

"How did you learn to use a sword?" Nan asked. "I do not understand it. I must admit that you did well fighting off those Viwa stewards that entered my home. I had become terribly ill when I saw them standing in the doorway."

Nan stared in the direction of the raging battle. A sudden thought crossed her mind.

Had not Eolande recently hinted that Emma was doing a certain something because of the Viwa blood in her veins? Was this it?

Emma smiled awkwardly at Nan and hung her head.

"Remember when you did not know where I was sometime?" Emma said. "You remember, Nan. Like when I came late to supper. I was practicing my best at becoming a soldier like the rest of the men."

"What!" Nan drew in her breath. "I do not know how you did it, but much trouble would have come to you had you been caught. Lord Robert would not have been pleased to know what Lady Catherine's maidservant was doing."

"Aye, I would have been dismissed from my position as maidservant to her ladyship and sent back to my mother in shame," Emma said "I was fearful to carry out my plans at first, but I am thankful that it worked out after all. Let me explain everything from the very beginning.

Remember when Eolande firmly said that I could not come back with you to Lamington to get the emerald? Well, not long afterward, while I watched the men practicing at war, a brilliant thought came to me. At least, I felt 'twas brilliant. I wished so much that I was one of them. If I was, I could bring you back to Eolande's castle after finding the emerald. There you have it! I *would* become one of them in time, but not without its dangers and unforeseen trouble ahead. I knew that I was not allowed to partake in anything they did out in the fields behind the castle, so one day, while exploring Eolande's castle, I happened upon the armory. I saw stacks and stacks of swords and shields. So I picked up one of the swords and practice I did! There was a large, empty room next to it where I pranced around and fought imaginary Sir Erlings and the most evil Viwa that I had ever come across. When I was not practicing in the room, I watched closely how the men fought in the meadows. I copied how they fought . . . how each of them swung a sword and held a shield. I did it just by studying their actions alone. What other way was I able to do it?"

"I wish I had known this sooner," Nan said. "I would have stopped you. I was foolish to think you had put your battle maiden plans behind you."

"If you had, then you might not be here safely away from Lamington with the emerald," Emma declared triumphantly.

"There is truth in your words," Nan answered. "I cannot say that I would not have made it alive out of Lamington without you, but it does not matter now, does it? In a way, I am happy that the reason you had acted very oddly toward me sometimes during supper was not because you had been upset with me over something."

"Oh, Nan!" Emma exclaimed. "Did I do that to you? I am very sorry if I misled you. Like you said a moment ago, you might have stopped me from what I was doing had you known. Eolande almost did. I was practicing one afternoon when he found me, much to my surprise. I thought my heart would stop when he stood there, his eyes fixed in a frozen stare. What made it worse is that I was wearing chainmail from the armory. It fit me perfectly when I tried it on. I believe this made it all the more disastrous for me. He demanded to know what I was doing, so I told him quite reluctantly. He was not happy. He listened patiently to what I was telling him, but in the end, he said he wanted me to stop this nonsense, as he called it. 'Twas my choice if, in the end, I wanted to continue playing at being a soldier. 'Twas then that he left me. I was so scared, but my mind was made up. I went on as if Eolande had never seen me, though I knew in my heart he was right."

"You risk too much for my sake, Emma," Nan declared. "I must confess something to you about Eolande. I spoke to him one afternoon about where you might be, but he would not tell me. His only words were that he did not approve of what you were doing, but he did not prevent you, because you had your own free will."

"'Twas his way of warning you of my misadventures in so few words," Emma said laughing. "I suppose he has not told anyone of my being a battle maiden. If so, I would not have been able to set off from the Land of the Diamond Sea at dawn today. Can you imagine me facing Richard and those men, had they found me out sitting atop one of Eolande's horses and pretending to be one of them?"

Nan did not answer, but looked up at the lovely blue sky and bright golden sunshine filtering down on them from the sky above.

"Such a beautiful day and such unnecessary fighting going on," Nan whispered. "I kept praying almost every hour since it began that 'twould end soon."

"I did not enjoy having to ride in the midst of it," Emma said. "There was no way to avoid the sights and sounds of it. I cannot wait to get back on the horse and take leave of this place."

"Nor can I," Nan said.

"Nan, I get the feeling that you think I enjoy being dressed as a soldier. To be honest, 'tis not at all comfortable in this armor and sitting like a man does on his horse. I have accomplished my duty as a soldier. I will now become Emma again."

Going over to her saddlebag, Emma reached in and pulled out the gown and cloak that she had worn when she arrived at the Land of the Diamond Sea.

"Wherever did you find those?" Nan asked with surprise. "I was certain that Eolande had thrown out your things, especially since he had given you quite a supply of beautiful gowns afterward."

"I actually found my things quite easily," Emma answered. "They were at the bottom of the big chest in our bedchamber, all washed clean and put away. We just did not bother to look in it. Let me go and change behind some trees there. I will return shortly."

Emma disappeared for what seemed like an eternity to Nan as she waited. While standing around, Nan examined the buds forming on a nearby tree. She smelled the fresh, strong scent of earth coming from the ground beneath the patches of snow. Nan then heard a snapping of twigs and the crunching of some leaves nearby. Her eyes darted around to see if someone was there, but she saw no one.

"Emma!" Nan called out. "Are you finished?"

Nan was about to start looking for Emma, when her companion came out of the trees and walked toward her. Emma was dressed like her old self, which brought relief to Nan.

"I tossed my armor and shield under a pile of old branches so nobody will find them," Emma said. "I decided to keep my scabbard and sword, though. They are hidden under my cloak. You never know when we may need a sword again. The shield would be too large to carry on my back, so I had to grudgingly dispose of it."

"We should leave here immediately, Emma," Nan said in a fearful whisper. Her skin began to prickle at the back of her neck. "I heard something or someone nearby. We make for the Land of the Diamond Sea without any more delays."

Emma looked around quickly as the girls mounted the horse. She then swiftly galloped her horse through the forest without looking back.

"Did you see anything?" Nan asked nervously.

"I did not, but that does not mean there is nothing to fret about," Emma said. "Mayhap 'tis a spy or two of Sir Erling's milling about, but who can say for sure. I will keep riding as far and as fast as I can, then we will slow down when I feel 'tis safe to do so. I do not want to wear out my horse. He has had enough excitement for one day."

They rode on through the forest until they went past the old cottage of Walter and Helene and the one used by Lord Robert where he hid as a hermit.

They traveled through the gorge with the waterfall and went up the high hill beyond it.

"Emma, how long do you think 'twill take us to get back to the Land of the Diamond Sea?" Nan asked. She wanted to be there before dusk settled as she glanced around at the terrain they were covering.

"We will be there in plenty of time, long before the sun sets over the plain," Emma replied. "I am finding that Eolande's horses are different from ours. This one is swifter and stronger and is a true pleasure to ride on."

Across the plain they went at full speed. Nan was becoming ecstatic that time and space was widening between the battle in Lamington and the plain. Then a bit of uncertainty filled her mind.

"Do you truly believe we are *that* safe?" Nan asked. "I cannot shake this odd feeling I have. Mayhap 'tis coming from the bad experience we had the last time we were out this way. I am not sure. I must think about this further."

"I command you to put that odd feeling out of your head, Nan!" Emma said confidently. "If I had to judge, we are halfway to the end of our journey. Does that make you feel better? We will soon be in the Land of the Diamond Sea with the emerald safely with us. What a wonderful a feeling it is! Do you know, Nan, when I saw you holding that jewel in your hand at the cottage, I almost wept from happiness? All the suffering we have been put through since we left Lamington will be rewarded. Every problem Lamington has faced will be wiped away. Christmas will return. Naturally, the book needs to be found as well, but I feel hopeful that one of the men has found it already. I prayed 'twill be so. Those are brave men out there fighting, Nan. I saw them fight and fight well they did. Nan, why are you so quiet? Why do you not answer me?"

Nan sat silently thinking and allowed several minutes to pass before responding. She reflected on how assured Emma was about their journey back to Eolande's castle and carefully mulled over her companion's words.

The wind ripped through the girls' hair and cloaks as Emma coaxed her horse to race even faster across the second half of the plain. The animal's galloping hooves went thundering underfoot with a constant sound that had an almost hypnotic effect to it.

"Emma, I do not believe we are as safe as you think," Nan answered. "We have forgotten about the very thing Eolande warned us about. Remember the One from the Onyx Gate?"

CHAPTER 33

"I remember Eolande telling us," Emma remarked. "I need not be reminded of the One from the Onyx Gate. Any thought of him will make me too upset to focus on what is at hand."

"I nearly forgot about him until you mentioned how we will be arriving at the Land of the Diamond Sea before nightfall, as if nothing else stood in our way of getting there," Nan murmured. "No one, not even Eolande, said that I would be getting back there safely. What is worse is that 'tis unknown how the One from the Onyx Gate will show himself. Eolande was worried, Emma. Now I am."

"Pray be optimistic for once, Nan. Before the One from the Onyx Gate rears his ugly head, we will be riding over the white bridge to Eolande's castle."

"You do not sound in the least bit worried, Emma," Nan said, becoming fearful of the growing fog forming on the barren plain. "The risks you have taken for me is more than I could ever have done for another—except for getting the emerald, which I had to do because there was no way around it. Even so, you cannot forget the warnings Eolande kept reminding us of over and over about the One from the Onyx Gate. He made it very clear in the presence of Richard and the men what the One from the Onyx Gate might do if you were here with me. You cannot tell me you have forgotten that?"

"Hush, Nan!" Emma snapped. "I have a good head on my shoulders. I will not let the One from the Onyx Gate tempt me. How little Eolande knows me! The Diamond Sea is not far off and Eolande's horse is a strong animal. Together we will outwit this evil being."

What more can I say when she is in control of the horse? Nan sighed to herself. She was tired of arguing with Emma, so she let her have the last word.

The girls rode on for about an hour longer when Emma reined in her horse. She gaped out at the fog, which had grown so thick that her horse was struggling to find his way through it.

"There is something I loath to share with you, Nan," Emma announced. "Not only can I not see in front of us, but I am not able to locate the Land of the Diamond Sea. A little while ago, I was so sure we were getting closer to where the plain would turn into the white sand beach of the Diamond Sea, but . . . but . . . ."

Emma's voice began to tremble. She was near to tears as she unwillingly admitted her shortcoming.

"Oh, Nan!" she cried. "I do not know what to do! We are doomed!"

Nan's heart began to pound loudly in fear at Emma's dire prediction.

What would they do if they could not find the Land of the Diamond Sea? Were they as ill-fated as Emma had said?

"And here I was thinking I was such a help to you," Emma bemoaned. "We are going to meet our fate of death out here. Nan, I have failed you!"

"Do not say such a thing," Nan said calmly. "The Diamond Sea must be here somewhere."

"I do not know about you, but I am becoming ill," Emma stated. Getting off the horse, she sat on the foggy, damp ground and grasped at her stomach.

Nan, who was still seated on the horse, sniffed the air. A sweet odor, almost like that of a flower, filled the air. The scent became more potent by the minute. She thought it odd that something was growing in a place where nothing grew at that time of year.

"I am sure I am not imagining that beautiful smell," Nan said. "Do you smell it, too, Emma?"

Nan clumsily unmounted the horse and sank down next to her companion whose eyes were now closed.

"Why am I so sick?" Nan whined. "I felt perfectly well a second ago." She pressed at her own forehead. "Oh, how my head aches! I will look and see if there is something for us to eat in the saddlebag. We must be hungry as we had not eaten since dawn."

Emma did not reply, but continued to sit motionless on the ground until she heard the sound of a horse's snorting. She sluggishly opened her eyes and looked up. Nan turned from the leather saddlebag and saw a figure coming out of the dense fog. It was Lord Robert pulling up on his horse as he sat staring at them from his saddle with a glazed look in his eyes.

"Your lordship!" Nan cried out in surprise, pulling her hand out of the saddlebag to face him. "God be praised that you have found us! We thought we were lost."

Emma forced a smile to her lips at the immediate appearance of Lord Robert. His death came rushing back to her.

Did she imagine his passing back in Lamington? Was it another soldier whom she saw being slain on the battlefield instead?

Emma desperately wanted to speak to his lordship but she felt too drained to try.

Lord Robert grinned. "I have found the lost book, lasses! You know of what I mean." He laid a hand on his leather saddlebag hanging by his side but did not show them anything. "Come! Follow me. We make for the Land of the Diamond Sea. We won the battle in Lamington! Where is your excitement over my news? Come, come! Emma, do not sit so on the ground. You must listen to your lord when he speaks to you."

"Emma!" Nan exclaimed. "His lordship has come to help us. He has the book, too! Do as he says."

Lord Robert waited as Nan pulled a limp Emma to her feet and pushed her up onto the horse. Nan nearly fell off trying to get herself on the animal until a pallid Emma held out a shaky hand for Nan to grab onto.

"Nan," Emma whispered. "I feel like I am going to die. This illness is consuming my body."

"You will not die, Emma!" Nan cried out. "I am as ill as you are. This dizziness is making it difficult for me to sit on the horse straight. When we get to the Land of the Diamond Sea, we will both rest and get better. Eolande will know what to do. We must try to keep up our strength and follow behind his lordship."

"I am happy that he is here with us," Emma stammered. "When we were leaving Lamington, I thought I saw him being attacked from behind by Sir Erling on the battlefield. I know now that Sir Erling has not done him any harm. Her ladyship would have been terribly grieved if he was badly wounded or . . . or . . . killed!"

"Killed?" Nan asked deliriously. "His lordship *killed?* Never! He is too great a man and brave a knight to have his life taken from us so soon, Emma. Did you not hear what else he has said? The fairies have been driven from Lamington. The battle there is over!"

Emma nodded slowly.

"I have heard. I am glad of this. I also must have been confused with someone other than his lordship when we were riding away during the fighting."

The girls trailed close behind Lord Robert on the plain as they swayed weakly to and fro on the horse in their unwell state.

"I am sorry I could not find anything for us to eat in your saddlebag, Emma," Nan said.

Emma shook her woozy head.

"I forgot that I ate everything that was in it after we met with Lord Roger and his army of soldiers," she said softly. "'Tis best you found nothing for me. I am too nauseous to take food."

"Emma, you will never guess! His lordship has found the Diamond Sea!" Nan exclaimed. "We are here at last."

Nan saw the castle of the Land of the Diamond Sea from a distance, white and shining in the sunlight. She was anxious to get to the castle and return the emerald to Eolande where he could dispose of the detestable object, which she had gone through so much trouble to find.

Emma's half-closed eyes opened slowly to look out ahead.

The three riders came to a white sandy beach, but when they rode over it, the girls found that the air was not balmy as it should have been in the Land of the Diamond Sea. The bridge at the end of the sandy beach was different than the one they had gone over to Eolande's castle. The astonishingly wide bridge neither rose out from blue ocean water to meet its visitors, nor was it erected out of white stone. This stationary bridge was of shiny, dark stone that glistened in the cool sunshine and spanned over a low-lying creek where the water was mossy green and very dank. And flowers did not grow out of it like Eolande's bridge did. A putrid fog seemed to permeate from the water, which forced the girls to hold their noses, while they crossed over this most peculiar bridge. A mist ascended from out of nowhere and when they looked out in the distance, they saw a large, bulky castle that was in great need of repair. Some walls were broken here and there and most of the bridge they charged over was crumbling in sections.

"Emma, this does not look like the Land of the Diamond Sea," Nan whispered. "At first I thought I was looking at Eolande's castle, but once we set out on the bridge, everything started to look different. All except for the sun that is above us."

"Nan, we have been deceived!" Emma said. "We *must* be going to the One from the Onyx Gate! We made a terrible mistake coming here. Nan, I meant it when I said I could get us back to the Diamond Sea. I could have, if only . . . ."

"Emma, I believe you," Nan said, trying to keep her fear under control. Remembering that Lord Robert was with them, she asked, "Does his lordship know where he is taking us?"

"His lordship has been duped, too," Emma stated. "Your lordship!" Emma screamed out with all the strength she could muster. "Your lordship! We must speak to you. Pray turn back. This is *not* the Land of the Diamond Sea!"

Lord Robert did not listen to Emma. He kept facing forward as he rode stealthily ahead on the bridge to the rundown castle.

With anxiety growing within her, Emma raced her horse quickly next to Lord Robert's as she tried to warn him a second time. He did not look at her, but kept riding as if he did not hear a sound. Emma reached her hand out and attempted to tug at his scarlet cloak. Instead of stopping to see what she wanted, his lordship galloped off with lightning speed ahead of them.

Nan was perturbed.

"How strange of his lordship to do such a thing."

Emma had no other choice than to keep up with Lord Robert as they rode toward the tall, yellow stone castle with its many turrets and watchtowers. At length, his lordship and the girls found their way off the bridge and went up a steep road that led to a drawbridge ahead. A strange, large creature with a thick lizard's head and mighty bird's wings soared gracefully across the sky. The sun's rays reflected off the creature's iridescent greenish-gray skin that covered its muscular body. Had it not been for the rest of its hideous form, the beauty of the creature's wings alone could have been mistaken for an eagle gliding through the heavens. The creature flew high in the sky above the topmost tower. It swooped down occasionally to get a curious look at the girls with its probing eyes of the same color as its body. The thing was unlike anything the girls had ever seen before. They screamed whenever the creature came close to them, while Emma's horse neighed in fear at it.

"What is that?" Nan cried out in horror. "I never saw such a thing like it in my life."

"Nor have I!" Emma replied, rubbing her weak stomach. "It reminds me of a mythical animal I once saw in a stained glass window, but I doubt 'tis the same thing. Whatever it is, it had better stay away!"

Lord Robert boldly trotted his horse across the drawbridge and through the castle gate where he disappeared from sight. The mist became heavier and got into Emma's eyes as she followed his lordship inside the castle walls.

"Come, lasses," said the gruff voice of Lord Robert from someplace in the mist. "Do not keep me waiting, you foolish geese!"

"I am afraid to obey him, Nan," Emma whispered to Nan, shivering incessantly beneath her cloak as they came to a castle courtyard full of weeds and dead grass. "If I were not so ill, I would leave this place with, or without, his lordship."

"We *should* leave," Nan insisted. "There is time to do it. Turn your horse around, Emma! We have been foolish to come here. The longer we stay, the worse 'twill be for us. I have a horrible feeling that he who dwells in this castle made us sick. 'Tis part of his plan."

"If that is true, Nan, we are in terrible danger!" Emma answered. "We *must* go now."

Emma spun her horse around and galloped back across the courtyard. As she made her way for the drawbridge just beyond it, a figure stood blocking her way. It was Father John smiling back at them.

"Welcome, lasses!" Father John said cheerfully. "Where are you going? I am delighted that you have made it safely back to the Land of the Diamond Sea. Eolande is waiting for both of you."

Emma glanced back at Nan apprehensively.

"Father," Nan began, "this is not Eolande's castle, and this is *not* the Land of the Diamond Sea. I tell you, this is not the castle we first laid eyes on!"

"We will not get off this horse for you, nor for anybody," Emma said stalwartly.

Father John laughed. "You are mistaken, lasses. This is most unquestionably the Land of the Diamond Sea, and this *is* Eolande's castle! Eolande has sent me out here to wait for you. His servants have prepared a large feast for you in the great hall. He has filled me in that you were to arrive here with the emerald. Do you have it?"

Emma and Nan looked at one another. They refused to answer Father John.

"Ah, I see you still think this is not where you are supposed to be, because the Land of the Diamond Sea is warmer and the castle looks much different than this one, is that not it?"

The girls slowly nodded in response, but they remained quiet.

Father John laughed aloud a second time until his whole body shook.

Lord Robert, with his tall, striking figure, had returned to the girls without his horse. He stood glaring up at them, feet apart with arms folded at his chest.

"I command you to the great hall at once!" Lord Robert roared in such an unyielding way that it frightened Emma and Nan. "You must not fear the Land of the Diamond Sea, lasses. Eolande has temporarily changed it, along with his castle, to make it look more like the Onyx Gate because of Sir Erling. Sir Erling knows that the emerald has been found and is on its way back to Eolande's castle. He has left the battlefield to come after you, Nan. Lord Hallam's soldiers had heard him say so. Sir Erling does not want the jewel placed back into my book. He knows what the consequences will be, but we have outfoxed him. He will not find you and neither will the real One from the Onyx Gate. They have lost. When Sir Erling thinks you have found your way into the hands of the One from the Onyx Gate, who wants the jewel as much as he does, he will stop pursuing you over it. Our makeshift Onyx Gate will fool him greatly! After the feasting, hand the jewel over to me. I will place it in the cover of the book myself."

Emma and Nan breathed a sigh of relief as they slid down from their horse.

"So this is how things have been plotted for us," Emma said, her illness fading away bit by bit.

"I am sorry, your lordship," Nan stated as she dropped on bended knee to Lord Robert. "We had not known. Pray forgive our ignorance."

Without saying a word more, Lord Robert turned and strode into the great hall.

"Emma! Nan!" Father John said in a hollow voice. "Why do you linger? A warm meal in front of a blazing fire awaits you!"

"I am so happy that our ordeal is over," Emma uttered to Nan as they followed Father John to the feast. "No matter how we got to the Land of the Diamond Sea, all has ended well. Has it not, Nan?"

"Aye, it has," Nan replied. Taking note of her companion's excellent demeanor, she added, "You are well, too, Emma. I am feeling much better myself."

"I am well," Emma said. "I do not know what made us so ill, but I am not complaining now. Nevertheless, we know 'twas not caused by the One from the Onyx Gate. Whatever the case may be, it has left me feeling very hungry. I am eager for this feast that Father John is taking us to."

"I only hope that Eolande has forgiven you for your bold behavior by rescuing me in Lamington," Nan chided Emma.

"I believe that he would be waiting crossly for me already if it were otherwise," Emma said confidently. "And not have such a wonderful feast made for us before we got here."

They entered the great hall where torches were burning brightly in the walls. Rows and rows of food fit for a king were laid out on linen covered tables. The girls saw no one but themselves and Father John.

"Father, will the others be eating with us, too?" Nan asked curiously. "Has Richard returned to the Land of the Diamond Sea? What of Lord Hallam and his men? Where is Eolande?"

"When I saw that the battle was turning in our favor, I left it to return here, before Lord Robert's arrival," Father John replied. "The others have made it through the fighting. They will arrive here sometime today. Eolande is busy. He will come by later, he has informed me, for the grander feast, which will be held for the soldiers."

"Father, I find it worrisome that his lordship has come back with the book," Emma stated. "After all he had put Lamington through, he should not have brought it here by his own hand. 'Tis still in his possession. He can still be tempted to read from it. You know what this can lead to."

"I do not believe that will happen," Father John said curtly. "He understands what he did. He has told me so. More than anything, he wants the jewel back in the book, lass. Eat, both of you, and say no more!"

Father John walked off as Emma and Nan sat down at one of the tables.

"How strange of Father to answer us like that," Nan said, feeling bothered by his strange behavior. "And to leave us so quickly. 'Tis not like him. Do you not think so, Emma?"

"Nan!" Emma exclaimed. "How can you speak of our castle chaplain like that? Let us be truthful. We are so tired of this senseless battle. It can bring out the worst in anyone, even Father John."

Nan sat sullenly as some servants entered the hall and poured out something to drink for the girls.

Emma is right, she thought. *I should be happy now that the battle is over. After supper, I will speak to Eolande—wherever he is—about when I shall go back to Lamington to see my family. How I long to see them!*

Picking up the goblet in front of her, Nan put it to her lips and took a small sip of her drink. Emma, whose throat was parched, enthusiastically took a large mouthful of hers. Finishing every last drop, Emma's head became foggy.

"'Tis a very potent drink, Nan," Emma said. "I cannot place what it might be, but it cannot be wine, even the weakest sort."

"Mayhap this is what wine tastes like," Nan replied. "And I do not feel well from it, either."

"Nay, I can assure you *that* is not wine," Emma contended. "I have had it many a time before. I am beginning to feel very much like I had earlier on the plain. My stomach is feeling ill all over and, oh! My head! My head! I see two . . . nay, three of you sitting there. Nan, I cannot handle it."

Nan felt an awful feeling of tingling ripping through her entire body within moments of her sip. She fell off the bench and onto the floor. Her mind was in a terrible muddle as Emma's was.

"Emma! Pray help me!" Nan called out, but Emma did not help her. She was fast asleep and snoring soundly with her head down on the table.

CHAPTER 34

As she lie on the floor, Nan saw a pair of leather shoes walk up to her and stop. Struggling to gaze upward, she saw Lord Robert with a sly smile on his face. Behind him was Father John standing next to an old man with a long, graying beard whom she did not recognize. He wore a dark velvet tunic and had a cruel-looking, shriveled face with penetrating eyes that scrutinized Nan carefully.

"Do you have the emerald, lass?" Lord Robert asked. "I see that your drink has had quite an effect on you and Emma. Wine itself would not work so fast if we had not placed a little something into it. The herb garden here has many things in it for our use."

"Give him the jewel, you foolish lass!" the strange man with the graying beard hissed. He bent down and peered at Nan closely. His drooping eyes were so frightening that she saw the red veins in them, which made her shudder and back away from him the closer he came to her.

"Nay, I cannot do that!" Nan screamed, but it did not do any good. She was merely a small lass up against the others who were much stronger than herself, particularly his lordship whom she knew she could not get away from so easily.

Wanting to rise from the floor, Nan crawled on her hands and knees to the edge of the table and tried to pull herself up from there. She failed and went back down on the floor. Her head was spinning and her eyes were becoming very blurry. The figures speaking around her sounded more like the buzzing of bees rather than men.

"Give me the jewel, lass!" Lord Robert shouted. "I am waiting, but my patience runs thin."

"Do you have the book?" Nan asked feebly. She rubbed her eyes, but she still did not see properly. "I cannot give you the jewel without placing it back into the front of the book first. I must see it."

Nan's endless questions seemed to enrage his lordship all the more. His eyes flashed and his face became more crimson with anger.

"Does it matter if I have the book or not?" Lord Robert asked impertinently. "I will get it when I am ready. Who are you to tell me what to do! Give that thing to me, you brazen peasant girl! If you give me the emerald, I will do much good for your poor family. Your father may have as many sheep as he wants. Think of all the money 'twill bring in for himself and his family. You may even have a better home to live in. Mayhap a stone one would suit you better than that straw one that needs constant fixing. I can provide all this and more if you do as you are told."

Nan's heart leapt for joy upon hearing Lord Robert's promises to her. A stone cottage to live in! It was too good to be true. Her mother would be forever grateful to the Lord of Lamington for his generosity. More money meant a better life for them. Her father would be bestowed a new life tending over flocks of sheep rather than slaving over a plot of land that did not always yield a good harvest.

Nan did not understand why his lordship wanted this emerald so badly like he did. Why could he not ask it of her in a kindly manner? Something was just not right about what was happening. Nan was becoming scared and indecisive over his persistent demand. She knew she was able to trust Lord Robert, but she remembered that there were other times when he had acted in a not-so-very amiable way. Nan decided that she had no choice than to hand over the jewel.

"I will give you the emerald, your lordship," Nan said, as she dropped her shaking hand into her dress pocket.

Pulling out the emerald, Nan held it up for all to see. Lord Robert's eyes grew wide as he greedily beheld the little green holly leaf-shaped jewel. Outstretching his hand, he waited as Nan placed the gleaming object into it. He rolled his hand into a tight fist around the holly leaf and walked over to Father John and the other gentleman. Opening his hand, the other men crowded triumphantly around his lordship as he showed them the jewel.

"Thank you very much, lass," Lord Robert stated with satisfaction. "The One from the Onyx Gate thanks you as well. Now you will get *your* reward. You will stay *ad infinitum* in the dungeon here. No one will ever find you or that maidservant. Who would dare rescue two foolish lasses from the One from the Onyx Gate? You will be tormented for the rest of your lives. Richard will not save you, nor will many of the other men who were with him. They were all killed in battle. All of them! Lord Hallam did not survive, either. Sir Erling is much too strong a Viwa fairy to let the others live."

Nan glanced up at Lord Robert with her bleary eyes and sadness filled her heart. They were hoodwinked after all. She and Emma have found themselves in a much darker place than the Land of the Diamond Sea. The temptations of the One from the Onyx Gate were far too great for anyone to overcome. It did not matter whether Nan had tried to return to the Land of the Diamond Sea alone or with someone else. The One from the Onyx Gate would have tricked her nonetheless on her way back. Now they were never to leave the Onyx Gate. To live out the rest of their lives in a dark prison was far too frightening to imagine.

Nan saw the hazy shape of Emma still slumbering at the table. Emma was oblivious to the dialogue between Nan and Lord Robert. She was not even conscious to see that the emerald was out of their hands and into those of the One from the Onyx Gate!

Emma! Emma! Nan cried out inside her mind. *Richard is dead! The others, too! Nothing has changed. Sir Erling still reigns in Viwa and his lordship still has the book. Christmas is still forbidden in Lamington and from the hearts and minds of those who live there. Why did his lordship and Father John turn to the side of the One from the Onyx Gate? Who is that other man who stands next to Father? I suppose that does not really matter. No one will come to save us, like his lordship has said. Emma, you and I cannot escape now.*

Lying dazed on the floor, Nan vaguely became aware of a distant pounding coming from someplace within the One from the Onyx Gate's castle. Her eyes fluttered open as the pounding became louder and louder. A door was thrust open and a rush of cold wind came sweeping through the room. Shouts were heard and horses' hooves came clop-clopping into the great hall. Nan lifted her head toward the direction where the noise was coming from. Richard came into the room with his sword and shield held out in front of him as if he were ready to take on anyone who got in his way. His dour face was caked with mud as was his armor from fighting. He appeared to be in no mood to play games with those whom he confronted.

"Give the emerald to Nan, you imposter!" Richard bellowed to

Lord Robert from his horse.

Several of Lord Hallam's men who were following behind Richard surrounded Lord Robert, Father John, and the third man in the great hall.

Lord Robert's face became enflamed as the veins in his head protruded with rage.

"I will not give it to that farmer's daughter!" his lordship retorted. "How dare you call *me* an imposter? The One from the Onyx Gate is posing as Richard, and you are he. The Onyx Gate is where you are from. You are the imposter, Richard!"

"Give it to her!" Richard exclaimed all the more louder.

"Richard!" a weak voice called out. "Is that you I hear?"

Nan saw that Emma had awoken and was trying to get up from the bench she sat on. Instead, she wobbled and grabbed onto the corner of the table as she forced herself to sit down again. Her eyes were glassy and her skin was sallow.

"I do not know if he is Richard, Emma," Nan said. "I am so confused by what is being said to me. Richard is no longer alive."

"I *am* Richard, Nan," Richard declared steadfastly. "Do not believe the others and who they say they are. They are a part of the One from the Onyx Gate. All of them!"

"I am Lord Robert of Lamington and no other," his lordship said firmly. "'Tis you who is not Richard. He has been killed in battle. I, myself, have seen him die."

"I have not died," Richard maintained. "You are part of him who lives here, and this is the Onyx Gate. You lie! Now you must pay for what you have done to these lasses. I have come to free them from this dreaded place."

Nan turned from Richard to each of the men. She did not know whom to trust. She watched as Lord Robert pulled a sword from his scabbard as he lunged at Richard. Richard jumped from his horse and began to take on Lord Robert in the fight.

An angry shriek came from Emma. With a sudden burst of energy, she reached for her sword, which she had hidden under her cloak, and ran from the table toward Lord Robert. His lordship did not see Emma coming. His back was facing her as she plunged her sword at him. He went falling to the floor in a crumpled heap.

Nan saw that Father John and the other man were dead as some of

Lord Hallam's men peered down at their dead bodies. Two of the soldiers had taken the other two men down just as Emma's sword had gone into Lord Robert.

"Father John is dead!" Nan cried, placing her hand over her mouth in shock. "Emma, you have killed his lordship!"

"Emma has not killed his lordship, lass," Richard said. "Nor has Lord Hallam's men killed Father John. The third man's identity is unfamiliar to me, but he is undeniably a part of the One's evil inner circle. Let me prove I am Richard and how I got here. I found my father's book in Sir Erling's tent. Though the battle was still raging, I knew I could not stay there. I had one last thing left to do. I had to leave Lamington immediately and bring the book back to the Land of the Diamond Sea as Eolande had instructed. After departing with some of Lord Hallam's men, we came upon you and Emma in the forest nearby. I wanted to join in your company, but a funny feeling of sorts came over me that told me not to do it. I am glad that I told the men that we should follow you instead. How little we knew where you were truly going, and Eolande's castle 'twas not! What is worse, if we traveled together with the jewel and the book, the One from the Onyx Gate would have vigorously tempted all of us to get them both back into his possession. Eolande said so. Can you just imagine it! What chaos! Finding you, defending ourselves, and preventing evil from grasping hold of those valuable items we carried on us! The One from the Onyx Gate would have liked nothing better!"

"How much worse, indeed!" Nan said. "We would have lost the book and the emerald more easily than we almost did a minute ago!"

"Not to mention that all our accomplishments would have been for nothing," Richard added. "We would be back where we started with the book's spell still hanging over us. I admit that we took a chance in coming after you to this place—bringing the book in here was dangerous enough, but at least the One from the Onyx Gate was not expecting me with it, and we still had to save you no matter what. Having you both remain here with the emerald was not something we wanted. I am sure Eolande would understand."

"Richard, Nan did say that she heard something—or someone—in the forest," Emma stated. "'Twas you all along! How courageous of you to come for us."

Color was returning to Emma's cheeks as the weakness in her body started to disappear and her head began to clear.

"Had you not, we were to be made prisoners here forever!" Nan said. "To never see the light of day in a dungeon was something I was not liking. Richard, can you show us his lordship's book?"

Nan was suspicious that Richard might be an imposter, which the figure of the so-called Lord Robert, who lie on the floor, said he was. This Lord Robert had not shown them any book. Could Richard do it?

"I do not think showing you the book here is the best idea," Richard said. "But I will show it to you quickly if that is what you wish me to."

Richard reached into his saddlebag and held the book half way out for the girls to see. He then replaced it in the bag for safekeeping.

Nan breathed a sigh of relief that he was, indeed, Richard with the book.

"I can feel the evil in these very walls," Sir Ivo observed. "It never sleeps. Its eyes are fixated on us. Leave we must!"

"Where is the jewel?" Richard asked the girls, his eyes darting from one to the other. "We cannot leave here without it."

"I believe 'tis in the hand of Lord Robert," Nan said in dismay. "I gave it to him before he fell to the ground."

"Nan!" Emma cried in fright. "His lordship is moving. It cannot be!"

Everyone turned to look at the lifeless body of Lord Robert. It began to stir as an odd, transparent grayish fog began to form around it. The same inexplicable manifestation started to occur to the bodies of the other men who lie dead on the ground. A loud whooshing sound came from them as they began to stand up. Each of the men's eyes, now glassy, opened as they turned to face the others with a long sword that appeared from nothing in their hands. They rapidly, yet woodenly, advanced toward Richard and Lord Hallam's men.

Emma let out a loud scream that sent shivers down Nan's back. Nan's eyes fell to the floor. She gazed upon the tiny holly leaf emerald laying near the edge of Lord Robert's foot as he rose up.

"Richard!" Nan squealed as she pointed to the ground. "I see the holly leaf over there!" She was afraid to grab the jewel for fear that his lordship would see her do it.

"The book!" Richard yelled, racing to his saddlebag. "I do not know if we need Eolande's castle to do this, but if the jewel is here, we can place it back in its rightful place immediately. We will end this madness before we return to the Land of the Diamond Sea. We can do this, lasses! Hurry! Time is not on our side!"

Emma sprung for the emerald. She was weary of the evil Viwa controlling their lives and did not care what the One from the Onyx Gate did to her. Her fingers reached for the jewel as Lord Robert changed course and ran to her with his sword. Meanwhile, Father John and the unknown man went after Richard as several of Lord Hallam's men came to his aid.

"Nan, pray take the emerald!" Emma called out. She reached out to Nan with a shaky hand and gave her the jewel.

Richard came to Nan and held up the front of the book where the little cavity for the emerald was visible. Nan had stood up as she was gradually regaining her health back after being ill just moments earlier. Her fingers trembling, she put the little green holly leaf back into its proper spot.

Richard nodded at Nan for doing so fine a job, but all was not over. The man who had been with Father John changed into a great, frightening lizard creature with bird's wings. It was the same creature that had observed Emma and Nan before they had entered the castle of the One from the Onyx Gate. It flew high in the air as it made a shrieking sound and spun in a dizzying circle above everyone's head. The creature then flew out of the castle window and disappeared.

The evil Lord Robert and Father John spontaneously changed into similar airborne bird-like creatures. They flew high up into the recesses of the windows with a noisy flapping sound. They perched themselves there and scanned the room with their eerie greenish-gray eyes for what seemed to be an eternity before making another move. Their screams were equally, if not worse, than that of the first creature that had left earlier.

The two creatures flew out of the castle, leaving Emma and Nan huddled on the floor together in fright. Richard and Lord Hallam's men stood about recoiling to the earsplitting sounds that were coming from the creatures. Their horses reared up in fright and wanted to run off. After silence descended upon the great hall, hundreds of Viwa maidens instantaneously came dancing into the room with their colorful gowns and white flowers in their flaxen hair. Ignoring Emma and Nan, they surrounded Richard and the other soldiers with their half-closed eyes and uncanny smile. Out of their mouths came rushing their proverbial scream. They were louder and more pronounced as there were at least a hundred or so of them crying together. They ran toward Richard and the men who pulled out their swords to protect themselves from danger. To everyone's bewilderment, the maidens became ghost-like and went through each person like a cold mist where they vanished through the back wall of the great hall.

Richard, Lord Hallam's soldiers, and the girls were momentarily dumbfounded and shaken by the unnatural events that had befallen them. The room had grown quiet and only until it seemed safe to do so did everyone start to talk and move about.

"'Tis truly over," Richard announced. He wiped dripping beads of sweat from his forehead with the back of his hand.

Nan and Emma were still too afraid to arise from the ground until Richard came to their assistance. Helping them up, it took the girls a while to regain their balance and their sanity.

"I do not want to stay in this loathsome castle any longer!" Emma exclaimed. Her fingers were still quivering as she placed her sword back into her scabbard.

"Wha— What has happened?" Nan asked.

"I . . . I do not know," Richard answered. "Off to the courtyard and onto your horse, lasses! We do not need another showing of these creatures or the fairy maidens. Mayhap this was the last of them."

The girls nodded in agreement as they rushed back to the courtyard with Richard and the other men and mounted Emma's horse.

"Promise us one thing, Richard," Emma pleaded as she sat down in her saddle while Richard helped Nan up behind her. "Pray do not lose his lordship's book as I had. Keep it safe where it belongs. Do not take it out until we get to the rightful Land of the Diamond Sea."

"That I can promise you," Richard said, as he slipped the book back into his saddlebag.

CHAPTER 35

The riders galloped their horses as fast as they could out of the One from the Onyx Gate's castle. They rode through the castle gate and across the drawbridge, taking note of the castle changing into something much more foreboding than what it originally was when they had first entered it. The castle transformed itself from rough yellow sandstone into one of polished black. Exposed on the castle gate were glittering black stones.

"I know why they call it the Onyx Gate!" Emma said, riding close behind Richard. "I am seeing onyx all over its walls."

"Here I was starting to believe that his castle was really that ugly yellow one!" Nan said. "How glad I am that he did change his black one into one of yellow. It might not have been *perfectly* nice, but anything was better than what we are now seeing."

"What were you expecting, Nan?" Emma asked. "He could not tempt us with a black castle. He knew we would not make our entrance into a repugnant one, though the yellow one did not look like Eolande's castle in any way, nor did anything around the yellow castle look like the Land of the Diamond Sea. I am indebted to you, Nan, for noticing those things, though we did end up going into the castle despite it all."

"We can thank those two charlatans at the Onyx Gate for doing *that*," Nan stated. "Their lies were too convincing for us not to do so."

"Do not forget about that sickness that was put on us before we arrived here!" Emma said. "Our minds were so muddled from it that we did not know up from down. But, as long as we were entrapped at the Onyx Gate castle in the end, nothing else mattered to the one who made us feel that way. Yellow castle or not!"

"I hate to disappoint you, but the One from the Onyx Gate misled you all too well, lasses," Richard told the girls. "Let us hope that we get to the *real* Land of the Diamond Sea today without any more setbacks."

"What were those beasts that flew like birds?" Nan asked. She was chilled by the thought of those winged creatures they saw at the Onyx Gate castle, but was unable to dismiss their fear-provoking image. "I was so frightened when I saw those men turn into them."

"They were most unpleasant, indeed!" Emma exclaimed with a shudder. "I was afraid that they were going to swoop down and carry us off to their den somewhere."

"They are somehow associated with the One from the Onyx Gate," Richard said. "What else could they be?"

"We keep talking about him, but where was the One from the Onyx Gate?" Nan wondered. "Was he there, too? Why did he not show himself?"

"He could have been there with those men and turned into one of those creatures afterward," Richard replied. "We just did not recognize him, which is how he may have wanted it. We will never know for certain."

"He could have been the man who was not the fake Lord Robert and Father John!" Nan speculated. After a pause, she then said, "Sometimes 'tis best not to know. If I did, I would have been more scared than I already was then."

"At least the emerald is now in its proper place in the book," Emma stated. "We can all be thankful to Nan for that."

"This must mean the battle in Lamington must be over!" Nan cried. "Sir Erling has met his just end."

Richard grinned. "I should think so, but we will not know for certain until later on, will we? Incidentally, both you and Emma have shown quite an act of bravery. I overheard how you saved Nan from the Viwa stewards in Lamington, Emma. I would not have expected it of you. I know Eolande will be impressed with your abilities as a she-knight, both in Lamington and at the Onyx Gate castle. Imagine that! You, Emma, killing off the bogus Lord Robert who, unbeknownst to us, came back to life!"

"I pray that Eolande is not too upset with me after what I had done," Emma said. "If anything, I plan on returning as maidservant to Lady Catherine very soon. She will need me more now that she is with child. My days as a she-knight are over. My only regret is that those abilities did not stop Nan and I from being tempted by the One from the Onyx Gate. We almost did not survive the trials that we were put through in his castle."

Nan smiled inwardly. If only Richard knew that some of Emma's distant Viwa blood might have played a part in her act of courage, but Nan dared not reveal this because of her promise to Eolande.

"When I think back over it, if I was supposed to be tempted by the One from the Onyx Gate, as Eolande had said, then 'twas best that I was not confronted by him alone," Nan said. "I am glad you were with me, Emma, during that time."

Emma turned around on her horse and gave Nan a cheerful smile.

"'Tis over, lasses," Richard reassured the girls. "There is no need to worry about the One from the Onyx Gate any longer. We are free of him. Off to the Land of the Diamond Sea we go!"

Everyone then sped their horses away from the Onyx Gate castle and over the wide stationary bridge where, eventually, they saw familiar territory on the horizon. Nan was filled with excitement as she gazed at the plain where low shrubs were starting to show themselves from underneath the snow because of the coming change in seasons. She was also happy, because she was thankful to Richard for risking his life with Lord Hallam's men and rescuing her and Emma before their situation in the Onyx Gate had grown more precarious.

The air was cool, but not uncomfortable, and there was a light breeze blowing as the party rode along. Nan and her two companions felt safer that they were riding on the barren plain at the height of a bright, cloudless afternoon and not when the sun was going down. They were confident that they would soon find themselves at the dunes of the sandy beach that would carry them over to the Land of the Diamond Sea. Nan turned to Richard who seemed much more relaxed since leaving the Onyx Gate. As Nan was seated behind Emma, she was not able to determine the other girl's emotions from where she was. Nan took a glimpse at Lord Hallam's men. She saw that some of them looked exhausted from the battle that took place in Lamington and their chainmail and shields had been worn a bit from the fighting. Others had bandaged injuries, but most seemed to have fared well during the battle. A few of the men spoke in a low voice amongst themselves, but many of them journeyed on in silence, anxious for food and rest at Eolande's castle.

CHAPTER 36

Everyone was soon within reach of the edge of the plain where the invisible line was drawn between the human world and that of the white sandy beach of the Land of the Diamond Sea. From their vantage point, they saw a pitiful figure of Lady Catherine walking by herself on the plain in a bright green gown without any cloak on. Her hair was hanging disheveled around her shoulders and down her back. She was not wearing a veil and she looked as if she had been crying.

"Lady Catherine!" Richard exclaimed, his eyes wide in disbelief upon seeing her.

"I do not see anyone with her," Emma said. She saw a sad Lady Catherine staring at them. "How could she have come this far by herself? Where is her horse?"

Emma galloped her steed ahead of the others.

"I hope something did not happen in Lamington," Nan declared with concern. "I cannot think of how she was able to find us and on foot, too."

Richard and Lord Hallam's soldiers raced up behind Emma and stopped to speak to her ladyship as she came walking up to them. Richard leapt down from his horse and went on bended knee to her. The others, following suit, came down from their horses to pay her homage as well.

"My lady!" Emma cried out. "What brings you here at such a distance from Lamington? Do you need any help? I am thankful to God that we have found you."

Lady Catherine did not answer Emma. Instead, she pointed a finger straight at Richard.

"'Tis all your fault!" she cried out. "My husband is dead because of you, Aric!"

Richard grimaced when he heard her use that name. He knew it to be his birth name, but he preferred if she used the name of Richard. He supposed she learned it from the Viwa stewards at Castle Lamington while she was being held prisoner there by them.

"Aric!" Lady Catherine screamed louder and louder. "You will pay for the loss that has befallen all of us. You are evil, Aric!"

Richard was taken aback. Lord Hallam's men were disgusted by Lady Catherine's behavior. She hissed at Richard and tried to scratch him with nails so long that they caused Emma to give them a second glance. Richard jerked away just as Lady Catherine reached for his face with her cat-like nails.

"Your ladyship, I do not know what has happened to his lordship or any of the men yet," Richard said in defense. "We left before the battle ended. Someone should have come to you to tell you the outcome of it. We have excellent news, however! Nan has found the emerald! She placed it back into the very book that his lordship read from that caused the blue snow to fall. Those terrible events, which were caused because of it, should be over and gone for good. I have the book with me, so I know this to be true."

Lady Catherine continued hissing like a snake. Next, she reached up and succeeded in scratching the side of his face much to the revulsion of Emma and Nan. They stood by helpless as Richard felt some blood on his hand from the deep wound that Lady Catherine had inflicted on him. A few of Lord Hallam's men got in between her ladyship and Richard to protect him from further harm. Her ladyship continued to keep a watchful eye on Richard. She seemed oblivious of the others around her.

"So *you* have the book, Aric," her ladyship said with a shrewd smile. "I demand you to give it to me. Where is it? Pray be a good lad and give it to me now! If you do not, then much trouble will await you."

"I cannot give it to you, my lady," Richard replied. "It no longer belongs to us."

Something was amiss with Lady Catherine. Richard became suspicious of her motives for wanting Lord Robert's book.

"If you will come with us to the Land of the Diamond Sea, which is not far off, you may see the book for yourself," Richard promised her. "I must have it returned to Eolande. He needs to do something with it. I was told the book will never leave the Land of the Diamond Sea after that."

"Eolande!" Lady Catherine screamed so deafeningly in Richard's ear that it began to ring. "That Eolande will never get his way with me. That book will never find its way back to *that* place of which you speak of."

From underneath a cloak that was tossed on the ground nearby, she lifted a shield and threw it at Richard. It was Lord Robert's shield as Richard was the only other person on the battlefield who had one with the coat-of-arms of Lamington on it.

Lady Catherine laughed while pointing to the object, which scarcely missed hitting Richard's head.

"I bring you great news, lad! Lord Robert *is* dead. 'Twas brought to me after he was killed."

Emma and Nan looked at one another with saddened eyes.

"So it is true!" Emma said. "Lord Robert *has* perished! How awful this day is, indeed!"

Was the new lord of Lamington in their midst? Nan asked herself with a quick glance at Richard. *Was her ladyship upset that he would take the place of her child and had lost her mind over it?*

"Your ladyship, how can you be happy about his death?" Emma murmured as tears rolled down her cheeks. "A moment ago you said how upset you were about it. I do not quite understand."

"I lied!" Lady Catherine screeched.

Abrupt changes began to take place before the shocked eyes of those around her. Her ladyship's face started to twist about violently. It altered itself from Lady Catherine's and into that of the face of an evil Viwa maiden. She opened her mouth to bare her ugly teeth. With her lips, she created that impossible sound combination of a screaming woman and a hooting owl. Hundreds of Viwa maidens began to rise up from the ground in wispy shapes until wholly formed. They encircled Richard, Lord Hallam's soldiers, and Emma and Nan. Their intent was to prevent anyone from escaping. They forced the riders to huddle closer together to the point that they could not move an inch without feeling the very breath of the evil fairies at their backs.

"Richard, I thought our worries had ended!" Nan cried out.

"I do not know how we can get away from them!" Richard shouted. He hardly heard himself above the peculiar call the evil Viwa maidens made harmoniously. He feared to look at any of the fairies straight in the eye. He worried that one of them would place him under a spell and force him to hand over the prized book, which he had in his saddlebag.

"We are trapped!" one of Lord Hallam's men said with discomfort at being so close to such evil. "I believe they want you, Richard, to give the book to them. Do not dare do so!"

"I know! I will never give them the book!" Richard retorted with glowering eyes.

"How can you not give us the book?" one of the Viwa maidens asked. "After the book, sure death for you, lad. You will join your father, fool! No son of Lord Robert of Lamington will reign on our throne. Ever!"

"What will we do?" Emma wailed. "I thought that all evil left us when Nan replaced the emerald in the book. We all saw the Viwa maidens disappear through the One from the Onyx Gate's wall in his great hall. How can they come back to us?"

"Mayhap you found the wrong jewel, lass," spoke another of Lord Hallam's men accusatorily toward Nan. "What if the one you found in the cottage was not the proper one?"

"'Twas the *only* one I found in the ashes at home," Nan replied, almost near tears. Nan rubbed her forehead as she thought hard. What if someone took the rightful emerald and substituted it with one that did not have a spell? She prayed in her heart that this was not so, but she was not certain. Perhaps those Viwa stewards who had shown up at the cottage did it. They were not trustworthy and might very well have been responsible for such a wicked act.

In-fighting broke out. Every person there, from Lord Hallam's soldiers to Richard and the girls, became angry and blamed the other for the impasse they found themselves in on the barren plain. The Viwa maidens smiled at Richard with their half-closed eyes. One of them grabbed at his arm and began to pull him out of the crowd. She had almost succeeded when the sound of a deafening windstorm was heard.

Eolande's figure appeared on the plain. He raised one of his arms over the group surrounded by the Viwa fairy maidens. In a loud voice, Eolande muttered something in ancient Viwa. The evil Viwa maidens let go of their suffocating grip that they had on the others, including Richard, and dispersed into thin air. If Richard and those with him thought that their troubles were over, nothing was further from the truth.

"Eolande! Eolande!"

A voice, which went from sweet to guttural, called from the plain across from where Eolande was standing. To their disbelief, everyone saw that it was the Lady Catherine herself who had turned back from being a Viwa maiden. A cold, raging wind came from her direction making those standing nearby unable to turn away from it and stay warm in their cloaks.

"Eolande, you fool! You thought you were so clever with my maidens, were you! I told you that you would not get your way with me. Now, take this!"

Reaching from inside her cloak, she pulled out a large, shiny onyx and held it up.

"'Tis the One from the Onyx Gate!" Richard exclaimed.

"Oh, I pray he does not hurt Eolande!" Emma murmured. "He is beyond our power if Eolande is harmed."

Nan became paralyzed with fear. A lump was in her throat and she could not speak.

A blazing ray of black and silver light streamed from the onyx and hit Eolande, which first encircled him, and twirled him around and around without end. A few of Lord Hallam's men drew back in fear, but courageously came to their senses to run to Eolande's side. It was no use. The One from the Onyx Gate, acting out in the disguise of Lady Catherine, triggered the onyx's power to do the same to the good Viwa knights. Richard became concerned that they had been killed and Eolande with them.

"Richard, do something!" Nan said, finding her voice.

Just as Richard nervously fumbled for his sword in the scabbard at his side, a luminescent light broke through the black and silver rays surrounding Eolande's spinning self. He stopped spinning and with an outstretched arm, he was holding a large diamond. He said something in ancient Viwa again. Shimmering waves came from the diamond and shot right through the Lady Catherine who was standing with the onyx. She howled loudly and disappeared on impact with a crackling sound and was seen no more. Lord Hallam's men stopped spinning and returned to their usual selves. Then there was silence.

Eolande stood smiling at the fatigued assemblage in front of him.

"I am sorry this had to happen," Eolande declared. "None of you would have made it to the Land of the Diamond Sea had I not come to your aid. When I saw the maidens at my doorstep barring your way, I knew

I had to step in. They are always a last resort for trouble. I also should have realized that the One from the Onyx Gate would try one last attempt of his own. However, he has learned his lesson. He should know I am more powerful than he is, though he believes otherwise."

"Eolande!" Richard shouted, waving his arms high in the air. "You do not know how happy we are to see you. We should have noticed sooner that we were not dealing with the real Lady Catherine. I did not believe for one moment that she knew my birth name to be Aric."

"It feels as if it has been a long time since we left you," Nan said, her throat parched with thirst.

"Will you ever forgive me for being such a foolish maidservant?" Emma asked Eolande. "I should not have left your castle to go romping about as a soldier."

Lord Hallam's men started to laugh with relief that they had come to their journey's end. A few of them rubbed their eyes as they tried to hide their own tears of joy, which was what they were feeling as they stood at the entranceway to the Land of the Diamond Sea, after seeing the sight of their old friend, Eolande.

"Eolande, let us in!" Sir Aswin, another soldier of Lord Hallam's, complained with an impatient smile. "Our energy is waning and we are about to drop from our horses. We have had a most difficult day."

Eolande chuckled as he motioned to them to follow him back to his castle, though he knew that what they had gone through was no laughing matter.

"Come! Get yourselves refreshed!" Eolande said. "I insist upon it. But, before you do, I want to share with you something which, I am sure, you will not want to wait to hear—the battle in Lamington is over! Victory there has been won! The rest of the battle-weary men will be coming back tomorrow. I have foreseen it. They are yearning to celebrate in their triumph with you. There will be a feast like no other that evening."

Oh, the cheers that rose through the air until everybody's throat became hoarse! Lord Hallam's men, so close to the battle since early morning, were especially delighted to hear that the battle was a success. It implied that they were going to do something that they had not done in years—go home to Viwa! Eolande had given them the best news in years. They were grateful for everything that Eolande had done for them since they had come to the Land of the Diamond Sea, even if helping them overthrow Sir Erling did take a long time to accomplish. They knew that Eolande, whom they had known for many long decades, would not fail them and there was proof in the words he had just spoken.

Nan smiled as she turned to Emma. She was humbled by the realization that their long adventure was coming to a close. Emma would return to Lady Catherine and Nan to her family's cottage. Back to the old familiar life with its days of hardship and toil, and other days of festivities and laughter when time allowed for it.

"Nan, we are going home!" Emma cried out. "Christmas *will* arrive again! All will be well again in Lamington."

"We *are* going home!" Nan said excitedly.

Thoughts of seeing her mother and father and little sisters and brother were no longer something of a far-off dream for Nan. They were becoming a reality. How happy her family would be to see her return home. How much they would have to say to one another when they saw her. Nan's only worry now was whether or not she could sit patiently enough through a long feast before they left to go!

The small company trotted their horses as Eolande walked with them the rest of the short distance down the plain, where they crossed that invisible line, which took them to the Land of the Diamond Sea. While Richard and the men went off to the castle stables with the horses, Nan stood basking in the warm sunshine of the balmy air until she and her companion were escorted by a servant back to their old bedchamber. Leaving behind the continual summer season of the Land of the Diamond Sea made Nan disheartened, but she knew she had to return home where she truly belonged.

The girls, fatigued from their long day, fell onto their beds without scarcely a word to one another and slept until late the next morning when a hardy meal was served to them. Emma was offered another beautiful gown to wear as well. Nan was happy that there was none for her, but the other girl decided to change into the periwinkle satin one that was laid out for her.

"Emma, I thought you made up your mind that your old gown was good enough," Nan said.

"I did," Emma replied, "but right before Richard left for the stables, he told me that Eolande has forgiven me for what I have done. Giving me this gown was Eolande's way of showing his forgiveness. He told Richard all this when we were making our way across the white bridge, and I do not want to disappoint him."

"I am so happy for you, Emma!" Nan smiled. "At least you can put your worries about being a she-knight to rest."

For the rest of the afternoon, Emma and Nan spent their time in the castle gardens while Richard and the men were somewhere in the castle deep in discussion over important future matters.

"I overheard Eolande telling Richard that that Viwa maiden was correct about his lordship's death," Emma said softly, bending over to smell a large, fragrant lily. "The shield was brought to Richard as proof of his father's passing. 'Twas not something that was made up to scare us. Now that his lordship is gone, there is no one left to become heir of Lamington, unless it be Richard or his lordship's second child by Lady Catherine. But, I suppose, that remains to be seen."

"So 'twas true after all! Poor Richard!" Nan exclaimed, shaking her head. "How sorry I am for her ladyship."

Emma nodded as she sat down on the grass. Her eyes were pink as if she were trying to hold back tears. After some hesitation, she blurted out, "There is something I have to admit to you, Nan! I already knew of his lordship's death before we ever got to the castle of the One from the Onyx Gate—I saw him being slain by Sir Erling when I was taking you out of Lamington. You see, Nan, we might have had a very good chance to evade the One from the Onyx Gate, and right from the very start, had I told you about his lordship's death, but I was in such denial over it. I did not think Lord Robert could ever perish. Then when we saw him—or, thought we did—at the Onyx Gate castle, this helped to keep me falsely believing that he was alive, even after we realized that the Lord Robert there was not the real one! How senseless of me! 'Twas only until Eolande confirmed his passing away did I really trust that he was gone. Can you understand that?"

"I do, Emma, and I forgive you," Nan answered. "I do not find fault with you. I remember telling you something similar around that time—that his lordship could never be killed, but it looks like God had a different plan for him."

"There is a second part to this which hurts me just as much," Emma whispered sadly. "Lord Roger is gone! As if seeing Lord Robert's end was difficult enough, I saw Sir Erling taking Lord Roger's life, too. 'Twas only seconds after Lord Robert was killed. Poor Lady Catherine! It breaks my heart thinking of her losing both her husband and brother all in one day. As with Lord Robert, I could not speak about Lord Roger until now. Pray do not make this known to anybody, Nan. Lord Roger's death has not been announced yet, but I am sure 'twill be."

Nan's eyes filled with tears. "What tragedies for you to see, Emma! Aye, poor Lady Catherine! I promise I will not tell anyone about Lord Roger. May the souls of the two lordships rest in peace." Turning her ear to a sound far away, Nan abruptly said, "I hear some men coming back! Lord Hallam and the rest of the soldiers are returning to the Land of the Diamond Sea."

Emma got up from the grass and running to the edge of the gardens with Nan, they peered around the garden wall. They watched an endless army of bedraggled men walking or riding their horses across the white bridge and making their way to the castle. Some they recognized, like Lord Hallam and Pell and a few others, but there were many they did not. Most were Lord Hallam's men and others were from Siddell. The girls spied Brother Alexander in the throng and were elated to see him return safely with the other men. They wondered where Father John was and hoped he had made it to the Land of the Diamond Sea with them.

Nan then caught a glimpse of a man she was all too familiar with. She gasped when she saw him clasped in chains and riding on a horse closely between several of Lord Hallam's men on theirs.

"Look, Emma!" Nan pointed. "Over there!"

"'Tis Sir Erling!" Emma said with surprise. "What an unhappy fellow he is!"

The Viwa pretender had been stripped of his sword and shield and rode clothed with only a plain tunic on. How unsettling this must have been for someone such as Sir Erling—accustomed to being ruler of a fairy kingdom and having his way for his own gain, even if it meant bowing to a dark lord in exchange for a holly leaf emerald in hopes of destroying those in the human world. Instead, Emma and Nan saw nothing more than a lowly prisoner at the mercy of a local Viwa lord who was Lord Hallam. Sir Erling was scowling wretchedly. His empty eyes were staring straight ahead at the soldiers who were taking him somewhere where his fate would be determined for him.

"No longer will we ever have to worry about Sir Erling," Nan stated. "He is powerless now."

"Aye, he will never again be known as Prince Erling of Viwa," Emma said.

Emma and Nan smiled to each other. They were thrilled that this day had come and that day, spent with danger and uncertainty, at the Onyx Gate was behind them.

CHAPTER 37

Later on that evening, the grand finale of all feasts was held in the Land of the Diamond Sea for its visitors. Emma changed into yet another gown that had been given to her. It was an attractive one of yellow-gold with both an embroidered neckline and sleeves. The hem at the bottom was also trimmed with intricate embroidery that would be the envy of any regal woman.

"'Tis our last evening spent in the Land of the Diamond Sea," Nan sighed. "How I shall miss it."

"So shall I," Emma replied, "but just think! No more worrying about lost emeralds or evil Viwa lurking in the shadows. I would much prefer to start sewing things for the new baby with her ladyship. 'Twill be much more exciting."

"Much more exciting than wearing all those beautiful gowns?" Nan asked disparagingly. "I cannot fancy it, Emma!"

"Well, this fun has to come to an end sometime, too, does it not?" Emma declared soberly.

In the great hall, Eolande had outdone himself with the main courses, and while everyone ate at the sound of minstrels playing, Nan decided to enjoy herself to the fullest as she and Emma sat at the foot of the dais where Richard, Eolande, and Lord Hallam sat. She knew that once she left the Land of the Diamond Sea, feasts such as these would become far and few.

Richard sporadically looked down at the girls and smiled at them. He himself had been exquisitely dressed in a red silk tunic, colorful hose, and the best velvet shoes for the grand supper laid out for them. His fair hair had been smoothed back until it gleamed to perfection. He stood out from the crowd of men seated around him, and the girls could only guess what this meant.

Lord Hallam arose from the dais as many fine, delectable desserts were being served.

"I want you all to know that the rule of Sir Erling in Viwa is officially over!" he said with great pleasure as he held high his goblet of Eolande's finest wine.

His eyes sparkled as those around him joined in the raising of their own goblets. They roared and drank merrily to the mentioning that Sir Erling was no longer their prince. Suddenly Lord Hallam's demeanor changed.

"I need not tell you that there is a painful absence of two men who would be here if their lives had not been taken from us so prematurely. Lord Robert of Lamington and Lord Roger of Siddell had died bravely defending Lamington from the evil Viwa. A message was sent out yesterday to the young son and heir of Lord Roger about his death."

Heads bowed silently in the room. A few of the men had discreetly wiped their eyes as they tried to compose themselves. Emma and Nan had been emotionally prepared for the bad news, especially for that of Lord Roger, but in the end they broke down and wept quietly over the two losses.

Eolande stood up solemnly from his seat to speak.

"I agree with Lord Hallam," Eolande proclaimed. "Their deaths were not some hopeless act by Sir Erling that happened when we least expected it to. Lord Robert and Lord Roger were strong men who will never be forgotten."

"We went to see Lady Catherine after the battle was over," Lord Hallam then added. "She was thankful that we had arrived to overthrow the evil Viwa who had tried to bring down Lamington. She took the news of Lord Robert and Lord Roger's deaths stalwartly. She also said that the two Viwa, who made her prisoner in her own castle, had fled once the battle was being lost. Father John is with her ladyship. He decided to stay behind with her at Castle Lamington. She needs his support after the ordeal she went through."

"Oh, Nan!" Emma burst out. "I am so happy for Lady Catherine! Praise God that the two fairy stewards are gone. I was sick with fear for her from the first day I was made aware of their presence at Castle Lamington."

"I, too, am glad that they are gone," Nan responded. "I am so pleased that Father John is alive and with her."

"We can be assured by this that he was never at the Onyx Gate," Emma said happily.

"And the best is being kept for last!" Eolande declared. "Sir Erling has been brought to my dungeon here. He will never escape the Land of the Diamond Sea for as long as he lives."

Lord Hallam quickly changed the morose subject of Sir Erling.

"A new era in Viwa history has begun!" he cried out.

The other Viwa in the room joined in his euphoria.

"Eolande, we must not forget that Richard has returned Lord Robert's book to you with the emerald in it!" shouted someone from the back of the hall.

"Aye, the book has been relinquished to me at last," Eolande confirmed. "I took it, like I have taken all other evil books with spells in the past, to a secret room here in the Land of the Diamond Sea where it has been destroyed. 'Tis gone forever!"

Eolande smiled as he laid his eyes upon Nan who sat quietly listening.

"None of this would have been accomplished without the help of this young lass here whose name is Nan," he praised. Turning his attention to Emma, he added, "It could also not be done without the help of Emma, though she did defy me a bit here and there."

Emma blushed in her seat and looked away from Eolande's gaze.

"Before this night is over and you return back to your world, Nan, there is something you must be told," Eolande said, leaving the dais—a customary habit of his anytime he had something important to say to her.

All eyes in the room were quickly fixated on Nan.

"I realize that you and Emma were tempted by the One from the Onyx Gate," Eolande began. "I saw it all from afar. Though I could only do so much from keeping you both from being tempted by him, I want you to know that if things had gotten much *much* worse, I would have been there for you, like I was when those Viwa maidens came to the edge of the Land of the Diamond Sea and caused trouble for all of you. But, in the end, you were a brave girl, Nan. You did not fail us. And with the help of Richard and some of Lord Hallam's men, you and Emma were rescued!"

Nan blushed a deep scarlet as Eolande and the entire party in the great hall stood up and raised their goblets to her. When they all sat down again, Eolande said austerely, "However, be forewarned, lass. This evil may have gone away, but 'twill not be gone forever. The One from the Onyx Gate and his underlings have had a temporary set-back, but they will leave us alone for a time."

"Eolande, I do not always understand fully what you mean by your words, but things always right themselves when you are there," Nan said.

"Eolande, if I may say so," Richard began, "with my good hearing, I cannot help to overhear some of what you say to Nan about those Viwa maidens." Frowning, he then said, "The lasses and I will *never* miss them! They had given us enough grief . . . disappearing and reappearing without notice. Our nerves were frazzled by them. I pray they will never show themselves in Viwa."

The girls glanced at one another questioningly.

Was Richard hinting at something? Was their traveling partner dropping a hint about his future?

"Richard, you do not have to worry about seeing Viwa maidens anywhere, unless you beg for the dark assistance of the One from the Onyx Gate as Sir Erling had," Lord Hallam interjected. "Without Sir Erling's power over Viwa, the maidens have nowhere to go but back to their master at the Onyx Gate where they belong!"

Jubilant cries went up from the men as they raised their goblets high in the air a third time that evening. Eolande himself took part in the festive atmosphere by raising his goblet once more with the others before returning to his seat.

After the feast was nearing its end and the last bits of food were devoured, Lord Hallam intervened by saving the best for last. He stood up and lifted his hand to quiet the lively exchanges going on in the hall.

"Men of Viwa," Lord Hallam cried, "you know of what I am about to say!"

Lord Hallam looked at Richard proudly as he spoke the following words, "Richard has decided to take on the great responsibility of becoming our prince in Viwa. He was a little reluctant at first when we asked him to consider coming back to Viwa with us to become our prince. When asked why, he gave us some valid reasons, but one did not make much sense. He said he did not truly know our language. We taught him a few words since he came to the Land of the Diamond Sea, but he said 'twas not enough for him to know fluently. We told him that this did not matter. He can always use his scepter to converse with those around him. If he does not agree with something said to him, he can always use the object upon our heads until he can find a suitable word!"

The most deafening sound of laughter came from the mouths of the men around Emma and Nan, which left their ears buzzing. Every man in the room, including Eolande, got up to kneel down to their future prince. The girls smiled at one another. They were not surprised by Richard's decision. It was only fitting that Richard would eventually find his way back to his mother's land and take on her duties as ruler there. They did not believe for one moment that the throne of Viwa would be left empty after Sir Erling had been removed from it.

Nan became saddened that they might never see him after tomorrow, but change was a continuous part of life, whether it be bad or good. She knew she had to accept it or become caught up in the past, never seeing the good that was occurring at the present time. Nan reminded herself that there would be memories to remember him by and that was good enough for her. She could always reflect upon them during the daily grind found in the life of a farmer's daughter.

Feeling some pressure to have a few words himself, Richard arose from his chair. His eyes darted about the room as he was tongue-tied for a moment or two, but it did not take him long to find his voice. Composing himself, he spoke flawlessly as if he had been giving such speeches his entire life.

"My plan is that as soon as I tie up some loose ends to my affairs in Lamington, I will immediately return to my new home in Viwa to take on my princely obligations," Richard said, flashing a princely smile. "The coronation will be my very first duty to my people. They must see that they have a new prince in their fairy kingdom. They will no longer live in fear and misery as they had under the evil Sir Erling. A new day is awaiting them. Only happiness and great prosperity will be found in Viwa as long as I shall live."

"Lad, do not speak of Sir Erling," Lord Hallam declared. "His name alone stands for the past. You are our future!"

Many of the Viwa men repeated Lord Hallam's words as they pounded their goblets loudly upon the table tops.

"You are our future!" they shouted over and over until Richard raised his hand to silence them.

"Becoming a prince of Viwa was the furthest from my mind after I had been knighted last night after our return," Richard stated. "I thought I might be arriving in Lamington to become lord. Instead, the men begged me with such earnestness to return with them to Viwa as their prince. I knew that I could not turn my back on them. I have changed much since the battle in Lamington. And so has my experiences and my thinking with it. Before the battle, I did not want to be prince of any land near or far. After the battle had ended, I was starting to feel otherwise. I will be returning to Lamington first thing tomorrow to let Lady Catherine know that I will be vanquishing any potential title of lord. 'Tis her ladyship's child who should be the new lord of Lamington, not I. I cannot think of anyone better as Lamington's lord than the very child of Lord Robert and Lady Catherine. She will be pleased when she hears of this."

"There is one more thing that you need to think of after you get to Viwa," Lord Hallam reminded Richard. "You do remember what that is, do you not?"

"Aye, I do," Richard responded. "You wish me to take on my birth name of Aric. I will use it, but only amongst the people of Viwa. In private, I wish to be known as Richard. 'Tis what I am most used to being called. Aric will be a befitting name during and after my coronation in Viwa, but I still want to openly be called Richard for a few more days."

Emma and Nan were silently listening, their hands folded neatly in their laps as they took in every word that Richard spoke.

"I just knew he would become prince of Viwa!" Nan said softly to a nodding Emma.

Emma and Nan admired Richard for making the hard decision of going back to Viwa to become prince. In due course, Prince Aric would come to embrace his new position in life and the rewards that would follow. He had come a long way from the lowly farmer's foster son, who was hidden from the world, until Lord Robert brought him to Lamington. Only did his long adventure with the girls truly lead him back to his birthright in Viwa.

CHAPTER 38

The pleasant evening of feasting had concluded. Everyone was eager to get back onto the road the next morning and start their lives anew back home. Nan was disappointed that Richard did not say anything to her or to Emma when he retired that night, but she knew that things were changing for him. He was no longer their old traveling partner, who fought off evil Viwa knights and maidens, or went looking in the forest for a hunter's lodge for them to stay in for the night. Recollections of their adventures together would become more and more distant in Richard's mind as more important duties took their place.

Emma and Nan were too sleepy that night to say much to each other. The moment their heads hit their pillows, they were awoken by a knock on the door by a servant to prepare for their final journey.

"Nan, I will miss you sorely when I return to Lady Catherine," Emma said. "I will never forget you and neither will her ladyship, although I wish I had been more pleasant at times. If I see you somewhere in Lamington, I will be sure to wave."

"As I will, too!" Nan exclaimed. "Things have worked out for the best in the end. You delivered me out of a battlefield in Lamington. I will never forget that."

"I know we will miss Richard," Emma declared. "If 'twas not for him, we would have been rotting away in a dungeon at the Onyx Gate, unless Eolande came to our aid. How tragic that would be! Before the feast this evening, Richard said to me that according to Eolande, the old man with the beard, who was with the false Lord Robert and Father John, was the *real* One from the Onyx Gate. The rest were definitely his minions, acting on his behalf."

Nan shuddered. "How truly frightening! I am so happy to be out of there."

"I am, too!" Emma replied. "Mayhap Eolande did not want to tell us about who the old man was. He knew we were terrified enough after what we went through at the Onyx Gate. I forgot to mention this to you earlier, Nan, but it does not matter anymore, does it? The One from the Onyx Gate is something we would rather forget."

"We have Christmas to look forward to!" Nan said, changing the subject. She was giddy with excitement. "How wonderful that will be. If there is a Christmas feast at the castle, I may finally get my chance to go there with my family. Ah . . . my family! Seeing them today is my greatest joy. And you, Emma . . . look at that chest over there! It looks quite heavy with all the gowns you have to take back to Lady Catherine. She will be quite shocked at them."

"I will give them to her," Emma said. "They are fit for a lady, and so she should have them. My old gown suits me just fine. I am starting to sound like you, Nan!"

The girls went out into the courtyard where Richard and the men were getting ready to leave. Richard was dressed in shiny, new chainmail with a shield of Viwa to fit his status. It had a coat-of-arms on it very similar to that of what Sir Erling had on his when he was prince of Viwa. Only this time, the *proper* heir of Viwa had it hanging by his side. Richard was also carrying a large sword with a jewel-encrusted handle placed in an intricately-engraved gold scabbard. His hair was washed and combed back neatly as he mounted the gift of a beautiful white horse, which came from Eolande's best breeds.

Eolande helped Emma and Nan up onto their horse. He then reached up and handed Nan a fragrant pink flower.

"I know you will want this to remember the Land of the Diamond Sea by," Eolande grinned. "It comes from the bridge over yonder."

"Thank you, Eolande," Nan said softly as she smelled it. "You have been a good friend to all of us."

Eolande took a deep bow. "You are very welcome!"

"I shall not forget either of you, lasses!" Richard said, coming over with his horse to the girls. "Emma, I will be coming to Lamington to pay a short visit to Lady Catherine, then off to Viwa. Nan, I cannot say I will see you after we get to Lamington. I will keep you in my thoughts and prayers for as long as I shall live. I shall always want you to think of me as Richard.

As I said in the great hall last night, 'tis the only name that I want my friends to remember me by, and I meant it."

Nan nodded her head as tears filled her eyes. Emma's eyes also became misty with sadness as Richard, with a bow of his head, turned his horse around and went back to join Lord Hallam and the others. They began to ride out of the courtyard and toward the bridge that would take them home.

Nan turned around and watched as Eolande waved them off to a safe journey homeward. His eyes sparkled in the sunshine, and his mouth formed into a broad smile as they went. She waved to him one last time as she memorized the gentle face that she wanted to keep etched in her memory forever. She was glad he gave her a flower from the bridge. However did he know she wanted one?

Eolande knows everything, Nan thought. *He saw it from afar, as he always said about things.*

After everyone crossed the bridge and alighted back onto the sand dunes, Nan turned again to watch the castle disappear into the sea and the bridge with it. She did not know if she wanted to cry over departing from that odd, yet wonderful place called the Land of the Diamond Sea, or to smile and laugh, because she was returning to that old familiar place called home.

CHAPTER 39

By late afternoon, the company of riders came within reach of the forest road before the farmland began at the edge of Lamington's walls. It was as if the battle with Sir Erling had never taken place. The farming folk, who left when the battle started, had returned and were clearing the land for the spring growing season. Many had either rebuilt, or had begun building, their cottages and other farm buildings that had been destroyed during the melee. The forest nearby was becoming greener, the first spring flowers were blooming, the sun was brighter, and the air was getting warmer. It was here that the knights from Siddell parted from the group to make their way back to their lands.

"Nan, we are going to take you to your parents before going off to the castle," Richard remarked as they rode through the partially destroyed gatehouse of town. "After this journey, 'tis the first place you will want to return to."

The damaged gatehouse shocked the girls who knew it could only have gotten that way after they left Lamington with the emerald. The travelers then ogled a large hole in the town wall that was made during the fighting. There were dozens and dozens of men around the hole busily repairing it.

"I would be quite pleased if you took me home first!" Nan said with sparkling eyes, in spite of seeing the horrid aftermath of the recent battle.

Turning off the main street, the riders came to the corner of the narrow cobblestone lane where Nan lived. They reined in their horses in front of the quiet cottage. A rooster and some chickens were heard out back, while a shadow of someone was seen moving about inside the house.

"Simon the farmer, we have come to deliver Nan, your daughter, safely to you!" Richard cried.

Richard dismounted his horse as Simon and Isabel came outside. Nan's little sisters and brother came running out with them and peeked out from behind their mother.

Richard pulled Nan's parents aside as he discussed something quietly with them before calling Nan over. Simon and Isabel beamed proudly at their daughter as Richard climbed up on his horse and waved to Nan before riding off with the others in the direction of Castle Lamington.

"Well, Nan," Isabel sighed as the riders disappeared down the lane to the main street, "'twas quite a story that Richard has told us. I do not know what to say. Seems you have saved Lamington from quite a misfortune, by returning something important—very secret, he said—that ended the battle we had here lately. I would not have believed that a daughter of ours would have done it, but you did."

"You are not upset with me then?" Nan asked timidly.

"There is nothing to be upset over, Nan!" Simon declared, embracing his daughter. "Lady Catherine did tell us that you were sent on some mission far from Lamington. Little did we know it had something to do with Lamington itself. What a terrible mess this battle had been and his lordship losing his life over it, too. May his soul rest in peace. At least you did not have to see it, though we did miss you quite a bit, while you were gone."

"What a good lad that Richard is, bringing you here like that, but a prince, too!" Isabel exclaimed. "My goodness, who would have ever believed that. Going from castle guard to a prince. How things change."

"Did he tell you where he will be crowned a prince?" Nan asked inquisitively. She wondered if Richard had been honest about Viwa, where the fairies lived.

"Nay, he did not," Isabel replied. "Well, no matter. Wherever he shall go, I hope he rules his land well there."

I am not surprised that you did not tell them, Richard, Nan thought. *They would not believe there was such a place. I am sure you did not tell them about the Land of the Diamond Sea, either. They would have believed that even less, especially if they knew of the man who lived there by the name of Eolande.*

"Your mother has prepared some of her good soup and hot bread to go with it," Simon remarked. "You know, Nan, when Christmas comes around again, I hope we can all go up to Castle Lamington to the Christmas feast. I suppose our supper has reminded me of it somehow, though Christmas is a ways off."

"That is a fine idea, Simon," Isabel praised him. "I hope I can find another sprig of holly to decorate the door with, too. Now enough worrying about Christmas! Come inside. Nan must be starving after a long day on the road. Nan, we are thankful to God that you are alive and here with us."

Nan's eyes slowly became heavy. She was not only hungry, but exhausted from so much traveling. She knew it would not take her long to fall asleep after supper. She nodded inattentively to her mother's words, as she followed her parents inside the cottage, and shut the door.

CHAPTER 40

True to Emma's words, Lady Catherine did not forget Nan. Her ladyship granted Nan's family a compensation for Nan's brave act, by bestowing on them a new stone cottage and all the sheep that her father could tend. Nan laughed when she thought of where the idea for the stone cottage and sheep came from.

Eolande gave it to her ladyship, through one of his many mysterious ways that he worked through people. Only such a good friend as he could have done it. As with everything, he saw the idea from afar, when the false Lord Robert suggested that he would give those things to me, if I gave him the emerald. How clever of Eolande!

A belated Christmas feast was held for the townspeople of Lamington, while another feast was held a week later in honor of Nan for putting an end to the battle, which an enemy of Lamington had started. During the small amount of exchange that Nan had with Emma during the Christmas feast, she learned that Richard had written a letter to Lady Catherine lately. He stated that although he was busy with many matters of state, he was quickly settling down into his new home, which he was learning to love tremendously as prince of Viwa.

Nan had become a bit of a heroine in her own right by this time. Everywhere she passed, the people of Lamington spoke highly of this simple peasant girl, who quietly lived in a cottage at the edge of town. Nan's parents were also appreciative of their daughter for their sudden good fortune.

Sometime in late September, word went out from Castle Lamington that Lady Catherine had given birth to healthy twin babies— both a boy and a girl. All of Lamington rejoiced! The boy, heir of Lamington as was expected, would be named Robert, in honor of his father, and the girl would be named Isolda. Food was sent out to the townspeople from the castle the next day, as part of the celebration, for the birth of the noble children. A public christening, officiated over by Father John, was held later that day, which Nan and her family attended, at the Church of the Holy Angels for little Lord Robert and Lady Isolda.

After all the excitement that Lamington experienced had quieted down, Nan fell back into her usual routine at home. One day as the leaves were blowing to and fro down the streets of Lamington, Nan glanced outside the window. She saw some colorful cloaks billowing from the backs of some men on horseback going down the main thoroughfare toward the direction of Castle Lamington. There appeared to be at least a hundred men with fair hair that fell to their shoulders. They carried banners with a coat-of-arms on them that left Nan's memory in a fog as she stood thinking as to whom it might belong to. She ran from the window and opened the door of the cottage to get a better look at the pageantry taking place.

In the midst of the riders, Nan quickly caught sight of a younger man who was dressed more elegantly than the others in a dark blue cloak. He had on his head a small coronet. At either side of him were two knights who held a larger banner as he rode. The banner had a background of gold with a brown boar pictured on it. The animal had a small sword in its mouth while a large pink rose rested on its handle. Many of the townspeople had stopped what they were doing and stared at the newcomers that had come to town. They whispered amongst themselves about who the men could be. After several minutes of trying to jog her memory, Nan remembered as the last man disappeared from view.

"Viwa!" Nan said excitedly. "The lad riding with them was Richard, or Prince Aric. If they are from Viwa, I wonder what brings them here."

Weeks went by before anyone found out who the visitors to Lamington were. When they did, the first of those to know was the family of Simon the farmer. A messenger arrived at the stone cottage announcing the presence of Nan to Castle Lamington. It left Nan and her parents perplexed at what this might mean. Nan went alone to the castle this time, and what she was about to learn was more than she had anticipated. She was ushered into the great hall where Emma was waiting with Lady Catherine. Emma wanted to announce the good news to Nan that Richard, or Aric, as he was known in the kingdom of Viwa, had asked for her hand in marriage. Nan was taken completely by surprise, as she had not expected Emma to have even the smallest interest in the lad, who since had been crowned prince in the fairy country he now resided. If Nan believed that this was the only purpose in which Emma had called her to the castle for, she was terribly mistaken.

Emma drew Nan aside to a window seat in the great hall. Lady Catherine then left them so they could have some private time to themselves.

Turning to Nan, Emma asked demurely, "Nan, would you like to become *my* maidservant after the marriage takes place?"

"*Your* maidservant, Emma?" Nan asked softly. "How can I be your maidservant? I am only a farmer's daughter. 'Twould not be proper for me to take on such a position."

You need not worry, Nan," Emma vowed. "I will teach you how to be a maidservant. Do not forget that I am Lady Catherine's, but not for long! Going to Viwa will be an adventure that never ends, much like the one we had recently. Richard has said that the weather there is much like the Land of the Diamond Sea, which you liked. You will not regret it, Nan."

"If I accept, may I come back to visit my family?" Nan said reticently. "I would forever be indebted to you, if you would allow me to see them sometimes."

"Aye, of course!" Emma answered. "I think Richard will allow it as well."

"I accept your offer!" Nan declared.

"I knew you would!" Emma cried, happily embracing her old companion. "I had not expected to become a princess of Viwa." She was undoubtedly enthusiastic about her prospect of becoming a princess, and it shown in her eyes as she spoke. "Her ladyship said that she was aware, from the very moment Richard left Lamington to go to Viwa, that he would return in search of a princess to take back to his kingdom. He told her so. Little did I know 'twas me, Nan! My parents approve of the marriage wholeheartedly. They also told me that they had recently discovered that we have a Viwa ancestor from my father's side. They were in disbelief that a fairy was found in our bloodline. They are even more shocked that my future husband is from a fairy kingdom!"

"There is something I have to tell you, Emma," Nan confessed.

She noticed that Emma was wearing the Robin egg blue gown that Eolande gave her. "Eolande had told me about your ancestor, but I was supposed to keep it secret. Mayhap 'twas because he thought I would notice the unusual strength you had when you fought our way out of Lamington, after I found the emerald. If there was something more to it, he never said."

"That sly Eolande!" Emma said with a giggle. "Well, I never did think that my strength came from the Viwa. Eolande was full of secrets, was he not? Anyway, her ladyship has returned all the gowns that he gave me. The gowns are more fitting for a princess, she said. They will be coming with us to Viwa."

"You are beautiful, Emma," Nan said with candor. "You will make a suitable princess for . . . er—Richard, or Prince Aric."

"He still wants us to know him by Richard," Emma stated. "You remember how he insisted upon it. So Richard it shall be between us in private."

"Aye, I remember," Nan said. "Are you happy, Emma?"

"I am happy," Emma replied. "Very happy. I decided to marry Richard of my own accord. I did not realize how I felt about him until after he left Lamington. I do not regret my decision, Nan."

"You deserve much happiness, Emma. I hope I can add to it by becoming your maidservant in Viwa."

"I hope you will, too," a familiar voice said. "My kingdom will be a whole new experience for you, lass. You will come to like your new home."

Looking up from the window seat, Emma and Nan saw Richard approaching them. He was dressed regally in a moss-green tunic with a jeweled belt and white silk hose. On a few of his fingers were various gemstone rings, their facets flashing dazzlingly in the sunlight streaming through the window above them. As Richard stopped in front of them, Nan immediately sensed a vast change in this lad, who had gone through quite a transformation, since his departure to Viwa. His manners were polished, his speech impeccable, and he carried himself with a poise and grace that only a prince possessed. He was also very courteous and had a more kindly nature than Nan remembered. Richard had become more of a man and less of a lad full of mischief and adventure since his return to Lamington. Though he was now known by his birth name of Aric, underneath it he was still Richard. Nan still detected some of his old personality, which was to a greater degree masked by his princely self.

Nan quickly arose from the window seat and went on bended knee to Richard whose tall figure loomed above the girls.

Richard stood chuckling at what Nan had done.

"I still find that sort of thing difficult to get used to," Richard said with a wave of his hand. "I almost wish that you had not done that, Nan."

"But you are prince now, so I must," Nan declared solemnly, standing back up. "I remember having done it many a time at the feet of his lordship, your father. 'Tis something those of us from town do."

"You will not be from the town of Lamington any longer," Richard concluded. "You will be leaving with Emma as her maidservant in a few weeks. Before that, there are many preparations to be made for the upcoming wedding. Emma's parents will be arriving here in another week, so there will be numerous guests to entertain. I have invited Susanna and her family as well, and Lord Eustace, whose presence I have made recently, and who now believes in the fairies. Father John will preside over the wedding ceremony here in town, too. A grand feast will be held afterward at Castle Lamington with food generously handed out to the townspeople by her ladyship. When that is over, Lady Catherine has promised to send us back with lots of gifts. I told her 'twas not necessary for so many, but she insisted."

"I see that my life will never be dull as maidservant to a princess," Nan said with a sigh.

"There is one more thing that *you*, Nan, must promise me from this moment onward," Emma said, looking hard at Nan.

"What might that be?" Nan asked.

"Since you will be my maidservant, you *must* wear a fine gown for your position, and I know just the one," Emma said. "I found the gown you refused to wear in the Land of the Diamond Sea. 'Twas in the chest we left there with."

Emma was determined for Nan to wear the garment as Nan's days as a farmer's daughter were about to come to an end. She knew that Nan could not back herself out of a corner this time.

Nan began to nod her head slowly as she smiled coquettishly at the future Princess Emma.

"Of course, your highness," Nan replied as she tried to suppress a grin. "I cannot fight you anymore about this as I had at Eolande's castle."

"Your highness?" Emma asked with surprise. "Aye, 'twill be my impending title, will it not?"

Emma began to laugh at the thought of it, and even Richard joined in the merriment. Nan did not hold back any longer and burst out giggling.

"That Eolande!" Emma said. "He knew all along what would happen to us when he laid out those fine gowns."

"I must say that does seem likely," Richard replied. "He saw things that nobody else did."

Nan sighed. "Gowns perfect for a princess and her maidservant."

Turning around to the window of the great hall, Nan's mind wandered beyond the walls of Castle Lamington and far past those of the town to her new homeland in the fairy kingdom of Viwa. She knew it would be an adjustment to live there, but as long as her treasured traveling companions were nearby, anything was possible.

ABOUT THE AUTHOR

Debbie Kelahan lives in eastern Pennsylvania with her husband, daughter, and two feathered friends who really compete for attention, especially the feisty cockatiel. When she's not writing or reading, she likes to grow beautiful flowers, go on long walks, and contemplate on the world around her. This is her first novel.

47360863R00202

Made in the USA
Middletown, DE
22 August 2017